Georgina

ALIDA LEACROFT

MAGIC ISLE PRESS

To Johanna Alida and Dorothy Hermione

Contents

Principal Characters

Georgina Ross – daughter of Dorothea Ross (nee Weatherly) (deceased) and Rev. Thomas Ross (deceased) granddaughter of Frederick Weatherly of Westmead House, Hamps.

Frederic Weatherly. Local landowner with a small estate adjoining that of the Kelling family

Arthur Weatherly – Nephew and heir apparent to Frederick Weatherly.

Mr. Thaddeus Winter – Frederick Weatherly's man-of-business

Mrs. Louisa Salmonds – Georgina's aunt, half-sister of Thomas Ross. With two daughters, Elvira and Maude.

Captain Edward Kelling – second son of Sir Gerald Kelling and his wife Elizabeth. Brother John, Sister Augusta (Gussie).

Minor Characters

Dr. Selby – The local doctor, living just outside Hurstbourne Priors

Mr. Tadswell – the magistrate from the small town of Whitchurch.

Penn – groom to Edward

Mary – personal maid to Georgina.

Mrs. Lessing – housekeeper at Westmead, and her husband is the butler.

Will – groom at Westmead.

Acknowledgements

My principal thanks go to the forever anonymous person who said I couldn't do this. Without them I probably would not have. Thanks go to my first readers who put up with my typos and my ability to ignore prepositions as far beneath my notice, Barbara Freer, Carmen Willis Belanger, Larry Bauer, Sabrina Garrison, Curtis Scott, Melissa Siah and Sarah Hoyt. My thanks also go to Amy B, who helped me to check the manuscript. Any errors are mine not hers. I appreciated input from Dr. Mark Baldwin and Dr. Alex John on the medicine of the 19th century. I think it made them appreciate how far we have come.

Chapter 1

Georgina Ross walked down the gangplank from the ship into the crowded, noisy seethe of Southampton Dock, with little more than four pounds and seven shillings in her reticule. It was as different as possible to her boarding the vessel. That had been by a winch, from the tossing surf-boat that had carried her out to the vessel. On the wild coast off Port Elizabeth in the Colony of the Cape of Good Hope, that had been the only way to get onto a ship, there being no quay like this!

She looked around at the crowds of people, hoping against hope there was someone there to meet her. She knew that her father had sent letters both to his family and to the Edinburgh Mission Society, when they had been evacuated to Grahamstown. They had sought refuge there, after the mission station in the Katberg valley had been attacked. She knew that her mother had sent a letter to her grandfather telling him of father's wounds, and again, of his death, and her plans to get a passage back to England for the two of them.

Only her grandfather had replied, which he had done tersely after the initial accident, saying that it should be a lesson to them both and they ought to leave this foolishness and come home. Erratic and slow mail on a remote mission station had been nothing unusual for them. It could take eight months or more for a letter from England to reach them.

Georgina had no idea what to do now. Their plans, such as they were, had hinged on her mother being alive, and not buried at sea two weeks before they'd even reached Biscay. Georgina could barely remember England. Places and distances had meant little to her as a child. Everything had seemed very big then, even the ship they'd travelled out to Africa on. The ship hadn't seemed large, this time around. She had spent much of the time on board nursing her mother, and finally, when mother had died, retreating into herself. She had been grieving, afraid and alone, a world away from the mission station in the Katberg valley. For all that it was now tinged with horror, it was really all she had known, where she had been herself. There she'd been 'a trifle too spirited'. Here? Here she was just scared and lost.

A sailor came and deposited both her trunk, and her mother's trunk, at her feet. "Want me to call one of them hacks for you, Miss? Or get you a porter?" He asked, jerking a thumb at the row of black hackneys whose drivers were now engaged in loud and largely incomprehensible transactions with several of the other passengers. Georgina pulled herself together, aided by the rough kindness in the sailor's voice. "I... I don't know. I have my Aunt Louisa's address, but I do not know how far away it is." She fumbled in her reticule and got out her mother's diary. "Oak Crescent. Number 220." Taking a deep breath she added. "I don't have a lot of money."

The sailor nodded, with an understanding kindness written on his face. There were no real secrets in the small world of one ship. They knew something of what she and her mother had fled, of who they were. "You've had a rough time of it, Missy. But you're back in England now. Away from them savage murdering heathens in Africa. I'll go and chaffer with one o' them jarveys for you. Thems a thieving bunch o' rogues."

She stammered her thanks, grateful, despite the fact that she'd far rather be back in Africa. She knew what to do there, and could have managed easily enough, even among the 'savage murdering heathens'. A few minutes later, she was in a rather malodourous, elderly, hackney-cab, jouncing across the cobbles, trying to steel herself for the next step of her journey. What she knew of her aunt was not encouraging. Her father's half-sister had not approved of his decision to become a missionary, had quarreled with him about their inheritance, and never replied to the letters which he had sent every year. Still, Aunt Louisa was here in Southampton, married to a sea-captain. Georgina had no idea how to reach her grandfather, living out in the countryside in Hampshire, or indeed how much it would cost. Her mother had showed her on the map. To someone raised on the distances in Africa, it had not seemed far. But mother had seemed to think that it was.

Her Aunt Louisa's house, when she arrived there, was tall and narrow, just like all the tall and narrow houses it adjoined. The hackney driver tried to cheat her, but she held firm to the price the sailor had told her, and finally with a sour face he offloaded the trunks onto the curb, and urged his sorry-looking horse to a trot, leaving her to climb the three steps and face the knocker, alone. The weather was as bleak as her spirits, with thin flurries of cold, fine rain, adding to her welcome.

She was about to try the knocker for the second time, when a housemaid opened the door, looked at her standing there in her rather old-fashioned clothing, and started to close the door again. "Wait!"

said Georgina desperately, holding onto the door. "Please take this card up to Mrs. Salmonds."

Perhaps the card, perhaps the desperation in her voice, perhaps the fact that she knew the name of the mistress of the house, or perhaps just the fact that Georgina was stronger than the housemaid, made the servant stop. The maid paused and looked at her, and at the card being proffered to her. It was one of father's last calling-cards, and quite precious to Georgina. It had not been something one needed at the mission station. Mother had found his card case in the crate of things that had been recovered and sent to them in Grahamstown. The girl – and, looking at her little, sharp-planed face, Georgina realized she was just a girl, who could hardly even be her own age, stopped trying to close the door, and took the card. "Yes, Miss. Who am I to say it is, then?"

"Georgina Ross. Mrs. Salmonds is my aunt. I have just returned from Africa. From the Cape of Good Hope Colony."

The last part plainly meant little to the maid, but Georgina being a niece obviously did. "Yes, Miss."

"May I come in out of the rain? And could someone please carry my trunks inside?"

The girl looked at her. "There's only Cook and me, Miss. John's been sent out to get some fish."

"Perhaps we could manage between the two of us, then," said Georgina. She had little enough. She couldn't leave it in the street, and she wasn't at all sure her aunt, or even this maid, would return to let her in.

By the look on the maid's face, if she'd said: "I am an elephant," she could hardly have caused more surprise. But the girl did put the card carefully on the hall table, and between them they hauled the two trunks up the three steps and into the hall. The hall smelled faintly of cabbage, and also furniture polish. "If you will just wait here, Miss. I will go and take this card to the mistress," said the girl.

Somewhere upstairs Georgina could hear the inept tinkling of the pianoforte. She stood, resolute and nervous, but at least grateful to be out of the weather. It might be coming on toward spring, but it was still bitter outside.

The wait seemed interminable. She heard the music stop and then raised voices. And then, finally, the maid came back, looking as if she'd had a peal rung over her. "You're to come up, Miss." So, Georgina followed her down the hall, and up the stairs, to a drawing-room where she found herself the object of the curious, but not particularly welcoming gaze of a large woman wearing a lace cap slightly askew on her head of iron-grey hair, and the bright blue eyes like those that Georgina had inherited from her father. A young buxom blonde girl sat on the piano-stool, and another rather alike in appearance, had a tottering pile of ladies' magazines on the couch beside her. The maid scurried away like a timid mouse, saying nothing. No-one had got up, and no-one had said anything to greet her. So, Georgina did her best to smile and say "Aunt Louisa? I am your niece Georgina. I was hoping..."

"What on earth are you doing here?" demanded her aunt.

"And where did you get such awful clothes?" said the girl at the pianoforte. She was dressed in pink, which did her, Georgina thought, no great service.

Georgina couldn't help her clothes. Mother had made dresses for both of them, with the help of a couple of native women. "We... we came home, after father died," she said, limply. "Mother wrote to tell you." It did not feel much like home. Mother had desperately wanted to come back, wanted to leave the horror of the Frontier War and her husband's slow death behind her. But for Georgina, this place was alien, cold and unfriendly. If she could have gone back right now, she'd have done so in a heartbeat.

"Where is your mother?" asked her Aunt Louisa, in a chilly voice.

"She... she died on the ship. She was buried at sea," said Georgina, in a small, stony voice. That was all that was left. "Please," she said, feeling broken and lost. "I don't know what to do. I don't know anyone in England. I didn't know where to go."

"Well," said her aunt, "You can't come here. You need to be off."

At this point of despair, an unlikely angel came to her rescue, in the shape of a rotund gentleman who entered the room, rubbing his hands and smiling at her. There had been no shadow of a smile on any of the other faces. "Well, Louisa, what's this Mary tells me, that poor Stephen's daughter has just arrived!" He walked up to her, took her by the elbows and kissed her cheek. "You're the spitting image of your mother, m'dear. Welcome back to England. A terrible business, with your father. Just dreadful."

"Thomas," said her aunt. "Her mother is dead, too! I..."

"No wonder that she looks ready to fall over," said the rotund gentleman putting an arm around her. "I am so sorry, my dear."

Georgina found herself quite unable to speak, but smiled tremulously at him, tears starting in her eyes. Her aunt was not similarly bereft of words. "She can't come and stay here, Thomas. We can't afford it. Why, the price of coals..."

"She's our blood kin, Louisa," he said, sternly. "Your brother's child!"

She snorted. "I remind you, Captain Salmonds, that we have our own children to raise! We can't afford this. Let her go to her other relatives! My brother wasted his entire inheritance on being a missionary. Let the Mission Society or the Church look after her. We have husbands to find for our own daughters."

"Now, now, Louisa. Something can be arranged, I am sure," he said, calmly. "What other family have you got my dear?"

"I don't know, besides my grandfather. There's a great aunt... I should have her address..."

"Aunt Edith has been dead two years gone," said Aunt Louisa, with a sniff.

"I am sorry, mail took a long time to get out to us. We did write... to you, to my grandfather, to my great aunt, to the mission society, to say my father was injured and again later, to say he was dead, and then to say we would be leaving as soon as we could find a passage on a ship. The only reply we got was from my grandfather, my mother's father, saying we ought to get out of Africa and come home." Plainly her aunt had got the letter about her brother's death, she'd known of that, and obviously told the Captain. Her mother had received no reply. Perhaps the reply had missed them, perhaps... her aunt just hadn't replied. Postage was expensive. Perhaps the others had not replied either.

"Your grandfather, where does he live?" asked Captain Salmonds.

"Westmead House, near Hurstbourne Priors," she answered mechanically, reciting the names of unfamiliar places, places that she barely knew where were on the map, although she'd heard descriptions of them all her life.

He nodded. "Ah yes. I remember now. Well now, that's not more than twenty or thirty miles off. I would say you should direct a letter to him, aye, and to the mission society, saying you're back, and explaining the circumstances. Maybe there's a pension of some kind, or a fund to help you get settled. In the meanwhile, Louisa, no arguing, she's to stay with us."

"Didn't your mother have a younger brother?" asked her aunt, plainly still looking for any alternative.

"My Uncle George... he sent us gifts," said Georgina, her heart aching at the memory of the huge excitement of receiving something all the way from England. "Unfortunately, he died three years after we got to the Katberg Mission. Mother was terribly upset."

Her aunt cocked her head, speculatively, but said nothing further.

Sheer nervous exhaustion, and the knowledge that at least for now, she had somewhere to stay, and perhaps could find her feet in this confused, unfamiliar world she found herself in, made Georgina want to sit down and cry. She wanted to be alone with her thoughts and memories. That was not an option, however.

Chapter 2

On that chilly April morning, Edward Kelling had got himself out of his bed and dressed, long before first light, while his valet snored – he wanted to be at the river by the time the sky turned pale. These days he was getting more sleep, but the injury to his leg did make lying in one position for too long uncomfortable. It was a great deal better than the agony of the first few months. He could walk some distance, ride again, although a few hours in the saddle would leave him in pain, and with a sleepless night to follow. Still, as the months had passed, it was a great deal better. And now, at least, there was something to get up for. The dawn rise at the river was not perhaps   exciting   for   many,   but   Edward   loved it.

In the stables, however, he was expected, and Penn already had their horses saddled. His "Good morning, Penn" got a nod. Penn was nothing if not taciturn in the early morning - but there was no stopping his former batman from coming along, Edward knew. Not without offending a loyal man to whom he possibly owed his life. Still,

Penn was happy to sit with the horses in the shed next to the stream, and get a fire and a brew going, while his master got wet and cast for rising fish.

They rode out down the drive, and onto the lane that led to Whitchurch, and then into one of the water-meadows that would lead them to the Bourne rivulet on their neighbor's lands. Edward had carte blanche to do so, and he had fished here since he was old enough to be trusted with a rod.

His interest was focused on getting to the water, on thinking of which of his prepared casts of flies to use... when suddenly Penn called out: "Captain! Look!"

Something was on fire, over toward Westmead House.

"Back to the lane. We'll make better time along it." In daylight, perhaps over the fields and hedges would have been faster, but in the pre-dawn, the lane would be the better way.

The lane, and then the carriage-way brought them rapidly to West-mead House, and the fire. The house itself, or at least one of the front-wings, was spitting flames. There was no sign that anyone was aware of it, beside themselves. Old Frederick Weatherly kept most of the big house shut up these days, with only a couple of maids from the village coming to assist the elderly housekeeper and her husband. There were still the old fellow's groom and a couple of stable-boys and gardeners living in the outbuildings – but plainly no-one was yet awake.

"You go and wake the groom! Get buckets!" Edward ordered, as they pulled their horses up and dismounted – well clear of the fire that made the horses balk nervously – in front of the house, at the end of the rill that was enclosed by the carriage-circle. He handed the reins to Penn, and ran to the nearest window which was not already gushing fire and smoke. He had seized up a small ornamental statue of Minerva from the head of the rill. It was marble and heavy, but he swung it and smashed the window into the library. He used the statuette to break the hole wider, took a deep breath and climbed in.

He'd have to go in through the library and then down the hall and up the stairs, along the gallery and to end of the wing to reach Mr. Weatherly's chambers. He wondered if his breath would last.

He didn't ever find that out. In the dimness he stumbled and fell heavily over something. It knocked the breath out of him, and he fell into the closed door. The object he'd fallen over groaned.

On his knees, coughing at the smoky breath he'd drawn, he realized that at least he would not have to go upstairs. He gathered the old man up in his arms and staggered back with his burden, to the window he'd come in through.

He was glad to breathe the fresh air, while he struggled through the opening. Penn and two of the stable-boys rounded the corner as he carried Mr. Weatherly away from the house, to set him down somewhere safe. Edward was still coughing, but able to call out: "I've got the old man."

"Groom has the back-door key, Master Edward. He's gone to see if he can get the housekeeper and his master."

"One of you boys, run and tell them I've got Mr. Weatherly."

Soon the housekeeper's elderly butler husband, the cook, the grooms, the footman, the scullery maid and the stable-boys were bucketing water from the ornamental rill of which Weatherly had been very proud. It was certainly doing him proud, at the moment. The housekeeper and the other maid were left in charge of both the old man, who appeared unconscious, but was still breathing, and his diminutive valet, who, in his panic to flee the attic, had fallen down the stairs, and broken his collar-bone. More people came – farmers on their way to their fields, a couple of maids up to do the milking –

some ran to fetch others, and some stayed to join in the bucket chain. The fire only had a hold on the ground floor of the wing that held the blue drawing room and the library on the ground floor, and seemed to be at worst in the blue drawing room – but even that had not yet spread to the upper story.

Edward was able to send one of the younger boys to his own home, with a message to tell his mother to bring the landaulet, and of course, more help. The ornamental rill, fed by a pipe and a channel from the Bourne, provided some water, and a pond yet more. Before the sun was fully up the fire had been reduced to a few smoldering timbers, and Edward's mother had arrived to take old Mr. Weatherly away.

The front door was still intact and locked, so, as they'd now entered the drawing-room via the windows, Edward thought he'd open the door to make it easier. But there was no key in the locked door. "Mrs. Lessing must have taken it to bed with her," said the younger stable-boy, knowledgeably. "She allus locks up."

"Run and ask if she has it by her, lad," said Edward. The wide hallway itself had been spared most of the effects of the fire, the blue drawing room having been the most seriously damaged. The window-drapes and window-frames and part of the floor had caught, but most of the paneling had not. He decided that he'd better check the library again – someone had been in the window, and said it wasn't afire, but he went to open that door off the hall, and found that it too was locked. A few moments later the plump housekeeper was helped in through the window. When she'd finished panting and arranging her garments – and looking in horror at the room – she turned to him: "No, Master Edward, the master always insisted the keys was left in the locks. He wouldn't abide them being taken out. Roust me out of bed once, when I dared lock the library. When he had one of his nights he'd go down there." She sniffed. "Which one of you brought one of the kitchen lamps in here? Master hates that fishy stink! He says it gets in the drapes."

Considering the room smelled of fire and ash and steam, Edward thought the master of Westmead House might not notice. Besides, the drapes had largely burned. "Well, at least the house is still standing!"

She looked at him with all the firmness of a woman who had known him since he was in short-coats, and was allowed to ignore his rank. "Yes, Master Edward. But one of them smelly lamps in here... And they've broken it! There on the floor!" In one of the worst burned patches of parquet lay a smashed lamp. "Which one of you was it?" She demanded, inquisitorially.

"But, Mrs. Lessing, we only come in this way, not through the kitching," protested the stable-boy. "We come in through the winder, just like you done."

"Well, I am going to check on the library. Through the window," said Edward, with a slight smile, seeing as battle royal was about to be joined. "Check everything is out, and put more water on, if there's any doubt."

"Not with that nasty smelly pondwater!" snapped Mrs. Lessing, to the lads. "And Joe, why, look at yer boots! Fancy coming into the house like that."

Chuckling to himself, Edward left. A strategic retreat, as it were. Mrs. Lessing, when roused, could rout a battalion. He climbed out of the window and then into the library.

It was dim and smoky in there. Looking around, Edward took in the scene... and turned straight back to the window. "Get Penn for me," he yelled.

Penn came running. "Captain?"

"You need to ride to Hurstbourne Priors, and get the constable to come up to Westmead. And then ride on to Mr. Tadswell, the magistrate in Whitchurch, and give him the message I will write for you. There's a writing desk in here. You're to give it only to him, and tell him with my compliments that I would like to ask him to come as soon as possible. Tell him that I think Mr. Weatherly has been assaulted, and that I believe we've got a case of robbery, attempted murder, and maybe arson, on our hands."

Once Penn had left: Edward looked around the room, careful-ly. The cabinet in which old Mr. Weatherly kept his collection of snuff-boxes had been left ajar and the various little flat drawers left open. One little ormolu gilded box lay on the handsome Turkey car-pet. And on the floor near it, and near the bloodstains from the old man's head, lay an ebony cane with a silver Ibis head, which the old man had habitually used. There was – as Edward could see, peering at it – blood visible on the head of the cane. Edward looked around the room, trying to ascertain whether the thief or thieves had taken anything else. He was not really familiar enough to be sure of what could be missing, and there'd be time enough to get an inventory from Mrs. Lessing later. The key was not in the lock on this side either. Plainly, the attacker had locked the door behind him, before setting the fire in the blue drawing-room – possibly having opened the front door to escape with his loot, before he did so. The fire had not taken hold very well, so it could not have been very long before he and Penn had arrived. What Penn had seen must have been the flare of the drapes catching fire.

He called Mr. Weatherly's groom, Will, a solid fellow who had been there twenty years at least, and set him on guard at the window, and went off to inspect the rest of the damage and see what measures were being taken to set things to rights, albeit temporarily. It was full daylight now, and looked to be a bright day. Despite the events of the morning, and his shock at seeing the evidence of robbery and the assault, he still regretted missing the dawn rise on the water. He felt faintly guilty to have even been aware of missing this pleasure, but, well, last year he'd thought it possible he would never be fit enough to cast a fly at a rising fish again. Every day now, he felt he was walking better, and he could spend up to an hour in the saddle, without a sleepless night of pain as a reward. He put it down to wading while he fished. The desire to cast a line got him exercising, slowly, and the cold of the clear water seemed to help. And, well, it had helped his mind as well. He'd known he would have to find a new direction, his military career being over. He'd little liking for indoor pursuits, and with his older brother set to inherit the estate, the Army or Navy had seemed like the sensible course. For the long painful months of autumn and winter, he'd been firstly too sick, and then too despondent, to think far ahead. But as the days grew longer, he'd become more involved in the running of Mr. Weatherly's property. It was no long-term prospect, and had happened purely because the old man had called at Bournelea to have words, as it were, about livestock from Bournelea tenants straying onto his lawns.

As Edward's father was out exercising one of his hunters, his older brother John away in London, and his mother had gone to visit one of his aunts, Edward had received him. The old man had not been next-or-nigh them for some months, the previous call had been while Edward was still confined to bed. It had been some years before that, before he'd been sent to Spain, that he'd last seen Mr. Weatherly. There was a certain coolness in the relationship between the two neighbors, although Weatherly's son George had been a frequent visitor at Bournelea, before his death.

Edward remembered the visit well. The old man had been taken into one of the parlors, and had been pacing around, plainly full of choler, and rather red in the face. He'd turned, on seeing Edward limp in, and his ruddy face had gone quite pale. He'd been near to a chair, and promptly sat down on it, looking at Edward all the while. Edward had hurried over, asking if he was all right, but even then Weatherly's color had been recovering. He'd made to rise, but Edward had pressed him back into the seat. "Sit for moment, sir. Let me get you a glass of wine. I haven't seen you for many years."

"You've changed a great deal, lad," Weatherly had informed him. "You were a round-faced boy when you left, but you look very like your father as a young man now. Startled me. Does the leg trouble you greatly?" Plainly, the heat of rage had been somewhat quelled by seeing Edward. Edward wasn't entirely sure why.

There had been little point in denying he was still in some pain. It showed. "It troubles me less than a few months ago, sir," He was at least able to say.

"Well, I wish you the best with it. This hip of mine only gets worse." They'd drunk a glass of madeira together, and on hearing about the cows, Edward had offered to come over, find out which of the tenants they belonged to, and see to the matter, little though he'd felt like even riding in a carriage, let alone bestriding a horse at the time.

The cattle had proved an easy matter – when he arrived he'd found a scared-looking boy trying to herd them away, and he proved to be the son of one of Weatherly's own tenants.

Edward might have been away from the Hampshire countryside for years, but he'd been raised to it. There were signs of neglect all over the Weatherly's estate. The old man had admitted as much, when Edward had gone to tell him about the cattle. "I lost heart for the place after my son George died. And my health hasn't been of the best. This cold does not help. I must apologize, my boy. The groom said he thought they were from one of the farms on Bournelea. I don't get about as much as used to. I should, but this cursed hip... I wish I hadn't come out today. It is plaguing me again."

Edward had offered to go around with the bailiff, and rapidly got to the root of the problem. The man was new, the third in as many years, since the man of Edward's boyhood had died. The bailiff did not know the area, or the tenants, and was sick to the back-teeth of the job and his rather demanding, elderly master. He was, Edward rapidly decided, not doing anything about the state of the hedging or the cottages, and was probably stealing his master blind – and he was also as resentful as possible at Edward going around with him.

The riding had been hard on Edward's leg, but the outcome had been his involving himself with Mr. Weatherly's estate. It had given his mind something to focus on, when he'd been finding despondency hard to shake off. Bournelea could not use another manager. His father ran Bournelea estate, and his elder brother John would inherit it. The openings for a younger son of the Squire were the Army or Navy, the Church or perhaps academia, or entering government as the secretary to some person of note. The latter would be difficult enough if one's family moved in the right circles, but the Kellings did not. They were just a respectable Hampshire family. As for academia or the Church... well, he could have gone up to Oxford, but really, he had no turn for it. At least, setting Weatherly's estate to good order had occupied his mind and, incidentally, reaffirmed his *carte blanche* to fish some excellent water, which he hadn't ventured onto since Weatherly's son's death.

His thoughts were taken from the past to the present, when the constable arrived, red faced and panting, as well as distinctly alarmed. The vicinity of Hurstbourne Priors was not one that took much policing. Edward was able to show him the scene and leave him to await the arrival of the local magistrate. Edward doubted that gentleman had attended to anything of the kind either. Rather tiredly, he had the groom bring his horse, and mounted up, and rode home.

There he was greeted by his father and brother, when he came in from the stables – his mother being in conversation with Doctor Selby about their elderly neighbor, now bestowed in the best spare bed-chamber. "Well, Edward," said his father. "What news of Weatherly's place, my boy? A lucky thing you came upon it."

"The fire is out, Father," he answered. "But there is more to it than just a fire. I'll be down to talk to you about it once I've put off these clothes. They're smoky and covered in ash."

"Were you already wet?" asked John, who regarded the dawn rise as an eccentricity best suited to his crazy younger brother.

"No. We were on our way there, but I'll tell you all about it when I come down. Here, Matthews," he said to the butler, "can you ask Mrs. Hawthorne if I can have some coffee and bite to eat. I sent Penn off to Whitchurch with my breakfast in his saddlebags. I'm devilish sharp-set."

The grizzled butler smiled. "I shall see to it at once, Master Edward."

He was glad enough to get down to the breakfast parlor and be greeted by the arrival of the coffee pot, as well as his curious parent and brother. They had already breakfasted, but were plainly waiting on the story. "Why has Penn gone to Whitchurch?" asked John.

"To fetch the magistrate. Old Weatherly was assaulted, left for dead, I would guess, and the place fired. It looks to me as if he interrupted a robbery in progress. His rooms are just above the library."

"What?" exclaimed his father. "In this district! You are not serious, Ned?"

A footman arrived, bearing chafing dishes of sliced ham, some excellent-looking sirloin and at least four eggs. "Ah, the best sight I have seen all morning," said Edward, eagerly.

"What a lovely thing to say," said his mother, entering just behind the footman. "Hello Edward. I have just this minute sent the Doctor away, so I am glad to see you with such a healthy appetite!"

"Well now, mother, just yesterday you said we were eating you out of house and home," he said, smiling at her. "How is Mr. Weatherly?"

She flicked a warning glance at the footman. "As well as can be expected," she said. "Simon, can you have a tray of tea brought for me? I cannot be drinking coffee at this hour of day."

"Yes, ma'am," said the footman, and left, which had plainly been mother's intention.

As soon as the door closed she said: "Gerald, you'd better send for Mr. Tadswell from Whitchurch. Doctor Selby says that it looks to him as if Weatherly was attacked! The injury is such that it is very unlikely he could have done so, falling."

"Edward was before you, Ma'am," said his father.

"Yes, Mama, I have sent for him. It looks as if Weatherly interrupted a robbery. He was hit with his own cane, and then the fellow, or maybe fellows, started the fire. Is he likely to recover?"

"The Doctor holds no very strong hopes, I am afraid," she said quietly. "His pulse is weak, he is still coughing a great deal, and is deeply unconscious. Dr Selby advised me we'd better contact his next of kin. To think of something like this happening here, of all places."

"Well," said John, "I can take a message to Arthur. I was going up to London anyway." He pulled a face, as he said it. "If I get there early enough I can avoid searching the Pall Mall hells for him."

"Still playing hard, is he?" asked his father. "I'm surprised he hasn't run aground. He can't have inherited that much from his family."

John shrugged. "He's a gambler by nature, I think. Always believes he'll win, somehow. And, as you said, one don't, or those banditti would not still be in business. Still, he could have run aground twice over, and we'd never know unless he was clapped up. I'll give him this much, he never gave much away, even when we had him dead to rights. Do you remember when he stole those pastries, Ned?"

"Yes, denying it to the last. He nearly got away with that one too. Bold as brass in the face of it. I got a thrashing for it, before we found his boot-print in the flowerbed outside the pantry."

"And then he still claimed you must have stolen his boots to do it." Arthur Weatherly was not much liked in the Bournelea household. A few years younger than Weatherly's son George, he'd been a relatively frequent visitor to Westmead House, in his youth.

"As if I could have got my feet into those tiny boots," said Edward.

John chuckled. His younger brother's enormous feet were something of a family joke. "If I didn't wish Frederick Weatherly the best anyway, the thought of Arthur inheriting Westmead would be enough to make me hope he recovers. Is there anyone else we should notify?"

"Well, the old fellow has a daughter," said his father, with a wry smile. "In Africa somewhere."

"Goodness," said Edward's mother. "Africa. I had no idea. This was your *cherie amie*, wasn't it, Gerald? She fled that far to escape you?"

Father laughed. "I'm better off with you, m'dear. At least you never fled further than Devon. Yes, that was Weatherly and m'father's idea. Well, Weatherly was very keen on it. He was very angry with her for not fitting in with his plans. And, to some extent, me, for not having taken her fancy. But she lived in Edinburgh for some years, so she plainly found Scotland far enough. She married some fellow who decided to be a missionary."

"That quite explains it," said mother. "You would have made a terrible missionary, my dear, and if her tastes ran that way, you must have been a sore disappointment to her."

He laughed. "Actually, nothing surprised me more than that. Dorothea was always so lively, I couldn't imagine her marrying some prosy parson, and a Scotsman too. I suppose we should try to send her a letter, but for the life of me I cannot remember the name of the parson, or have any idea where in Africa." He grimaced. "Perhaps Arthur will know. Or maybe Mrs. Lessing will have an idea."

"She's due back from Africa, I believe," said Edward. "The old man was very pleased about it. He got a letter just after Arthur's last visit. The one where he had that little contretemps in the Priors."

His father snorted. "Bad business, that. Well, I wonder if we should send a message to Arthur. If he shows his face and the old fellow has recovered consciousness, the old fellow might just have apoplexy," said Edward's father. "But we'd better send word to him, none-the-less."

"And I'd better get back up to my patient," said his mother, getting up from the table. "I've left Betty with him. Doctor said to apprise him of any changes. I only came down because I wanted you to call for the magistrate."

"I'll send your tea after you," said Edward, cutting a piece of the ham. "And I will come up and see how you go on, once I have finished with this breakfast which I need badly. It is a little belated."

As the tea-tray arrived just as he said this, he was spared that necessity. A little later, having eaten, and discussed the events of his morning with his father and brother, he went upstairs to see the patient he'd thrust onto his mother. He was feeling some aches from the exertions of the day, but at least did not also have to deal with the pain of his stomach telling him that his throat might have been cut. The return of a healthy appetite was one of the benefits of his recovery and increased capacity to exercise. He certainly had seen his share of exercise today.

Old Mr. Weatherly was not looking – or sounding – at all good, when he got up there. His breathing was rasping, and plainly an effort, broken every now and then with weak coughing. He was as pale as the sheet drawn up against his chin, as he lay, propped up against the pillows on the bed. His head was swathed in bandages, and no-one had tried to put a nightcap over it. "Doctor Selby said to keep him sitting upright as much as possible. It does seem cruel," said his mother.

"Selby knows his business, mother," said Edward. "I owe him my leg, after all."

"Yes dear. Indeed. Although I will never forget the mess that treatment made of the sheets! I only hope we do not have to pack Mr. Weatherly's wound with honey, too."

There was a tap on the door. It was Simon, the footman. "Captain Edward. Mr. Tadswell is below. He is wishful of having a word with you."

The local magistrate was sitting having a glass of wine with his father when Edward entered the room. He stood up and took Edward by the hand, eyeing him critically. "Well, Captain Kelling. A bad business. Indeed, a terrible business. How came you to be there?"

"I'd gone to fish," said Edward.

"To fish?" said the magistrate, looking skeptical.

"Yes, I fish the dawn rise. The trout come to feed on new-hatching nymphs..." Edward realized he might as well have been speaking a foreign language. Not classical Greek, of course. The magistrate was a known scholar of that. "It's quite common among fishermen, sir. The fish feed actively first thing in the morning, and the poor light helps us to catch them. So: in order to get onto the Bourne in time, I got up at four. First light is just before five at this time of year."

The plump magistrate, known as a late riser, looked at him with horror on this revelation of his matutinal habit. His father laughed. "Ned's always been an early bird, Mr. Tadswell. I did it myself when

I was a young man. But the older I have got, the more attractive my warm bed seems to me in the early mornings."

"Ah," said the magistrate, still looking rather dubious. "Continue, young man. Were you alone?"

"No, Penn – my groom, comes along with me, and takes care of the horses, and makes me coffee and breakfast. He learned his cooking in the army, so it's always the same fry up. He caught sight of the flames through a gap in the trees, and we made as much haste there as we could, and roused the household."

"I will speak with him a little later," said Tadswell, "You've employed him for some time, Sir Gerald?"

"He was with me in Spain," explained Edward. "He was one of my troopers and ended up as my batman. He was the one who staunched my wound and stopped me bleeding out at Avila. He's a good man," said Edward, crossing his fingers behind his back. Penn was a good fellow. He was also very good at finding a chicken in a Spanish village when none were for sale.

Tadswell nodded. "So, now tell me: how came you to find Mr. Frederic Weatherly?"

So, Edward told his story. In the process he heard that a window to one of the store-rooms adjacent to the kitchen, which Mrs. Lessing had been complaining 'forever' of a broken catch to, had been found open. One of the kitchen lamps was missing from the kitchen – presumably used by the thief, and later used to start the fire. And the keys to the library and front door had not been found. Tadswell's suspicions were, naturally, focused on anyone who might have known that window to be open and that Frederick Weatherly's snuff-box collection existed and was in the library. "There were various other valuables not disturbed," said Tadswell. "Mrs. Lessing is doing her best to do an inventory. But, while she seems an adequate housekeeper, she has little idea of what was in the collection."

"I've seen it," said Edward. "He showed it to me. To be honest, sir, I wasn't very interested. You could try asking Reverend Hornby – he was a friend of the old man's and shared his interest – but as you may know, he's gone to visit his daughter in Leeds."

Tadswell made a note of it, and said: "I'll follow up on that. I'll also be talking to Dr Selby. I gather from your father that Mr. Weatherly himself is unable to speak with me?"

"I can take you up, sir. But he is deeply unconscious," Edward paused. "Selby told us to prepare for the worst, Mr. Tadswell. We have someone sitting with him at all times, but there seems to be nothing much that we can do, but keep him warm and wait."

Tadswell nodded gravely. "If he recovers his senses, could you please have me called? And, of course take careful note of anything he may say. I assume his family has been notified? Does he have any relations in the district?"

"No one local, sir. My brother has taken a letter from my father to London to the nephew living there. Um, Arthur Weatherly. You may know of him."

If Tadswell had heard of Arthur, he made no sign of it. He just wrote it down. "Does he often come down here?"

"Not very often. I don't think he's been here since before Christmas, as far as I know. Mrs. Lessing would be the one to ask."

"I shall do that. I will return there on my way back home."

"Do you have any idea who did this, sir?" asked Edward.

Tadswell looked at him, cocking his head on one side, thoughtfully. "Suspicion, naturally falls on those who might have known the window to be insecure, or to have some idea of where the collection was – I gather he did not show it to many people. It does not seem as if it could have been a chance robbery. Have you any ideas? Any suspicions? Do you know of any grudges?"

Edward had actually not given the subject much thought. But when it came to grudges... "Well his last bailiff left under something of a cloud," he said. "He would have been into the library – Mr. Weatherly conducted his business there. And he could possibly have known about the window. You'd have to ask Mrs. Lessing. She might know more."

"That would be," said Tadswell, consulting his notes, "One William Grove. Yes, Mrs. Lessing did mention him. I will set enquiries about. Have you seen him recently?"

"Not in a month or so," said Edward. "He came to demand payment for something and Mr. Weatherly threatened him with the constable. I was there in the library talking to Mr. Weatherly at the time. Grove is a big, belligerent fellow. I and the groom... helped him leave."

"Ah. Any idea where he might be found?"

Edward shook his head. "I can't help you, I'm afraid. Mr. Weatherly's man of business might now. Winter. Thaddeus. I've met him. He lives somewhere in Winchester. Or Mr. Weatherly's attorney. I am afraid I can't help you with a name right now. I know he was up to see the old fellow just after Christmas. I expect Winter might be able to give you some more information."

A few more questions and Tadswell asked if he might speak with Penn, so having sent for the man, Edward took his leave.

John had already set out for London, and Edward, restless after his morning, had a light luncheon with his parents and rode back across to Westmead House. Old Frederick Weatherly was at least no worse, and there seemed little point in merely sitting about at home. At Westmead he found himself greeted like a relieving force. Without anyone to give orders, or certainty of their future, the people of Westmead House looked to the Squire's younger son as someone to take decisions, give instructions, and above all, to calm them in the uncertainty that this had cast into their normally very ordered lives. Mrs. Lessing and the housemaids had already been cleaning and airing what could be cleaned. The library, to Mrs. Lessing's distress, she was not allowed to touch. That distressed her almost as much as having the Captain enter the house via the kitchen – as the key to neither the front door nor the library had been discovered.

The window Edward had broken had Joe Suggett, the constable, standing in front of it – also plainly not knowing quite what to do next, Mr. Tadswell not having informed him, and this sort of thing being far out of his experience. He was relieved to have Edward order one of the grooms back to Bournelea to have Samuels, who saw to the repairs about the estate, come and board up both the broken and burned windows. Once that had been made secure, Constable Suggett would be free to get back to his not very arduous duties, an idea that the bucolic officer greeted with great relief. There were a dozen other minor decisions to be taken. They weren't, Edward reflected, really his to take, but someone had to, in the absence of Arthur Weatherly, who was not to be expected until the morrow, at the earliest.

It didn't take long for Edward to become well aware that that was in no small part their worry. Country folk were not overly fond of change, and change must follow, if Frederick Weatherly died. The future, with Arthur as their new master, looked... uncertain. "The place will be sold, surely," said Mrs. Lessing, wringing her hands. "For he's not likely to want to keep it. He doesn't like it in the country. He said so. Said it was a rubbishing old place."

Westmead was a relatively modest country house, and, certainly, some of the rooms could use refurbishment, but it was a solid Queen Anne house, with an attractive prospect and what could be a pleasant park. But Arthur Weatherly was unlikely to live there, Edward had to agree. It was possible he might keep it, but more likely he'd sell it, or possibly rent it out. He admitted as much to Mrs. Lessing, but pointed out that there was a chance that her old master might recover, and also that whoever bought the place, might well employ at least some of the staff. He wondered if Weatherly had arranged a pension for Lessing and his wife, but he had no idea how things were left.

He was about to take his leave, when Mrs. Lessing said: "Master Edward, I mean Captain Edward," – she'd known him as a little boy, when she'd been a housemaid at Bournelea. "I clean forgot. Will the groom went as he always does, to the Priors, to the receiving office. He said he'd not have been knowing what to do with himself otherwise. There's a letter for the master, that he paid for." She thrust it into his hands. "Normally, I'd be leaving it in the library. I don't know how to manage all this." She started her crying again.

Edward patted her on the shoulder. "Send Will into Whitchurch in the morning to get the locksmith to come out. Otherwise he'll have to go on to Winchester to find someone. Those locks must be replaced if the keys cannot be found," said Edward, looking at the letter. "I suppose there is a chance that the old fellow will regain consciousness soon. Otherwise, I must turn this over to Arthur, I suppose. I imagine he will come to Bournelea, to see his uncle. Or perhaps I need to give the letter to his man of business... or his attorney. I am a little out of my depth, I am afraid, Mrs. Lessing. But I'll ask my father."

He bore it home and handed it to his father, who scrutinized it and answered his question with: "I am not sure, my boy. Probably the attorney. It doesn't look like any matter of business. It appears to be from one G. Ross, from somewhere in Southampton. The name rings a vague bell, but I can't place it."

The address was neatly written in a careful round hand that re-minded Edward of his younger sister's script. "It'll keep a day or two, in any case," said his father.

Chapter 3

Georgina had not even got as far as the receiving office to send her letters, since she'd arrived. She had no idea if they had been posted, or if her grandfather would pay to receive the missive she had sent to him – or how often he might get any post. She considered, not for the first time, taking what was left in her slender purse, and going to a posting-house – that she was not sure how to find, and taking the mail-coach to the nearest town to her grandfather's house. But she had no idea how far the house might be from the point where she would be set down, or if she could hire some form of transport there, or would have to proceed on foot. She had memories of life in Edinburgh as a child, but these stood her in poor stead for information on how one got about between places in rural England. She'd happily ridden far greater distances in Africa, but the idea of a lady doing so, here, seemed wholly alien to her cousins – and they were her only view on the wider world of the country which was supposed to be her 'home'.

She had found the wait to get any form of reply from her letter interminable. Her aunt's house might provide shelter from the rain, and meant that she had food, but that was where any good points ended, as far as Georgina was concerned. Her aunt would rather have welcomed smallpox into her household, and lost no opportunity in letting Georgina know that. Captain Thomas, who she'd viewed as her rescuer, she had come to be nervous about. He kept... standing too close, putting an arm around her. Patting her. Even kissing her cheek. Perhaps this was how men in England behaved. They certainly did not on the mission station at the foot of the Katberg, or in her mother's company when they'd fled to Grahamstown, and certainly not on the ship. But perhaps her manners were as provincial and out of fashion as her clothes. She was limited to blacks, and there were only five dresses – two of hers and three of her mother's – that she could wear. The style of them was – as to be expected from a remote mission station, several years out of date, with gigot sleeves and they had a modest style and were high cut on the bodice and shoulders, and had full skirts, when her cousins had sleeves tight to the arm, were ornamented with ribbon, and were low-cut, with their skirts showing their feet.

Her complexion too gave the cousins, cousins she had not known she had, something to sneer at. "You're as brown as a gypsy," Elvira disdainfully informed her. "How do you ever expect to get a husband looking like that?"

It had not taken Georgina long to establish that there were few thoughts in the heads of her cousins – or their mama, except about forming a respectable connection, the wealthier the better. Liking, let alone love, seemed entirely subservient to wealth.

Georgina hadn't actually given a great deal of thought before to marriage, or indeed love. When the border wars had started she'd been getting to an age where this was a consideration. There were certainly not many young English women in the border regions of Beaufort. She knew that some of the officers who had attended the church services at the mission when their duties took them into its vicinity, had certainly made an attempt to be very friendly, and smile on her. But, with the wall of her father, and her mother's watchful eye, she'd never had more than a polite public conversation after church. She'd briefly been quite doe-eyed about one lieutenant and had been quite breathless with excitement when she'd seen him return to a service at the church. It was only when he'd turned his head that she realized it was someone else, that she'd discovered the unfairness of regimental dress.

It was still deeply instilled in her, by a mother who had taken just that decision, that happiness in marriage rested on common values and loving your husband enough to follow him to Africa and the privations of a frontier mission station, five days of wagon travel from the military outpost in Grahmstown. Her Aunt Louisa having set her to work turning sheets she spent a great deal of time listening as she sat and sewed linen – turning sheets – that being the work that Aunt Louisa had set her to. She came to realize that her Cousin Elvira was untroubled by the fact her current beau, whom she and her mother were increasingly sure could be brought to propose, had a mistress. Moreover, he was more than double her age, and was, it seemed, the owner of a manufactory producing gin.

It also appeared that the one thing that Elvira and her mother wanted to avoid at all costs was her Mr. Vinery meeting Georgina. She couldn't think why, as he sounded just like the sort of person she had no wish to meet, and being sent to the poky little attic-room given her as a bedroom, was no particular hardship, when he arrived to call. It left her with little to do but to look out of the tiny window over the rain-wet roofs of the town, and ponder her next move. That, barring a reply from her grandfather. She'd written to the Edinburgh Mission

Society as well, as she knew her mother had held some hope of some kind of small pension. She couldn't see how it would descend to her, but her mother had been insistent, right up to her dying breaths, that she contact them.

She had to find some way of making a living, of providing for herself. Not for the first time she desperately wished that they not left Africa. Even when they had evacuated to Grahamstown they had known a few people. She could perhaps have found a position as a housekeeper, and in that society would have met people, even if only at church. She'd have had some chance of finding a husband that she could feel some affection for...

Her aunt had laughed at her, rather scornfully, when she'd tentatively asked about the possibility of applying for some such work here. "You're too ignorant to be a governess. They'd want you to have some experience. And you're far too young and inexperienced to be a housekeeper."

"I did most of the housekeeping while mother was nursing my father," she said awkwardly.

"In Africa," said her aunt with a sniff. "You lack the conduct required for an English house. Why, earlier you were in converse with Mary. A servant!"

"I am sorry, Ma'am," said Georgina, biting back a retort that she actually liked Mary, and felt the way she was treated was shameful. Or the fact that Mary had confided that she was off quick-smart as soon as she could find another post. If she'd learned anything from Mary it was that the life of an abigail was a hard one, at least in this house. The maid slept in the next attic room, but was seldom there in waking hours. So, Georgina was surprised to hear sounds from it now. Sounds that included sobbing. She went to see what was wrong. Mary was in the act of packing up her small pile of possessions. "What is the matter?" asked Georgina.

The little, sharp face was pinched and red from crying. "Oh, miss. Not another hour will I spend in this house. That man!"

It took some patience to get the story out of the girl. She was even younger than Georgina, and a good few meals short in growing, and now very distressed. Apparently, the suitor had placed his hand somewhere decidedly unsuitable on Mary's person. "As if I was some tavern lightskirt, miss. I'm a good girl." She'd set up a screech, she informed Georgina. "And I tried to box his ears, miss, and what's to happen but the mistress come in and yells at me, and tells me off, and threatens to turn me off without a character!"

Mary started crying again. "Oh, miss. I don't know what to do! Me mother... she needs the money, she's got four to feed besides herself. We'll end up in the poorhouse. Oh, Lord." She buried her head in her hands.

"The Captain, he seems..." offered Georgina.

"He's off to sea again, Friday, on the tide. She'd wait until he's off, for sure," said Mary bitterly.

Indeed, it was only three more days. Georgina had been aware it was due to happen, but not quite aware of when. That added a fresh tier to Georgina's own worries. But her first task was to help Mary. The girl was in terror of what Aunt Louisa might do, once Elvira's suitor had left. On the other hand, she was worried about the fact that her week's wages would not be paid, and, although this was a very small sum, it went to feeding her family. Georgina felt so terribly helpless that she could not even help to shelter Mary from her aunt. There was no telling what might happen to her own shelter, after Friday. She took a deep breath and made her decision, and spoke hastily, before she could change her mind. Father had always said one must have the courage to do what was right, no matter the cost. "Mary. I don't have much money, but... I can give you a pound. That... that might help you to have a little time to find new work. And... I could write you a character reference. I haven't known you very long, but I could say I found you good and honest and hard-working while I was in my aunt's house. It's true so I am happy to write it." She patted the girl's shoulder. "They wouldn't know I have only been here a week." She felt even her father would have forgiven that. It was hard being a missionary's daughter. She was expected to be saintly, and, being truthful with herself, she felt she fell far short of it that.

She was quite un-prepared for Mary's incredulous look and to find herself being hugged. Mary backed off hastily. "Oh Miss. I do be taking liberties. I'm sorry."

Georgina patted her shoulder again. "There. Don't worry." She smiled wryly. "I'm from Africa, as Aunt Louisa will tell you. I don't know how to behave."

"Oh, Miss!" protested Mary. "You're far more of the lady than her! And so much prettier than those daughters of hers."

"No, I'm not. I don't know how to behave, here. And my clothes are old and dowdy."

Mary shook her head. "It's not for nothing that they want you out of there, when there's men visiting, Miss."

"More like because I'd embarrass them," said Georgina, ruefully. "Now, Mary, I must just go and get my money, and... and we'll need to find a quill, and ink and some paper."

"Miss! You can't be giving me your money." It was plain that even the housemaid knew how poor she was, and how dim her prospects.

"I can and I will," said Georgina firmly, wishing it would not be making such a hole in her slender funds. "Now... to write a letter of commendation. I have my mother's writing-case. I'll need some new ink, and to sharpen the quill."

"I could get some from the master's study," offered Mary. "He'll not be back until this evening. He's with his ship. They're loading. And the mistress is not likely to come up here unless it is to look for me. But she'll do that, soon enough." She shivered.

"Well. I'll not take a chance it happens before I can do this for you. I don't know how I could find you otherwise," said Georgina. "Go and get the ink and come to my bed-chamber." Seeing the look of trepidation on Mary's face, she said: "You can hide in the cupboard if we hear her coming. She has a tread like an elephant."

That was enough to get a little start of a laugh out of the girl, and send her racing off while Georgina went back to her little room and took her meagre funds from the little hiding place she had in her trunk, and then struggled to get it off the top of the one that still held her mother's possessions, to get out the writing-case. By the time she had it out, Mary was back with some ink and she was able to carefully pen a letter commending her, and to give her the money. It was more than six weeks wages for the maid, and she eyed it with a mixture of relief and guilt. "Take it," said Georgina.

"Oh Miss. But you do need it."

"I'll have to trust to God to provide," said Georgina. It was what her father always said. Not that what He'd provided had been easy.

"You're a saint, Miss." Mary proclaimed, tucking the money away carefully.

"No," said Georgina, "My father was a saint, or at least my mother always said so, and she said it made him hard to live with. I'm... I'm just rather scared and alone. My father always knew where he was going. My mother was always willing to be going wherever he went. I... have no idea. It's all so strange. I don't know anyone or anything at all. I don't know quite what to do. All the way from Africa, and now, I'm as lost as a child." She drew a deep breath. "But that is my problem. Now: what are you going to do, Mary? Do you need help packing up?"

The housemaid looked at her, with something Georgina was shocked to realize was hero-worship. She took a deep breath. "I reckon, Miss, that I'll wait for that old besom to throw me out. And if she doesn't... I'll look for another place and give you your money back when I find one! I've your beautiful letter now, and it'll do my ma proud to read it. And you needs someone to stand by you, and what I can do, I will."

Georgina felt too choked up to speak. Yes, Mary was just a housemaid, from some poorer part of town. But she'd been feeling so isolated and alone. She squeezed Mary's arm again. "Thank you. You... you better put that letter away safely and... and...

"And get myself back to work, before she finds me up here. And I'd better take that ink back," said Mary.

It actually worried Georgina even more, knowing that she had an ally... that she might lose at any moment. But, oddly, against both of their expectations, the feared expulsion did not come. Thinking about it, Georgina decided that either her aunt had decided to wait until the Captain left, or she'd decided that replacing Mary – at the wage the girl had accepted – would be difficult. Mary was indeed a good worker, and kept hard at it, by both the other three servants and the family. She did get time off to attend church on a Sunday, and an afternoon off every second Tuesday, which she used to visit her mother. That would have been the next day, but had been pushed off a week, because the house was at sixes and sevens preparing for the Captain's departure. Mary had her tasks from early morning until the evening meal was served, and could be called for at any time – it was why she was given the little cubby of a room in the eaves – to be available and not off home every evening, as John was. Cook – who called herself the housekeeper, as well as the kitchen maid who also helped with the cleaning, and the other maid, who was Aunt Louisa's personal maid, slept in the other wing of attics.

During the day, Georgina saw Mary occasionally, as she too was kept busy. But a quick smile, given after a nervous look around, did lighten the day. In the evening, when Georgina was able to go to her bed, Mary too was in the attic, and Georgina was able to call her into her bedroom, close the door, and the two could talk. "If anyone should come or call for you, I shall say I called you in to help me pin a flounce," said Georgina. "Which is true. My father would think I was a shocking liar." That was also true, but Georgina knew it would be essential for Mary's protection, let alone her own. It took a little while to persuade Mary to sit on the very end of her bed. She wondered if Mary would be more comfortable in her own room, which had two tiny cots – but only held Mary at the moment. It was smaller and colder than this room, and besides, Georgina's presence there would be even harder to explain.

Georgina soon discovered that the servants, at least, had an enormous curiosity about where she'd come from and what her experiences had been. Her aunt and cousins had affected disinterest. Well, it was possibly not affected. The truth was they were little interested in anything that wasn't fashion or a possible hope of matrimony. Her uncle had asked some questions – but these had centered on trade and the sea-ports – which as a girl from a frontier mission-station she knew little about.

She was able to satisfy... or rather disappoint, Mary's very vague ideas about Africa – which it appeared was a place which was all much alike, very hot, and full of black people, jungle and savage beasts. The idea that Katberg mission got snowed on, and that while there were wild animals – Georgina had seen elephants, zebras and lions, and many different antelope, the 'jungle' was either thorny semi-desert, or grassland. It was still a tale of wonderment to someone whose world had never moved beyond five miles from where she was born, although Mary's parents, she gathered, had come from Ireland.

Georgina, on the other hand, was able to learn, at least through a housemaid's eyes, something more of her Aunt's establishment as it compared to others, something of the city of Southampton, and a little of employment prospects and how one tracked them down.

Both were yawning copiously before they parted and went to sleep. Georgina enjoyed a better rest than she had, up to now. Her mind was full, and her dreams were somewhat confused. She thought, with amusement as she woke in the morning, probably less confused than Mary, who had some curious ideas about the wildlife of Southern Africa, some of which she hadn't known existed until yesterday.

Georgina knew now, that the house had fewer servants than the one next door. She knew that Cook was stealing from the mistress, and that Mary was terrified of being blamed. She knew the manservant was often drunk in the morning from his potations in the gin-sluiceries, and that Mary was scandalized by the carryings-on between him and the mistress's maid. She knew, too, that advertisements of employment were carried in the Morning Post, which was, when the master was home, taken up to his study. She knew which posting house the mail and accommodation coaches left for London, and where one could procure a ticket. Times and costs were beyond Mary's ken. Indeed, she'd looked a little upset at the idea of finding out, but had promised to attend to it when she had her next afternoon off.

Chapter 4

Arthur Weatherly arrived at Bournelea the following day, while the Doctor was upstairs, paying his second visit of the day to the patient. Courtesy to the old man made them receive Arthur with the semblance of politeness and consideration. He might, after all, end up as their neighboring land-owner. Edward thought, despite his fashionable attire, that Arthur was looking a little wan. But, to give him the benefit of the doubt that could be merely because he was upset at the news.

Awful Arthur lost no time in living up to his nickname, demanding to know who had dared to incur the expense of sending for a locksmith and boarding up the windows of Westmead House, as if it were in some back-slum.

He seemed, to Edward, to be exceptionally tense and almost eager to quarrel. Normally, Arthur could put on a reasonable semblance of a well-bred man, although he'd always rubbed Edward up the wrong way. "If you'd been up at first light," said Edward, "You'd know that it was pouring with rain from then until well after ten. I sent one of our people over to board up the windows, to keep everything inside secure and dry."

"The glass needs to be replaced!"

"By all means, I suggest you get a glazier from Winchester to come and do so. The window frames on the saloon are quite ruined too," said Edward. "That'll need a skilled carpenter. You'll want to get the timbers in the floor joists and ceiling checked, and possibly those replaced as well."

Arthur chose to ignore all this: "And that locksmith! He dared to say he should be paid for his time, after I sent him packing. He went as far as to ask that damned magistrate to open an action of law against me."

"Well, he'd come a considerable way to do the job," said Edward, reasonably.

"I didn't employ him. As I said to that encroaching magistrate, let him approach whoever did!"

"That would be me," said Edward, keeping his calm. "And I shall settle it."

"How dared that magistrate enter my property without my consent!" said Arthur, cheated of that complaint.

"It's not your property," said Edward, growing rapidly – as he always did – tired of Arthur's manner and conduct. "And there was an attempted murder, as well as robbery and arson at Westmead."

"That valuable collection of my uncle's. I knew it should have been under lock and key. Those snuff boxes were worth a great deal of money and the Ming bowl that was taken, thousands of pounds."

"I didn't even know the bowl was missing. That would be that one that stood in the corner, with all the colors? He did say it ought to be locked up, but he liked to look at it. So: how is Tadswell's investigation going?" asked Edward, trying to turn the conversation to more neutral ground.

"Futilely," said Arthur. "The man is a nincompoop. Even asked me where I was two nights ago! As if I would ride down here from London in the dark. Fortunately, I spent most of the night with friends, who can testify to that effect. The effrontery of the fellow! How could he suspect me!"

Edward held his tongue. Arthur's willowy form did make assault less than likely. And, admittedly, burglary would have taken more courage than he thought Arthur possessed. It was not, he admitted to himself, that Arthur lacked nerve. He had that, to a degree of barefaced effrontery. It was simply the physical intrepidity that was natural to the Kelling brothers, that he'd always shied away from. But these points, he felt, would hardly have soothed Arthur. "Anyway," said Arthur. "I've come to enquire after my Uncle Frederick. Your brother John informs me he is unconscious and unlikely to recover. Why did you remove him from his own home? I hold you responsible for conduct that will lead to his death."

"When I removed him from it, his house was on fire, and I had no way of knowing if we could save it. It was a lucky chance that we caught the fire early. We brought him here for my mother to care for. He was gravely injured, you know. Arthur, we've actually done our best for him and his property," said Edward, evenly, keeping himself in check. "Whereas we haven't seen you here since before Christmas. Do you remember that?"

Arthur eyed him with what could only be described as malevolence. "That was totally uncalled for. Besides, why anyone should believe some lightskirt provincial..."

Edward was spared giving an answer by his parents, accompanied by Dr Selby, entering the room. The greetings that were exchanged were politeness itself – but frosty, withal. "How is my Uncle Frederick? I would like to remove him as soon as possible," asked Arthur.

"He remains comatose," said Dr Selby. "And I cannot advocate moving him anywhere. His condition is grave, Mr. Weatherly. I do not hold out any high hopes."

Looking at the play of emotions quickly darting across Arthur's face, Edward was surprised to see the man looking worried. He would have thought Arthur would rejoice in his uncle's demise, but it appeared not. Edward thought rather the better of him for that.

"I may assure you," said Edward's mother. "We will give him the best care possible, following Dr Selby's orders to the letter, until he is ready to go to his own home."

"Maybe you should see to making his house as safe and comfortable as possible," said Edward's father. "He's a tough old bird, you know. He'll pull through, if anyone can."

"I... I, um, I shall see to it," said Arthur, sounding discomforted. "I will be coming down to stay in the house in a day or two. Unfortunately, I have to be back in London tomorrow... a matter of business, you understand."

Edward wondered just what business that could be, as his brother John had told him that Arthur's chief occupation was patronizing various gaming hells, and could seldom be seen abroad before evening. But perhaps Arthur had reformed his ways. It was always possible.

"We will send you a message should anything transpire," said Edward's father. "Which puts me in mind of something: we have a letter for your uncle. From a G. Ross."

"Ah!" said the Doctor. "Ross! Weatherly's son-in-law. Oddly, we were both up at Cambridge together, in the same college. I knew him slightly. As well as any medical student knows someone studying theology, that is. An oddity he was, in that he came from Edinburgh.

He's in Africa. A missionary I believe. I heard he'd been injured in one of the native wars."

"The letter is from a receiving office in Southampton," said Edward's father. "Didn't you say you'd heard the missionary chap died, Edward?"

"Yes, the old fellow... Mr. Weatherly, said he was expecting his daughter to come back to England. He seemed pleased about the idea. They were... estranged, but he seemed to welcome the idea of healing the rift. He's been preparing for her to come to Westmead House. Mrs. Lessing says she's opened up two of the bed-chambers in the West wing. I'm sorry... I didn't realize her surname was Ross. He always just talked of 'my daughter'."

"Good Lord, what a terrible homecoming for her," exclaimed Edward's mother.

"It can't be her," said Edward's father. "His daughter's name was Dorothea. I ought to know," he said with a wry smile. "Must be another Ross."

"He did say something about a grand-child," said Edward. "I'm sorry, we didn't really discuss family matters. We mostly talked about his land and the management of it. And fishing."

"Which is no business of yours," snapped Arthur. "My uncle does have a daughter and granddaughter, called, as I recall, Georgina. You had better give the letter to me. As his heir, I will be dealing with his affairs anyway."

Edward could not but feel uncomfortable about this, but his father went and fetched the letter and handed it to Arthur. Arthur, then and there, almost as if to make his point broke the wafer and opened it. It was a single sheet – and not, as Edward's sister always did, crossed, but more than that they could not see. Edward noticed the man was... tense. His hand was tight on the chair-top he had taken hold of.

Odd, thought Edward. But the hand relaxed, and so did Arthur's face. "Georgina Ross. Well."

"What about her?" asked Edward's mother.

Arthur looked as if he was about to say: "None of your business," but he caught his breath, and answered civilly enough. "It is a private letter to my uncle, to inform him of the unfortunate passing of his daughter, my cousin, on her way back from the Southern African colonies. The result of some unpleasant tick-borne disease."

Doctor Selby was the first to break the silence. "A very unhealthy place, Africa. Sad to hear that. I never knew her of course, but a great pity she and her father never got the chance to heal their rift. Well, I daresay they'll get their chance soon enough."

"What's happened to the granddaughter?" asked Lady Elizabeth. "I assume if she is writing to him, she must be alive and have arrived in Southampton."

Arthur nodded. "Yes, she is situated with an aunt there. She had hoped to come and visit her grandfather. Well, I shall have to see the girl and break the news to her."

"She's welcome to come and visit him. I mean, it would be distressing for her, but she would be welcome."

"I will see to it," said Arthur, firmly.

There was little to say to that. Arthur did not go upstairs to see his uncle, and shortly took his leave, along with the Doctor. He did promise to return within a couple of days.

Whatever else that letter had contained it did seem to have made Arthur a great deal less eager to pick a fight, and he even summonsed the grace to thank Lady Kelling for her care for his uncle before departing.

After he'd left, Edward's mother shook her head. "I never understand that man, I am afraid."

"Well, he usually manages to be all too popular with the ladies," said Sir Gerald, dryly. "Never understood why, myself, but then your sex has always been something of a mystery to me. A pity that he is likely to be our neighbor."

"Actually," said his spouse, tucking her arm in his, "Possibly not. I don't know what came over Dr. Selby, except maybe a desire not to have Frederick Weatherly moved, but he was considerably less discouraging about Weatherly's condition to me than he was to Arthur. His breathing is much improved, and his pulse a little stronger."

"Ah. I can't say it wouldn't be good news if he recovered. A pity about his daughter, though."

Edward's mother nodded. "Yes. I have a good mind to write to the grandchild, tell her of the situation and invite her to come and visit him. There's no telling what Arthur will do about it. It's unfortunate that I can't."

His father smiled. "Why not?"

"Where would I address it to?" asked his spouse.

"I was intending to send a letter saying that Mr. Frederick Weatherly could not at present read the missive, and that if the matter was of any urgency they could approach Mr. Winter, his man of business. I had got half way through composing it, and when I went to fetch the letter, I wrote the address on my pad, because I wondered if Arthur would deal with it appropriately. It's on my writing desk."

"I will write to her at once, then!" said Edward's mother.

Chapter 5

The perusal of the Morning Post with reference to finding herself some form of a position had not, so far, been very rewarding for Georgina. The Captain tended to take the latest copy to the ship with him, so what she had managed – with Mary's assistance, to get ahold of, were weeks old, at the very least. Then, deciphering quite what was meant or wanted was also a little difficult, given her ignorance of localities and the roles occupied by the various degrees of English society. She had found several positions she considered possible, had even sent a letter to one requiring a young lady of quality to assist an elderly employer – only to be told the position had been filled – which was more than she'd heard from the other   two   enquiries,   as yet.

In the meanwhile, she had found herself 'employed' in a manner of speaking, at a vast amount of mending, darning and sewing. These were things she knew how to do, but had not, herself, done much of. On the mission station there were several of the native women who had embraced such work: they were paid to do it, a novelty in their society, and, Georgina came to realize, it would be one in hers. Also, having made some comment about the pianoforte to Maude, the second daughter, she had been disparagingly told not to opine on something she knew nothing about. They didn't have such things in Africa!

"Well, actually, we did. It came by sea. We played it a lot. It was very popular with the congregation. The native women have such beautiful voices, and harmonize wonderfully," she said, briefly transported by the memory, to the dark night and a tiny Church against the edge of the mountain, filled with the sound of voices lifted in song.

"I don't believe you!" said Maude.

Nettled, and somewhat lifted by the memory, Georgina seated herself at the pianoforte and began to play. It lifted her spirits further... "Stop playing!" snapped Maude. "I didn't ask you to."

"Well, you should," said Captain Salmonds, who had plainly heard the music, and put his head in to see who was playing. "She could teach you a thing or two. You play well, young lady. Do you know anything a bit more cheerful, eh?"

"I only really learned hymns, Captain," she answered. "I can read music though. If you have the score for something else, I will try."

"I have no idea. I am not musical myself. But see if you can teach this puss of mine to play as if she wasn't beating the poor thing to death, eh?"

"I don't think I can teach..." started Georgina, doubtfully.

"Now, now, give it a try. Maude needs a bit of help."

Georgina soon decided she was quite right in saying she was not able to teach. Her reluctant pupil was certainly not eager to learn. However, it was borne upon her by her aunt that she was expected to succeed. So, she tried. She was able to reflect that at least one of them was trying.

On the Thursday, with Captain Salmonds was due to sail on the next morning tide, several things changed in her life, rather dramatically. The first was that she received a letter – for which she had to disperse three pence, but she hoped it would be some prospect of getting herself out of the Salmonds' household and able to support herself. She was accustomed to rising early from life at the mission-station, and the habit had never left her. She was up several hours before the rest of the household, and had accompanied John, whose task it was to check the mail at the receiving office for the Captain, especially so close to his departure, long before the family had even exited their bedchambers, let alone gone down for breakfast.

In the privacy this afforded her, she was able to open the letter and read it. It was not the hoped for reply either from her grandfather, or the application she'd made to be an elderly lady's companion. It was a letter from someone she had certainly never written to, who styled herself Lady Elizabeth Kelling of Bournelea. The content certainly made her no more settled. Lady Elizabeth began by offering her condolences on the death of her mother, informed her that she was the neighbor of her grandfather – and that the old man was in her care and, sadly, had been injured and was still deeply unconscious, and in some danger of death. She invited Georgina to come and visit her grandfather at any time, and to stay for a few days if she so desired. It was a very polite, kindly letter, and left Georgina in a quandary as to what to do. She felt she ought to go and see her grandfather – whom she'd never met. It was a duty, she believed. On the other hand... how was she to get there? What could it do to her already slender purse, and what good could it possibly do her?

She was wrestling with these problems and had just decided that the cost must be borne, because her mother would have expected it of her, when matters took an even more unexpected turn. She was trying to focus her attention on Maude's playing, and wondering how best to bring up the subject with her aunt, when John, the manservant, came and announced to the ladies in the drawing room that a gentleman had come to call, hoping to have speech with Miss Georgina. He presented the gentleman's card to her aunt who was reposed on the sofa. She held it out at arms-length, to avoid reaching for her lorgnette. "This will be your grandfather," she said, looking at it. "A Mr. Arthur Weatherly. Show him in, John."

The slim gentleman shown into the room was such the epitome of sartorial elegance as to make her aunt... and her cousins, draw breath. He was also plainly not her grandfather, being far too young for that role. He was handsome too, and had beside an air of fashion and an elegant hairstyle, a charming smile. He bowed over their hands, and took both of hers in his, on being introduced. "So, pleased to meet you," he said, smiling. "We are cousins, I believe, if once removed. My father was your grandfather's younger brother."

Georgina recalled vaguely hearing of something of her grandfather's nephew from one of Uncle George's precious letters. She looked back at him in some relief. "What news, do you have, sir, of my grandfather? I..."

"It is rather grave news, I am afraid. He's not in what you might call plump currant. In fact, he is very ill."

She nodded. "Yes. I had a letter from Lady Kelling, telling me so."

He looked slightly taken aback, but recovered himself with a small smile. "Well, I am glad I don't have to break the news to you at least. Your letter was given to me, so I know you hoped to go and stay with my Uncle Frederick, but he is not at home, so unfortunately that won't be possible yet. However, I will keep you apprised, and I shall come down regularly to tell you how he goes on."

"Thank you," she said: "Lady Kelling invited me to go and visit him."

He paused briefly. "Well, it could be arranged, but you know he is deeply unconscious. He would be unaware of your visit."

Georgina nodded. "I, I am not sure what good a visit would do, but, well, I believe my mother would have wished me to do so. And," she added, drawing on a painful memory, "The military surgeon in Grahamstown told me... during the time when my father was in his last days, when he did not really seem to know what was happening, that he had a patient, whom they thought deeply unconscious, who told them later that he had heard every word they said, but had been unable to reply. So, I would very much like to go."

"I shall have to make arrangements then," he said, "You may leave it to me."

"Oh, thank you so much. I must write to Lady Kelling to thank her."

"I shall happily convey your message to her," said her cousin, leaving her to reflect how much of a relief it was to have someone to take care of these matters, and to feel even more grateful to him. He did not remain above half-an-hour, but the entire event left her feeling up-lifted and as if things might well be improving, although that too was contrasted by the fact that the refuge of staying with her grandfather was now a closed door. By the tone of Lady's Kelling's letter, it had not seemed there was any great hope of recovery. With that in mind, she had begged Cousin Arthur, on his leaving, to please arrange for her to visit her grandfather as soon as possible. He assured her that he would, and also would deliver the hastily written note of thanks she had excused herself to pen for Lady Kelling.

After his departure she found her aunt and cousins similarly con-
flicted. Plainly they were all very impressed by Mr. Arthur Weatherly, Maude describing him in rather awed tones as 'A great swell,' an
expression she was told off for by her mother... who plainly shared
her opinion of Cousin Arthur, as he'd insisted that Georgina call
him. She'd rather nervously made him free to address her as Cousin
Georgina. It did make her feel a little less alone in this unfamiliar
England. She regarded him as something of a relieving force, that
would help her to at least leave this house, even though it was only
temporarily.

It was plain, however, that her cousins and aunt had found a new
worth in their unwelcome cousin from Africa. She could bring them
into contact with a far wealthier tier of society than they had previously had entry to. The references her cousin had made to attending
a soiree with a name she'd never heard of, and of what Lord so-and-so
had said to him might be lost on her, but had deeply impressed them.
Her aunt had wanted nothing more than to be rid of her: now she was
finding reasons why Mr. Arthur Weatherly should rather visit here to
carry news to Georgina of her grandfather, than she go there.

Elvira and Maude had absorbed every detail of his dress and were
happy to tell of its merits... as well, of course, as mentioning the poor
impression her unfashionable appearance must have made on him.
It was... uncomfortable. She wanted her cousin to think well of her,
but at least he seemed kindly disposed towards her. That... she had
to admit to herself, was something that mother had been very unsure
about her grandfather being. His letter had been terse, and while he'd
said they should come home, it was anything but clear whether he'd
meant 'back to England' or back to his home.

And, while Arthur Weatherly had seemed kindly, she really had no
claim on him at all. She wasn't sure how he fitted into her grandfather's

life, but he plainly had been to visit him often enough, and was thoroughly familiar with his house, Westmead, and had been deputized to open his mail. With her Uncle George dead, he was probably her grandfather's heir, she reflected. She knew her mother had been disinherited for marrying against her grandfather's will.

It had been good of Cousin Arthur to come and see her to tell her the news – which he certainly was not obliged to do in person. He could simply have sent her a letter, or not replied at all, she supposed. He obviously hadn't known of Lady Elizabeth writing to her.

She had received a scold from her aunt for having ventured into the receiving office, but it had been a minor one. She had no way of knowing if and when Arthur would make good on his promises, but at least it did reassure her that her aunt would not send her packing the minute Captain Thomas's ship had sailed.

She was quite relieved not to have to wait too long. A message, delivered by hand, reached them the very next day. Mr. Arthur Weatherly would escort her, himself, to visit her grandfather, if she could be ready to set forth at the hour of nine o'clock? It was early, but they had some distance to travel.

Taken to her aunt, the message caused no small amount of uproar in a house already in some chaos with the Captain about to sail and, as was their tradition, his wife and children going down to the dock to wave him farewell. Georgina had politely declined to join this expedition, as she felt it was something which belonged to the family. The Captain had hugged her and kissed her soundly – and wished her well with this new beau, her cousin, that he'd heard so much about from his wife. It was rather odd to hear Cousin Arthur thus described, but it would make a pleasant daydream, Georgina had to admit. It was very uncharitable, but that would certainly make the Captain's daughters green with envy.

Mr. Arthur Weatherly's note raised the immediate problem of how a young woman could possibly go off, alone, with a gentleman. Two days ago, Georgina thought, her aunt would have happily seen her run off with a coal-heaver. Now, needs must, she must take Elvira with her, to be a chaperon. Not, by any slight chance, thought Georgina darkly, to allow Elvira to cast out her lures at Cousin Arthur!

She suggested, politely, that it might not be convenient for Cousin Arthur to have to transport both of them, as they had no idea quite how he meant to travel. Perhaps they should enquire? For once Aunt Louisa actually listened to her, but made it abundantly clear that, without adequate chaperonage, the journey was not going to happen. As the note had been borne by a messenger who had waited for a reply – as he'd been instructed to, this proved quite easy. They were rewarded, some half an hour later, by receiving a visit from the gentleman himself. He was all smiles and acquiescence. "I had assumed Georgina's maid would travel with her. But of course, your daughter would be a very adequate companion, Mrs. Salmonds. I shall be riding, they can travel in the chariot I have hired. I hope we should be able to accomplish the journey there and back in one day, because I hardly feel my cousin would wish to impose on Lady Kelling." He tugged at his chin. "She can be, how can I say, quite prickly. She is caring for my uncle, but, well, I cannot like it. There's been some conflict between the Kellings and Weatherlys. Land issues, you know. Our acres march alongside theirs. It's rather difficult having my uncle in their house, due to the circumstance of his indisposition. But I will say no more. You understand me, I am sure."

Georgina didn't, fully, but nodded anyway. She was sorry that she would be unable to stay away from her aunt for longer, if not permanently, and Elvira would rather get in the way of the frank conversations she wanted to have with her cousin, asking his assistance in

finding her a post she could support herself with. But there was little
she could do about it. She wondered what her aunt would have made
of some the things she'd done, in perfect safety, around the mission
and even in Grahamstown. Well, there was no-one to disapprove of
her out there. Here, it seemed, people were all around all of the time.
It came to her suddenly, how desperately she missed the space, the
solitude and the silences of the Katberg valley. Perhaps to those who
had never known them, living in these tall, narrow houses, surrounded
by noise and people was just natural and acceptable. She would have
to take whatever life dealt her next, but she had to hope it would not
be a life in the city.

She was ready in ample time the next morning. Needless to say, her
cousin Elvira, not an early riser at any time, was not. In an odd way this
worked out very well for Georgina, as she was able to join her cousin
in the downstairs parlor, with her aunt, who was called away to attend
to some problem her daughter was having. They were left together,
in some privacy.

She plucked up her courage. "Cousin Arthur, forgive me, I am
ignorant of the mode of acceptable behavior in England. I find it very
confusing here... and... and I find myself in desperate need of advice."

"I will of course be very happy to help, Cousin Georgina."

"You know... my mother and I came back from Africa, and, well,
doing so was very expensive. Missionaries have very limited funds,
and mama had spent most of what she had, caring for my father. She
sold her jewelry to pay for the journey," admitted Georgina, twisting
her fingers, awkwardly. "And now I find myself... in very straitened
circumstances. I was hoping that my grandfather might..." she found
herself coloring and at a loss for words.

He looked grave, and sucked air between his teeth. "This is awkward, my dear Cousin. Forgive me for being so direct to you. But,

if you had hoped my uncle... well, the truth is he was still extremely angry with your mother. Said it served her right for her bad decisions. I wouldn't refine too much on hopes of his charity, should he make a recovery. It is not to be looked for, to be honest."

"Indeed, I wasn't hoping for charity. I was just hoping for some assistance in... in finding something I could do to provide for myself. I... I am not at all proud, you know. We had to do many tasks a lady would not consider, it seems, back in England. I just have no idea how to go about the thing. I hoped for, I don't know, perhaps some recommendations, or even character references. I am, unfortunately, rather young for many positions, and, while my father did give a great deal of time to my education, I don't really have a formal education that I could refer people to. I am woefully ignorant of... of so many things that even an English housemaid would know," she said, thinking of Mary. "At most I had hoped I could stay with him for long enough to find some kind of position. I can work hard, and I am willing to do so."

He smiled. "You should be thinking of getting married, not of entering into some lifetime of drudgery!"

"Oh, I have no prospect of that!" said Georgina, hastily. "I have no dowry, and... and I have no likelihood of meeting anyone, let alone them liking me."

He patted her arm. "Now, now. Of course, I will stand your friend. I am sure..."

The door opened, and Elvira made her entrance, dressed in a pink crepe that looked, Georgina thought, more as if she was heading for a ball than a long drive into the country. But the opportunity for confidences was at an end. They were soon bestowed in the carriage, behind a pair of horses, and heading out along the cobbled streets, only three-quarters of an hour late. Elvira was animated enough to point out various sights and buildings to her, as well as several people she recognized as they passed through the fashionable quarter of town.

Georgina was able to enjoy the experience, secure in the knowledge that in Cousin Arthur she'd at last found a champion worth having. It was a mild spring day, with scattered cloud, but at least none of the rain that she'd come to think of as England's central characteristic. Once they were out of town, they picked up speed a little – and the country, Georgina thought, was so much prettier than the city had been, with trees in new leaf, green fields, and fruit trees in blossom. She said as much to Elvira, who yawned. "It's rather dull really. I have never understood what anyone sees in the country. It's so empty and boring.

"But... I can see houses everywhere!" said Georgina. There was at least greenery and trees, but there were frequent houses on the road-side, sometimes on both sides. And others were to be seen in the fields, with the prospect of several larger houses in the distance. They'd left the coal-fire scent and cloak of smoke of Southampton behind, but there were still many habitations visible, to someone used to the tens of miles of the emptiness of the Amatola ranges, to say nothing of the vast bleakness of the dry and thorny Great Fish River valley, where there was easily twenty miles between settlements on the track back to Grahamstown.

"Yes," admitted Elvira. "But very few of them. And there's nothing else. No balls, no theatres, no entertainments and absolutely no shops at all. What do ladies do out here?"

Georgina was about to tell her that maybe they did something use-ful with their time, but fortunately managed to swallow the comment. She had a number of hours to spend with her Cousin Elvira, and a brangle at this stage could only make the journey unpleasant. So, she looked out of the window, and Elvira settled into a squab and fell asleep. She snored. After a while Georgina wondered if an argument might not have been a more peaceful way of passing the journey.

They stopped in Winchester to change horses, and to partake of some refreshment. Looking at the clock, Georgina decided that their journey must be taking far longer than Cousin Arthur had anticipated or the extra time Elvira had added to their departure, unless of course they were only to spend minutes with her grandfather before turning around.

They resumed the journey, proceeding along the London road, and through several villages. Georgina could only be glad she'd not had to navigate this on her own. Perhaps to the English it was all obvious and easy. They came at last to a stone gateway, and turned into a well-kept carriageway, heading towards a rather extensive roof-line visible above the trees. Bournelea, when it came in sight was a large building that straggled off from a central block. It bore all the signs of being added to over the years, and boasted an impressive number of chimneys.

It also had a porte-cochere and there, once the step was let down the ladies were able to alight from the carriage, while they waited for Cousin Arthur to deal with the post-boy. That individual led Arthur's horse and their chaise away, and they made their way up the wide shallow steps to the front door. These were opened by an elderly butler, in livery, very slightly out of breath. "Ah, Matthews," said Cousin Arthur, rather grandly, "Please inform Lady Elizabeth that I have brought Miss Georgina Ross to see her grandfather. I trust we are not too late."

The butler looked at the party, bowed and invited them to come into the yellow saloon while a message was sent to Lady Elizabeth. A few minutes later, he returned and said: "Lady Elizabeth sends her regrets that she is unable to come down to you right this moment, as the Doctor is with Mr. Weatherly, but asked if Miss Ross could accompany me upstairs."

"I'll come with you," proclaimed Arthur.

The butler shook his head. "Lady Elizabeth said I was not to bring anyone but the young lady."

"I need to talk to that Doctor," said Arthur.

"I shall desire him to come and have speech with you, Mr. Weatherly, as soon as he is finished with her Ladyship," said the butler, firmly.

So, Georgina followed him down a hall lined with portraits, and to a slightly worn but broad stair, wondering if her grandfather was perhaps at death's door. She ventured, somewhat nervously, to ask. The butler favored her with an avuncular smile, "Indeed, no, young lady. Doctor is quite surprised at his progress. He is still not himself, his wits are still disordered, but he has come a long way from when Captain Edward hauled him out."

"Hauled him out?" she repeated.

"From his house. It was on fire."

"Goodness!" exclaimed Georgina. "I did not know. Lady Elizabeth just said he'd been injured and was not conscious."

The butler nodded. "Yes, Miss." He knocked on the door.

"Come in," said someone from inside.

So, the butler opened the door for her and Georgina went into a handsome bedchamber. If the white-haired man with the closed eyes, pallid face and bandaged head, lying propped up on the pillows was doing better... from her experience he must have indeed been very close to death, before. The room had two other occupants, a man in his fifties, she judged, and a slightly plump grey-haired matronly woman, who beckoned her from where she stood in the threshold. "Come in, dear. You must be Mr. Weatherly's granddaughter. Let me make you known to our good Doctor Selby."

Georgina walked across to them to make her curtsy. "Lady Elizabeth? Thank you so much for your kind letter."

Before she could reply the man in the bed – whom Georgina had assumed unconscious, or at best asleep, said in a tremulous, cracked voice: "'thea? Dorothea?"

"Good heavens," said the Doctor, stepping over to his patient. "That's the first coherent thing he's said!"

Lady Elizabeth took Georgina's hand in hers and squeezed it. "Your mother's name was Dorothea, I believe. Your voices must be similar. My dear, come and speak to him again! He has opened his eyes a few times today, which is why I called Doctor Selby, but he still seems terribly confused."

So, Georgina went closer to the bed, and stood beside the old man, wondering quite what to say. If he was expecting her mother, and he was this frail... "I am back from Africa," she said taking the parchment-like old hand.

Her grandfather opened his eyes, and she felt the faint pressure of him squeezing her hand. "My dear. See if you can get him to take some water," said Lady Elizabeth, holding out a glass to her. "Dr Selby says that, chiefly, is the most urgent thing he needs now."

Georgina took the glass, and from memory, using the same tones her mother had used nursing her father, held it to his lips, and said: "Please, now take a little sip of water for me, sir."

He did. A little spilled on his chin, and she was handed a napkin. "Another little bit, sir? For me?" she offered, and again he drank and swallowed.

"Thank you, my girl," said the patient, weakly but audibly.

"That's capital!" said the Doctor. "If we can get him to sit up slightly more, between us, and get him to take a little more... Lady

Elizabeth, if you can adjust the pillows, this young lady and I can support him."

They did, and the old man struggled slightly. "Now, now, sir, it is all right. I am right here," said Georgina, again echoing her mother. "We just need you to drink a little more." Her grandfather seemed to calm at her voice, so she kept talking to him, telling him he'd be better presently and to please have a little more water.

"He responds well to you!" said the Doctor. "You've nursed people before, have you, Miss Ross?"

"My mother. And I helped my mother with my father... he, he was delirious for some of the time," said Georgina.

"Well," said the Doctor, "If you can get fluids into him I will hold out some hope of his recovery. His brain may still be injured, but he is recognizing something and co-operating. Now, another mouthful, and we will lie him down a little again."

They did that. The old man just seemed easier in himself, but it was hard to tell. He continued to hold her hand, but then his grip slackened. His breathing, though shallow, seemed even.

"I think," said the Doctor, quietly, "That he may actually be sleeping. It's hard to tell of course."

Lady Elizabeth smiled warmly at her. "I hope you will make a long stay, my dear Miss Ross. I am sorry to throw you straight into deep water like that."

"I... don't think we planned to visit for more than just very briefly, as I said in my letter," said Georgina, awkwardly. She thought she'd made that plain. "I... I must thank you for letting me come to see him. My mother would have wanted that. But, I don't think I can stay."

"Frankly," said the Doctor, "Miss Ross, I would urge you to do so. Lady Elizabeth and her maid have both tried for several hours to get him to drink something and failed. And if he does not get sufficient

fluids soon, he will die. I'm sorry to be so brutally direct, Miss. I gather
you've been through a horrid time, already."

"Can you not stay for at least a few days, Miss Ross?" asked Lady
Elizabeth. "The poor old man. Such a terrible thing to have happen to
him."

"I... I would like to remain, but I came up with my Cousin Elvira,
and, and Cousin Arthur promised my Aunt Louisa that we'd be back
by this evening."

"Back where?" asked the Doctor.

"Southampton."

"You'll not do that by dark," said the Doctor.

"No indeed!" said Lady Elizabeth. "And a terribly long, fatiguing
day it would be too. You really must all remain here. We can send one
of the grooms down with a message." She chuckled. "Nothing they'd
like better than a night in the big city."

"It is so very kind of you," protested Georgina, "And I feel it is my
duty to care for him. I really would like to, but..."

"But me no buts," said Lady Elizabeth firmly.

"I can't so inconvenience you. And my Cousin Arthur, put to all
this expense and trouble, and..."

"You leave Arthur to me," said Lady Elizabeth firmly. "He should
have had you here days ago."

"Oh no," protested Georgina. "He's been so kind. And there is my
Cousin Elvira too. She... she will be wanting to get back to town. And,
and I didn't bring any luggage."

"You leave it to me," said Lady Elizabeth. "Now, we have not left
Mr. Weatherly unattended, and I daresay the Doctor will wish to have
a talk with you. Would you care to remain here and do that? Then I
can go and deal with your problems. I can't tell you what a relief it
would be to me. Betty and I have not had a great deal of sleep in the

last few days. I've had a few of the other housemaids helping as well, but he's been rather restless."

"Oh Ma'am! You haven't attended to him yourself all this time?" exclaimed Georgina, feeling profoundly guilty.

"Well, I am somewhat practiced," said Lady Elizabeth. "And he is our neighbor."

"It is my duty to look after him," said Georgina, resolutely. "He is family, and mother would have wanted me to. And I must. Yes, Lady Elizabeth. If I can stay here, if it is not going to be too difficult... thank you."

She was rewarded by a smile. A rather tired smile, she realized. "Thank you, my dear. Anyway, let me go and attend to the matter. Really... Arthur." And on that note, she left.

The Doctor looked keenly at the patient, felt his pulse. "I suggest if we could withdraw to the window a little Miss Ross, so further talk does not disturb him." When they got there, he looked speculatively at her. "You know, I knew your father. Not well, but we were up at Cambridge together. I was very sorry to hear of his passing."

She swallowed. She knew, a little, from her mother, of what her father had given up to follow what he believed to be his calling. She'd never met anyone who had known him before the mission – or at least not that she could remember. She wondered how to answer this, and resorted to something she'd heard her mother say. "He died doing the work he believed in."

"You should be very proud of him. And your mother too, going out there, with him. It must have been hard for you all."

"Not as hard as coming back to England has been," she admitted, ruefully. "I left here when I was a child. I don't remember it well, and have found England very confusing. But... my grandfather. Could you tell me exactly what happened to him? I was merely told that he had had some kind of accident and was unconscious."

"You've encountered violence before, out in the colonies?" he asked looking at her with slightly narrowed eyes.

"Yes. My father was speared trying to quell an attack. The Xhosa attacked the settlement of our converts. Many fled to the Church for sanctuary. We did as well. My father was injured trying to get Macoma's men to... to respect sanctuary of the Church." She paused, eyes closed briefly. "They were coming in to attack us, and... and then there were shots fired. A patrol from Fort Beaufort had seen the smoke. They rescued us."

He was silent for a full minute. Sucked air between his teeth. "What a terrible experience!"

"We survived. Many of our Khoikhoi converts did not," she said. "Unfortunately, my father's wound became infected. He..." She shook her head, unable to continue.

He patted her shoulder. "I am sorry. And here I have to further distress you. You appear a very level-headed young lady, and I still think it best to be direct with you. Your grandfather was assaulted in the course of a robbery, and his attacker left him for dead, and attempted to set fire to the house. He suffered a head injury from which I did not expect him to recover, and the smoke-inhalation aggravated matters. He's doing far better than I expected, but is anything but out of the woods. He may recover... or not. I did not expect him to get this far. He's a tough old man, but here is the truth: He is old and he suffered a grievous injury. He may well never recover completely. He may well die, because the body it seems will only fight for so long. It's too early to tell, and likely to be a long road. Are you ready for that? Because you must be."

She nodded. "As you say, I must be. Mother said... mother said England was so safe. It was one of the things she wanted so desperately, after, after what happened."

"It just doesn't happen, here in the country. Believe me, I've been in practice here for twenty years, and this is the first time I have ever seen anything of this kind. I had never encountered the like of it before. People fall off horses, or get diseases, or get trampled by cows or fall into the river after too much to drink... but this doesn't happen here. Highwaymen, and footpads maybe. In the metropolis or larger cities maybe. But houses are often unlocked out here. Your grandfather's house was not one of them, but it is common practice. I doubt if Bournelea even has a key to every door."

She shuddered. "I would think... do they know who did this? Have they caught him?"

"Suspicion falls on an ex-bailiff of your grandfather's. He had made threats. He was apparently seen a few nights before, in one of the villages relatively near the area. He'll be caught. Anyway... to the matter in hand, I have prepared a paregoric draft in case the patient does become restless, but I would avoid it unless absolutely necessary, as I am not a believer in narcotics with head-injuries. If you can keep him drinking and possibly see if he will take a little light gruel. Otherwise, it is merely a question of rest and keeping him calm. He's been very agitated, and you seem to have done him a great deal of good." He smiled. "I'll repeat all this to Lady Kelling, of course. She will have me called if there is need. My home is only a mile off."

Edward, having ridden out with his father and John after luncheon, was regretting this action, by the time he came home. Both his father and brother were bruising hard riders, as he himself had been, once. The ride was an exercise in them forgetting his injury, realizing it and then treating him as if he were as near death as old Mr. Weatherly, and then forgetting it again. The being treated as if he were a total invalid nettled his temper, the harder riding he did so that that did not occur, hurt his leg. He was both sore and irritable by the time he returned home, to the news that Awful Arthur was visiting, along with the old man's granddaughter. And they had not even bothered to let mother know, he thought with annoyance. What a rag-mannered pair.

Elementary good manners, however, dictated he should join his father and brother in going to meet their unexpected guests, so as soon as they'd put off their riding clothes, they came down to join Arthur and the young woman, enjoying some wine and cakes in the yellow saloon. If he hadn't already been sore and irritable, the company certainly would have rapidly induced the latter. Arthur, he concluded, simply had to breathe in his company, to annoy him. The young woman, to whom he somehow failed to get introduced, except as 'one of my cousins' had a laugh that reminded him of a donkey braying, which she employed a great deal too often. She was dressed in the height of fashion – as of course, was Arthur. Edward, who was normally as blind to such things as a man could be, to the annoyance of his mother, noticed, and decided that her dress did not suit her. She seemed set to flirt with everyone, including his father, and, it would appear, was having a wonderful time, despite having come to visit an ailing, and potentially dying relative. "Oh la, Sir Gerald, so many fine portraits! I do declare I have never seen such handsome gentlemen."

Edward Kelling was, naturally, proud of his ancestors, but 'handsome' was not a term that was much applied to the Kelling line. 'Big' or 'solid' or 'broad-faced', maybe. According to his father, thatch-gallows would be more appropriate! He was spared having to make a reply by the entry of his mother. "Ah. Arthur, I am glad to find you here. I need to talk to you. Goodness, Edward. You look decidedly pale."

"Trotted it a bit hard today, Mama. But I am fine," he answered, knowing she worried, still.

She looked at him, sternly. "I don't need two at death's door in this house! Now, Doctor Selby is still here. You go up to your room and I shall have him attend you shortly."

Edward shook his head. "Really, I am fine. I just rode a bit further and harder than I should have. I just need to rest it a little..."

"Go and rest then, son," said Sir Gerald, looking guilty. "Please your mother and me. It's entirely my fault, Elizabeth. It was the pleasure of having both my boys ride with me again, I just forgot Ned's not up for that long in the saddle, yet."

So, Edward took his leave of them. He was in truth quite glad to do so, even if just to avoid being annoyed by Arthur and this vacuous granddaughter of old Weatherly. His mother, as usual, got her way, and Dr Selby came up presently, and gave him a thorough examination. Selby was at least comforting about it. "You are, in fact, greatly recovered. You must realize however, that you can expect pain from your wound, and it will take time for the muscle to heal. You lost enough for a good Sunday roast from that leg. The bone itself may still be infected. It will either heal or it won't, but overdoing things won't help it. Elevate it, rest it, put a hot compress on it. Eat a quiet dinner here in your chambers, take this draught I am going to prepare for you, and you'll likely be as right as rain tomorrow."

Edward knew he had no chance of avoiding the quiet night, once Selby had had a word with his mother. Oh, he could have gone his own way on it, but it would hurt her, and she'd been through enough worrying about him, without that he'd now landed another patient on her. He had spent a little time watching Frederick Weatherly, but then, mother reckoned the sick room was no place for men, let alone young ones. A rest this evening would be welcome, rather than the company of Arthur and that girl, but he was damned if he'd drink the potion. They always left him feeling sick, and he'd rather endure the pain. And tomorrow, he would go out early and fish the dawn rise.

He wondered how long their guests would remain. Hopefully, not above a day or two. He'd thought they might relieve his mother and her faithful Betty of some the night-watches. He wondered vaguely if the girl was hoping for some kind of inheritance. Not the estate itself, because that was surely entailed – besides, come to think of it, he'd had it from Frederick Weatherly in conversation back when he'd started helping the old fellow out, that Arthur was his heir. Well, he had no idea how the rest of the estate had been left. It wouldn't be likely to be that much of a plum. A competency at best.

On that thought, he went to sleep, and got up at his usual hour, and had a less than good morning on the river. It was bright quite early, and something had put the fish down. He only had a brace to take home, and he had kept trying later than was really worth his while. He and Penn breakfasted, and they set off home at what was really quite late for him.

He soon discovered that it was not late, for their house-guest. Penn had informed him that one of the grooms had ridden all the way to Southampton yesterday afternoon to take a message and, apparently to arrange for the visitors' portmanteaux to be sent up with a carrier. He met the girl his way into the house, yawning, asking her way to the breakfast parlor. Out of politeness he escorted her there, rang the bell to get fresh coffee sent, and made polite conversation, naturally on how she had slept. "Oh, it was far to quiet. And so dark!"

He blinked. "Ah. Yes. I suppose it is quite peaceful."

"Well, except for in the morning! All of those birds. That's why I am up so early."

The arrival of the coffee fortunately spared him from having to answer, but he was less lucky with her other comments and questions, before he was able to make his escape, as she tried to persuade him to take her to look at the flowers. "Because your mama said I must particularly see the spring flowers."

Fortunately, the hall clock chimed just then, and Edward was able to hastily say: "I am sure someone will show you around, Miss. Forgive me. I have to go. I am running late."

He was glad not to have to invent what he was late for, but went upstairs, thinking he would at least look in on Mr. Weatherly, and perhaps his mother, and find out how long this... person would be staying. He met his mother on the landing, having just left the guest chamber Weatherly was ensconced in. "How is he?" he asked.

She smiled at him. "Edward, I do think Dr Selby is going to be pleased and surprised."

"Oh good. Then perhaps we can get that insufferable baggage of a granddaughter of his out of the house," said Edward, savagely.

His mother looked much shocked and put her finger to her lips, and walked him away from the door. Once they were a little distance away, she said, quietly, "Dearest, what has come over you! She's done Mr. Weatherly the greatest of good. She seems to know just how to handle him, and he responds so well to her. He's still terribly confused and does not stay awake long, and thinks she is her mother, but she is so kind and patient with him. Her manners seem very nice..."

"Nice? She was asking me how much money father earned!" said Edward.

His mother seemed amused. "Oh dear."

"You weren't the one trying to answer her, and be polite. Oh, she also finds the birds disturbing and the silence and darkness at night keeps her from her sleep. And she considers ten in the morning early."

"Well, you know there are many country houses where the gentry do not get up until noon, Ned. I'm surprised you took her in such aversion, but still, she has done him a lot of good. You're hardly likely to see much of her."

"Not if I can help it anyway!" he exclaimed.

Inside the sick-room, Georgina sat, rigid with shock and indignation.

It had been a long hard night, and she'd only had a few hours of sleep, when Betty had come to relieve her. Her grandfather slept for short periods, and woke confused and determined to get up, and it seemed only her voice could soothe him. They had been kind enough to set up a truckle bed in the room for her, but Betty had been unable to manage on her own, and she'd got up several times, dozing rather than sleeping, in between. It had been shortly after she'd heard the first sound of morning, a cock-crow, and the then sound of horses on the drive, and then the welcome dawn chorus of strange – to her ear – birds, that Lady Elizabeth had come in, somewhat distressed and still in a dressing gown. "Oh, my dear. I am so sorry. The stress of the last few days and nights, and just the relief of having you here. I slept. I asked Betty to wake me."

"I told her not to. She said that you were worn to the bone."

"And now you are. You should go and rest. Or perhaps you need something to eat and cup of tea or chocolate first."

"Tea," said her grandfather. "Tea, Dorothea."

So, they had got him some tea. Weak, sweet 'nursery' tea, cooled a little with lots of milk. It had seemed to help him a great deal, and to settle him, and after that Georgina had been persuaded to lie down, even if not to leave the room.

She had just woken again, and Lady Elizabeth had sent a maid scurrying for water and a basin. Then after she'd refreshed herself, the lady of the house said she was going to order some breakfast for Georgina, and that she was to go down and eat it, while her hostess sat with her grandfather, secure in the knowledge that she'd be called as soon as needed. She'd send for Selby, too, because the patient's condition had plainly changed.

'Insufferable baggage'! he had called her. It rankled. She was still seething when she went down to the breakfast parlor, where a breakfast the likes of which she'd never seen, ranging from devilled kidneys to fresh trout, mushrooms, bacon, sausages, eggs... there seemed no end to it. It was even more sumptuous than the dinner that had been brought to her the night before. Georgina enjoyed a healthy appetite, and it did take the edge off her resentment at being referred to in that way, by someone who was obviously the son of the house.

As she was finishing her repast, she was joined in the parlor by Cousin Arthur, who was shown in by the butler. "How does my uncle do?" he asked after greeting her.

"So much better!" she said, pleased to be able to relay such good news.

He looked a little startled. "He has recovered?"

"Well, he is still very confused. He thinks I am my mother, and he doesn't recognize Lady Elizabeth or Dr Selby, or know quite where he is. But he is able to take nourishment and his color is much improved."

"Good gracious. So, he does not recall the fight or the events that led to him being attacked?" asked Arthur.

"Not so far, anyway. The magistrate, Mr. Tadswell, will come and see him later, possibly. Doctor Selby says in such cases it is not unknown for people to lose their memories completely or their recent memories at least. He does seem to know who he is, though."

"Well," said Cousin Arthur, "That is a great comfort. So: tell me, Cousin Georgina, what is his prognosis? And how does it affect you? I had hoped to set things in train to help with your security and well-being. For, you must realize, that should my uncle recover his wits entirely... well, I don't know. But it could be very awkward. I would like to have your affairs happily settled by then."

He smiled kindly at her, and she was comforted to finally have a friend, here in this strange country. "Doctor Selby says it is too early to tell, yet. He holds some hope, but says some patients never recover their memories. There is also still some possibility of a relapse. He is an old man."

"And how does this affect you, Cousin? Do you plan to stay much longer?"

"Oh, I can't tell," she said, biting her lip and then shaking her head. "He, he responds to me as he doesn't to anyone else. As if everyone else is unfamiliar and, and strange to him. It's as if I am the one island in a sea of unfamiliarity he is clinging to. And I know exactly how that feels," she smiled at him. "You're the one island I have found in this my own sea of bewilderment. Thank you."

"It is easy to want to help you," he said. "So, the Doctor gave no idea on how long you have to remain here? I am not entirely happy with this situation."

She pinched her lips. Then said: "I am not either. And some people can't wait for me to be gone. But Lady Elizabeth has been very kind."

"Ah. Who has been unkind to you, Cousin Georgina? I've a good mind to call them to account," he said with a smile that said he was funning – but encouraging her to open her budget to him.

"An individual called Edward. I believe he feels I am an insufferable baggage," she said crossly.

He looked slightly warily at the door. It was solid and firmly closed. "The younger son of the house. I..." he paused. "I don't know how to say this to you but I harbor the deepest suspicions about him myself. He, well, let us say he enjoys something of an unsavory reputation. I hoped to shield you from his company, but I thought you would not be here above an hour or two."

"I will avoid him with great care, believe me!" said Georgina.

He looked at her slightly askance. "He and I have had clashes before. Um. Look, this is very hard to say, but I wonder if he is not the villain in this piece? He... and that groom of his, Penn, who Tadswell said had a...chequered background, they were there, on the scene in the small hours of the morning when the alarm was raised about the fire. Edward claims to have carried my Uncle Frederick out of the building."

Horrified, Georgina clapped her hand to her mouth. Then asked... "but why?"

"I don't know. I gather he's been around at Westmead House a lot in the last while. Inveigling his way in, if you ask me, as relations between the houses have always been prickly. My uncle's son had made friends here, but my uncle did not entirely approve. And, well, there was a robbery. Valuable snuff boxes and some precious Chinese porcelain stolen. I've heard rumors of deep going in the various clubs." Seeing her expression of puzzlement, he expanded on that. "Gambling."

"But surely... if he was involved, he would not have..." protested Georgina, shocked.

"I think the he was caught. Surprised in the act by my uncle, and when challenged seized the old man's cane and hit him. The lamp fell over when he was escaping – or maybe he set the fire a-purpose. Then when the alarm was raised, he came back and carried the old man out, and fought the fire. It all fits so well. And it was he who cast blame on this bailiff. And of course, around here, his father is the squire, and cannot be questioned," said Arthur, bitterly.

"But..."

"It is why I want my uncle out of here, back in his own house. I have engaged the Runners to investigate the attack. They will track down the stolen property and report to me. I believe Tadswell is in Sir Gerald's pocket. So: keep calm. I am handling this," he said in a manly, authoritative tone.

She nodded at him, wide eyed.

There was little time for further confidences because one of the maids came to say that Lady Elizabeth was asking for her to come when she had finished her meal. She went, hastily, thinking that her grandfather must be restive, or they were struggling to manage without her. But instead she was taken to a chamber one up the passage from the room her grandfather occupied, where Lady Elizabeth was engaged in arranging some flowers in a pretty vase set on an oak chest of drawers. Her own – and her mother's sea-chests, were set in the corner. "They arrived a little earlier. They managed to get them on the coach that left at first light. My dear, will this room do for you? It's a little small, but quite convenient for your grandfather."

Georgina felt she was going to burst into tears. It was a beautiful room, full of sunlight, hung with bright curtains, with a lovely rug on the floor, and contained a four-poster bed with a magnificent quilt. Filled with information that made her want to flee the house, and yet unable to desert her grandfather, and then faced with this kindness and care, flowers being arranged for her... It was too much. She swallowed hard, trying to speak. Her hostess noticed. "You poor dear! You've had a horrid time of it, and I fling you into this situation. It was just that you said you wanted to look after him."

"I do." She took a deep breath. "I am sorry. You're being too kind to me, Lady Elizabeth. I can't impose on you like this. It's a beautiful room. Far too good for me! Better than any I have ever had. I am quite happy with the truckle-bed until we can move grandfather back to his own house... it is still habitable, isn't it?"

Lady Elizabeth nodded. "According to Ned, it could be very rapidly. He'll see to it, if you like."

She wasn't too sure who 'Ned' was. It could be the dreadful Edward. "I would have to ask Cousin Arthur." She suddenly thought how thankless she must appear. "I... I am so grateful for you organizing my trunks. Mine and mother's really. I, I hope my Aunt Louisa wasn't too difficult."

"It seems the letter your cousin wrote was a powerful persuader, although your aunt did apparently, according to the groom, throw the house into sixes and sevens organizing the trunks. Your cousin has four. And several bandboxes. I had to find her a larger room."

Georgina had to laugh. "She's... fond of clothes."

"My dear, aren't we all?" said Lady Elizabeth, laughing herself. "But maybe not quite that fond."

"I must settle the cost of bringing them up here," she said, suddenly stricken – and horrified at the thought of the probable cost. "Lady Elizabeth..."

Lady Elizabeth patted her hand. "Now, now. We can sort all of that out later if you wish to. I'm sure your aunt..."

"Oh goodness, no!" said Georgina, horrified. "I can't... I mean she mustn't... I don't think I can..." she lost herself in a tangle of half-sentences.

"There. Now, don't worry. It's no great sum, I am sure. And look, I do want you to have a little comfort and rest. And I need to feed you up a little. You're too skinny, child," said Lady Elizabeth. "You need a little looking after, if you're going to look after someone else."

This time Georgina did tremble into tears. She'd had some kindnesses, but no-one had been as motherly as this. How could she reconcile this with the sheer nastiness of Lady Elizabeth's son? She found herself being hugged and patted on the shoulder. "You've been bearing a lot, my dear. In an unfamiliar place and with unfamiliar people. Don't worry! We'll help you find your feet."

There was a knock on the door. It was one of the footmen. "If you please, Lady Elizabeth. The other young lady wants a bigger looking-glass. Can I move the one from Miss Augusta's old room for her?"

Lady Elizabeth nodded. "Get Jem to help you. It's quite heavy. Yes, Patsy, what is it? Is he awake?"

The latter was addressed at a young housemaid, who had peered around the footman to attract their attention. She nodded, and rushed away. "Silly girl," said Lady Elizabeth. "I said just to call out, or ring the bell. We'd better go."

They found Mr. Weatherly determined to get up, and the little maid trying to stop him. It took all of Georgina's tact to establish why he felt the desperate need to get up. Then they had to get two footmen in to assist, while the ladies withdrew. "It is an encouraging sign, I suppose," said Lady Elizabeth. "He's at least in control of that aspect of his life. It does make caring for him a great deal easier. I do think he's on the mend, you know."

"I hope so," said Georgina, thinking that it would at least give her a chance to decide on a course for her own future.

Indeed, the rest of the day proved this to be the case. Her grandfather both ate and drank – sparingly, as considered by Lady Elizabeth suitable for an invalid, and then was persuaded that he was unwell and ought to rest. He remained firm in his conviction that Georgina was his daughter, but was at least well-disposed to the ministration of others, as long as she was around. As both the Doctor and Lady Elizabeth said that it was best to let him retain this delusion for now, rather than subjecting him to further shocks, Georgina went along with it. When he fell into a deep sleep, Lady Elizabeth suggested she take a walk in the gardens to give her a bit of respite. "We missed church this morning, but Sir Gerald and John went. If you would like my dear, I could have Edward take you and your cousin to Evensong. As for me, I shall get my book, and some embroidery, and sit here in peace, knowing Sir Gerald won't talk to me while I am in a particularly interesting or exciting part of my book," said Lady Elizabeth.

That drew a laugh from Georgina. "I wouldn't want to go far away, yet, Lady Elizabeth." Which was true, and besides she wasn't going anywhere with the abominable Edward. She'd almost forgotten the very existence of Elvira. Let this Edward have the joy of her. They would deal extremely, she thought. "But I do envy you your book."

Lady Elizabeth clapped her hand to her forehead. "Oh, my dear! What a terrible host you must think I am. I should have thought! There is a whole library full of books!" She looked faintly guilty. "Although Sir Gerald will tell you far too many of them are romantic tales. I am somewhat addicted to them," she said with a mischievous smile, "And he does not realize I am on the mailing lists of several of the publishing houses. Are you fond of reading?"

"Very," admitted Georgina. "But, well, very few books came my way, out on the mission station. I was lucky enough to be able to read one of Mrs. Edgeworth's works on the voyage. I read it several times," she admitted.

"Go immediately to the library, child! It is directly below us, here. If you can't find it, one of the servants will show you," instructed Lady Elizabeth, with a twinkle. "If I can't find you in several hours I will have a rescue mission sent. I will make Matthews do it. He is elderly, the library large, and you should be able to avoid rescue for some time."

The laugh that drew from her was so welcome after the months of stress, sadness and fear that she'd been through. She'd forgotten how good it was to laugh, she realized. She had to reply in kind. "Oh, I think all he would find would be a pair of shoes. My father always said he never met anyone as completely devoured by books as I was."

That made Lady Elizabeth laugh in turn. "I think my daughter Augusta, Lady Stonehaven these days, would give you stiff competition. Edward, since his injury forced inactivity on him for so long, has shown signs of it too. John and my husband won't read much beyond the newspapers. Now, off you go. I expect you to return eventually with a suitable stack of books. Take a few to your room and have a good read. I shall have you called when I need you, and I hope they find more than your shoes."

So, thus adjured, Georgina proceeded downstairs to the library. The door was slightly ajar, and she was able to glimpse the book-lined shelves before she went in.

Edward was comfortably ensconced in his favorite chair in the library – one which had excellent light from the tall windows and allowed him to stretch his feet toward the fire on winter evenings, when the door opened, and a young woman came in. She didn't even notice him, her gaze taken up in rapt attention at the bookshelves. She was wearing black, had dark hair, which was very simply dressed, if you could call it dressed at all. She was a slim, fairly slight young woman, and she only noticed him when he got to his feet. She had, he observed, rather brilliant blue eyes, and a firm set of dark brows. Her expression, on seeing him, was one of... well, trepidation. "Hello," he said. "Can I help you?"

She looked almost as if she might turn and run. "Lady Elizabeth said I was to come and find myself a book to read."

"Then you're definitely in the right place. Just as long as you don't want mine," he said, carefully setting it down. Curiosity overcame him. "If I may ask, who are you? I feel very remiss in not introducing myself..."

"I am Georgina Ross. I am here looking after my grandfather," she said. It was both chilly and... defensive.

"Oh, I thought..." he started. "Well, I am Edward Kelling, at your service. How is the old man going on?"

"He is recovering. Something I plan to see he succeeds in doing. Now, if you will excuse me, I wish to find a book and go back upstairs to him."

If ice could have formed on her voice it could scarcely have been cooler, Edward thought, wondering what on earth he'd done wrong. Then it came to him. Arthur. Well, it scarcely mattered. She had drawn herself up to her not very considerable height to make this pronouncement and was staring at him as if daring him to challenge her. He noticed her hands were tight clasped and trembling slightly, but she stood her ground. "Be my guest," he said. "I was just going to leave, as it cannot be long before luncheon. Will you be joining us?"

"I have just eaten, thank you," she said, somehow managing to inject chilling hauteur even into that.

Somewhat taken aback, he bowed. "Well, I shall leave you to it," he said and beat a hasty retreat.

He was at first somewhat offended, but then he recalled the shaking, clenched little hands, the expression and the obvious control being exerted... it took him back to his time in the army. To raw recruits facing their first engagement. She was plainly frightened near out of her wits, but still standing bluff. Well, he supposed she had just come out of Africa into what must be very unfamiliar ground. But then who was that other woman?

He met his brother John coming back from the stables. "I just met old Frederick's granddaughter. Who is that other female? I was laboring under the delusion that that was his granddaughter. I missed her name in the introductions the other night."

"Oh, that is some cousin of the granddaughter," said John. "Came up to keep propriety, and now seems to think we exist to dance attendance on her. I haven't met Miss Ross yet. She's spent pretty much every hour with her grandfather. Is she much like the other one?"

"As unalike as chalk and cheese! And, unless I am much mistaken, filled with horror stories from Arthur about how evil we are. She looked on the edge of flight when she met me in the library."

"Oh. Bookish, is she? Or just getting another tome for mama?"

"I don't know. She did her best to freeze me solid," said Edward, with a laugh.

"Well, it seems both of our guests want for conduct," said his brother, amused.

"No, I can't say that," said Edward, ever honest. "Just wishing me in Jericho in the politest way possible!"

"Pastry faced, like the other one?"

Once again, Edward's innate honesty made him say: "No, a neat figure and, I suspect if she wasn't being so severe, an attractive face. Her dress is the inverse of the other one's garb: austere, black and simple. Well cut though, I'd say. Not that I am much of a judge."

"No, Ned, you're not," said his brother, laughing. "Well, I suppose that's appropriate for a missionary's daughter. That other chit is pestering me to be taken for a drive in my curricle. You don't fancy doing the honors for me, Ned?"

"Absolutely not! Why not deputize Arthur, if he is still hanging about?" suggested Edward.

"Trust him with my bays? Over my dead body. Anyway, Arthur Weatherly turned down our hospitality and has gone to rack up somewhere else. Maybe at Westmead House. He came this morning merely to inquire about his uncle, but took himself off pretty quickly."

"And how long are we to be blessed by the one demanding you drive her about the countryside for? I think I might shab off and visit Gussie."

"Mama would take that very ill, or I'd be with you," said his brother. "She – Miss Ross's cousin, said something about her mother coming up on Wednesday, to see how they went on."

Edward rolled his eyes to heaven. "I wonder how rapidly Frederick Weatherly can move home! I could see to repairing the place in a trice, but Arthur is likely to have a fit if anyone else – especially me – touches the place. So, we shall likely have them cloistered with us for a twelve-month."

Georgina was still shaking as she made her way to the first book-shelf. She hadn't expected him to be here. When he'd stood up, large and against the light, she had got quite a fright, anyway. Once she'd been able to see his broad face, it had in fact been quite benign – not the monster she'd envisaged. Nothing he'd said had been anything untoward, but it had still upset her composure. She took a book off the shelf at random and fled. She took the opposite direction to the large figure retreating down the hallway, which in this rabbit warren of a house got her through to a door that she realized had led her out to the stable-yard. She paused, about to turn around, when she thought a breath or two of fresh air might actually do her some good. Her incorrigible sense of humor – and the smell of stables, which naturally included that of horse manure, made her laugh at the thought of it being fresh. That too did much to ease her state of mind. And it put a little smile on her face, as she turned to greet a groom with a deeply lined face, who had come trotting up to her. "It's all right. I just got lost and took the wrong turn and ended up out here. I rather enjoy stable-yards, although I know that's supposed to be terribly un-ladylike."

That speech plainly did her no harm in the eyes of that groom, anyway. "Eh. Missy. Miss Augusta was always coming down here. Would you like to come and meet the horses? Couple of prime ones, if I says it meself."

"Oh, I would! But I had better get back. My grandfather..."

He nodded. "They was saying he was properly perking up at you being there, Miss. And it is true, you do have the look of your mother. I worked over at Westmead when I were a lad, as a stable-boy. She always had a smile for us, your mother did. You're very like. Very like, indeed. It were terrible sad to hear what happened. But you're a comfort to old Mr. Frederick. He were properly gutted when his son come to grief. We're glad you're back. Oh, and that puts me in mind...Young Jem had something for you. He went down to Southampton to get your gear. He's been wanting to get it to Betty to give to you... Let me call him." He bustled off, hastily, and she walked over to the nearest stall to talk to the horses and pet noses. A younger – but still not young – groom came running up. It seemed they grew old in service here. He bowed and held out a note to her. "Miss. The housemaid at your aunt's place give me this for you."

"Mary!" said Georgina.

"That'll be the one," said the groom cheerfully. "she give me a shilling to be sure to give this into your own hands."

"A shilling!" said Georgina, taken aback, knowing how little money the maid had.

Jem grinned. "Aye. I give it back to her, telling her not to be a silly clunch. She give me pepper too, but I won."

"You're a very good man!"

He grinned. "You tell me missus that, Miss Georgina."

"I'll tell her, if I see her," Georgina promised.

"She's the mistress's maid," he said with just a touch of pride, making Georgina realize just how inter-connected the people here were. And also, to understand that Jem was not just any groom. A lady's maid, she knew, would generally be above a groom's touch.

"Then I will tell her, indeed!" she dug out her purse and took out two shillings. "And at least I can double it. And don't you dare argue with me!" she said, smiling up at him. "You were very kind to her, and she was very kind to me. I wish I could help her too."

He took it with good grace, and she wished it could have been more. She put the note in her newly borrowed book, which proved to be something called 'The Hungarian Brothers' and went back in, cheered and lifted by this encounter, and found her way, successfully, back to the passage which led to her grandfather's room. She was tempted to simply go back into her new room and read the note and luxuriate in a book, but instead she knocked quietly on her grandfather's door. He was still asleep, and Lady Elizabeth waved from her own book, so she left.

In her own room she settled herself into the chair provided, and opened the book and took out the note. Mary was indeed a step above the run-of-the-mill housemaid, in that she was lettered. Her writing was labored, but clear. Her letter showed some signs of at least a rudimentary education somewhere.

"Dear Miss, I hope this finds you well" – obviously that was how you started a letter. "They tells me your grandfather is sick and dying, and I am hoping they are wrong. The mistress was cross as crabs, when you didn't come in, but Miss Elvira's letter put her in high croak. I am not knowing if I am going to see you again, Miss. I am missing you, but hoping you can find a situation. I was feeling bad about what you give me, so when they sent me to pack for you, I put it in your shoe. I am not sure how long I'll keep my place here, but I have your character, which I give to my mam to keep safe for me. She was proud."

Georgina held the letter, thinking to herself that not all of England's people were out to rob you, and not all were like the abominable Edward, or even her aunt and cousins. She was still dreadfully insecure, and uncertain what her future held, but at least she had the goodwill of her Cousin Arthur. She wondered if finding a respectable position for a housemaid was in his power. Probably, she decided. He had been so good to her, though, that she hesitated at the idea of asking. She unpacked a few things, hoping to hang the creases out of them, but not seeing the point in unpacking completely.

She settled in to read a little of Miss Porter's book, and was rather sad to be interrupted by a gentle knock on her door. It was Betty. "He's still asleep, Miss," she said, answering the question before it was asked. "But her ladyship wanted to know if you'd like to go down to take luncheon with the family? Or whether you wanted something brought up? Her Ladyship said not to wake you if you was asleep, but reckoned I'd find you with your nose in a book. She said I was to help you dress if you wanted."

"I should sleep," said Georgina, guiltily. "But please don't worry about food. I have barely had breakfast."

"Miss, you need to be eating! You need a bit of feeding up," said Betty, who was comfortably padded herself.

Georgina could not help but compare the rosy-cheeked woman with her dear Mary, who looked much shorter of good meals than Georgina was. "I hope you say that to Jem. Who is a good man, I want you to know! You tell him I told you so."

Betty blushed like a school-girl. "He is, Miss. But it wouldn't do to be telling him that. It'd go to his head," she said, beaming at Georgina.

"He was very kind to someone for me. And I appreciate it. But seriously, I am going to lie down for a while. Is Lady Elizabeth going down?"

"Yes, Miss. She says if she doesn't, the men forget their manners. They'll be tearing the roast apart and eating it with their hands," said Betty, plainly thinking this a capital jest. "Miriam will be sitting with the old man while I help her dress, and then I'll sit with him while she goes down to eat. She needs to eat as well."

"You'll call me instead. I can read there just as easily," said Georgina.

Betty shook her head. "You can have a bit of sleep miss. Miss Augusta liked that daybed," she pointed. "We'll call you as needed."

So, Georgina took her instructions, and was soon dead to the world. She hadn't realized how the stresses and near-sleepless night had drained her.

She was woken by a loud knock and struggled to her feet, for a moment disorientated by coming out of deep sleep, but knowing that it must mean she was needed.

As it happened, she wasn't. It was merely her Cousin Elvira. "Lying asleep at this time of day! Why didn't you come down for lunch? It looks very ill-mannered. They could have used another lady to even up the numbers at the table!"

"I was tired. I spent most of the night attending to my grandfather, and Lady Elizabeth suggested I sleep."

"There are servants who could do that," Elvira informed her.

"I feel I have to do it myself. They also have work to do, you know. Anyway, Lady Elizabeth's been sitting with him, herself. I can hardly do less."

"Well," said Elvira. "I don't really mind having all the gentlemen to myself, Georgina, but it doesn't look good. Your Cousin Arthur came, just after luncheon, but he wouldn't stay and talk to me. He just wanted you. He says he will call again in the morning. He has to go to Winchester, to arrange for some tradesmen to repair his house."

"His house was damaged?" she asked, sympathetic. No wonder he had other things to attend to.

"Well, no, not his house, he lives in London. In chambers. Very smart. But the house he's going to inherit. Your grandfather's house. It's prettier than this one, but not nearly as large. Also, I don't think there are as many servants. I saw it when I went out driving with Mr. John Kelling. I asked Captain Edward – that's the younger son with that ugly limp – but he was quite disobliging. I don't like him nearly as much, besides, he's a younger son."

"Well, I am glad the house is being repaired, Dr Selby says familiar surrounding sometimes help a patient recapture their memories, so it would be nice to move my grandfather back to his home," said

Georgina, not mentioning that there she would at least avoid Edward Kelling. Captain? She wondered at that title. Anyway, it was none of her business.

"So, I came to find out if you were going to come to church this evening? I wanted to know what you planned to wear for it? Not that old gown again, surely?"

"I don't really have much else appropriate to wear in my circumstances," said Georgina. "It's been long enough to leave off blacks, but too soon for colors."

"Well, you'll have to get something made up! You're an embarrassment in this kind of company."

Georgina shook her head. "Be comforted that they won't see much of me. I don't think I can go far from my grandfather yet. He doesn't know where he is and I am the only person he finds familiar. Thank you for waking me, I had better go to him. Unless you would care to join me there?"

"I don't care for sick people," Elvira informed her.

"Well, I must," said Georgina, picking up the book from the dresser where she had set it down.

Mary's note fluttered out and landed at Cousin Elvira's feet. She swooped on it like a heron might a on a frog – well, with the speed, but less grace. "What's this?" she asked, opening it. "A love letter?"

"Nothing to do with you," snapped Georgina, appalled, both at the sheer effrontery of Elvira, and the content of the note. "Give it to me." She reached for it.

Elvira instead opened it, holding it away from her. "I hope this finds you well," she said, mockingly. "Good gracious... Mary?"

Georgina, furious, grabbed Elvira's arm as she tried to hold it out of reach. Elvira was taller and larger, but had lived an indolent life. Georgina had not. She pulled the plump arm down and whipped the piece of paper out of Elvira's hand. "You had no business reading that! It was addressed to me."

"She's our maid! I will tell mama. Fancy getting a letter from the maid!"

"She is good and kind, and I was very pleased to have got her note. Now go away."

"You've bruised my wrist!" complained Elvira

"I should have slapped your face. And I will in a minute," said Georgina, crossly.

"Consorting with the lower orders! It's not ladylike," said Elvira, with a sniff, feeling her plump wrist and beating a retreat.

Georgina was too angry to speak – for which she was grateful a few moments later. She closed her door on her cousin and paced about, trying to compose herself. She took a deep breath, picked up the book she'd dropped, and put the note into it, and went out and knocked on her grandfather's door. Lady Elizabeth was there. "Ah. He was just asking for you again. I said you were having a rest, and would be in presently. He seemed to accept that. He still has no idea who I am, but he had a cup of tea, and a piece of bread and butter, and a slice of chicken."

"Oh, that is so good," said Georgina. "I mean, not that he can't remember, but that he has eaten."

"Yes, the body needs its strength." She looked enquiringly at Georgina. "What has cut up your peace, my dear? You are quite flushed."

"It's nothing, Ma'am," Georgina answered, tersely.

"I can try to help. Often telling someone helps."

Georgina sighed. "It's nothing important. Just my Cousin Elvira being obnoxious."

"That," said Lady Elizabeth, dryly, "I can well believe. She does seem to have a talent for raising hackles. She has both John and Edward running for cover, poor men. She even put Sir Gerald quite sadly out of countenance with one of her utterances. Never mind, my dear. I can see no reason why she should remain after Wednesday, when I believe her mother is coming up."

Georgina smiled wanly. "I can't fight with her. I may have to return there, Lady Elizabeth. And... well I think I may have left the only person who was kind to me there... one of the maids, in an invidious position. I didn't mean to do so."

"What happened?"

"She... Mary, the housemaid, sent a note up with Jem. She was just being kind. But... but Cousin Elvira doesn't approve. And her mother won't either. I shouldn't consort with servants. It's not ladylike."

"Good gracious!" said Lady Elizabeth. "A good thing your cousin never met my daughter then. She was always running tame in the stables. So were the boys, of course. Don't let it worry you for an instant, dear. You conduct yourself very well, and your mama would be proud of you."

Georgina laughed shakily. "I'm sure she would say I had behaved like a hoyden... as usual. The thing is, Lady Elizabeth, I... am not really used to England."

"England will just have to get used to you, then," said her hostess. "I loved that book, by the way," she said, pointing to the book. "I hope you enjoy it."

"Oh, I am, already. I feel I should be savoring every word, and here I am gobbling it down. I am so grateful to you for allowing me to borrow it."

That made Lady Elizabeth chuckle, richly. "Oh, my dear. There are plenty more. Now you sit and read. I have found there are very few problems that do not seem less intractable after a good read. Except possibly being interrupted in the best bits!"

Georgina bowed her head, meekly. "Yes, Ma'am. I shall do as I am told." She looked up with just a little dimple of a smile. It was impossible not to like Lady Elizabeth.

Her cheerful laugh and waggled finger said they understood each other perfectly.

The book did distract her, and she was grateful for it, but she could not but help being upset for Mary's sake. Mary would indeed probably lose her place, and all because the person she'd been kind to had not been more careful.

A little later her grandfather woke. Georgina was fairly sure, by now, that this was indeed sleep he was slipping into. She talked to him, got him to drink some more and listened patiently to him ramble about things that had happened before she was born, she suspected. He was still somewhat confused, and seemed somewhat put out at it. He asked her the same question several times and seemed not to remember that she'd answered it before. It was a little wearing, but, honestly, there were worse things, she reflected. Perhaps he would soon get better, and would remember his anger with her mother. Perhaps... perhaps he would die. Cousin Arthur had promised to help, but it would be a difficult period until he succeeded. She would have to go back to her aunt's home. And that would not be pleasant, especially with her only real ally there sent packing.

He dozed for a bit and then woke and told her he felt hungry, so she rang the bell and a simple meal was brought. He ate reasonably well, and then fell asleep.

Later, Betty came in, saying her mistress had given strict instructions that Georgina was to join the family for dinner, after they'd been to Evensong, so she should dress, and that she would be called if there was any need. Did she need help dressing or preparing her hair? Because she, Betty, was itching to get at Miss Georgina's hair with a pair of curling tongs.

"I've never had my hair dressed. Or myself for that matter," admitted Georgina. "I will be fine, truly. I don't need to be any extra trouble."

Betty, trying hard to keep a straight face, said: "Trouble! Miss, how you can say that after giving my Jem a swelled head, I wouldn't know! Now, I'd like to do it, Miss. I'd not offer otherwise."

"Well," said Georgina, trying for a compromise, so as not to hurt Betty's feelings. "I will dress myself, but could you do my hair, please?"

"Is there anything you're needing pressed, Miss? Not but Young Molly may have seen to it when she unpacked your trunks."

"Unpacked my trunks?" said Georgina, startled.

"Yes Miss. We always do so for visitors, if they haven't brought their own maid or dresser. The housekeeper sent her up to do it about an hour ago."

"Oh. I wasn't planning to unpack completely. I have no idea how long I will stay, but I don't think it will be above a few days."

"Then we will help you pack up again," said Betty.

So, Georgina retreated to her room. There she found her fire had been kindled, and Young Molly – a woman in her mid-forties at least, but so called to differentiate her from Old Molly – now apparently long retired and gone to live with her daughter in Winchester, still unpacking. She had set all of Georgina's shoes from the trunk outside the door, to be taken and cleaned – so Georgina hastily searched the toes before going in... And found nothing.

"Good afternoon, Miss," said Young Molly, "I'll be done before the cat can lick its ear. Honestly, those maids at your aunt's house did a very dismal job. Things all rumpled!"

As Georgina or her mother had packed the trunks, neatly, and little had been unpacked, that told her that someone had rifled through them. Georgina clenched her hands, nails digging into her palms, forcing herself to control her tongue. It would have been Mary who packed up the last items into her trunk, and she would hardly have taken the money. Likewise, little though she liked finding her clothes being unpacked, it would be outright stupid for Young Molly to have taken anything. It was, she felt, unlikely that any of the other house-maids would have come up, on a Sunday afternoon. That really left... It was just so petty! But... Elvira could well have done so, inspired by curiosity, and knowing that the servants would bear any blame, unless she was caught red-handed. Elvira's room was further down the passage. She'd probably have had some excuse ready... and would have been able to hear through the door of her grandfather's room, if he'd been awake and they'd been talking. So, Georgina smiled mechanically at Young Molly, and asked if she wanted her to go away, or to help.

"You just sit for a minute, Miss. The laundry maid will be up with those two dresses you had hung up. I asked her to press them for you."

"But it's Sunday!" protested Georgina.

"The good Lord said you should not leave your beasts without water on the Sabbath, Miss. And ironing's not water, but it's needed as much," said Young Molly, firmly. "Besides, it will keep that young snip out of trouble."

Georgina was left with nothing to do while the maid bustled about, and a few minutes later the dress she had been intending to wear – one of her mother's – in dove-grey and black, now years out of fashion, but still well-cut and of good fabric, arrived. Young Molly too, offered to help her dress, but was dismissed with thanks, and Georgina was ready, and composed, although still angry, by the time Betty arrived with the curling tongs.

After a while she said. "There miss. You go and have a look in the mirror."

Georgina found her hair had been braided *a la Didon*, with little curled bangs at the sides of her face. "Goodness! It...it doesn't look like me at all!"

"It looks very elegant," said Betty. "My lady is going to be very pleased. She asked me to give you a new touch."

"You've certainly done that! I'm not sure it is appropriate, with me still in mourning for my mother..."

"Your mother, Miss, would be glad to see you looking so beautiful," Betty informed her. "Now, I've heard the dinner-bell, you go down, I'll stop by with Mr. Weatherly."

So: rather nervously, Georgina did. She was conscious that her leg-of-mutton sleeves and the height of her waist made her dress conspicuously old-fashioned. It was, however, her mother's best, which she'd worn to a dinner given in honor of the Governor-General's visit to Grahamstown, many years previously.

Georgina was still seething about the theft. Petty, perhaps, to someone else. Perhaps she was wrong, perhaps one of the carters had done it? No, everything had been in good order when she had taken out the dresses to hang up. Perhaps the maid unpacking had found it and made up the story of the clothing being rumpled? Perhaps it had fallen out, and she would discover it? That she could not know. There was still reasonable doubt, she concluded. But it still made her angry: a large sacrifice on Mary's part, a large sacrifice on hers, all for nothing.

The family were in the drawing-room, and Georgina apologized saying she hoped she hadn't kept them waiting. "Not at all, my dear," said Lady Elizabeth. "We still wait on your cousin, and Edward only beat you by seconds. He his still out of breath, hair disordered, from that headlong sprint."

"I collapsed from exhaustion when I got here," said that gentleman. "But I have revived, miraculously, at the smell of roast goose. Your servant, Miss Ross. I trust you found a suitable book?"

She colored slightly. "Yes, thank you."

Lady Elizabeth inspected her hair. "Betty has worked wonders with your hair. I do like that braid, my dear."

"I hardly recognized myself in the mirror," said Georgina. "It was so kind of her. Thank you so much."

"One of her favorite pastimes, my dear. I think she misses my daughter for just that reason."

Just then Elvira made her entrance, and shortly after that the gentlemen escorted them into the dining-room.

Edward found himself pipped at the post to offering Miss Ross his arm, by his brother, and was obliged to do the honors instead with her cousin. He reflected that Miss Ross was not the only one to hardly recognize herself. With her hair done, the bangs framing her face, and blushing at the compliment from his mother... well, she was a remarkably taking little thing, he had to admit. Her gown, he recognized as being less than modish – but then he was no fashionable peacock himself. And, after all, she had just got off a ship from the Cape. She was fairly quiet at the table, not setting herself forward at all, but her amazement at the food was amusing and quite charming. No pretended ennui from Miss Ross. She exclaimed over all of it, and explained that their diet on the mission station had been rather plain, and on the ship, likewise. "And there seems to be such a lot of food," she said, naively.

"The joys of the home farm," said Sir Gerald, plainly finding his guest's enjoyment pleasing. "Now what about one of these woodcock, my dear?"

"I don't think I know those. Do you farm them too? Served speared on their own beaks, too."

He laughed. "No, that's John's shooting. You'll watch your teeth on them, in case of shot."

"We do add some variety with a bit of game," said John. "Did you eat any game in Africa?"

She nodded, which was enough to lead the conversation off in that direction. Elvira's attempt to bring it back to fashion, or, later, the failing health of the King and what effect this might have on society could not capture the interest of the gentlemen, especially when Miss Ross said how much she had enjoyed the fish that she had been served earlier that day. "We never really saw fish," she admitted.

"Well, you've got your office, Ned," said Sir Gerald. "Fresh trout for Miss Ross's breakfast, eh boy?"

By the time the ladies withdrew, and the gentlemen were left to enjoy their port, it seemed that Miss Ross had won acceptance and some liking from all of them.

"Nice little gel," said Sir Gerald. "Bit of a different cut from the other one, eh?"

"Well," said John. "I could deal with her staying in the neighborhood, if she means to look after old man Weatherly?"

"No matter how well Weatherly is doing, he can't really move back, not with his house in disrepair," said Sir Gerald. "What's the situation there, Ned. Can you lend a hand?"

"Not while Arthur remains in charge. It wouldn't take that long to fix it, but he's not willing to do it," said Edward.

"Well, I hope Winter – Frederick's man-of-business – will put in an appearance soon. I wrote to him, you know. We had some slight dealings over the property down near Bristol. He travels a bit, so he may be away. He may be able to put some pressure on Arthur."

"Arthur does what Arthur will," said Edward.

"Unfortunately," said his brother. "Are you going after some fish tomorrow, Ned? I've almost a mind to join you."

His father laughed. "Trying to make a good impression with Miss Ross, John?"

"Well," said John. "She seems to like me more than Ned. He's welcome to t'other one."

"Thank you very much. It's so nice to know my big brother is looking after me," said Edward. "I suppose we'd better join the ladies." He had, indeed noticed that Miss Ross, while perfectly polite, tended to answer him in monosyllables and converse with the others. Well, he'd have to make a recover, if only to tease John. His older brother had come close to the parson's mousetrap a year ago, and hadn't quite got over being rejected for an older but richer suitor. At the time he'd said he'd sworn off women. It was good to see that was wearing off a bit. Edward didn't see himself getting married, and someone had to carry on the name.

But when they went through to the ladies, he found that Georgina had gone back up to her grandfather. "She is a very conscientious young woman. It could be her background perhaps, or just her nature," said Lady Elizabeth, approvingly.

The gentlemen soon found reason to retire, too. Edward saying that as he was going to fish the dawn rise, he'd need a little sleep, and he kindly offered Miss Salmonds a nice ride at first light.

"There should be a lovely freezing mist down by the Bourne, to add to its charm," said John, encouragingly. "And you get to spend three hours sitting with the horses in a charming un-heated shed, while he fails to catch fish."

She shuddered. "I don't think my mama would approve."

"Not unless she wants you to catch your death of pneumonia," said Lady Elizabeth.

Her grandfather woke several times during the night, and each time she had to patiently explain, again, that he had had an accident, had hit his head and was recovering, and yes, she was here, and he would be fine. Other than that, Georgina had a peaceful night. She slept on the truckle bed, to be on hand, and turned down the offers of relief. The last time her grandfather woke, the sky was just paling, and she heard the sound of horses going off down the drive. Well, someone was up early too, she thought, wondering if it was worth going down to the kitchen to try and find herself a cup of tea. She resolved to go back to sleep – but as sleep avoided her, she decided it was worth the attempt, and that her grandfather was relatively unlikely to wake. She could have rung the bell but that might have woken someone else. So, she took a candle -it still being rather dark in the passages, and went in search of the kitchen – not being too sure where that was. As it turned out she just had to follow her nose. The kitchen was awake – at least some of it, getting the new bread ready, and preparing for the morning. She got a cheery, if surprised welcome, and was asked if her grandfather needed anything – and got a promise of tea to be delivered to her shortly.

It did indeed arrive soon, along with some fresh pastries. She was sitting enjoying this wholly unlooked for luxury when a yawning Betty came in. "You've never been awake all night, Miss Georgina? Why didn't you call?"

"Oh no. I am just quite an early riser, and I was enjoying a cup of tea and my book. My grandfather slept most of the night."

"Well, you've finished your tea, Miss, and I'm here, so now you'll go and climb into your own bed and rest. It's three hours before most of the family will be awake," said Betty firmly.

Georgina, recognizing that she had somehow become one of Betty's nurselings, and that this was a rare honor, did as she was told, meekly. She did not expect to sleep, but closed her eyes in the luxury of the bed – and woke to another cup of tea being brought in, together with warm water for her morning ablutions. It was, she thought, indeed, a far cry from her aunt's house, or, for that matter the ship or the mission station, or the lodging in Grahamstown.

She washed, dressed hastily and took herself next door, with her cup of tea, where she found her grandfather awake, having had some tea, and now looking at some breakfast, which she was able to encourage him to eat. A few minutes later saw the admission of Dr Selby. "I have extensive rounds to do today, and I thought I had better come and see how he went on before I was hard to reach or find," he said, by way of an explanation. He gave his patient a thorough examination, exhibiting both tact and patience. Georgina, who had only ever known rather brusque military surgeons, found him absolutely wonderful. She said so, afterwards, when he asked her to come down and talk over the patient's condition. That in itself was surprising, as he had not hesitated to speak in the room before.

"My father was an army surgeon-general," said Selby, with a smile. "Most of his patients were young and fit and had physical injuries. All too many of mine are old and suffering various ailments. It requires a different approach. He is much more *compos mentis* today, he knows who he is, and it is apparent he is eating and drinking and in full control of his bodily functions... but he appears to be showing signs of brain injury. Short term memory loss."

"So, what do we do? What can we do?" asked Georgina.

"Be patient. Time sometimes heals. Perhaps more familiar surroundings. Do you know if his house has been restored to being habitable? While I worry about the bumps and bouncing in any carriage, I think sufficient time has passed to try this. To explain: That was a vicious blow he was struck, his skull was possibly fractured, and as a result he may have blood clots... these can cause a blockage of the flow of blood to certain parts of the brain – an aspect of the condition of apoplexy, which you may have heard mentioned. That could kill him. On the other hand, patients are generally happier surrounded by the familiar, and that may contribute to their recovery."

"My Cousin Arthur is supposed to be going to Winchester today to get some tradesmen to fix my grandfather's house. I do not know how long that may take." She looked him directly in the eye. "Doctor Selby. I have just been through the death of both of my parents. You need have no scruples about speaking directly to me. If I understand you correctly, there is no great hope of recovery. You are saying that while there is risk in moving him, it would be better for him, for his happiness, for us to take that chance?"

He nodded slowly. "You are quite an unusual young lady. Older than your years. May I ask if you plan to continue to nurse him?"

"As long as I can, I will. My Cousin Arthur, his heir, will have to take the final decision. I can't expect... to... house myself on his charity, indefinitely."

"I see," said Doctor Selby, thoughtfully. "Let me say I believe it essential for Mr. Frederick Weatherly to have you caring for him. I know he takes you for your mother, but that has a calming effect on him. I would not advocate moving him without you. I will speak to your cousin." He paused. "I will also have a word with Sir Gerald. I will also, I believe, need to speak with Mr. Frederick's man of business and his attorney. He cannot be considered *compos mentis* to sign any documentation."

There was a knock on the door. "Miss Georgina, please come," said the maid. "He's asking after you."

So, Georgina left the Doctor, and returned to her grandfather.

Doctor Selby's visit proved merely to be the first for her of the day. She had barely had a chance to have some breakfast, which again included some of the trout she'd so enjoyed the day before, when Reverend Thorpe arrived. He was standing in for the usual parish priest, and had come to inquire after Mr. Frederick. He was considerably interested in the fact that Georgina had been on a mission-station in Africa, and would have stayed longer, had not the magistrate, Mr. Tadswell, arrived to see if Mr. Frederick remembered anything of his attacker – which he did not. Then, barely had he left, than a message was sent to Georgina, that if possible could she come down to speak with Mr. Winter, her grandfather's man-of-business.

Georgina faced this meeting with some trepidation, her knowledge of business being non-existent. She felt it might well be about her future prospects, which she suspected were also non-existent.

Thaddeus Winter was a very small man, not quite her height. He was balding, and had a slight pot-belly, but could not have been much past forty. He looked rather un-threatening – but she knew little of 'finance' - except how slender her purse was.

He had a very slight stammer, which, once again, might have disarmed her, had she not been so wary. "P...Pleased to meet you, Miss Ross," he said, bowing. He extended his condolences about her parents' deaths and asked questions about the mission station, and of her return to England, and what she planned to do here. He was calm, patient with her nerves, and knowledgeable enough to ask just the right questions, to set her at ease. It took her a little while to realize that she had told him a great deal more about herself, her life, and hopes, than she had confided in anyone, and also that she'd betrayed that her pockets were almost entirely to let, and she knew little of England. He, on the other hand, had told her very little. She stopped. Looked at him slightly askance. "You are very good at getting me to talk, Mr. Winter. I know nothing about the normal conduct of business. Is this how it is usually done?"

He gave a small prim smile. "Y...You are very astute, Miss Ross. It's a great help to me in my line of business to be a good listener. People then tell me a great deal, which helps me to understand them and their business. I manage the affairs of several gentlemen, but your grandfather was my first client. My father – who was in the same line of work, handed him on to me."

He looked at her thoughtfully. "In the course of managing my client's b...business... I have spoken to Sir Gerald, and made a stop with Doctor Selby, as a result. I was fortunate to catch him returning to his home for luncheon, and he was good enough to give me of his time and his professional opinion of my client's health, and the care he will need. He recommended that I should endeavor, for my client's welfare, to get you to remain with him. While I respect the good Doctor's opinion, it was necessary for me to assess you for myself, so I can speak to Mr. Frederick's attorney. I was concerned about your youth, and, frankly, of your connection with a man you have not known." He tugged his chin. "It is a great deal of responsibility to place onto young shoulders, young lady, and you may be sure of my help and support, should you undertake it. I will consult with Abraham Lawrence, who is your grandfather's attorney, as to how things should be best managed. Dr Selby says Mr. Frederick is suffering some degree of injury to his brain. There are various legalities..."

"Legalities?" said Georgina, blankly.

"From my point of view, in the m...managing his affairs. Decisions that need to be taken. Authority to withdraw monies, and so on," explained Mr. Winter. "The estate will need to be managed. Investments have been made which will need decisions on what should be done, when they mature. Your grandfather had shares in certain ventures, outside of the more conventional investments."

"Oh, I am sure Cousin Arthur... Mr. Arthur Weatherly, would be the right person for you to talk to. You've rather wasted your time with me on that, I am afraid. He's my grandfather's heir and has been arranging everything. You had better speak to him."

Mr. Winter nodded politely, his face expressionless. She could see how he conducted business for his employers now. He gave little away. "I...I will talk to Mr. Lawrence, and proceed from there," he said. "But it is your intent to care for your grandfather? To stay with him?"

"Yes. If it is at all possible for me to do so. I think it my duty and what my mother would have wanted. But it is not my decision, really."

He steepled his fingers and nodded. "Th...That would, I believe, be best, for both him and the estate. Now, Miss Ross, my advice to you: Please take no actions, sign no documentation without first consulting me, or Mr. Lawrence. Please promise me that."

She was slightly amused. "I can't see what actions I would take, or what I could sign, that would be of any relevance."

"Well, you might decide to return to Africa, or sign a marriage certificate," He said with what was plainly his attempt at humor.

She shook her head. "I do not wish to return. I do miss that life in some ways, but... I need to move forward. Besides, how would I get there, and what would I do? As for marriage, I believe nothing could be more unlikely!"

He nodded, again showing no clue of his thoughts on his bland face, as he said: "None-the-less, Miss Ross. It is a duty of care I owe Mr. Frederick Weatherly." Then he surprised her utterly: "Now, Miss Ross, in the short term, you will be needing funds. I will consult with Mr. Lawrence about the longer term, but I do have certain discretion."

While the idea of any money was welcome, Georgina did not see quite why or what for. She said as much.

"M...Miss Ross," he said, with just the hint of a smile. "I... I am not frequently surprised. I am now. I do not think I have ever had such an offer repulsed. The opposite is usually true. Look, Miss Ross: other considerations aside: You will be taking care of my client. If someone else were hired to do so, they would have to be paid, and I, under the circumstances, would be paying them out of the accounts I hold for Mr. Frederick Weatherly. You will have a great deal to see to, and I shall talk with Lady Elizabeth and Sir Gerald to ask if they can help you to get settled. You will need additional servants in the house to help you. You may need other things – medications or special foods. It would be inconvenient for you to have to call on me every time you wish to buy some small thing. Accordingly, I am going to give you a sum to be going on with. I had hoped you would tell me how much you needed me to disperse to you. But I think that will not answer, because you would not tell me. This," he said, with the prim smile again: "Is a novelty. You have the charm of great novelty, young lady." He stood up. "I am going to give you fifty pounds."

Her mouth fell open, and she had to force herself to close it. And then to protest. "That is far too much!"

He shook his head. "H...how much, then?" he asked, still smiling, drawing a roll of bills from his pocket.

"Ten pounds?" she said warily.

"That is far too little for the costs you are likely to incur."

"I could ask you for more... and... if my cousin thinks I am not doing a good job he might send me packing."

"That would not be in his authority," said Mr. Winter. "Only Mr. Lawrence could do so, if he feels my advice to have been poor. You are, regardless of the will, his next of k...kin, while he is alive. But yes, I will be coming up again in a week, and you will then have a better idea of what you need, Miss Ross, I hope. But I suspect I am wrong, so I will give you twenty pounds." He counted it out and handed it to her. "Now, would it be possible for me to visit Mr. Frederick? I hold him in some affection. He taught me a great deal. And, indeed, so have you."

"Thank you, Sir. I will go and see if he is awake. I warn you, he may well not recognize you."

"Th...That Dr Selby has told me. None-the-less, I should like to see him, even if he is asleep. I would feel I had not done my duty, otherwise."

"Then come with me, sir," said Georgina, who felt that what she really needed was to sit down quietly somewhere.

Her grandfather was awake, and greeted her with: "Dorothea, why am I here?" He looked at Winter. "And who are you?" he demanded.

"Thaddeus Winter, at your service, Mr. Weatherly."

Her grandfather paused. "I know a Samuel Winter. You have the look of him."

"M...my father, sir."

"Ah. That accounts for it. Dorothea, why am I here?"

She explained again. Shortly, Mr. Winter took his leave, and she accompanied him downstairs, to where Sir Gerald was waiting to speak to him. He bowed over her hand. "D...do not hesitate to contact me, Miss Ross, should you need any assistance. And please remember my advice about consulting me or Mr. Lawrence about any actions you wish to take, either in your own case or for your grandfather." He paused. "My father has been dead fifteen years. Good bye, Miss Ross. It was an honor to meet you."

She was left in a conflict of emotions. There was some relief that Mr. Winter seemed at least to want her to remain with her grandfather, which in a way relieved the pressing worry of where she could find shelter and food, once her small funds ran out. The money he'd given her was an enormous relief – to the point that it worried her. What if her grandfather died? She could return the money, as long as she had not spent it. Of course, that would leave her in as bad a position as she was now – unless, she thought indignantly, someone stole it. She decided to either carry it with her, or hide it extremely carefully.

Her real issue with Mr. Winter was, that despite him having been a sympathetic listener, and, it seemed, generous, and even kind, that he was very hard to read. She wanted to think him a good man, but there was a niggling doubt. Why would he wish to help her? Perhaps, it was merely that she was unable to believe – after all that had happened in the last year, that anything good could in fact come her way. She resolved to follow her father's advice and count her blessings. Part of her said: and prepare for them not to be blessings.

The next visitor, later that afternoon, was Cousin Arthur. One of the footmen came to call her, saying he desired a private word with her, about his uncle. He was waiting in the yellow saloon. Arthur looked somewhat tired, and she said as much to him.

He sighed. "It has been a very tiring day, between dealing with certain of my own matters of business, which has meant going back to London, and my Uncle Frederick's affairs. Talking to the Runners because I am determined to capture the miscreant! Anyway, the tradesmen from Winchester should be there to do the glazing tomorrow. The floors and other work will have to wait. The library and blue drawing room will have to remain off limits for a while, I am afraid. How do you go on? I will say that seeing you lifts my spirits! And how is my uncle today?"

"Wondrously improved!" she said, thinking that too would lift his spirits.

"He is... remembering things?" asked Arthur.

She had to shake her head. "Not of the attack, no. Doctor Selby says he may never remember that. Sadly, he could tell Mr. Tadswell nothing. In fact, he did not even recognize him, and they knew each other. And he did not recognize Mr. Winter, either."

"Winter! He has been here?" said Cousin Arthur.

"Yes, he left about two hours ago," said Georgina. "He said that he planned to see you."

Arthur looked very concerned. "There are irregularities in the accounts I have looked at. Monies not accounted for. In short, I believe Winter has been feathering his own nest at my uncle's expense. I would not be surprised if this assault somehow ties to him. I must urge you, dear Cousin, to treat him with a great degree of caution."

"He... did make me a little uneasy," admitted Georgina. "But he was very kind."

"Honeyed words, Cousin Georgina," said Arthur. "Anyway, what I came to say was that I plan to remove my uncle to his own house as soon as the repairs are done. That could be as soon as Wednesday, when I believe your aunt is coming up to collect you and your good cousin. I believe you've been called on to work like a black slave caring for my uncle. You'll be relieved that I have found a nurse to care for him."

"Oh no!" she said in real dismay. "That is, not that I'm not grateful, dear Cousin Arthur, and you mean it for the best…"

"I am sorry, Georgina, I cannot be at ease while he is in this house! He must go home."

"Oh yes. I agree that he must go home. And so does Doctor Selby. But I plan to care for him."

He looked startled. "That is very good of you, but quite unnecessary, I assure you. He will be well looked after, I promise. And you have a life of your own to pursue. It is not to be thought of that a beautiful young lady like yourself should be immured in some little country house, caring for an invalid. You'll be bored to death. You should be at balls and parties and plays, and enjoying the metropolis. I am persuaded you will like London excessively, and I am looking forward to taking you there."

She had to laugh a little. "Now, Cousin Arthur. I'm a poor missionary's daughter. There will be no parties or balls for me. My purse is very pinched, and I will be lucky to find a position somewhere that allows me a roof over my head and to feed and clothe myself."

"I'd like to change that, Cousin Georgina," said Arthur.

Her heart beat a little faster. "Just what do you mean, Cousin Arthur?" she said, aware that he was standing quite close, and feeling slightly uncomfortable and not knowing quite what to do.

"I mean I would like to offer you my hand in marriage. I have been entranced by you from the moment I met you."

She could only gape at him and step back, as she was very unsure of how to react and what he was going to do next. "C…c…cousin!" she exclaimed. "You hardly know me!"

"Even a few minutes in your company would be enough for any fellow. I'm surprised not to find you surrounded by suitors," he said, earnestly. "I had not meant to speak so soon, but it's all holiday with me! Thought... I'd get in as soon as possible. Look... I have a great deal to offer. You would never have to worry about a roof or feeding and clothing yourself, ever again. You could shop in the finest of modistes. I would not keep you short of pin money, I assure you! We would live in London of course, somewhere in the first stare of fashion. You would take the shine out of all the other ladies." He advanced, holding out his hands.

She retreated as far as she could. "Cousin Arthur... I, I..." She fell over her own tongue, not knowing quite what to say. She'd never had as much of a hint of a proposal of marriage before, and never thought, seriously, to get one. Oh, it was a daydream, with a handsome suitor, who would sweep her off her feet. But... reality was not quite what it seemed in the daydreams. Was he going to kiss her? She didn't know how to respond to that, let alone the proposal. "I promised my grandfather I would look after him. He gets so confused. I cannot abandon him. And... and this is too soon. I can't... And... and we're cousins."

"Once removed. We can marry, dearest Georgina," he said, taking possession of her hands. "I went up to London and prevailed on the Bishop to grant me a special license." He leaned in, to kiss her.

"Excuse me, Miss Ross," said a voice, making Arthur back off hastily and release her hands, to her relief.

It was Sir Gerald and, just behind him, his son Edward. "Miss Ross, I am sorry to interrupt, but Lady Elizabeth was looking for you. And Mr. Weatherly, you are just the person I needed to see. Can we have a word?"

"Yes, er, of course," said Georgina. "Where is her ladyship, Sir Gerald?"

"Edward will escort you to her," said Sir Gerald, waving a hand at his son.

"Oh. Thank you," said Georgina, aware she was blushing to the roots of her hair. "I must go, Cousin Arthur."

"We shall see each other again, soon, dear Cousin," said Arthur.

Edward led her down the hallway and through several odd twists and turns, to what proved to be a large linen store. Georgina had had time to recover her composure by then, and her hostess's calm smile of welcome did much to reassure her. "Goodness. I didn't mean she had to come at once, Edward. I just said when it was opportune. I am sorry, my dear. Men!"

"It seemed a good time," said Edward, with no hint of an expression crossing his broad face. "We thought Miss Ross might find it convenient, now."

"Yes, Ned," said his mother. "Now, I daresay you have something else to do. Miss Ross, we went over to Westmead House with your grandfather's man-of-business, to see what needed doing to make it possible for Mr. Frederick to go back home. Mr. Winter tells me you have agreed to return with him and care for him. My dear, that is very good of you!"

"I do think it is my duty," said Georgina, her mind still a turmoil from the turn of events in the yellow saloon.

"He is family," said Lady Elizabeth. "But all too many people shirk that, my dear. But Mr. Winter is quite right, it must be made as easy as possible for you, because it is not a light thing for a young girl to take on. Mrs. Lessing, the housekeeper, is a good woman, who has done her best. But she's not young. She's is not, in her own words, much up to caring for invalids all night. You are very short of staff to run the house. Mrs. Lessing had a young girl from the village to help her clean, and her husband who combined duty as butler and footman, there is a groom and a couple of stable-boys and old Ted, the gardener... but you'll need at least two more indoor maids, and at least another footman. Your grandfather had most of the house shut up and under Holland covers, but Mrs. Lessing tells me it had a staff of nine, when Mr. Frederick's wife was alive, and the children were young. Things have been rather let go, as old Mr. Frederick had no interest in housekeeping. As long as the library, his bedroom, the blue saloon, and the morning room – where he took his meals, were in good order he was satisfied."

"I am sure I will contrive," said Georgina. "I will only need a room and a bed."

"No, you don't!" said Lady Elizabeth, firmly. "You will need some degree of comfort, and so does old Mr. Weatherly. Mr. Winter says the estate is in perfectly good enough financial shape to afford to run the house normally, and being properly cared for will enhance its value for the future heir. He's quite correct. The place is going backwards."

"But, surely that is Cou... Mr. Arthur's Weatherly's prerogative? He is the heir. My mother told me so," said Georgina.

Lady Elizabeth shook her head. "I assumed you knew. According to Mr. Winter, while Mr. Frederick Weatherly remains alive, you are his nearest blood relative, and will have responsibility for his medical decisions, if he cannot make them himself. Indeed, really, the Doctors would have to certify him mentally fit again, before he could assert legal authority. Selby says it is quite a process, fraught with challenge! It goes down the bloodline, and then up to parents, and then only to siblings or children of siblings. Unless Mr. Weatherly instructed his attorney that Arthur would be acting for him, which, apparently, he has not... it is over to you, my dear. I am sure old Mr. Weatherly's attorney will be coming to see you, but Mr. Winter says he is quite laid up at the moment. Sciatica, I believe. He is not a young man."

This, coming on top of her day of shocks and surprises was almost too much to deal with. "I don't know what to do. Or how to do it!" she blurted out.

Lady Elizabeth smiled kindly at her. "Sit down, dear. Mr. Winter reposed great confidence in you. He was very impressed, and said you were a great deal older than your years. That's a great compliment from him. And don't worry about telling Arthur. Sir Gerald has undertaken to explain it to him."

Georgina did sit down. She felt she needed to. Taking a deep breath, and thinking back to her conversation with Mr. Winter, she supposed he had said much of this. It did not seem quite right to her that Cousin Arthur would not be there doing the organizing and she really was not sure how she could manage. She said as much.

"We'll be here to help you, dear. And Mrs. Lessing is a good house-keeper. She just needs someone to take decisions. Now, what I was doing down here was selecting some sheets to lend to you. Westmead House is very short of linen, it seems! More will have to be ordered, but that will take time. Or do you think your aunt would rather see to it?"

"No!" said Georgina, firmly. It was good to have something she could make an easy decision about.

No wonder Mr. Winter had said she would need money. Well, that was better. The money wasn't really for her. She must keep careful account.

A sudden thought occurred to her. "Lady Elizabeth, you spoke of servants. Could I, could I... hire someone that I wanted?"

"Of course you could, my dear! You will definitely need a personal maid. Look, you will have to keep up appearances in the district. You are his granddaughter and there is a certain decorum to be maintained. And you should – if you're willing – choose the other staff. I would get Mrs. Lessing to help you, because it would be difficult if there was conflict about that. She is very excited about bringing the house back to the way it used to be."

Georgina took a deep breath. "Lady Elizabeth, could I borrow Jem... or, or hire his services, I am not sure how these things are done – to run an errand to Southampton for me?"

There was a twinkle in Lady Elizabeth's eye. "I'm not sure that you should poach your aunt's household staff, Miss."

"It's likely she will be given her notice for her kindness to me, anyway," said Georgina, firmly. "Mary may not want to come out into the country, or to be that far from her family. It would be very rural for her, here. She may want to stay in the city."

"And you, my dear?" asked Lady Elizabeth. "Do you find it so?"

Georgina was moved to laughter. "To be honest, I find it quite full of people here, let alone in the city. I mean, I am used to places where one would not see another house, or even a trace of smoke from a fire, for as far as the eye could see. In Southampton I felt as if the buildings were crowding over on top of me. I didn't realize how much it was bothering me until the carriage took us out of the town." She saw the look of surprise on her host's face. "Not that I wouldn't want to visit a city, occasionally, but I wouldn't choose to live in one. Of course, one's choices are not always what one gets."

"True enough, my dear. Of course, most people hold that the city is far superior to the country. I love going there, but I am always glad to escape it myself, as is Sir Gerald. Poor dear, he is just not at home there. If he can't hunt or shoot or fish, he gets restive, and nothing is worse for a marriage than a restive husband. Now, this linen..."

Chapter 6

Edward had been relatively unsurprised to see Arthur Weatherly crowding Miss Ross into a corner. What had surprised him was the look on her face. He had thought she liked 'Cousin Arthur', by her tone and comments about him.

He was also mildly surprised, that, if she hadn't wished to be kissed, she hadn't let out a screech. This was Bournelea, not some back-alley in London – or Madrid, for that matter. But then, perhaps in Africa help had not been so forthcoming. He'd been close to stepping past his father and planting the fellow a facer. He would have done so, if it had not been for his father's restraining hand. He'd not known quite what to say to her, taking her to find his mother, and had decided to follow the advice of his old commanding officer, who had, at one of Edward's attempts at explanation of the sort of mess only a green lieutenant can get themselves into, advised: "If you don't know what to say, Lieutenant, don't open your mouth. You'll only make the situation worse."

She had seemed terribly embarrassed by the situation. Rather like his sister Gussie, when he'd walked in on her kissing one of her suitors. But there had been relief on Miss Georgina Ross's face when they had entered the parlor, of that he was sure. Gussie had merely shown chagrin, he thought, smiling to himself. His sister had been, without a doubt, something of a hoyden. Now she was married and had her first child she'd settled down, somewhat.

It had been something of a momentous day, he reflected. Firstly, there'd been what could only be considered a damned awkward interview with Tadswell. It was Penn, of course. Something about him had roused the magistrate's suspicions. He'd found out Penn's place of origin, and then written to the magistrate there, asking about him. Which had revealed Penn's career prior to his military one, to have been 'successful poacher'.

"Yes, Mr. Tadswell. He told me."

"But you did not see fit to tell me, Captain," said the magistrate.

"I didn't see it as relevant. He's been with me for six years. I would trust him with my life, and indeed, he looked after all my possessions, and his care kept me alive. He told me he was up before a magistrate, caught trespassing under suspicious circumstance, and while the magistrate was unable to tie him to anything but being where he shouldn't be, he was given the choice of taking the King's shilling or being charged."

"The magistrate reports that poaching took a substantial downturn on his departure," said Tadswell.

This Edward could well believe, but he answered politely that he didn't really see what it had to do with anything.

"It has been suggested that you two might be implicated," said Tadswell, plainly trying for shock value. "I have to question the early hour you were on the scene."

"Mr. Tadswell, with due respect, why don't you ask the locals? My habit of fishing the dawn rise is well known. And as for my man, Penn, question the grooms at Westmead. He woke them to make them aware of the fire. If either of us had set it, we would hardly have rushed to wake them, to help to put it out."

"I shall follow up on these matters," Tadswell had informed him, plainly still regarding getting up before first light to fish as unthinkable.

Then his father had asked him to accompany his mother, and Mr. Winter, across to Westmead. That too had been full of the unexpected. It had been good news that while Frederick Weatherly was alive, but medically incapacitated, that responsibility for his welfare devolved to his granddaughter, rather than Arthur Weatherly. Eventually, Arthur would inherit, of course, but no one was in a hurry to have him as a neighbor. Admittedly he'd probably sell the place as soon as he could, anyway. The part that had shocked him, however, was the conversation that Winter had had with him, as they walked around the grounds, while his mother was talking with Mrs. Lessing. "I...I believe, Captain Kelling," said Winter, "from what my client told me, previously, that you have been assisting him in r...running the estate. As his agent."

Edward shook his head. "More like helping out as his bailiff! The estate is not large, as you'd know. Just five farms, all under tenancy. Far too small to justify an agent. And there was nothing official about it. Just... well, I was still recovering from my wounding, and his bailiff had been cheating him. The place was going to rack and ruin."

"I have actually seen the improvement – both in the land and returns. M...my client did talk to me about the possibility of making it official," said Winter. "And yes, I know you had turned it down."

"I am going to have to pursue some career," said Edward. "As you may know, riding any distance is... unpleasant."

"And how is your...recovery progressing?" asked Winter.

"It's been improving. I've gone from being bedridden, to struggling to walk, to gradually being able to ride a mile or two. But the Army is a closed door for me."

"Well, Captain, th...this is awkward, but if I can get Samuel Lawrence – my client's attorney, to agree, could we prevail on you to accept the position as his agent, *pro tem*? You see, Miss Ross, while an excellent young lady in many respects, does seem to attach considerable authority to Mr. Arthur Weatherly. H...he would, I suspect, assume the management of all your good work." Winter cleared his throat, and looked up at Edward. "The estate must provide for Mr. Frederick, and the young lady, possibly for some years. I don't expect you to do this for any length of time, Captain, but just to... to allow her to find her feet and to keep the value of the property intact. We will then appoint someone else, if you wish. I actually do have the authority to do this on my own, but I would confirm it with L...Lawrence."

Seeing Edward silenced, Winter continued. "I hate to spring this on you, but I did speak to your father about you continuing in the role you already filled, until things should be a little more settled. He said I would have to speak with you, but thought it a very sensible idea. At least for the s...summer."

"I am somewhat nonplussed by your suggestion. It seems... a bit underhand."

"You, and I, are quite well acquainted with Mr. F... Frederick. It is what he would have asked you to do. He had in fact asked you to do."

"And I had turned him down," said Edward. "Very well. He was kind enough to me. And frankly, although it galls me to improve Arthur's inheritance, he'll likely sell it immediately it is his, whereas if he were managing it he'd be doing all sorts of foolish things, just to annoy us."

"You will merely be continuing to do what you were doing – in an official capacity which would make it difficult to have you dismissed," said Winter. "I too... ha...have had dealings with Arthur Weatherly."

"I suppose so."

Winter was very good at keeping his voice even, and gave away nothing in his facial expression, which remained placid and urbane. But Edward was sure that those dealings had not filled Thaddeus Winter with any liking for Arthur. "It is going to make Arthur as mad as fire," he said.

"Captain Kelling, th...that is possible. May I suggest that in the interests of tact with Miss Ross, we need not point out that this is not a longstanding arrangement. It has existed for a while, just not on a formal basis. You n...need have very little to do with Miss Ross, as her responsibility is merely that which concerns the medical care of Mr Frederick. The estate continues to be under the responsibility of his attorney, and myself, as we are authorized to act for him. R...rest assured, I shall be available to you, at any time, and I will be giving this matter a great deal of my attention."

Edward remained somewhat troubled about it. What Winter said was true enough, Frederick Weatherly had wanted him to do the job. But it still seemed an underhand way of doing it. He had to wonder if there was more to Winter's behavior than met the eye.

He was still pondering this when he was greeted by Miss Elvira Salmonds. "Why, it is the gallant Captain Edward Kelling!" she exclaimed. "I thought you were avoiding me."

Tact prevented him from saying that for once, she'd got something absolutely right. "Good afternoon, Miss Salmonds. I trust you're enjoying the spring sunshine?"

"Mama says it's so bad for the complexion. But I have a new bonnet with a broad brim, and the sun is not so fierce, so I was hoping someone would take me for a turn about the gardens."

He could not escape, so spent half an hour hearing about fashionable dress, and having lures cast for compliments. He was somewhat comforted that she had little real interest in him, as the younger son, but was merely keeping her hand in. Her interest – by the leading questions, was in his brother, John, and to his amusement, Arthur Weatherly, with whom she was plainly deeply impressed. She asked after Arthur's fortune, and Edward was led into saying that he really didn't know, but it must be large or he must owe his tailor a mint.

"Yes," gushed Elvira. "He is of the first stare, isn't he!"

"He certainly attracts a great deal of attention. Women do seem to find him attractive," said Edward, feeling those answers were at least truthful. He could tell her less than she wished to know about Arthur, to her disappointment. He was relieved to be able to take her back inside, on the grounds that she had not brought a shawl with her, and it was getting chill out, this early in the season. He made good his escape, and took himself back to the library, to a comfortable chair and book, which offered a rest from dwelling on the events of the day.

Georgina, after checking on her grandfather, had also taken refuge in her book, seating herself in his room. But her mind was too disordered by all that had happened to allow her to escape the world into fiction. Did she wish to marry Arthur Weatherly? He was, in many ways the epitome of some of her daydreams. Had he, the smartly dressed man-about-town, really fallen in love with her, the little missionary's daughter, with no prospects and dowdy clothes? She'd looked at herself in the mirror. She was not precisely an antidote, she supposed. But he had to know many more beautiful girls than her. It made her smile, wryly. Here she was, one moment so sure she'd never have an offer, and the next questioning a very eligible suitor's proposal.

Thought on the subject eventually returned a conclusion: It was not that she did not like Cousin Arthur, or even disliked the idea of marriage – either to him or anyone else. It was just... she hardly knew him – or anything about men of her own order in this England that she found herself in. The little she did know suggested that courtship – outside of romance novels – usually took a lot more time. A part of her said it was so romantic and... well, flattering, for little Georgina Ross to have attracted the attention of a man of fashion and position, like Arthur Weatherly. And a more pragmatic, practical part wondered if he would fall out of love as quickly as into it. She resolved to ask him for time. Time to get to know him, time to let her own feelings develop. That was on one hand. The other said: marry him and you have ensured your security. That in itself was tempting. She knew exactly what her father would have said about such temptation... but then he hadn't left her very well provided for, so that she could avoid it.

It all left her restless and uncomfortable. Her grandfather awoke, and she set her book aside, and they talked, and she rang a bell to fetch him tea and something to eat. "I do not like to eat in bed," he informed her.

"That is a good thing," she said. "As I wish to talk to the Doctor about getting you up a little to sit in the chair. We hope to take you home soon."

"I want to be back at Westmead again," he said. "I am struggling so to remember."

"It will get better," she said, with a confidence she did not feel.

She was rather withdrawn at dinner that night, but Elvira made up for it, she thought, being happy to engage in most of the conversation.

That evening she wrote to Mary – at some length, because she felt she really needed to explain it carefully, and offered her the position as her maid, at what she was assured by Betty was a good wage. The next day Jem, entrusted with the letter, and a sum of money to cover any losses Mary might suffer in giving her notice, and also to pay for their return on the mail-coach, should Mary be willing, took himself on the mail to Southampton. He promised to return with the little gel, looking after her as if she was his own daughter. He seemed pleased and amused by the errand, plainly having been given the office to do this, forthwith, by his wife.

Under Dr. Selby's eye, her grandfather was given a fresh and less bulky dressing to the wound on his head, which had healed well, and was now mostly extensive bruising. He was helped from his bed, into a dressing gown, and to a wing-chair in the sunlight. At which point there was a knock on the door. It was Edward Kelling, with a newspaper. "I know this was his habit," he said with a smile. "How do you go on, Sir? It's good to see you up."

He sounded genuine in his concern. She knew he'd been up several times before, but usually when his mother only had been in attendance.

"Edward!" said the old man. "How are you my boy? Got any good fish lately?"

"A couple of fine ones. I hit on a good mayfly hatch this morning. They were rising all over the place. Didn't get a touch until I switched to teal and green. They were being very particular."

It must have meant something to her grandfather even if it might as well have been Greek to Georgina... Actually, worse than Greek. She knew quite a bit of that from her father, who had studied it in order to read the Bible in its original form. "Yes, a good fly this early in the year," her grandfather answered. "And the papers! Very good, my boy. Now, my eye-glasses..."

"I'll have to fetch them for you, sir. They must be at Westmead. Sorry. I should have thought of that."

"I will read to you, Grandfather," said Georgina.

He looked a little confused, but then said: "Eh, yes of course, Dorothea."

"Where would you like me to start?" she asked.

"The obituaries, of course. How else do I know I'm not dead?"

Edward withdrew – as did Doctor Selby. She did not read to him for much time – it was dull work, and he nodded off before long. Lady Elizabeth came back up, and beckoned to her. They went into the dressing room so they could talk and not disturb him. "Selby took his leave, said he was very sorry to go without speaking to you. But he is at one with us about moving Mr. Weatherly back to his own home. And he was very pleased at him recognizing Edward. He said it bodes well, once he is back in a familiar environment."

"I was really surprised by that," said Georgina.

"Well, Edward saw him most mornings. You know he's been setting the Westmead estate to rights. It's been good for my poor boy too. He was really... well, without direction, when he was invalided out of the army."

"Oh... I didn't know," said Georgina. "I am afraid I know so little about the entire situation."

"Edward's not one to talk about it. But I thought my little boy had come home to die," said Lady Elizabeth, quietly. "If it hadn't been for Selby... I believe he would have." She shook herself. Mustered a smile. "The mess of that treatment defies all belief, Georgina. Honey! Packed into the wound. If I hadn't been desperate enough to try anything...

But it worked. Anyway, my dear. Your grandfather saw most of us very occasionally, in church, when his health permitted. Ned, on the other hand, was over there a great deal. There is little for him to do here, with Sir Gerald and John running the estate, and him not feeling it as his business, and not being able to enjoy his various sporting pursuits. The Kelling men do not thrive on idleness, I am afraid. He has become something of a reader as a result, but he finds not being able to be as active as he once was a sore trial. So, helping Mr. Frederick with Westmead was good for him. I hope you will have no objection to him continuing. I know Mr. Winter has asked him to go on. The attorney desires it too."

Georgina felt she was in no position to contest this, but did put forward that really it wasn't her decision, meaning really the authority belonged to Cousin Arthur.

"Oh, I know, my dear. Winter apparently has power of attorney for the running of Mr. Weatherly's affairs. But you should be consulted."

"He hadn't mentioned it to me, Ma'am," said Georgina. "And surely my Cousin Arthur..."

"Oh, Arthur," said Lady Elizabeth. "Perhaps Winter wanted to talk to him first. Anyway, Arthur is a city man, not well grounded in country matters. I know he finds them tedious, so I am persuaded he'll be glad to have someone to do it for him."

Georgina did not know how to say that Arthur suspected Edward of the assault. And she reflected, the reaction of her grandfather to the man was hardly that of someone he had been attacked by. It would also take enormous effrontery and confidence to come up, face-to-face and trust he would not be recognized. Surely Arthur might be wrong? She resolved to watch Edward closely, whatever. She still had not forgotten his insufferable rudeness about her. That, combined with the politeness that he treated her with at dinner, showed him capable of being two-faced.

The rest of the day passed fairly peacefully and without further incident, with her grandfather glad to take to his bed after his time in the chair.

That evening, after her grandfather had eaten, and she'd settled him, she retreated to her room to await the dressing-bell. He was becoming more spirited and had demanded wine instead of these slops they were feeding him. She had been obliged to refuse, and he had not been happy about it. She was sitting there with her book, when there was a tentative knock at her door.

"Come in," she called.

The door opened and there stood Mary, looking, Georgina thought, both lost and terrified. Behind her stood Betty, smiling. Georgina rushed over and without a further thought, hugged Mary. "Oh Miss!" protested Mary.

"Mary! I am so glad to see you," said Georgina. "I was so afraid you wouldn't come."

"Jem says he had a fair job of it," said Betty, laughing.

"Come in and sit down, you poor dear," said Georgina, leading her in, and pushing her into the wingchair. "Oh Betty. Can you get me some tea for her? Have you eaten, Mary? Oh, I am so glad to see you!"

Mary stood up with great determination. "Now, Miss Georgina! I can't be sitting down! I'm just a bit mazed by it all."

"Jem got them a bite to eat in Winchester," said Betty. "And she'll take her meal with us in the underhall, later. I'll have someone show her the way, and to her room. One of the men will carry her boxes up. Now Mary, can you help Miss Georgina dress for dinner, or shall I come when I'm done with Lady Elizabeth?"

"She'll be fine," said Georgina, firmly.

"I will, indeed," said Mary. When the door closed, she modified that to: "I'll be doing my best, Miss Georgina. I don't know much about what I have to do."

"I don't need much. Honestly, Mary, I just wanted to fix any trouble I may have got you into. And to get you away from a place where I knew you were unhappy."

"Me mam says it's a great opportunity," said Mary. "Jem... he took me straight-away to her. I was supposed to be working! He told Cook I needed to see me mam, immediate like, and put me in a Hackney cab! I've never been in one in me life. I thought ma must be dying... and then I recognized him. And he did take me right home, then and there. I thought me mam would have a conniption."

"I begin to understand exactly why Betty married him! He is a treasure. I will have to reward him. And Mary, I will try to make this the opportunity your mother thinks it is. It... it may not be. It's only while my grandfather is alive, and even the Doctor can't say how long he will live."

"Miss, getting away from that woman, it was worth it. I go to give me notice... and she turns me off. Just like that. No pay, for the days I've done. Just 'get out of my house'," Mary said, indignant. "At least here, as Jem says, I can rise a bit in the world. I can put something by, because I have never been paid so much."

"How could she be so petty and mean! At least you will not have to see her again," said Georgina. "She comes tomorrow to fetch Elvira home. I will have to be polite, but I will be very glad to see her go."

The next day brought Georgina mail from the receiving office. Two letters on the same day! The first was from her grandfather's attorney, apologizing for the fact that he had not been to see her and his client, but explaining that he himself was temporarily laid up. He, in legalistic periods, confirmed that she was, in the case of caring for her grandfather, indeed the person responsible for decisions concerning his welfare. He also explained that Mr. Winter, having power of attorney for Mr. Frederick Weatherly, would control all of Mr. Weatherly's affairs, and disperse such monies as she should require to provide for the comfort and well-being of Mr. Weatherly, within the capacity of his estate to provide. The running of the affairs of the Weatherly estate would devolve onto Mr. Winter, and the property itself – the farms and tenancies, as previously, would be under the management of Captain Edward Kelling, whom he would write to under separate cover, to ask to consult with her about any needs she might have from the land. There was a great deal more authorities and whatevers, that she would have to grasp. Mr. Lawrence seemed inclined never to use one word where he could use ten, the longer and more obscure the better, and he never tried to be clear, except by accident. He did say that he would endeavor to visit as soon as he was able, or she was welcome to write to him or visit his chambers at any time. In the meanwhile, she was to repose all confidence in Mr. Winter, and to please convey his wishes to his old friend for a speedy and complete recovery.

The second letter was somewhat more of a surprise. It came from one Doctor McPhearson, and it took her a few seconds to realize that he was a Doctor of Theology not Medicine, and that this was a reply to her letter to the mission society. She had almost forgotten them. They offered their condolences and prayers, and their appreciation for the courageous work in the service of the Church and God that her father had done. It appeared that in one respect, at least, her mother was right. They did not intend to merely abandon her. However, their ideas of 'not abandoning' were quite different. It appeared that they were sending a missionary out, back to the newly annexed Queen Adelaide's Land, to build a new station in a 'somewhat more protected setting'. Reverend McLeod, who had been due to leave in April, had had his voyage delayed. There was some circumlocution – but when she got to the nub of the matter it was that they wanted her to meet the Reverend McLeod, because while doing God's work in Africa he stood in earnest need of a wife, and perhaps this could be a heaven-sent answer to both of them.

She could only sit and gape at that idea.

In one way, it would give her something she'd desired: an escape from this unfamiliar England. Yes, she would be provided for. And yet... she didn't even know him. She had not accepted Cousin Arthur's offer because she wished to know him better, to see if she could come to love him, rather than merely like him. Also: to go back? She would not easily forget that night in the Church – and the next day. It was etched in horror in her memory.

Yet... a week back she might well have seized on this as a way to free herself of the situation that she found herself in.

She was called to attend to her grandfather at this stage, and was able to put the content of the letters from her mind. The plan was to take advantage of his feeling slightly stronger in the mornings – based on the day before, to convey him, with plenty of cushions, in the landaulet back to his home.

She went up to Cousin Elvira's room, to tell her they were close to being ready to leave, to find her cousin still abed. She bade her polite farewell's saying that her cousin was welcome to join her, to await her mother. Elvira informed her that there scarcely seemed a point as mama would doubtless want to set out as soon as possible, and that she had to oversee her trunks being packed.

This left Georgina, accompanied by Mary, to travel with her grandfather. He seemed a little dazed by the entire process, but at least not unwilling to return to his home.

Her first view of Westmead House showed her a double-storied, neat, symmetrical house, of brick with stone-framing with large white-framed sash-windows and four dormers, and a selection of chimney-stacks, with a wide stair leading down to the drive and the ornamental rill, beyond it. It was an impressive residence, if smaller and very unlike the sprawl of Bournelea. The carriage did not stop at the front entrance, but instead went around the back to a far less impressive doorway.

"I am sorry, Miss Ross. The locksmith in Whitchurch refused to come out again, and while a man from Winchester is due later, the front door is still locked," explained one of the grooms.

It had been decided that Mr. Frederick was not up to walking very far, and certainly not up the stairs, at this stage, so four of the sturdiest men carried him up to his room on a chair from the dining hall. He was soon installed in his own bed, with his own nightcap, and informed her it felt good to be home. The move had tired him and he soon fell asleep, leaving Georgina free to go and see her new demesne. Mrs. Lessing, her face impassive, presented Georgina with the keys. Having been primed by Lady Elizabeth – otherwise she'd have had no idea, Georgina politely gave them back. "I hope you will continue to look after my grandfather, and the house, Mrs. Lessing. You have years of experience at knowing what they both want and need. I have no experience at running an English household, and I hope you will teach me."

The stiffness in the housekeeper unbent remarkably. "Bless your heart, Miss. You're very like your mother. We all missed her."

She was introduced to the staff, taken on a tour of the house – excluding the library, which was still locked. Much of the furniture was still under Holland-covers and she was happy to agree that it would need a couple more maids to bring it all into order. Georgina was not, herself, sure how much of the house was needed. Her grandfather had effectively shut off one wing of it, but she was reassured by the news that the master had planned to open it all up when he heard that his daughter was coming home. That was a great comfort to Georgina, as she'd been uncertain if they'd even have been welcome. She said as much.

"Oh yes, Miss Georgina! He talked of it often to me. Now, footmen..."

The conversation moved to the number of staff that Mrs. Lessing thought necessary for the running of the establishment. These were a little above what Lady Elizabeth considered necessary, and Georgina was glad to say that Mr. Winter would of course have to decide. Their life on the Mission Station had been quite frugal and simple, even compared to other settler's homes. Even by the standards of Africa, where labor was cheap, this seemed a bit much.

Mary was rapidly settling into her new role and position, even if she was rather shocked to find herself elevated to sitting next to the master's valet and not at the foot of the table, as she had been accustomed to, in Mrs. Salmonds's house. The food too was not at all what she had been accustomed to, in a good way. "Me... My, I have to speak proper, as your maid, Miss Georgina! My only sadness is that me...my mother couldn't have seen me so elevated! And the food is even better than at the big house!" Georgina found herself let into the rivalry between the two estates – where a fair number of the staff had worked at the other, at some stage. Apparently Westmead House was in a constant state of war to be better than Bournelea – 'the big house'. This was a war in which the Westmead staff thought they had had many years of severe disadvantage, and were now delighted at her coming to open the house up, as it should be.

Even if she was town-bred, Mary had more knowledge of her mistress than they had, and was thus the subject of considerable interest to them. "Indeed, Miss, the impertinent questions they was asking! I was never so shocked in me...my life," said Mary primly, working hard on filling the role she'd been cast into. Her eyes twinkled. "Oh Miss! To think I was scared of them and the country. Now... I don't know if I'm on me...my head or my heels. But I have a lot to learn. I can't be letting you down."

"You won't. I don't need much looking after, Mary. I've not had a maid on the ship, or when we were in Grahamstown. And you can't know less about this than I do. I'm supposed to be a delicately bred lady – not a missionary's daughter from a tiny little mission station in the middle of nowhere. My mama never taught me how to deal with this situation."

"You, Miss Georgina, can deal with anything!" said Mary, with glowing admiration.

The faith was comforting, but it was shortly to be put to the test. The first part of that test was of someone plying the knocker – loudly enough to make Georgina, who had been looking at the fire damage to the front parlor with Mrs. Lessing, jump. "Someone will run around, Miss. It's a sore trial that key being gone," Mrs. Lessing informed her.

Because the drapes had been burned, and not yet replaced, Georgina had a full view out of the window and could see a heavily laden travelling-carriage on the drive. "Is my grandfather expecting visitors?" she asked with some alarm, as the knocker sounded again.

"Good gracious! No, Miss. I wonder who it could be? We can't possibly be receiving anyone, with the house still needing work, and the master in bed, and you so new and all."

"Perhaps we should go and call from the window?" asked Georgina.

Mrs. Lessing shook her head, quellingly. "Lessing will send them right-about, Miss. Now, as I was saying about the color of drapes for this room..."

There was the sound of considerable acrimony from outside, including raised female voices, but Mrs. Lessing continued to ignore it, and went on about the virtues of a paler fabric than the nasty color chosen last time. As Georgina had no idea what that had been, she could agree, but really wanted to know what was happening on the doorstep.

She got to find out all too soon. A rather shaken sounding Lessing announced: "Mrs. Salmond, Miss Georgina."

Georgina's heart fell. Even before seeing her aunt – a startling figure in purple bombazine, with her two daughters peering around her, and, by the looks of it her personal maid behind them. "Aunt Louisa," said Georgina, trying to remain calm and polite. "How do you do?"

"What kind of hurly-burly household is this, that the only way into the house is through the kitchen? It's disgraceful, Georgina."

"As I am sure Lessing explained, we are getting a locksmith. It is very awkward, but it should soon be fixed," said Georgina. "I am sorry to be unwelcoming, but we're dealing with bringing my grandfather home and settled, as well as waiting on some repairs. The house is mostly closed up and we can't really entertain you."

"Oh, we haven't come to be entertained," her aunt informed her, beaming graciously. "I am here because I am your guardian. You cannot remain here alone, my dear Georgina. I gather from Elvira that you must remain here to care for your grandfather and cannot come home with us. So, we will have to remain with you. You cannot be left here without a chaperone. Besides, you are far too young to run such a house. You need my assistance."

Georgina looked at her incredulously, too stunned to speak for a minute. This woman had wanted to throw her out on the street! Finally, she gathered herself. "Aunt Louisa, I am in no need of chaperonage, I am in my grandfather's home."

"Unfortunately," said her Aunt Louisa, smoothly. "Your grandfather is, according to the Doctor, not in the full capacity of his senses. Therefore, I, not he, am your legal guardian until you are twenty-one. That is the law in England, my dear. I know it is not what you are used to. It is my responsibility to see you adequately chaperoned. A girl your age living on her own is simply not to be countenanced."

Georgina had absolutely no idea what the law said about it. "You can't do this. You wanted me out of the house!" she said, controlling herself rigidly.

"I never did!" said Aunt Louisa. "Why, you are my poor dear dead brother's only child. Now, Georgina, it is for your own good, I promise. You have no idea how to manage a house. The last thing your grandfather would want is for you to set the neighborhood in a bustle. Really, I cannot see what the fuss is about. Your grandfather is unlikely to live very long and then you will be returning to us, anyway. Now, I need to put off my bonnet and pelisse, and have some tea brought, while our trunks are carried to our rooms."

"All of the bedrooms except mine and my grandfather's, are closed up, and so are most of the rooms downstairs."

"Exactly why you need my help, Georgina. As I said to Lady Elizabeth, a most unfair load to put on a young girl's shoulders. It's only right that as your nearest relations we should help with it. She agreed with me."

"You can't stay. The house is not ready," said Georgina, sticking to her last.

"Then it may be got ready. I will assist," said her aunt. "Anyway, Georgina, we have already paid off and dismissed the coachman. He is on his way back to Southampton by now. So, we cannot leave, and anyway, I will not leave you un-protected in this house. It has been robbed once, and there might be any sort of desperate ruffian hereabouts."

Georgina's sense of the ridiculous came to her rescue. She could not help an inward chuckle at the thought of Elvira, if confronted with a desperate ruffian. She'd flirt with them. She turned to Mrs. Lessing who looked like she might burst a blood vessel at any moment. "Mrs. Lessing... I am so sorry to give you all this extra trouble. Could... could some beds be got ready?"

Mrs. Lessing nodded stiffly. "If you say so, Miss."

"I will leave it in your capable hands," said Georgina. "Lessing." She turned to the butler. "Please escort Mrs. Salmonds and her party into the morning room. If you could be as kind as to ask Cook to see some tea is brought to them?"

She had not been listening to Lady Elizabeth giving instructions for the past five days in vain. "I shall go up to my grandfather," she said calmly. "You will find it very dull in this house, Aunt Louisa. It is centered around an old, sick man."

Keeping rigid control of herself, she walked past them as Lessing was saying: "If you will step this way, Ma'am," to her Aunt Louisa.

Once safely up the stairs, Georgina went into her own room, determined to calm herself before going into see how her grandfather was doing. She found Mary there, carefully unpacking her clothes. "Mary! The worst thing possible has happened."

"Oh Miss! Not that your grandfather's dead?" exclaimed Mary, dropping the garment she was holding.

"No. No. Nothing like as bad," said Georgina. "You're right, there are many worse things that could happen. No, it's my aunt. I so thought I... we... had got away from her. She says she's my guardian and it's her duty to look after me!"

"That woman!" exclaimed Mary. "How could she, Miss Georgina? She can't do that, can she, Miss? She can't take you away from your grandfather!"

"It's worse. She has decided to come and stay with us. To chaperone me. And... she may be able to. I don't know." She took a deep breath. "I have to stay, Mary. But... but if you want to go, I can give you enough money to start looking for work elsewhere. I can't expect you to have to put up with her for me."

"Miss Georgina! As if I would run off and leave you!" said Mary.

"She will pick on you, Mary. She will," said Georgina.

Mary sniffed. "It is you I work for, Miss. You'll not tell me she'll be paying any of the staff here, because she's a nip-farthing."

"True. I must write to Mr. Winter and ask him what I am to do. And maybe the attorney as well."

"I'll bet, Miss," Said Mary, shrewdly, "That's why she's here. She's thinking she'll hang up her shot at your grandfather's expense. She'll have given the servants notice, and be thinking you'll feed and house her, and her daughters."

"You could be right," said Georgina, thinking to herself that it could also be the fruit of Elvira's boasting of the fine company she found herself in and the prospects of finding better-heeled suitors for her daughters. That was an uncharitable thought, but she would not venture a groat on it not being right.

As it was, she had barely time to finish the letter to Mr. Winter when Mrs. Lessing came in search of her, asking her to do that very thing. "That woman," she said, wrathfully, "is setting herself up in your place, Miss. She's demanding maids we don't have to be abigails to those daughters of hers. And she's complaining of the bed-chambers, and telling me she wants to look over the fare that will be served for dinners. I said I would consult with you, Miss, you being the person Mr. Winter and the lawyer gave charge to. That gave her pause, I'll tell you. I hope I didn't speak out of turn, Miss, but Mr. Winter did say it was you giving the orders. I can't serve two mistresses."

"Oh dear. I have written to him," she held up the letter. "If the groom can take it the receiving office, Mrs. Lessing?"

"Will can ride through to his office, Miss! That's how the master did it," she said taking the letter. "Now, I had planned a nice light meal for the master. Cook is at sixes and sevens with so many extra to feed, and that Mrs. Salmonds demanding what can't be had. It's to be feared he'll leave us in the lurch."

"I'll just stop and check on my grandfather and then go down to the kitchen and talk to him," said Georgina, feeling completely out of her depth, yet again.

Her grandfather proved to be awake, and wanting to talk, and then to her surprise, play chess. "Ask Edward to give me a game when he comes in."

"Uh. Certainly, sir," she said a little puzzled. "We could play if you liked?"

"You would have to bring the board up from the library," he said, tiredly. "I am feeling my age, Dorothea."

"I will have it done. Perhaps not immediately. I... I have a travelling set. I will go and fetch it." The Cook and her aunt could wait. This was progress, she thought. Her mother had a small folding chess-set that they'd played with many times over the years, and she went back to find it.

He was delighted in seeing the set. "I remember when I gave it to you!" he said, beaming.

They played for some time. Whatever else was wrong, his memory of chess-moves was unimpaired. But he fell asleep again shortly after they'd reached stalemate, and she had to go downstairs to face her various challenges. These proved that time would deal with many things: Her aunt, her aunt's maid and her two daughters had gone upstairs to oversee their trunks and valises being unpacked. The Cook, on her wary venture into his domain, was firm in his assertion that nothing would stop him from setting the master's favorite meal before him, and it appeared he felt he'd won the encounter with her aunt, and was triumphant about it.

On leaving the kitchen she encountered another unexpected visitor: her Cousin Arthur. He smiled reassuringly at her. "I have just been in search of you. The house seems to be in a state of chaos. I let myself in. Forgive me. I used to run tame here. Don't start away, Cousin. I intend you no harm, I promise."

"Oh. I am sorry. I was startled. It has been a rather trying day. My aunt, the house and all it needs to run it. Moving my grandfather."

"And all of it fallen on you," he said, sympathetically. "Come, let me take you out of it for a little bit, and walk around the gardens."

He sensed her hesitation. "Don't worry, I shall make no attempt to make love to you, my dear cousin. I merely wish to stand your friend. I realize I went on too fast. Come and enjoy the tranquility of the gardens after this hurly-burly."

"Um. I should not go alone, surely?" asked Georgina, looking, she admitted, for an excuse. Their last encounter had frightened her, she had to confess to herself.

He waved a dismissive hand. "In the country, cousin, no one thinks twice. It's quite different in the city, but if you feel you need a maid to trail along... well, the only problem is finding one in such a busy house."

"I will go upstairs and get my bonnet and pelisse. And my maid," said Georgina, helped by the pages of the romantic novel she had been reading, if not her own experience. "That will stop my Aunt Louisa having anything to say. I must admit, I feel I have been cooped up forever. First on the ship, then at my aunt's house, and then in caring for my grandfather. I am not used to being surrounded by so many people."

When a few minutes later, she and Mary walked out with Arthur solicitously giving her his arm she realized that she had indeed sorely missed the feeling of space and fresh air. She did not particularly enjoy the sauntering pace, wanting to lengthen her stride and walk, but the beds and spring flowers were indeed beautiful. It seemed that her cousin was set on repairing the distance that he had opened up by his sudden proposal, by being charming and amusing. She didn't, admittedly, know the people he was talking about, or indeed, the fashionable scene he referred to, but it was light and inconsequential, and after what she'd been through, seemed a soothing pleasant froth. It was... very different to the way papa had talked on the mission station, and that had been her largest male experience.

He was sympathetic about her aunt suddenly being quartered on her. "Not but that it is the right thing to do, I am afraid. They have rather shabby-genteel ideas of propriety out here in the sticks."

They came around to the drive and the ornamental rill, a sequence of tiny waterfalls, set with irises and ferns. The tinkling splash of the water was delightful, reminding her of the stream that had wound its way down from the Katberg heights to flow past the station. The upper area – closest to the house, the beds had plainly just been planted. "Trampled in the fire," Arthur said. "There was a huge gunnera plant here..." He paused and peered at the bed. "Hello. What is that?

It was the ornamented bow of a key, sticking out of the dirt of the bed. Mary bent down and retrieved it, wiping it carefully on her apron. "It's a key, Miss. Someone's lost it," she said holding up the large key.

"That," said Arthur, "I will hazard a guess, belongs to the front door. "Well, well. Right here where they were drawing water to fight the fire. I think we should go and try it, and then I must go and have a word with that magistrate."

"Why?" asked Georgina.

"Because it points to someone who fought the fire being involved in the burglary," explained Arthur. "They must have had the key and lost it while bucketing water!"

Georgina found that a horrific thought, as they made their way up to the front door. Sure enough, the door unlocked and opened on a startled Lessing.

"Cousin Arthur found the key!" she informed him.

"Well, Miss! That's a mercy. Where?" asked Lessing.

"Down next to the water feature. The rill. Where it has just been dug over."

"I'll have the gardeners go looking for the library key there. To think of the thief throwing it away so close. Mind you, Miss under the leaves of that giant rhubarb thing the master was so proud of would have been just the place to hide anything. Rare plant it was, rarely odd if you asks me."

"Well," said Arthur. "I must take my leave. I look forward to being able to call again, perhaps to stay, so we can become better acquainted, Cousin. I must go and tell the magistrate that you found the key."

"Well, actually, you found it, Cousin Arthur," said Georgina, eager to give credit where it was due.

"No, no, really all down to you," he said bowing, and exiting just before the two Salmonds daughters came down the stairs. "La! I thought we heard Mr. Arthur Weatherly's voice," said Elvira. "I was hoping he could show us over his house."

"He has just this minute left," said Georgina, reflecting that what Elvira said was in a way true. Sooner or later this would be his home. Maybe hers, if she married him. That, she reflected in a way that her father would have said was most un-Christian, would upset Elvira, no end.

"Oh, that is too bad of him, when I particularly wanted to see him," pouted Maude. "After he left on Tuesday, I thought of something I wanted to ask him about Pall Mall. He's such a London swell! He said he would see us here, and come and visit."

"I daresay he will call again, sister," said Elvira. "Cousin Georgina, you really need to get someone in to replace the drapes. They are positively shabby. And I will need a maid if we are to remain here."

"I don't think I can do that," said Georgina. "I will have to talk to Mr. Winter, first."

"But you have a maid," said Elvira, staring at Mary. "Don't you work for my mother? What are you doing here?"

"I pay her," said Georgina.

"But you don't have any money. Mother said so!" exclaimed Maude.

"Perhaps she does not know everything," said Georgina, enjoying the moment. "And now, if you will excuse us, we have things to do."

The return to a normal tenor of life at Bournelea was a pleasant thing, thought Edward. His mother, of course, could not simply let be. "I feel rather guilty sending that Mrs. Salmonds on to Georgina. She seemed perfectly aimable, but I do know Georgina and the cousin accompanying her did not see eye to eye."

"I didn't realize," said Edward. "Not surprising really. Cut from different cloth, as it were. Odd how one's relations can sometimes be so unlike those to whom they are related."

His mother laughed. "And be such dirty dishes at times. Look at my Cousin William."

He shuddered. "Do I have to?"

"Fortunately, not, unless you have a wish to visit Staffordshire. Now, I desired Cook to make up some of that raspberry flan of which the old man was so particularly fond. Will you be going to fish the Bourne again tomorrow?"

"Yes, but Mother, I would hardly wish to take that on horseback, have it sit in the shed with Penn and then carry it along to them. Or do you think four in the morning a suitable time to deliver it? Penn says he nearly got a chamber-pot flung at his head, last time, and that was for a fire."

"Oh, how very true. I will have to go over myself, tomorrow."

"I'll go later. I have to see if the work on the hedge-row along the south-side has been finished properly. I will take John's curricle then. It's a bit more saddle-work than I would want in one day," he said, ruefully.

She nodded. "But it goes on better, Son, does it not?" There was a hint of anxiety in her voice.

"Oh yes, chalk and cheese," he said, cheerfully.

The next morning, after his usual session on the river, he collected the flan, and he and Penn set out for Westmead House, taking it to the kitchen. The reception he got at the kitchen was a scullery-maid, telling him the front door was now once again the way for the gentry, and Mrs. Lessing would have a fit if the Captain was allowed in via the kitchen! "But I am dropping something off for the kitchen!" protested Edward.

"The front door," said the maid, firmly.

So: put firmly in his place, Edward went to the front door and plied the knocker, where he found himself admitted just as Mr. Tadswell was about to depart. "Captain Kelling," said the magistrate. "Could you show me where you were on the morning of the fire, when water was being bucketed?"

"Certainly," said Edward. "Here, Lessing. My mother sent this over for Mr. Frederick. Could you have someone take it to the kitchen. They won't let me in there."

"Indeed, Captain. We are very pleased not to have everyone come in that way," said Lessing, relieving him of the container.

So, Edward walked down the steps to the big sash window. "This, and then inside would have been where I spent most of my time, Mr. Tadswell.

"Not down near the ornamental water? The rill?"

"Other than taking the statue from it to break the window, and setting Mr. Weatherly down, no."

"Could you show me where you set him down, Captain? And exactly where the statue came from? Has it been returned to same place."

"Lord, I wouldn't know. There was that big-leafed plant around the statue. There's a couple of stairs down into the bedding. Next to that, where he was out of the way, and safe. We had a fire to fight, you know."

"Please show me."

Edward did his best. The large-leafed plant – which if he recalled correctly had been a botanical treasure from some South American country, was gone. The bed in which it and the statuette had stood had been dug over. The statue was back on a plinth, which pretty well said that was where it came from. He'd dropped it into the herbaceous border under the library window, but it seemed to have suffered no ill effects from window smashing or dropping. Mr. Tadswell eyed him askance. "That happens to be remarkably close to where the key to the front door was found, Captain Kelling."

Edward looked at him in puzzlement. And then as enlightenment dawned, laughed. "Mr. Tadswell, are you seriously suggesting that I robbed the house and then came riding back to break in and rescue Frederick Weatherly?"

"It was clearly someone who knew what the valuables were, and where to find them. That excludes any burglar who did not have some knowledge of Mr. Weatherly's collection. Moreover, you knew which room he was in... to find him. You were here at a most implausible time," said Tadswell. "The key was found by Miss Ross, just exactly where you took the statue from. And your groom – your only witness, has a very questionable record, Captain Kelling!"

"Mr. Tadswell..." said Edward, trying for patience. "Have you actually made a serious effort to find the dismissed bailiff?"

"Indeed, I have," said Tadswell. "And while he has not yet been tracked down, I do have a witness who saw him in Southampton, that very evening. I think you have been trying to lead me astray, Captain Kelling."

"I am amazed you haven't had me clapped in irons, Tadswell," said Edward, sardonically. "I go fishing early in the morning, something that is well-known in the district, even if not by you. The house was on fire. I rescued the master of the house, and led the effort to put the fire out. I sent for you, when I saw the evidence of the crime."

"Because if you had not, someone else would have. I do not have sufficient evidence to arrest you yet, Captain. No one is willing to provide testimony against the squire's son, no matter how implausible the story. But circumstantial evidence is piling up. I keep checking stories, and sooner or later, something will not tally! I must caution you not to try and leave the district."

"I have no plans to. I live a mile away," said Edward. "And frankly, you're barking up the wrong tree."

"We shall see," said Tadswell. "Now, I wish to speak to your groom again."

"He's in the stable-yard," said Edward. "Where I intend to be shortly, when you have finished wasting my time."

"I will take as much time as I require," said Tadswell, stiffly. "Or are you impeding me in the course of my duties, Captain?"

Edward sighed, "You have a bee in your bonnet, Tadswell. Nothing I can do, but to leave you to it. Very well, you go ahead and speak to Penn. I shall go and pay a visit to my supposed victim to see how he goes on."

"If you would call your man for me?"

"Call him yourself," said Edward, by now irritated. "One of the Westmead staff can help you, if you can't find the stables." He turned and walked off, back towards the front door, where Lessing was happy to admit him. "How is the master this morning, Lessing?"

"He has eaten a good breakfast, Captain," said Lessing. "Miss Ross is sitting with him."

"Could you ask Miss Ross if I might visit him, please, Lessing."

"Certainly, Captain. Can I show you through to the south drawing room? The Salmond ladies are in there."

"No thank you. I will wait here. I was just hoping to see how Mr. Frederick went on, to give my mother a report on his progress."

Lessing bowed, and went up the stairs. A few minutes later he returned and escorted Edward up to the master's rooms. Frederick Weatherly was seated in a comfortable wing-chair in the sun. Miss Ross, plainly dressed as usual, rose to meet him. She gave him a cool, unsmiling greeting, but Frederick Weatherly was pleased to see him, and seemed to Edward's eye, to have recovered his color a little. "How are the fish, my boy?" asked Weatherly, with a smile. He had been a keen angler himself once.

"A bit shy, this morning. I think it was a little bright. I did pick up a nice one around two and a half pounds where the half-fallen willow forms an eddy-pool. It is a difficult cast, that close under the tree-branches."

"Ah yes! There's often a good one down under the roots. You can't drift a cast into it, though."

They talked for some time about fish that had been caught before Edward was born, and, on that subject anyway, the old man seemed completely clear and rational. Edward found himself inveigled into a game of chess with the invalid. Miss Ross had taken a seat by the window, and plainly felt no need to intrude, but instead, after a while, picked up her book and appeared engrossed in it. The old man might have lost some of his recent memory, but chess, a lifelong passion, he still remembered the moves to. This game went to him. Edward hoped he'd been quite subtle about making that happen. At the end of the game he could see the old man was tiring, so he got up and took his leave.

"You'll come again, boy?" asked Weatherly.

"If I may," said Edward. "You need your rest, sir."

"I feel as weak as a cat," said the old man, irritably. "And they keep giving me cat-lap to drink."

Edward laughed. "Talk to the Doctor. Your servant, Miss Ross. I can see myself out. I know my way to the front door, now that you have found the key."

"I am not that rag-mannered," she said, calmly, setting her book aside. "I shall just tuck this shawl in around you sir" she said to her grandfather, suiting the action to her words. She tinkled the bell. "Mary will be in directly to keep an eye on you. Then I can see Captain Kelling off." As soon as the little maid appeared, she accompanied Edward out. On the stair she informed him: "I did not find the key. Cousin Arthur spotted it, sticking out of the ground in one of the flower-beds."

"A most fortunate find," said Edward, evenly.

"Indeed. It has made our lives easier."

"My mother did say that if we, over at Bournelea, can do anything to help, to send a message at once. She sent her best regards, and will come and call in a day or two, once you have settled in. If there is anything I can do, likewise. You know that I will be keeping an eye on the estate and tenancies, so I will ride over from time to time. If you feel it is of help I can sit with him for a while."

She colored slightly. "Lady Elizabeth is too good. Oh, I must send her a letter of thanks. I've just been... well the house, and, and my aunt. But that is no excuse."

"I think my mother will find it a good one," he said, comfortingly. "Besides, we just did what neighbors do. And you have already thanked her, a number of times."

"My mother said it was not properly done, unless it was done in writing," said Miss Ross.

"You miss her, Miss Ross?" he asked, gently.

"Terribly. We were... mother, father and me, well, she was my most frequent companion. We weren't isolated, but it was only Reverend Fenner and his wife who spoke English. I mean, many of the converts had a few words and we did see soldiers, and some of the traders, but mostly it was just us. And, well, mother longed for this life. She understood it. I don't."

"You conduct yourself very well," he said, rather taken aback at the picture she painted.

They were coming to the door by now – which Lessing was just opening to admit another visitor – Mr. Winter.

The finely-built man bowed politely to them both, took her hand, and said: "M...Miss Ross. I believe you have some issues to discuss. I...I am at your disposal. How is Mr. Frederick Weatherly?"

"A little tired, but doing well, I think," she said.

He then shook hands with Edward. "I am glad to see you too, Captain. We need at some stage to meet and discuss the f...financial aspects of your role, now that you do not report them directly to our principal. While I am here would be convenient for me, if you can find a time that does not impose too heavily on your plans."

"I was heading out to check on some of the hedging work we'd commissioned done. But that could be undertaken this afternoon. Could I suggest, sir, that when you've done here, you stop and have luncheon with us," said Edward. "That would save Miss Ross further complications with her catering," he said with a smile. "And it would be on your way towards home."

"That would be m...most kind. But I do not wish to put anyone out," said Winter.

"I will go and tell my mother that we are to expect you. Your servant, Miss Ross," said Edward, and took his leave.

Penn had the curricle waiting, and they drove off. Once they had rounded the first bend, Penn said: "Proper jobbernol that magistrate, Captain. Was pressing me hard to say you done the dirty on the old fellow."

"He's got rats in his attic," said Edward. "I'm going to have to do something about all of this."

"Aye, Captain. But shooting him might make things worse."

"Don't even joke about it, Penn," said Edward, grinning. "Some idiot's bound to hear you and repeat it to him."

Mr. Winter arrived about an hour later, and they were able to sit and discuss certain improvements Edward had thought might increase the long-term value of Weatherly's estate. "Though I am not sure why I bother, with Arthur likely to sell it the day he inherits, and me not likely to get much thanks for increasing the value of the place."

"Well, the new owner may thank you. I will be consulted, you know. And Mr. Frederick may live many more years. He remains a little confused, but his granddaughter does seem to be taking good care of him. The poor girl has had a great deal to bear with."

"The relatives, on top of it all," said Edward.

"W...we cannot choose our relatives," said Mr. Winter. "She is something of a change from most of my clients, in that she is extremely w...worried about spending the money of others," he seemed to find that amusing. "I hope you will continue to stand her friend, Captain. She has need of one."

Edward decided not to mention that Miss Ross's treatment of him ranged from apprehension to one of chilly civility. The most he'd seen her unbend was talking of her mother. Instead he said: "For as long as I remain out of jail, Mr. Winter. Tadswell is convinced that I attacked Mr. Weatherly, and set the fire, and then rescued him and put out the fire to cover my tracks. Oh, and I stole his collection, although why I did any of this I cannot imagine."

"Ah. Mr. Tadswell is r...rather overwhelmed by this crime. It is by far the biggest thing that has occurred in his career as a magistrate, and he feels it will make him... important," said Winter. "He questioned me at some l...length too. I offered to show him my books, which seemed to intimidate him, and I suggested he discuss it further with Mr. F...Frederick Weatherly's attorney. As to you: I believe he thinks you were interrupted in the arson and c...covered your tracks by staging the rescue and putting out the fire. As for the theft: you are supposed to have considerable gambling debts, incurred before your injury. And you're the younger son with no prospects."

"Good Lord. I got burned gambling once as a subaltern," said Edward, laughing. "And though they told me I'd make a come-about if I kept playing, I resented losing money so badly, I don't even like playing copper-loo, since. Now, before my injury, if it came to bets on my riding, I'd take a few, but the turn of a card... I've no luck, Mr. Winter."

"M...more people should believe that," said Mr. Winter. "Now, the leases on the paddocks on Southwell..." And the conversation moved back to land-matters.

At lunch they returned to the subject, when Edward told his family that it seemed he was now chief suspect. His mother was angry and incredulous. His father, resigned. "Tadswell always gets the wrong end of any stick," he said, with a grimace. "He doesn't really understand country people, and he's had some clashes with me in the past."

"I've reached the point," said Edward, "Where I feel I need to do something about it, Father. Although, exactly what to do, I don't know. Tadswell refuses to even believe I go fishing in the early morning. He thinks because you're the Squire, everyone would lie the devil out of hell to protect me."

"If I m...might make a suggestion?" offered Mr. Winter.

"By all means!"

"The goods stolen – snuff-boxes, are of little value for their precious metals, but of some interest to collectors. Amongst my clients, I do have one such gentleman, who has told me that he has his man scour pawn-brokers for these items."

"I suppose I could do likewise. Only Tadswell cautioned me not to leave the district – and I imagine there'd be little point in asking in the village, or even Whitchurch! They would probably sell them in Southampton."

"Possibly," said Mr. Winter. "B...but the largest market for such items would be in London. Which brings me to the second part of my suggestion: The Bow Street runners are being w...wound down. But they do still undertake to investigate and recover stolen goods, for a reward, naturally. It w...would be part of my role to see if they could be recovered for my client. Some detail of whence they came, m... might be obtained. Also, as I do not think you frequently go up to London..."

"John went up the day after the attack, to let Arthur Weatherly know," said Edward. "Next thing Tadswell will have him accused of being my accomplice."

"Well, naturally," said John. "I would have been with you, except I don't do early mornings. Seriously, I think it is a good idea if we hire one of these Runners. This investigating is not our trade, any more than it is Tadswell's."

Georgina had found – as usual, her meetings with Captain Edward
Kelling confusing. How could anyone be that two-faced? Yet... he had
undoubtedly done her grandfather a great deal of good. If she hadn't
heard him with her own ears condemning her care for him, she would
have had difficulty believing he was so duplicitous. If, indeed, he had
attacked her grandfather, he must be utterly brass-faced, to come and
visit and play chess with him. Perhaps he had hit him from behind?

She had quite forgotten her violent dislike of him after the way he
had conducted himself, and his polite handling of the matter of the
thank-you note, and his solicitude. But, she had heard what she had
heard.

Mr. Winter had in many ways not set her mind at ease in the least,
she thought, crossly.

"M...miss Ross, unfortunately, there is not a great deal I can do
about your relations," he'd said. "M...my authority extends only as
far as the estate, and Mr. Frederick's other financial affairs – and they
are complicated, he speculated in various things, but never to the
detriment of his capital, and that really is the end of it." He'd steepled
his fingers. "The law – and this is not my f...field – might well side with
you. You have not yet attained your majority, I believe, and would be
unable to enter legal treaties of certain sorts without your guardian's
consent. I have had very little to do with this – but I do see that having a
relative living with you, while your grandfather is incapacitated might
be seen in a positive light in the district. Of course, you are your
grandfather's nearest blood relation as far as the law is concerned, and
could it be demonstrated that your guardian was seriously impacting
your ability to care for him – not allowing you to be here, for instance,
when the Doctor has determined that is helping him a great deal, that
could be the subject of a court appeal. But that would be long and

arduous, and not really what Mr. W...Weatherly or you need. You are... how old now?"

She hadn't even thought of her own birthday, let alone celebration thereof, for a long time. Her nineteenth had been while her father's wounds were being tended, and there had been too much else happening. "I approach my twentieth year, sir."

"At w...worst you have a year to tolerate it, Miss Ross." He'd given his little prim smile. "I should think from my meeting of Mrs. Salmond's older daughter, that they will tire of the exigencies of country life very rapidly."

"They are going to be extremely expensive. Can I not get them to leave, or just leave Elvira with me, if I must have someone? I don't want to be spending my grandfather's money, and leave him without the means to support himself."

Winter shook his head. "That is r...relatively unlikely. Your grandfather was... is of a frugal nature, but he is not unable to support this household. You are entitled to spend reasonably on entertaining them."

"It is not my money to spend on entertaining. And I fail to see that either my grandfather or Cousin Arthur would thank me for not being frugal."

"May I assure you, that you will not d...deplete the estate," said Winter. "I will be settling the bills and I will let you know if you stand in danger of outrunning the c...constable, so to speak. Perhaps you can set your aunt to redecorating the damaged parlor, as I have found spending money – especially other people's money – exercises a soothing effect on many people."

"I don't think we should spend a great deal. My cousin seemed very concerned about spending money."

"It is not his concern. Your grandfather, when he comes downstairs, would find it distressing if it was not presentable. And, if a l...limit is set, and she is to attempt to return it to something like its former state, with the advice of the housekeeper, it would be wise – even if the house is eventually to be sold. The present situation detracts from its value and besides, must be very inconvenient."

He named a sum that quite took her breath away. They settled on somewhat less, but Georgina rather resented the idea of Mrs. Salmonds having the pleasure of spending it. On the other hand, it would perhaps keep her occupied.

"Now," said Mr. Winter, "To my correspondence with the attorney, Mr. Lawrence. He agrees with me that you should be receiving some sort of stipend. Do you have some form of banking facility that you can draw on? It would be easiest for such sums to be deposited directly into that, but I do appreciate that you are rather restricted in travelling at the moment."

"Oh no. I mean my father had a banking account. I think. I have not really gone through my parent's documents. I have all of them."

"I think, if you w...will entrust me with them, I should like to pass them on to Mr. Lawrence. There may be formalities to be dealt with, and certainly your father's bank should be notified. There is also the question of last wills and testaments, death certificates, and matters like that."

"The Doctor on the ship signed the death certificate for mother. I assume my father's is in the tin box. The Army surgeon in Graham-stown signed that," she said, feeling subdued.

"W...well, I think you should get it for me," said Winter. "I will see it all dealt with and returned to you. We can look into a banking accommodation for you in good time. In the meanwhile, I know your grandfather has one of these new Chubb safes. I know because he bought it on my advice! Do you have any idea where he kept the key? I will need to entrust quite a sum of money to you for the various expenses and wages."

"I think... that could be the key that we found in his bedside cabinet. I thought it might fit the library door. It does have the word 'Chubb' stamped into the bow. I did not know what that meant. But I have no idea where the safe could be."

"I would ask the housekeeper. But if I recollect correctly, it was in the l...library. That was his favorite room, where he conducted most of his business."

"We can't get into that room, yet."

He sucked on his teeth. "That could be difficult. I thought a l...locksmith was coming?"

"Well, he hasn't yet. Anyway, let me go and fetch my mother's papers," said Georgina. "If you will excuse me."

She found that the locksmith had indeed arrived and was busy in the passage as she left the breakfast parlor. That was the good part of leaving Mr. Winter. The bad part was meeting her aunt in a somewhat belligerent frame of mind, demanding to know where she'd been hiding herself. "In the breakfast parlor with Mr. Winter. My grandfather's man-of-business," said Georgina.

"I have a great deal to say to him!" snapped her aunt.

"Why don't you go in and say it?" asked Georgina. "I have to go and fetch some papers for him, and to look in on my grandfather."

"I shall do just that!"

Georgina felt slightly mean to leave Mr. Winter at the mercy of her aunt, but perhaps it would help him to understand what she had to deal with. She headed upstairs, and finding her grandfather comfortably asleep, collected the key for the safe, the tin box from her trunk, and went back down, meeting Mrs. Lessing at the foot of the stair. "Oh Miss! The mess in the library! And the master's collection! And the floor. And his Chinese bowl is missing. We never told Mr. Tadswell that.

"I will send a message, later," promised Georgina. "I am just busy with Mr. Winter. You'll be happy to know the front parlor is going to be redone." That did indeed please Mrs. Lessing, and it was only the excuse of having to take the papers to Mr. Winter that got her out of a lengthy discussion about it.

She found that she had severely underestimated Mr. Winter. He had managed to bring a smile to Aunt Louisa's face by dangling the prospect of spending money at her, and effectively got rid of her by suggesting she go and take measurements and consult with Mrs. Lessing. "It m...must of course be in keeping with Mr. Frederick Weatherly's tastes."

"Shouldn't Mr. Arthur Weatherly's be consulted? He seems to have excellent taste," said Aunt Louisa.

"He is unlikely to live here," pointed out Mr. Winter. "He is a London man, after all," he said after a moment.

"Oh, very true!" said Aunt Louisa. "Are you leaving us now, Mr. Winter? If so I must take my leave of you."

"I just have some personal business to complete with Miss Ross. Matters concerning her mother's death and so on, you understand. You will excuse us," he said, opening the door for her.

Once she'd gone Georgina set the box down on the table. "The library has been opened," she said. "And I have the safe-key."

"Very good. Could we have a look at these papers together?" he asked.

"Certainly," she said opening it.

He went through the box, setting aside bundles of letters, and sorting out various other papers. He made a careful note of these, and put 'taken for the attorney, Mr. A. Lawrence of Samuel and Lawrence" the address and the date, and signed it. "Paperwork, Miss Ross. Always best to have it in order. Anyway, that should let me wrap this side of it up. I suggest putting this document in the safe. Now, I have here a schedule of wages and payments, as well as the monies for making them, on Friday. I think we need to check the safe together, and I shall give your discretionary monies to you."

It had been quite alarming, not only because that was more money than she'd seen in her life, but also because the safe was anything but empty. Mr. Winter, being his usual careful self, itemized everything, signed for it, pressed the key into her hand, and then took his leave of her, saying he must get across to Bournelea.

Rather wide-eyed, Georgina went upstairs with the little tin box, and found a small broach of her mother's, with a double catch on it, and attached that to the key, and that to her petticoat breast, so the key hung inside, against her skin. It was uncomfortable to have charge of so much money belonging to others. She would never in her life be able to pay it back, should it be stolen. Thank goodness the thief had not got into the safe.

Chapter 7

The next day was blustery and squally, mostly spent indoors. Georgina found herself having to referee constant sparring between Mrs. Lessing and Aunt Louisa. The servants took their tone from this, and orders from the two daughters and Aunt Louisa were often met with "I will check with Miss Ross" – which most of the time meant supporting the order. She also found herself having to deal with other matters she had no idea of: the hiring of a new footman, and two more housemaids, and another helper for Cook.

She had Mrs. Lessing in for advice on this, which caused her aunt, when she interrupted one of the final interviews to start shouting.

"Hush. You'll disturb my grandfather!" said Georgina.

"I will not hush!" shouted her Aunt Louisa at the top of her very penetrating voice. "How dare you tell me to hush? You... you impudent, thankless..."

"Master's calling!" said Mary, bursting in the door, which Aunt Louisa had left open. Sound it appeared carried very well from the library. Georgina left at a run. He querulously wanted to know who the women were, who were creating a ruction in his house. Fortunately, he was distracted by a sudden flurry of rain, which made him comment on April showers, and her sitting with him a while and encouraging him to talk of being caught in one and the trouble he'd had trying to keep his gun dry. "Out after pigeons, George and I. Where is George? Oh." And a tear trickled down his lined face. "I forget. My head is so cloudy, dear. It's just so good you at least are here, Dorothea."

She'd been trying to get him to call her Georgina, a few times. Right now, it did not seem important. She comforted him, and, very uncharitably, wished her aunt in perdition. He settled back down to sleep, and she had to venture downstairs. There she was met by a fierce-looking Mrs. Lessing. "I told her her fortune. I told her that if that lawyer-fellow got to hear of it, he'd have them turned out of doors if any ill come to the master. Doctor said he don't need to be disturbed. I don't think that she believed me, but it shut her budget, and she left."

"Thank you," Georgina sighed. "I'll have to make the peace, somehow. My father had a temper too, but he always tried to keep it under control."

"She doesn't," said Mrs. Lessing with a sniff.

Georgina dreaded the outcome. However, her aunt – perhaps genuinely frightened that her free accommodation and saving on food and servants, to say nothing of status, might come to an end, was merely distant, when Georgina apologized for rushing out. "You need instruction in running such a house, Georgina. However, I suppose it unlikely that you will do so for long. Have you thought more about what you may do, when your grandfather does die?"

"Not really, Aunt Louisa," she resorted to one of her father's escape clauses, when confronted with difficult circumstances. "I am sure God will provide."

Her aunt snorted. "You would do well to start thinking about it. Even before this incident, I gathered he was not in the best of health. And he is very elderly."

"Did you finish measuring up in the front parlor?" asked Georgina, changing the subject.

This led to discussion on fabrics, and where best to get them, and how inconvenient it was in the country. Georgina then remembered she had letters to write, and went off to pen one of thanks to Lady Elizabeth, and another to the magistrate, informing him that they had discovered another missing item. These Mary took to the groom, and Georgina took refuge again with her grandfather. He was asleep, but she could read her book. She was, regretfully, coming to the end of it, and, of course, it was the first of three volumes. Her grandfather's library was downstairs, but firstly that meant going downstairs, and secondly, she doubted she'd find such books there. She'd read what was there, of course. She would read anything.

Her peace – and read – was interrupted by Maude, who came and tapped on the door. Georgina went out to see what the matter was, reluctantly putting her book aside.

"Oh, Cousin Georgina. I am so terribly bored. There is nothing to read, and nothing to do. Won't you come down and play the pianoforte for us? It's on the far side of the house, and should not disturb the old man. Mama said we must not disturb him. I want to practice my dance steps."

Mary who had come quietly along the passage, said: "You go, Miss. I'll stay with him. I want to do a little polishing and dusting in there, anyway."

"That's not your job, Mary," said Georgina, with a smile. Her own room gleamed to the point where Mrs. Lessing had commented on it.

"I know. But I like to be keeping busy," said Mary. "A shame the weather is so bad, or you could go out, but Cook says it'll blow out by tonight."

So, Georgina went. She thought it might make something of a peace-offering, and she was right. Besides, she enjoyed playing. Of course, the problem, as far as the two Salmonds girls were concerned – they planned to have her play music for their dancing practice... was that the only tunes she knew were hymns, some of which at least they could waltz to – even if it seemed wrong to her. And her keen ear said the piano needed the services of a tuner. She could have tried playing from sheet-music but there was none that was younger than a few decades ago. One of those was a minuet, that she was able to follow with some difficulty. The two sisters fell to bickering, with each other and their mother, and Georgina tried to lose herself in the music.

She was able to escape upstairs on some pretext, and went to her grandfather, who was awake. He had plainly decided that any audience was better than none, and was favoring Mary with a story about the hunting field. It was probably as distant from Mary as Georgina's tales of Africa had been, and Mary was making suitable 'Well I never!' and 'Really' noises as she polished. Both seemed happy, and Georgina was reluctant to disturb them – but she wanted her book. Her entry brought an end to reminiscences, but she was informed that he'd loved to hear her playing.

The evening had cleared, and she longed to go out and just be away from people for a bit, but instead she held herself to her duty, and talked to him, and then when she went down to dinner, was polite to her aunt who had seated herself at the head of the table, as if to make a point.

The next morning, she awoke in the pale predawn. There was not a sound in the house, her grandfather, if he'd shown one clear trait since the very earliest days in her care, was a late sleeper, being a little restive during the night, but sleeping deeply from around five – which she judged it to be now, until nine. She'd finished the book the night before. Perhaps the library would yield something. On the other hand, it looked clear outside... Accustomed as she was to being an early riser among late sleepers, she got out of bed, pulled on her walking-dress, and found her stout walking shoes – and with them in hand, stole downstairs... where she found the front door was locked, and the key removed. Irritated by this, she went to the kitchen. The fire there was down to embers – but the key was in the lock. So, she went out.

It was not her intent to go very far, and she was sure she had the world largely to herself at this pearly-pink skied time of morning, with the barest zephyr of a breeze, but cool enough to give her goose-bumps. Well, a brisk little walk would sort that out and some fresh air would clear too many people, too close, and too many dramas and uncertainty from her head, she resolved, and followed one of the footpaths.

It led to the river – more of a broad meandering stream, set about with willows and rushes, and lush green meadows, where the birds were already awake.

It was the first time and place in England that she'd felt the least affinity for a place. The beauty and peace of it was balm for a poor soul that felt bruised and battered by what life had flung at her. It was good to be out, and alone.

And then looking at the water, she realized that she wasn't alone.

Admittedly, for all the notice she got, she might as well have been. He was standing in the water, casting a line in a delicate arc that landed with barely a ripple. Edward Kelling was so intently focused on the

water, and the rise and swirl of a fish dappling it, that she thought
cannon-fire would have been un-noticed. She turned quietly to walk
away. But her movement must have caught his eye. He glanced up and
caught sight of her, and lost control of his cast, and had half of it splash
on the water. The flies managed to lodge on his hat.

"I am so sorry! I didn't mean to disturb you," she said, horrified. "I
was just enjoying watching so much."

He laughed. "And I had to cow-hand it."

She found herself catching the infectious laugh, but shook her head.
"Oh no, I watched the cast before. It was beautiful. Like a dance. Oh,
dear. What a silly thing to say."

By the broad smile he did not think it so. "It is, you know, when you
get it right. Anyway, good morning, Miss Ross. I'm sorry I didn't see
you. I don't see many people at this time of day."

"I didn't mean to disturb you. Please go on. I just wanted a walk...
before I had to deal with people."

He nodded. "I know exactly how you feel. Nice to have the world
to yourself for a bit."

A fish rose, a perfect circle on the water, as it sipped a fly. "Well, I
didn't put them off as much as I thought," he said.

"Please... please cast for it," she asked. "I will go away. Unless my
moving will disturb it. You said something about that, talking to my
grandfather."

"It's just a fish," he said still scanning the water, plainly. It rose again.

"Oh, cast. Cast. Please. I would love to watch," she asked, despite
herself.

"I'll just get the fly off my hat," he said, and did so. He shook the line
out, gently. The cast – long and easy dropped the three tiny flies onto
the crystal water, just as the sun peeped over the horizon. They drifted
down and she actually saw the fish rise, seemingly out of nowhere

among the stones, and suck the fly down. And then in a swirl of water, as the hook bit, it dived and then jumped and splashed and ran and jumped again, as the fisherman brought it in, and to the net.

She watched in silence, entranced, until he had it in the net. Then she clapped.

He waded closer so she could see it. "Here you are, Miss Ross. Bourne brown trout."

She looked at the fish in the net, the crimson red spots in the lustrous brown, the slightly hooked jaw, and bright eye. "Thank you so much. That is quite the loveliest thing I have seen in England. Not... just the fish. All of it. Now, I will go away and leave you in peace to catch more."

"You don't have to leave, Miss Ross." She realized that he was blushing slightly. "I am... happy to have you watch."

"I would love to. But I must get back before grandfather wakes, or I am discovered missing. And I am not properly dressed... but I didn't expect to see anyone. I am sorry."

"You seem very proper to me," he said, "compared to me in my wading-clothes."

"It's colors. I don't have any black walking dresses. And I haven't put my hair up, or got a bonnet or a parasol," she explained. "Anyway. I will leave you. It is the most glorious morning, isn't it? Catch some more of those beautiful fish."

"I will. May I drop it at Westmead House for your breakfast? Your own fish?"

She clapped her hands together. "I would, indeed, like that. Very... very much."

"Then it will be my greatest pleasure." He beamed up at her. "I don't meet many people who take delight in the early morning, Miss Ross, but it is indeed a glorious one. I won't suggest escorting you back, because that would spoil your quiet and enjoyment of it. Au revoir, Miss Ross. I'll stop by at the kitchens, later."

"Good bye, and good luck, Captain Kelling," she said, turning to walk back, carefully not looking back, until she'd gone some distance. Then she could not resist a glance. He was not fishing again, but staring after her. They both looked away, and Georgina made her way, hastily, back to the house.

She'd still beaten the household into wakefulness, and the day did not seem quite so intimidating as yesterday had been

On the bank of the Bourne Rivulet, Captain Edward Kelling did not immediately resume fishing, despite this being in the middle of the golden few minutes of the morning rise. Instead he stood and looked down the path she walked away on... hoping that, somehow, she'd come back. Then he whistled to himself. Well. So that was what it felt like to be on the wrong side of a hook, he thought, looking at the fish in the net. He took his priest and put it out of its misery.

He wasn't sure he shouldn't hit himself over the head with it next. He was lucky he hadn't fallen into the water. But that might have made her laugh, and she had an entrancing laugh. Actually, she was just entrancing. Or maybe enchanting... yes, that was better. Her simple delight had been so very unfeigned and joyous, her blush at realizing she was not appropriately dressed... Well. She had no idea, plainly, how beautiful she looked in the simple straw-colored walking-dress, with her dark hair down, and her speaking deep blue eyes and... He shook himself. Like a water-nymph among the rushes. It seemed appropriate that he'd fall for one. But if he was to catch fish for her breakfast, he'd better get to it.

And he'd never been more determined to succeed at that in his life.

Georgina did hear Captain Kelling making good his promise. "No, Lessing. I won't come in, I'm in my fishing clothes. But if you could take the creel through to the kitchen – I'll send Penn for it later. Now, you see you tell Cook that the fish with the rush-leaf tied through the jaw is for Miss Ross. No one else. Make double sure of that. It is her fish. And tell him he's to do the finest job he ever did of frying it in butter, or I'll have to fry him instead."

"Yes, Captain, I'll see to it." Even from the library, Georgina could hear the amusement in Lessing's tone."

"Good man," said Captain Kelling.

Georgina wondered if she should come out and thank him, but decided against it. She was still somewhat uncertain about Captain Edward Kelling. The happy, pleasant, smiling fisherman on the river had seemed so very different to the disdainful, angry person who had spoken so hurtfully of her, to his mother on that first day, when he had not known she could hear.

Besides, she had her day ahead of her. It would be her first day of having to pay the staff, and she was dreading it. On the positive side, she would be rid of her aunt, and daughters for some of the day, as they were going to Winchester to pick out material for the new drapes, and to try and find a suitable carpet to cover the new floor-boards.

It was mildly embarrassing to have Lessing himself come and present her with the fried trout in the breakfast-parlor, but he seemed very pleased with himself doing so, and she enjoyed the fish very much. The day passed with less stress and more pleasure than she'd imagined. The wage-paying was quite uncomplicated, and, while she failed to find anything as entertaining as Mrs. Porter's romance, a book on the life of Lord Nelson provided some entertainment. She went and played the pianoforte for a while, which her grandfather appreciated, and, by the time the Salmonds' expedition to town returned, themselves much cheered by crowds and shops – and being able to proclaim how superior Southampton was, she was able to greet them with a calm demeanor.

Before that could deteriorate too far, they had a visit from Sir Gerald, Lady Elizabeth, and their two sons, to see how they went on, and to hear if Mr. Frederick was making progress. Georgina was left with a dilemma of how to thank Captain Edward without raising the demon of jealousy in Elvira and Maude – who both considered themselves due any male attentions, and the ire of Aunt Louisa who would doubtless consider her behavior shocking, and ring a peal over her.

"Thank you for the gift of the fish," she said politely. "Lessing told me you brought them in."

"Most tasty," said her aunt. "Not as good as sea-fish of course. Where do your staff catch them?"

There was a moment's silence. Then Captain Edward said: "Oh, they have a pair of trawling vessels that ply the river. If you get up around five you can hear the cries of the fishermen as they hawk their wares along the banks."

Georgina had to fake an unconvincing spasm of coughing.

"Really, Ned," said Lady Elizabeth. "People will think I dropped you on your head as a baby. He's teasing you. We plant them in the water meadows. This is the early harvest."

"Oh, Mother," said Edward. "They have just been hiding the truth from you. It's netting or they harpoon them, like whales, but with really tiny harpoons."

"Why yes," said John. "One of them harpooned a salmon once, and it towed him but it broke the harpoon-line just short of Southampton."

This kind of jest had not come Georgina's way before, but she was enjoying it very much. The best part was the expressions on Aunt Louisa and the cousins' faces. She was unprepared, however, for Captain Edward's next shaft. "And how did your staff gather them in Africa, Miss Ross?" he asked.

"Um," she said, floored for a moment, but spurred to invention: "It was a tribal secret. But one of my maids told me they herded them with hippopotamuses and when they had all the fish trapped in a pool, they would get well-trained elephants to suck the pool dry with their trunks, squirting the water over their backs, until the women could go and collect the fish in baskets."

This was greeted with such a shout of laughter that Georgina said: "Hush. My grandfather."

"I'll go up to him and apologize," said Edward, still shaking with laughter. "I can't top that story, Miss Ross."

"I must apologize for my family," said Sir Gerald, smiling. "They do let their sense of humor run away with them. Forgive them for funning like this. And yes, Edward. You should go up, if that would not be inconvenient, Miss Ross. Frederick knows you best."

"I will take the Captain up myself," said Georgina, blushing furiously at the success of her sally.

She led him out, closing the door on Maude's rather plaintive voice saying: "But how do they catch them?"

She had to smother another snort of laughter. She cast a sidelong glance at Edward Kelling, to see he was laughing too. "That was too bad of you, Captain," she said, trying to look stern.

"I know. But your riposte was absolutely brilliant. I quite understand why my mother likes you so much, and I can't wait to introduce you to my little sister. You two will deal extremely."

Georgina was rather staggered by this. "Lady Elizabeth... is, has been so kind, and, and good."

"She is," said Edward, slowing slightly to manage the stairs. "I am glad you like her. And she is quite right, your grandfather is extremely fortunate, and you are an exceptional young lady."

She froze, briefly, and then walked on. "I thought I was an insufferable baggage?" she said raising her chin.

"Who dared say such a thing of you!" he asked, looking shocked and indeed, angry.

She paused again, her hand on her grandfather's room's door-handle. "You did, Captain Kelling." And she opened the door, stepped in and gestured for him to follow.

As a soldier, Edward had had to keep his head under fire. He felt at least that he'd been there before. For the life of him he could not think of ever having said that about her, and a few moments ago he'd been ready to plant whoever said such a thing a facer, if not call them out. And now he was having to be polite to the old man, instead of apologizing and trying to clear the matter up.

"I will leave you to talk with him," she said. "Mary can stay with him when you decide you need to leave. I had better go and be polite to your parents and brother, or my dear Aunt Louisa will give me a thousand words."

"Oh. Um yes. I, I am sorry," he stammered, "I...I would not want you in trouble with her, although... ah...er." He lost himself in a tangle of words, wanting to say the silly woman could go to perdition, and to beg for an explanation of how he could have said something like that, and that he certainly did not mean it. The best he could manage, feeling rather like a bad puppy hoping for a pat of forgiveness, was: "W...would you like more fish?"

He was very grateful when she nodded, but she had retreated behind the wall of polite distance again. "Perhaps sometime, when it is convenient," she said.

Never had conversation been so hard, but fortunately he did not have to say much. Frederick Weatherly was pleased to see him, pleased to tell him, again, fishing stories of yesteryear. And all he could think of was the best morning rise of his life, which he couldn't really tell Weatherly about, or that he had fallen head-over-heels in love with his granddaughter, whom he seemed to have offended. He would, somehow, get to the subject if the maid left, because come hell or high-water he was going to marry Georgina Ross, and he'd like Weatherly's consent and blessing. But that wasn't going to stop him... If he could ever work out how he'd insulted her.

By the time his mother came up – with Miss Ross, to say they were leaving, he was rather more composed. But he also had no opportunity for further private conversation with her, as the party left. The best he could hope for was that she would take a walk again in the morning. He was not – to judge by the little of her character that he'd seen, ready to bet on it. But he would be there. That might become the most flogged stretch of river on the entire Bourne.

He was rather silent for the first section of the ride. Finally, John said: "Nice girl, Miss Kelling."

He was plainly fishing, and got a rise in a terse. "Yes."

"Bitten bad, brother?" said his older brother. "I don't blame you."

Edward nodded. "But I am in trouble with her about something."

"Ah well, there are always the other two. The younger one was giving you the eye," said John with a grin.

"Go to the devil, dear brother," said Edward grumpily.

"It's rhinestones against a real diamond, isn't it?" said John with a chuckle. In a more sympathetic tone he added: "She seems a good sort of girl, Ned. Good sense of humor, anyway."

He nodded. "That surprised me a bit too. Wonderful. She'll fit in."

"To this menagerie anyway. No objection to sport, then?" asked John, to whom sport was central.

"Loves fishing. Well, watching it, anyway. And the grooms say she petted Thunder."

Thunder being a notoriously shy horse, that spoke to his brother, who gave him a stare and a chuckle, and said: "Well, brother, if you're clapped up for attempted murder, theft and arson, I'll have to have a crack at her myself!"

They were entering the stable-yard by now, so Edward was spared the need to answer that sally.

Georgina was, she had to admit, surprised at herself for even bringing Captain Edward Kelling's rudeness up with him. She'd certainly not planned it. And in fairness, he'd looked horrified and very embarrassed, but had made no attempt to deny it. That actually stood him in better stead than glib denials would have. Back in the large drawing room she had had little chance to dwell on it, as the party, now being entertained with wine and cakes, were very busy in conversations. She was quietly taking notes on how adroitly Lady Elizabeth drew people in, and, while the laughter of earlier was absent, the two girls were happily talking to John and Sir Gerald about their expedition to

Winchester, to which both were responding with what she suspected was spurious interest. Lady Elizabeth drew her into the conversation between her and Aunt Louisa, on the drapes and redoing the blue drawing-room.

The visit did not extend long, and Lady Elizabeth said to her, "Well, my dear, if you could take me up to see Mr. Frederick – I hope he remembers me, and I can relieve him of my son, and see how he goes on."

"Only with pleasure, Ma'am," said Georgina, getting to her feet. They walked up as the rest of the party were still in the drawing room, and Lady Elizabeth said to her: "My dear Miss Georgina. I realize you would not have wanted to go to Winchester with them. You can't leave your grandfather, just yet anyway. But I am going myself tomorrow. I would love to take you, but I quite understand. I could however bring you back some swatches of fabric. Mrs. Linsome, over in Whitchurch, made several dresses for my daughter Augusta. She could come and do some measurement and make them for you. Your grandfather would like that. He did comment about you wearing black."

"I am in mourning, Lady Elizabeth. And... And I really do not have, er wish to..."

"You're not imposing, Georgina. And I know Mr. Winter did provide funds for this, specifically. He said your grandfather would want you dressed appropriately for your station. And I agree. We all understand you've come straight off a ship from Africa, my dear. And I have been longing to interfere. It's what I do best, and I don't have a daughter at home to meddle in, any more. As for the mourning, there is black fabric, and black fabric. They are not all the same. Neither is the way a garment is cut."

They had reached the door to her grandfather's room by then, so there was no chance for her to say more. Georgina was glad of that respite. She had felt some yearning towards something new in her wardrobe, but prudence and lack of opportunity had both kept things as they were.

The next morning again provided a return to April showers, and though she was tempted to go for a walk early anyway, it was not really a good idea. She wondered if the fisherman would be out in this weather. It was probably just as well that she did not go and find out, she thought. Honestly, she was becoming like Elvira and Maude, chasing men. Ones who were beyond her in birth and means too.

She did notice, however, that there were no fish for breakfast. Perhaps the elephants were tired? Or maybe the harpoons blunt? It gave her a little smile, thinking of it.

They started on the stitchery for the drapes. Well, mostly, she did, with Mary assisting, her aunt supervising, and the two sisters bickering. She was getting used to that by now. She realized that it was just the way they were.

It was late afternoon when a carriage drew up, to the excitement of the Salmonds girls. It proved to be Captain Edward Kelling.

"Just a parcel from m'mother for Miss Ross," he said, explaining the purpose of his visit on being shown in. "And a book for you Miss Ross. The second volume of Mrs. Porter's trilogy."

She could not restrain her delight at this. "Oh, thank you! Your mother is so very kind. So thoughtful! I have been reading the A Life of Nelson, but it is not the same."

He bit his lip, restraining a smile. And then managed a very credible: "Not quite," with only the slightest tremble to his voice. "And I am sorry, no fish this morning. I did try. And the weather-wise say we're in for even more rain tomorrow, though it should clear after that."

"Will you take a glass of wine with us, Captain Kelling?" asked Aunt Louisa.

"No thank you. I will not stay long. Penn is walking the horses, but it is raining on him, poor fellow. I was hoping Miss Ross would take me to pay my respects to Mr. Frederick. If he is awake and wishing to see anyone, that is."

She did not, however, get even the walk upstairs to talk to Captain Kelling – which Georgina had a feeling might have been his plan – as Aunt Louisa accompanied them, and talked of the excellence of the seafood available in Southampton, a subject she obviously thought would be of interest to him. It made Georgina want to laugh. But she was very much in charity with him because it allowed her to leave her parcel and the book in her grandfather's room – he was asleep, and it enabled her to make the excuse of needing to get the first volume for him, to return. She went in, dashed off a note of thanks, while her aunt took Edward Kelling back downstairs. "And lobsters, you know, lobsters can be most aggressive, especially the large ones," she heard as she came down the stairs.

"I've heard they're of a tremendous size in Africa," said Captain Kelling, with a look that tempted her to offer tales of them sinking ships.

Instead she merely handed him the book and the note.

He took both, and then took his leave of them.

When Lessing had closed the door, her aunt said: "I hope you're not encouraging that young man to dangle after you, Georgina? He has very limited prospects, and you have none."

Georgina bit her tongue and did not ask why Aunt Louisa did not stop Maude trying to flirt with him then? Instead she meekly said. "I don't think anyone would wish to dangle after me, Aunt Louisa. After all, I am not fashionable, or modish and my complexion is too brown."

"As well you know it, girl," said her Aunt Louisa, not finding anything amiss in this. "But some men will fly at anything. Not that their intent is honorable, but they are just like that."

Georgina looked down and said nothing, already comforted by the thought of diving into the book that awaited her upstairs.

The parcel too gave her pause. The fabrics were indeed fascinating. She allowed herself a moment of desire: but resolutely put it aside. Perhaps one dress for Church, if her grandfather's health reached the point that she could attend. But she needed to be careful with her pennies.

Edward had had a cold, wet, fishless session that morning. That, of course, was not his only disappointment. He'd at least had time to think, and one of the thoughts had been that if Frederick Weatherly's attacker could be laid by the heels, that would be one thing done. He could not go looking for the ex-bailiff, and neither could Penn... but could ask his father if he could spare Jem for another trip to Southampton. The senior groom had worked in the port city for a while, and was a man who knew a thing or two and a few people. It was most likely that Grove had gone to ground there – he too had connections with the port.

The morning being fishless and cold and wet, Edward had retreated after drying off and warming up to the library, hoping to lose himself in his book. He found he was too distracted to do so, but it brought him to think of his meeting, there, with Georgina. What book had she taken? His mother might know. But looking for a gap in the shelves brought him to the fact that she had the first volume of Mrs. Porter's Hungarian Brothers. Well, he could take her the next volume.

He returned to the library after lunch, and a game of billiards with his brother. Reading still failed to bind him. He wondered if taking the book over would be sufficient excuse. And he wondered just how he would propose to keep a wife. He was going to have to find some kind of gainful occupation.

His mother returned from Winchester, bemoaning the weather... and asked him if he would take a parcel over to Westmead for Miss Ross. "You're a champion, Mother!"

Her eyes twinkled. "And also, not blind. So sits the wind, my Son?"

He saw no point in denying it. "She's as likely not to catch it in her sails, I am afraid. But yes." His thoughts from his reverie in the library still fresh in his mind, he spoke it. "I'm not much of a catch, Mother."

"A mother's opinion may possibly differ on that, Ned," she said fondly. "I like her. You two are quite alike in tastes, I think. And I don't think her expectations are in the least worldly, if that's what is worrying you. Talking with her of the mission station, she has lived very humbly most of her life. Mr. Winter says he had the greatest difficulty in persuading her to spend any money at all, which your father would say was a great advantage in a wife."

"Yes," said Edward. "But I must be able to adequately provide for my wife! I need to seriously cast about for new profession. I can't expect..."

She patted his shoulder. "When I married your father, things had been left at a pretty pass at Bournelea by your grandfather. Your father was similarly worried, but I would rather have had him if he were a pauper, than any other man I had met," she said, firmly. "And I did have other offers, you know. More than that... my portion was fairly paltry. And from what your father said, although he won't tell me who it was, he was in with a chance, with at least one heiress, and she could have pulled Bournelea out of the river tick easily enough."

"And you were the best decision of his life, Mama," said Edward, giving her a hug. "But I don't think I am much of a prize. But I am still very grateful for the opportunity to go and call on her."

"I shall have to find more errands for you to do, my Son," she said with her warm chuckle.

"I'm glad you don't disapprove anyway," he said.

"I am delighted your fancy should have turned to such a sweet girl, actually," said his mother. "She's kind, and has a sense of humor. That's hard to retain, through all she's had to bear. She's a brave child, who has had a rough time, which she had to carry largely on her own. She has said little of it, but it has marked her, Son. I kept wanting to give her a hug and say things are not so bad, or so frightening. Courage and kindness will outlast looks, I can tell you," she said touching her own face.

Edward blinked. "I hadn't really thought about that, Mother. I'd sort of assumed the aunt had stepped in... but now I have met her, I doubt it."

"Yes. I doubt it too," said his mother with a laugh. "Now, if it had been her daughter you had taken a fancy to... I would have been looking for a reason to send you to see how Gussie got on."

Edward shuddered.

His trip to Westmead house was less satisfying than he had hoped, but he brought the note to his mother.

She opened it, and cocked her head at him. "Lending books out, are you?"

"Yes, but I let you have the credit for it. And she was making do with A Life of Nelson."

"I can tell you were inspired by mercy. Well, I intend to betray you at the first chance."

"Mother! Don't go interfering," protested Edward.

She laughed at him. "What else do mother's do? Now, the dressing bell has already gone. You need to change."

Chapter 8

T he Sunday plan for the Westmead household was, as was the custom, to attend Church. Georgina had cried off, for the simple reason that her grandfather could not be left alone, and she was the only voice and person he automatically seemed to respond to, so he could not be left with a servant. She would have liked to have gone, if simply for the comfort and nostalgia of the familiar refrains. One of her father's stated beliefs was that the church building wasn't the Church. The building might be important to the church-goers, but the people were the Church. It had earned him a few puzzled looks, so she spared her aunt that, and merely said someone had to stay, and that they would meet people.

Her grandfather's elderly carriage had been brought around, so the ladies could depart in a mere spit-spot of drizzle. That did not improve, giving her a bleak view of misty drifts of fine rain from the window of her grandfather's room. The house was empty and quiet. The fire was lit, and the room pleasantly warm, and she had a good book to enjoy.

She sat down to read, and had been happily engrossed in this, when the door creaked, and a sudden chilly breeze stirred smoke out of the fire.

In the silence, only broken by her grandfather's breathing, that had been enough to disturb her. She realized the door was not quite to, and the fire could use a little attention. Setting the book down carefully, she got up to see to it, picking up the poker. Then she heard a sharp clanking noise, from downstairs. She walked to the door, pulling it open, and she heard it again, with what could have been a muttered curse. "Who is there?" she called out, gripping the poker. Surely it must just be a servant back from Church in the kitchen that had startled her?

Her voice had plainly alarmed someone, anyway. A door clicked open, and she heard hasty footsteps. "Who is it?" she called out, again. Then from some instinct, she called out. "I am armed and coming down!" They wouldn't know it was just a poker.

There was no answer except the door slamming open. Later, she would question her own judgement, but she raced down the stairs, three at a time, nearly breaking her neck tripping on a flounce at the bottom, and barely catching herself on the bannister. Finding her feet, she ran to the front door – which was open. Looking out, all she could see was someone running away in the rain towards the trees in the park. For a moment she actually considered chasing after them. Then reaction and common sense took over. Who had left the door open? She reached to close it, and realized that someone had left a key in the door. From the outside! Furiously she drew it out. Really! Had Lessing left the key in the door when her aunt and the servants had left?

Someone was going to be raked over the coals about this, Georgina thought savagely to herself, feeling the shock and reaction beginning to set in. She closed the door, locked it and took the key out. And then a horrible thought occurred to her. What if someone else was in the house? Putting the key in a pocket, every muscle tense, she stalked through the house checking rooms. The library door was open, and she knew from experience as her grandfather's room was straight above, some peculiarity of the building carried sounds from it up to there. She peered in, very cautiously. There was no-one there, unless they were behind the desk. She crept up to it, ready to strike. A part of her mind said: any sensible girl would be upstairs, barricaded in with her grandfather, until the staff returned. But the part that was not sensible, that was pure angry Georgina, strode up to the desk ready to hit any intruder with the poker.

There was no-one there. But she was so intent on that that she tripped and almost fell over the jemmy-bar dropped next to the safe, a scar on the wall showing where the thief had attempted to lever the safe off. She left it there, and continued her search. By this time reaction had set in well and truly, and she was shaking a bit, as she held the poker at the ready. But her search failed to turn up any other signs of anyone. So, she went to the kitchen, put a chair under that door-handle, and then went back to the front door and fetched out a chair from the dining room and did the same. Then she went upstairs, and settled down to wait. And to shake, quite a lot. She watched from the window, until she saw the first people walking back down the carriage drive. She went downstairs then, to open the door – the kitchen seemed most likely, and it was, but she was a little too slow, as the door was being furiously rattled, and someone was calling out: "Miss Ross! Miss Ross!"

She took the chair away and hastily got out the way as the burly groom thrust into the room. "Sorry Miss! The door was stuck."

"It wasn't stuck. I had a chair under it. We had a burglar in the house," said Georgina, with, she thought, remarkable calmness.

That calmness was not the reaction it provoked with the groom or Lessing, or the two housemaids who came scuttling up to get out of the rain. "Burglar, Miss?" said Lessing, incredulously. "This isn't London... or Africa."

"Come and have a look!" she said crossly, and led the entire troop – now growing, to the library. She pointed to the crowbar and the scratches on the wall and, she noticed, on the door of the safe. "Do you think I did that! And you left the key in the outside of the front door!" she pulled it out of her pocket.

They all looked at her, their mouths open... except for the younger of the two maids, who promptly fainted.

"But... Miss," protested Lessing. "I did lock up. I have the key here!" And he produced a key. The two were identical, except that hers had a plain bow, and was considerably newer.

"What happened, Miss?" asked the groom, while Lessing examined the keys, shaking his grizzled head.

"I heard a noise, I called out, thought I heard something and came downstairs with a poker."

"With a poker," he said, staring at her as if she had grown two heads.

"From the fire, upstairs. I had to have some sort of weapon," she explained.

Lessing turned to the groom. "Get on a prad and get across to Bournelea. Look sharp about it." The groom turned on his heel and ran. "Now, Molly," said Lessing to the maid who was being fussed by her companion. "You've no call to be sitting down. Get along to the kitchen both of you. Be telling Mrs. Lessing I want the footman to stand guard over Miss Ross. And the gardener can help me search the house."

"I've done that," said Georgina. "I saw him run off. It's far too late for a guard. Maybe you need to fetch the constable instead. And we can see if those two keys are actually the same. And, when it is convenient, I should like some tea. I feel I have earned it!"

"Indeed, you have, Miss Georgina!" said Lessing admiringly. "But you should come and sit down, Miss."

"I'll go and sit with my grandfather. He usually wakes about this time," she said and took herself upstairs. She was bracing herself for her aunt's arrival. That would be a storm, no doubt. Honestly, she'd rather face another burglar. At least she could hit the burglar with a poker.

She had managed half a cup of tea when the carriage drew up at the door, and so rather than wait, she went downstairs to greet her aunt.

"Many people inquired after you, Georgina," said her Aunt Louisa drawing off her hat. "You should have been there. It does not look good."

"Well, if I had not been at home," said Georgina. "We should have been burgled."

"Hmph. What nonsense. Burgled indeed. You are filling your head with rubbish moonshine. You read far too much."

"It's true, Ma'am," said Lessing.

"What!" exclaimed her aunt. "Impossible! What happened?"

Trying to keep it as calm as possible, Georgina said: "I heard a noise downstairs, so I called out. I heard more noise, and so I came down. They fled, leaving their crowbar at the safe. They had been trying to get into it, by the marks."

"I think I am going to faint," announced Maude.

"No, I am going to faint," said Elvira.

This was interrupted by a thunderous pounding on the knocker –
so loud that the two fainting candidates suddenly revived and took
shelter behind their mother.

Lessing opened the door cautiously and was pushed aside by Captain Edward Kelling who came in at what could only be called a charge.
He was as white as a sheet, hair disheveled, wet, and hatless. He ignored
the others, and rushed to Georgina, and took both her hands, staring
into her face. "Georgina! Uh, Miss Ross! Are you all right?"

She was quite as startled as she had been, when she'd heard the
noise downstairs, but as the look on his big broad face could only be
described as bordering on the distraught, she excused the liberties he'd
taken. "Absolutely fine," she said reassuringly.

"We were just saddling up... when your groom came in and told us
you'd chased off a burglar with a poker... I came to see if you were all
right."

He was examining her from head to toe, obviously set on establish-
ing this. And he was still holding both of her hands in his very large
ones. "I chased him. I didn't actually fight with him," she said, unable
to restrain herself from smiling up at him. "And could I have my hands
back, Captain?"

He dropped them, after a further second of staring into her face.
"So sorry! Sorry to burst in. I was afraid you might be hurt."

Aunt Louisa cleared her throat. He turned to her, and the two girls.
"I am sorry, Mrs. Salmonds. I didn't even see you there. Forgive me
for bursting in. If... if you're quite all right, Miss Ross, I'll leave now.
Perhaps I will pay a more dignified call, later, just to check," he said,
hastily.

"You'll take that wet coat off, and give it to Lessing, and come and
sit in front of the fire," she said firmly, before her aunt could utter a

word. Then despite herself, she said: "It is nice to have such a large person in the house."

"Indeed, it is!" said her aunt. "Why, we might be murdered in our beds."

Captain Kelling's tenor of mind, and reprehensible sense of humor – reprehensible if only because it made her want to laugh – and she was sure that would be deemed inappropriate by Aunt Louisa, had re-asserted itself. "Oh no, Mrs. Salmonds. Country hours here. You'd have had to have been murdered in the breakfast-parlor. But if you don't mind, I would like to hear the whole story. And it is a joy to find that, after a lifetime of being 'that great lump', my size has some purpose."

"Do stay, Captain," added Elvira.

Just then the knocker sounded again, and the rest of the party from Bournelea – plainly come by carriage and much drier and still in Church clothes arrived. "Glad to see everyone seems in one piece," said John, looking at his brother.

They were all invited in, as everyone wanted to hear the story. Georgina felt she'd coped well, but was comforted to have the house full of people. She was still processing Captain Edward Kelling's reaction, and the way he looked at her, and their previous meetings. She somehow found that the ideas planted in her head by Cousin Arthur about him having attacked her grandfather had receded into the bounds of the ridiculous. Perhaps... it would be worth finding out why... how... if, she had changed from an insufferable baggage, to someone to be looked at like that. She found herself flushing slightly at the thought.

They were all eager to hear the story, all trooped in to see the jemmy-bar and scratches made by it, and all examined the pair of keys.

But at this point, Captain Kelling rubbed his jaw, and asked if she had seen the individual."

"Not clearly. He was running off, and it was raining. A man. I would say his coat was black."

"On foot. That narrows it. Likely someone will have seen him," said John Kelling.

"Everyone would be in Church. It's a better time than midnight around here. There might be a poacher out and about at midnight," said Sir Gerald.

"And besides, if anyone were missing from Church, everyone would know, and the Reverend would probably be around to call later," said Lady Elizabeth.

"A poacher," said Edward, thoughtfully. "Miss Ross, did you see which direction he ran? Could you point it out to me?"

"Happily," she said. "Lessing, can you open the door? It will be easiest from the step."

"You went out?"

"The door was open. I stopped out there. It was raining."

He looked at her and shook his head. "I am grateful for the rain."

"I think the burglar might be too," said his brother, showing humor to be a family fault. "Or she might have hit him with the poker."

Captain Kelling cast him a fulminating look. "So where did he go?"

She pointed at the spinney she'd seen him run towards.

Captain Kelling looked at it carefully, and then said: "If you'll excuse me, I shall go and get Penn, before the rain obscures things any further. You might as well go in. I may be a while."

He wasn't though. He returned a few minutes later. "Not on foot," he said. "He had a horse tethered in the spinney. For some time, Penn says."

—————⟨✕⟩—————

Edward had been disappointed not to see Georgina at Church, but her absence made good sense. The rain had stopped briefly after the service and people were as usual engaged in the social exchanges that could go on for quite a while – but, before the service, one of the farmers had told Edward that he ought to have a look at the low bridge on Mr. Weatherly's place, as, he put it 'it didn't look good to him'. That tended to mean 'imminent collapse' around here, so Edward had put the word to his mother, and the Bournelea party had been among the first out and away, and Edward had got into his riding clothes immediately, and headed for the stables. Penn was just finishing off tightening Thunder's girth, when the groom from Westmead came around the corner at something perilously close to a gallop, reigning in the horse, hard. "Captain!" he panted out, "Lessing sent to call you. A burglary... Miss chased him with a poker!"

He had no memory of getting into the saddle or riding to Westmead, or of losing his hat. All he remembered was the enormous relief of seeing her, alive and apparently unharmed, framed by the hall. When she stood there, with him holding her hands, and her smiling up at him, it had been all he had been able to do not to kiss her, right then and there. That would have given that silly tabby of an aunt something to go on about.

Penn had found footprints in the mud, not that they had been much needed, because looking around the spinney, perhaps eighty or ninety yards from the house, they found a gap and a little opening in the middle of it, where Penn's keen eyes picked up chafe-marks on a branch – presumably where the horse had been tethered, a few chestnut mane-hairs on a branch suitable for scratching on, and of course, horse droppings and hoof-marks. Penn pointed out the number of droppings – and that some were much older, and had plainly come from a day... or night, when it had not rained.

"I'd say this was where the bounder who attacked Mr. Frederick left his horse while he went about his dirty business," said Edward.

"Aye. Must have known the spot, Captain. It's not obvious. I reckon he got here early and waited until everyone left."

"All we know is that he rode a chestnut horse."

"Aye. And his feets are smaller than yours, or mine."

"I'll get m'father to put the word about. Someone might have seen him ride in or maybe out."

Penn nodded. "What she needs about the place is a good dog, Captain."

"I agree. But what she needs more is this villain laid by the heels. I wonder if Jem has had any luck in Southampton."

They returned to the house, and he told the others of the finding where the horse had been tethered. "I suppose a letter to the magistrate is called for," said Miss Ross, with a sigh. "He hasn't been back to me about the bowl."

"Indeed," said Sir Gerald. "I do think he's a little out of his depth, poor man. Ancient Greek scholarship, is one thing. Practical matters are quite another."

"My brother, or I should say my half-brother," said Mrs. Salmonds, "Was himself a scholar of ancient Greek, and I cannot agree more. That is why poor Georgina has been left in such a parlous state. How she is to ever form an eligible connection I cannot think."

His mother and father both looked mildly horrified, as they must be, with this woman discussing Georgina's affairs as if she were not there. "For you know he wasted his entire inheritance on this missionary venture of his," the aunt continued, disapprovingly.

"He believed in it with all his heart," said Georgina in a low voice. "And I honor and loved him for that. And I won't hear anything bad said about him."

"Well," said Edward. "I think he did something very fine. You should be proud of him. You too Mrs. Salmonds. And any decent man would be a fool to let Miss Ross's circumstances weigh with them. I..."

There was a knock on the drawing-room door, and Lessing came in. "The constable is here, Ma'am. He'd like to speak with you, Miss Ross, if that would be convenient."

It was, as far as Edward was concerned, damned inconvenient. But a few seconds reflection were enough to make him realize that perhaps a proposal of marriage should have a little privacy, especially if she was to turn him down. He didn't have a lot to offer, after all. Her circumstances be blowed, by the time the story of the burglar and the poker got out, half the young men in the county would want a wife like that. And that was before they'd even seen her.

The Bournelea party took their leave while the constable was painstakingly writing everything down. Poor man, writing was not something he had to do often.

Chapter 9

G eorgina had had a lot of trouble getting to sleep that night, firstly, because of the day's adventures, and secondly for the ringing peal her aunt Louisa had rung over her. "My girl, you are being entirely too forward. People will think it very fast of you to encourage that young man."

"I haven't encouraged any young men," said Georgina, thinking of Aunt Louisa's own daughters, whose behavior had scandalized her, and who had been discussing the merits of the young men of the local gentry who had been in Church.

"You have to keep line, Georgina. Remember how totally unacceptable you would be to the poor boy's parents. The Kelling family are not rich, and he needs to marry well. If it is marriage that he intends," she said, sniffing disapprovingly. "I know, appearances can deceive. But I believe Sir Gerald's father mortgaged the place to the hilt, and while the older boy may inherit something, there is precious little left for the younger son."

"I have given the matter no thought," said Georgina, who really hadn't, or at least not the subject of how wealthy he might be.

"Well, you need to. You are giving him far too much encouragement and behaving like a coming, forward girl. Do not delude yourself he will come up to scratch. I imagine his parents are giving him a stern lecture right now. I was hopeful of finding you a parson or someone of that order, but if you develop a bad reputation... What are you laughing at girl?"

"Oh. Nothing," said Georgina, somewhat untruthfully. She had suddenly had the image of Sir Gerald and Lady Elizabeth giving Captain Edward a lecture. She failed to see it happening either from the point of view of the lecturers or him. They'd make a joke, and he did not seem the kind to meekly take orders. "I think you refine far too much on his concern, Aunt Louisa. He rescued my grandfather, they know each other well, and I hope he believes I provide him with good care. He regards me as an insufferable baggage, I believe. That is hardly endearment. And speaking of my grandfather, I had better go up."

"Do not think you can run off until I have finished speaking to you! My girl, you are letting your position here go entirely to your head. Remember, this is not yours, and your playing queen-bee here could end at a moment."

"I know. And I know I have no prospects. And I know you were willing to throw me out on the street, had not Captain Salmonds intervened. But at the moment, I must care for my grandfather," and she walked out, steaming.

She knew little of what acceptable behavior was. Mother had always kept the few men they'd met on the mission station at a distance from her. But she didn't think she was fast, or forward or a hoyden – as she had heard Elvira call her as she walked off.

That evening she discovered her other sins included exaggerating her role in the drama of the burglary. "You're just putting on airs to be interesting and heroic," Maude informed her. "I don't think you was in any danger."

"Probably not. They ran off, after all," said Georgina.

By some convoluted form of logic this too was wrong, because she had not behaved in a lady-like fashion. That seemed to comprise fainting. Or possibly being murdered in her bed. She was relieved to escape from that, even if sleep was as far off as murder seemed likely to be. Yes, she did put a poker at her bedside. And yes, she did have an impossible task persuading Mary not to sleep on a cot in the dressing room. She sensed that was as much comfort to the small maid as herself, so did not try too hard.

Her thoughts, before finally falling asleep, were that perhaps, as the rain had stopped, she'd take a walk down to the Bourne, early in the morning. Just to see the beauty of it in the dawn, of course, she said to herself, smiling at not having deceived herself at all. It was a rather pleasant thought to fall asleep on.

It was also thwarted by the fact that, as she discovered, Mary was a very light sleeper. Any thought Georgina had of quietly leaving was not going to happen. The sight of Mary in her night-clothes, a small smoothing-iron being swirled on a belt, ready to deal with anyone who dared murder her mistress in her bed, was some compensation, but not as much as she'd have liked.

"It's all right. It's just me," she said, soothingly, seeing Mary's mouth opening to set up a screech. "I get up far too early."

"Oh Miss! You nearly frightened me out of a year's growth, and me mam says I can't afford that! Can I be getting the fire up for you?"

"I'm thinking of going downstairs to see if I can get the range up enough for a cup of tea."

"Miss Georgina, you can't be doing that! It would not be right. I'll go."

"I'll get a dressing gown, and we can both go. It won't be the first time I have made a fire or tea, Mary. We did not live quite like this, and I may well find myself even worse off, when my grandfather dies or... no longer needs me. I will have to work for my bread and butter, on my own."

Mary cast a sapient eye at her. "Seems there's one who'd like to be taking care of you. Not that I'd be paying any attention to any below-stairs gossip," she said with absolutely no truthfulness, but a small inquiring smile.

Georgina didn't pretend not to know what she was speaking of. She shrugged. "I doubt it. I have no prospects, and I am just... the granddaughter of a neighbor."

"That's not what Penn said. And what he heard from Jem from Lady Elizabeth's maid..."

"No below-stairs chatter, Mary," teased Georgina, rather curious as to just what the household at Bournelea were gossiping about. "It is always wrong, anyway. You're making too much of it."

"She who lives longest, will see most, as my mam says," said Mary. "Now, shall we go downstairs. See if the house has been robbed while we slept? Me mam said the country would be safer than town. I've a tale to tell her!"

The house had not been robbed – or at least not that they could see. Georgina was amused to see the chair had been put under the latch again.

They went back upstairs, and, because it was early, and because Mary was awake as a result of her actions, Georgina felt she couldn't return to her book. So, she got out the swatches of fabric that Lady Elizabeth had brought her, and was soon surprised to discover that her maid not only had a keen eye, but a great deal more knowledge than she did, about dressmaking. "Me mam does some work for a seamstress. She makes dresses on Farthing Street. Mam was hoping she'd take me on. But it didn't work out."

Mary was far more persuasive than Lady Elizabeth about the possibility of getting Georgina new clothes, as she was happy to talk of the costs and issues like wear and durability. Some calculations were done, and measurements made. It was an odd, but pleasurable interlude, Georgina thought. She might as well enjoy it, and a few new dresses might make her more employable.

When the servants of the household had stirred, and work had begun below-stairs, they went down to continue on the drapes. Georgina did cast a longing look or two out of the new-opened windows at what looked like a cloudy but clear morning, as they worked. She did hear the horses arrive, the knocker tapped, but Lessing was there to open the door. She heard Captain Kelling say: "Morning Lessing. Some fish for your mistress. No more incidents last night?" and decided to step out of the dining room where they had been using the table, to greet him, as Lessing assured the Captain all had been quiet.

His face lit up on seeing her. There was no other way of putting it, really. He looked exceptionally pleased to see her. "Good morning, Miss Ross! Um. You're up early."

"It was five o'clock she was up this morning," said Mary, who had come out behind her. "Like I hear tell you are."

"Good morning to you too, Captain. Yes, I do keep what everyone says is odd hours. Will you come in?"

"No, thank you. I'm in all my fishing togs, and they smell, my mother has informed me, of fish. She says one should never talk to ladies when you smell of fish."

"Oh. Well. I... she would know better than I do. Was it good on the river, today?" she asked, trying to prolong the conversation, but very aware they were being watched with avid interest by both Lessing and Mary.

"Not my best day," he said with a twinkle in his eye. "That was last week, Thursday."

Despite herself, Georgina said: "Tomorrow, I hope, will be better. If the weather permits."

"I'll be out there," he said. "I would check the weather though. Anyway, I'll take my leave of you. There's some work on a bridge I need to see to."

"An excellent young man, Miss," said Lessing, when he had left. "I've known him since he was a boy, of course. I remember well a fine nose bleed he had here. A little hammer-and-tongs with him and young Master Arthur, in the stable-yard. Master Arthur's a few years older than him, but they give each other salt-and-pepper," he said with a chuckle.

"I didn't know... Well, of course, they must have known each other."

"Them Kelling boys followed Master George around like tantony pigs, Miss. He liked them and they was always over here."

The day proceeded, and, mid-morning, Mr. Tadswell arrived. He apologized deeply. "I have been away, to Oxford. A meeting, you understand."

"Scholars must meet," said Georgina, in Greek.

He beamed at her. "Your father's scholarship shows through, young *Kyria*."

"Her name is Georgina," said her aunt.

"I am aware of Miss Ross's name," said Tadswell. "I merely addressed her in Greek."

"I do not approve of foreign, heathen tongues sullying young ears."
Aunt Louisa sniffed.

Mr. Tadswell swelled visibly. "As your brother used it to study early
Biblical work, it was hardly 'heathen'," he snapped. "Ancient Greece
is the fountainhead of our civilization."

"A waste of time," snapped Aunt Louisa, straight back.

Before battle-royal could erupt, fortunately, Elvira came into the
room, and said: "I heard we had a visitor... Oh. Good morning."

Plainly he was a bit disappointing as a visitor. However, it did give
him time to recall his business. "Anyway. I need to speak with Miss
Ross. Perhaps we can go to the library, Miss Ross." He turned a cold
eye on Aunt Louisa. "Privately. I would be pleased to enlighten you at
some other time."

"I will take you through," said Georgina, before any further explo-
sions could occur.

Once they were safely in the library, Georgina rang the bell. "Mr.
Tadswell. Before we talk, I am going to get you a glass of wine," she
said. He was still very red in the face.

"Quite un-necessary, my dear," he said. "I shouldn't..."

The footman arrived. "You rang, Miss."

"Yes, Sarun. If you could bring Mr. Tadswell some Madeira,
please?" He bowed and went off.

She said: "Please, Mr. Tadswell, sit down. I am sorry about that. My
aunt... doesn't like Greek scholarship."

"Absolutely not your fault, Miss Ross," said Tadswell. "Just a shock.
I'd expect that from the rustics, but surely she must be proud of her
brother, your father?"

"They were half-siblings, sir. And she resented his going to Cambridge, and his share of the inheritance, and the way he spent it. I had
heard... but not really realized how deep the problem was until I came

back here. But she is my legal guardian, until I come of age. And my uncle is not unkind."

He nodded. "I sympathize. I..."

The footman returned with the wine and some macarons, which interrupted his revelation, and improved his constitution, markedly. "Now," he said, putting the glass down. "I received two letters from you Miss Ross. One saying you had discovered something else missing. A Chinese bowl, I believe. What can you tell me about that?"

"Very little, sir. Mrs. Lessing says it was very valuable, and should have been locked up, but my grandfather liked to look at it. Perhaps she could describe it for you. Or... or Mr. Winter may know more. Or Captain Edward Kelling. He was in here quite often."

"Captain Kelling was familiar with it?" said Tadswell. "Hmm. Alongside his suspicious presence. Fishing. Ha. At that time of morning!"

"He does go fishing in the early morning, sir," said Georgina, rising to his defense. She had seen it, after all.

He looked at her. "That's what they'll tell you here. The Squire's son! But no-one..."

It had given her a moment to think, and so, rather than say, 'Well, I have seen him myself, standing in the river, catching fish.' – a thought which made her smile – she said: "You should perhaps ask my grandfather, Mr. Tadswell. He himself used to do so. He has told me about various dawn rises and magnificent fish. It's a passion of the local fishermen."

He still looked a little doubtful. "If you say so, Miss Ross."

She smiled at him, working hard for the point. After all, Captain Edward had sprung to her defense. "It's 'Sport', Mr. Tadswell. You know how they feel about 'Sport'. They feel about it as you do about Ancient Greek. You can hardly not have noticed, sir. And please, do ask my grandfather. He would love to be asked. I have heard all the stories quite a few times."

Perhaps it was the touch of dryness in the last, that got through to him. "He does seem to repeat topics," said Tadswell. "Yes, I would grant he'd be an unimpeachable witness. Well... I am still not satisfied, but let us go on. This burglary. How exactly did the miscreant gain entry? And you are sure it was a burglary attempt?"

She showed him the scratches on the wall, where they had tried to lever the safe free, and the gouge in the safe door-frame, where the hinges had been attacked. "And the constable has the jemmy-bar that the thief dropped."

"They did not get into the safe, excellent! So, tell me the rest?"

She told the story again, wondering why she'd bothered to tell the constable.

"So, he ran off on foot, eh. Well, that restricts the possibilities," he said. When she got to the part of chasing the burglar out, he exclaimed: "That was brave to reckless, young lady. You're not a vengeful Athena! These miscreants can be dangerous."

"Well, I didn't think at the time. And, and it turns out he did have a horse, tethered in the spinney. Captain Edward's man, Penn, found it."

"He was here?" said Tadswell looking like a terrier, catching sight of a rat-hole.

"No. I was alone. Everyone was in Church. This was afterwards. We sent a groom to Bournelea for help, when the servants got back. Captain Edward and his man were the first to get here."

"That is convenient. Again."

Georgina bottled down her irritation. "They were in Church when it happened. Why don't you ask my aunt? Or my cousins. Or the priest. Reverend Thorpe came yesterday afternoon, and remarked on it."

"I will follow that up. But the matter of the key has rather focused my mind. A duplicate, you say?"

"Yes."

He proceeded to inspect the key, the place where the horse had been tethered, and to go up to speak to her grandfather, who had finished his papers, and wanted a game of chess. He did not know who Tadswell was, but was happy to tell him all about fishing the dawn rise, at considerable length.

Whatever the magistrate believed about Captain Edward Kelling, or did not believe, he certainly knew that, indeed, there were people who were mad enough to fish at first light, and ride to be at the river, by then.

When he departed, Georgina made the discovery that Westmead House was now on the calling-list again. The Cressell's had been, and left their card on being informed that she was busy with the magistrate. No, they had not wished to see Mrs. Salmonds, they had merely called to inquire after Mr. Frederick's health, Lessing informed her. "And if you asks me, Miss, they was curious about the burglary. You should have seen Mrs. Cressell's face, when I said you was with Mr. Tadswell. Story is all over the county by now, I reckon."

"Oh dear."

"Well, Miss Georgina, not much that's exciting usually happens around here. A two-headed calf is a nine-day wonder, hereabouts."

"I wish it would return to that!" she said. "I prefer it quiet. Anyway, who are the Cressells?"

"They lives half a mile the other side of Hurstbourne Priors, Miss. Part of the Hunt. They're liked hereabouts, for all she's something of a poke-nose." Lessing suddenly realized what he'd said. "I spoke out of turn, Miss. They are respectable people. You should go and call or she'll be offended, Miss. It's how it is done here."

The idea quite horrified her. "I can't really leave my grandfather. Could I send them a note apologizing?" she asked hopefully.

He considered this and nodded. "She can't take offence at that, Miss. Explain and invite them to call again. Maybe... Wednesday? You don't want it too soon, or too slow. You might ask Lady Elizabeth how to manage the swells, Miss."

Quiet was not something she was about to be granted. Looking out from her grandfather's room, where he had just dozed off after luncheon, Georgina saw not one but two vehicles drive up. The first, a carriage, stopped, and her Cousin Arthur got out and came to the door. The second, a small, one-horse gig, drew up, and an unknown gentleman... who had an unmistakable clerical look to him, was consulting a piece of paper. She'd been around priests and missionaries too much of her life not to recognize a priest. She wondered what he could want.

She went to welcome Cousin Arthur, who was already being enthusiastically greeted by Elvira and Maude, while their mama beamed on. "Ah, Cousin Georgina. I am so glad to see you looking in such good health," he said, making his bow, showing his perfectly pomaded blonde locks. "I have come down to spend a few days with you to help you settle in. If that is not inconvenient that is? Your aunt was just assuring me of a welcome, but I did want to ask you first."

"Of course, he is welcome!" said her aunt. "This is your house, after all, Mr. Weatherly."

"It is my uncle's home. I have spent a great deal of time here, though," he said urbanely. "Well, may I stay, Cousin?"

What could she say, except, "Certainly." Actually, she did feel another man inside the house – besides her grandfather and old Lessing, a footman and a valet with a broken collar-bone – might be welcome. "I warn you, though, we may apparently all be murdered in our beds."

She turned to where Lessing was speaking to the other new arrival. The butler bowed to her. "This gentleman says he is the Reverend McLeod, from the Edinburgh Mission Society, and he was wishing to see you, Miss."

The poor man looked entirely out of his depth and place. Georgina clapped her hand to her mouth, then said, "Oh good gracious. I... I did send a letter."

He bowed. "Indeed, Miss Ross." His voice had a distinct Scots burr, more pronounced than her father's but reminiscent. "But Dr. McPhearson felt I should come down and meet you anyway. Your father, after all, was one of the founding members of the society, and your Great Aunt Edith a generous donor. He felt I should come down and express our condolences on your loss in person, and to see how you were settled and that you were reasonably provided for. To arrange to the best of our ability, anything that you needed." He smiled – he was not an unattractive man, with a long serious face, perhaps a few years older than Cousin Arthur. "And, besides, I am off to the Cape Colony. I thought you could tell me something, firsthand, of what I will experience. You could tell me so much and it would help me and also the flock I must minister to, if I understand them."

"I will happily tell you as much as I can! And it was so good of you to come."

"We were concerned. But you do seem very comfortably situated, Miss Ross."

"It is not quite what it seems," she said. "Anyway, you must come in, Reverend. I really would like to talk."

Her aunt bustled forward, eyeing the priest with some dislike. "Did I hear you say you were from my brother's missionary society?"

"Yes," said Georgina. "He has come to talk to me about my father and about Africa. And I have just invited him to stay..."

She meant to end with "and talk." But her aunt promptly interrupted. "You can't just invite people to stay, Georgina!"

"I can, and I have," demurred Georgina.

"Look, I do not wish to cause any dissention," said the Reverend, holding up his hands pacifyingly. "I had no intention of intruding or staying with Miss Ross. I would merely like to talk to her about her father and his work. You are a blessed woman to have had such a brother, Ma'am – if, if I am correct in saying you are the dear departed Reverend Ross's sister?" He had a firm, carrying preacher's voice, that easily cut above the chatter.

"Yes," said Georgina. "This is my Aunt Louisa, Mrs. Salmonds."

"A fine Scots name," said Reverend McLeod, plainly ignorant of how desperately Aunt Louisa tried to avoid any sign of her origins. "I am most pleased to meet you." And he took her hand and shook it firmly. "So good of you to have opened this lovely home of yours to this poor child."

Georgina wished desperately she had someone to share the humor of the situation with.

Rescue came from Cousin Arthur, who said: "You must come in and talk to Georgina, and to my uncle."

In the face of this, Aunt Louisa folded. Reverend McLeod, however, said: "I would be happy to call tomorrow. I am sure I can find somewhere in the neighborhood to stay."

"You will stay here," said Georgina. "Please. I... I have not really had any opportunity to talk about my father or my mother or about what they did. They believed in it, and, and I am pleased you will be going to continue their work. Besides, I may need to consider my future."

She realized, belatedly, that what she'd meant as 'have some support and contacts in looking for employment' he could misconstrue as 'be willing to marry you, and go back to Africa'. Well, she would explain it to him, later. When he was not volubly expressing thanks.

"Yes," said her aunt. "She does need to consider her future. Come, Mr. Weatherly. Let us see you comfortably bestowed. You have a chamber which is reserved for you, I believe."

He did. Maude and Elvira had had a bicker with Georgina about not being put into it, each being convinced that they deserved better and larger accommodation, the issue only being resolved by the presence of Arthur's shaving brush and razor.

The next while was taken up in unloading vehicles – the priest had come in a gig hired from the local hostelry and it seemed Arthur's too was a hired carriage, and seeing the visitors bestowed in rooms. Georgina had to spend some time with her grandfather – who wanted to know what all the noise was about, but seemed satisfied that it was merely visitors. "House should be full," he said, firmly.

That at least took that off her conscience. She went down a little later and found that Reverend Donald McLeod might be capable of missing a few social cues, but he was equally capable of holding his own in a hostile environment. Her aunt's barbs went simply un-noticed, it seemed. And the effect of his comments on the worthlessness of frivolous fashion to the Salmonds girls were a joy to behold. Perhaps not a particularly holy joy, but a joy none-the-less. She was almost sorry to carry him off to the morning room. "For you would hardly all wish to hear about my father's work and death," she said, and her aunt made no objection.

"I was hoping to make myself known to your grandfather," McLeod said, once they had got out of the drawing room.

"He is asleep again at the moment, sir." She paused briefly. "It may not be a good thing, Reverend McLeod. He... he should have no sudden shocks and upsets, while he is trying to recover. You see, he was exceptionally upset with my mother marrying my father. He refused to countenance the marriage. He wrote her out of his will, he never replied to her letters – although she wrote, regularly."

It was his turn to be silenced. Finally, he said: "I see. His condition is very bad? I was studying medicine before I decided I was called to ministry, so I understand and you may be frank with me. I had no idea of the situation. His sister, Mrs. Edith Haggerty, left quite a considerable sum to the Society, so I thought we were in good standing with the family."

She shook her head. "I've heard the story many times. Mother... mother was being pressured into a marriage she could not like. So: she went to stay with Mrs. Haggerty – my Great Aunt Edith, in London. She was very involved in Church work, and was hosting a young man who planned on going out on a mission to Africa. My father. They met, fell in love, and my father came down here to ask my grandfather for her hand in marriage, to be his bride and to go to Africa with him. Things did not go well," she said, feeling that was probably the understatement of the generation.

He sighed. "From what I know, Reverend Ross was such a fine man too. There was no reconciliation? I wish there could have been."

"Mother tried hard enough," said Georgina.

"But surely, surely now that he has his granddaughter home..."

"Let me explain, Reverend McLeod. He is recovering from a brain injury. He does not remember clearly, and he thinks I am my mother. He... has moments of clarity, and he seems to be improving. But, well, when he recovers, he may simply turn me out of doors. And if he dies, I am similarly going to be homeless. So: I know it looks like I am well situated, but really, I may not be. But I am still not going to marry you and go to Africa," she said, determined to get that out of the way.

He nodded. "I... thought Dr. McPhearson went far beyond what should have been proposed. I will need to think and pray on these things, Miss Ross. Tell me instead of your life on the mission station."

So, she did. It was a relief to talk of it, to get it out. The story of the attack on the mission-station shocked him, as she meant it to. She was graphically open about the rapine and killing, and the horror of it all. He was badly shocked, as she also meant him to be. And he was further shocked about the attack on her grandfather, when she got to that. "This does not happen in civilized countries," he informed her.

"It would seem that you are wrong," Georgina said to him. "I fear the villain may yet return, because he obviously is still looking for something. I know what is in the safe, and I cannot think what it could be. I am grateful for a full house, for that reason alone."

Chapter 10

E dward's Monday had followed a somewhat broken night – the hard ride had not helped, and his head was full of speculation. Still, as Penn had pointed out, a few months ago that ride would have had him in bed for a week, instead of out fishing, hopeful, the next morning.

Edward hoped he had correctly understood her about seeing him the next day. He had been whistling and cheerful when he got home that Sunday afternoon. A little later, one of the maids came to him in the library, and told him Jem was back, and wishful of speech with the Captain.

He went to see the groom, who was back from his trip to Southampton. "Well, I tracked that rascally bailiff, Grove, down, Captain," said Jem. "But I was just a little bit slow. Far off after the fair as it were. I'm sorry."

"Dead?"

"No, I didn't find him, so he's still warm," said Jem, cheerfully. "But he shipped out on the tide early this morning. By the time I got to the boozing ken he's been racked up at, all that was left of him was his shot, that he skipped without paying. Ship bound for Danzig. Works the Baltic trade. The Maid of the West."

"Skipped the country? The timing is suspect, enough," said Edward, thoughtfully.

"Could be, Captain. He's been at sea afore this, though. Penn was telling me about a chestnut the thief were riding. Not much sign o' the gelt to hire a horse. Or he wasn't spending it anyway. Drinking on tick, and the landlord was getting mighty peevy."

"We might need to try and find out where he was on Sunday. Or tell that magistrate, if he'll listen."

"Not much chance o' that," said Jem dismissively.

Edward suspected he was right. The next bit of news came from Mr. Winter. A brief, precise note, saying that three of the snuff-boxes had been found and recovered from a pawn shop in Bermondsey.

Edward was armed with these bits of information when Mr. Tadswell came to call later that afternoon. Tadswell seemed a little subdued, and while his patience with the plump man was more than a little frayed, Edward did his best to be civil. "A couple of questions, Captain. It has come to my attention that a bowl was missing from the library at Westmead house, and that you were often in there. I have a very limited description from the house-keeper, Mrs. Lessing."

"Ugly, heathen thing?" asked Edward, knowing her feelings on the subject well.

Tadswell looked somewhat taken aback. "Er. Yes, words to that effect. And that it should have been locked away, somewhere in a dark cupboard, preferably. She did tell me that Mr. Frederick said it was extremely valuable, and that she had to caution the maids about dusting it."

"I wish I could tell you much more. You might try Arthur Weatherly, or one of the old fellow's cronies – the lawyer I think had an interest in porcelain. Winter might know. I can give you the color and a vague description, but, to be honest, I didn't have much desire to know more. He did show it to me. It was on that lacquered rosewood table with cabriole legs, in the near corner, as I recall. He used to keep the chessboard in the drawer under it. You might check if that is there too. It was of some antiquity, I believe, and probably valuable."

"How do you know this, Captain?" asked the magistrate.

"We played chess together, two or three times a week. I have been overseeing his estate, and I would often stop and spend a little time with him a couple of days a week," said Edward. "You know, Mr. Tadswell, I have been in and out of that house since I was a boy. His son George – the one who died on the hunting field – encouraged us to run tame there. George was nine years older than me, seven years older than my brother, and we thought the world of him."

Tadswell blinked. "I thought there was bad blood between the houses?"

"My father is the master of the local Hunt, Mr. Tadswell. George was hunting mad. We were all gutted when he died."

"I see. Now, would it be possible for you to call your man, Penn, for me. I wish to ask him about the signs of a horse tethered in the spinney."

Edward rang the bell. "Certainly." When the footman answered, he sent for Penn, and then said to Tadswell. "And I have a further lead for you. We've tracked down William Grove – but not caught him."

"Ah. That is a loose end. Where is he, and I will arrange for him to be apprehended for questioning.

"On board a ship, a merchant vessel trading with the Baltic ports. The Maid of the West."

"That would exclude him, then."

"He sailed on the morning tide, this morning. One of our grooms spoke to the ship's agent, and he's on the crew list. The big question is whether he comes back."

"How did you happen to find out all this?"

"Mr. Tadswell, you've as good as told me you suspect me of attempted murder of the father of a man I hero-worshipped, because you don't believe anyone goes fishing early in the morning..."

"I have had to re-assess that, Captain. Miss Ross provided me with testimony of the fact that at least it is possible that you were going fishing."

"Good of her," said Edward.

"Captain Kelling, finding a criminal means assessing matters of motive, opportunity, and means. To me..."

"I don't have any debts, nor, I admit, prospects," said Edward. "But I doubt if the old fellow's collection was worth more than a few monkeys, Tadswell. It's not that large or rich an estate. I should know, I've had a lot to do with running it. To a rogue like that Grove it might have seemed worth it. For my family reputation, no. I don't see that as a plausible motive. Half a dozen people have motive, and..."

"I have been investigating the possible suspects, from yourself, Mr. Grove, even Mr. Arthur Weatherly, to various collectors. It's the combination of knowledge as to where the valuable collection   was kept – they are typically better secured, the motive, the opportunity, and means. In your case, I felt you had the knowledge, the opportunity and means, and I was informed you had the motive."

"Arthur Weatherly," said Edward, sapiently. "He doesn't like me, Tadswell. That's all. You might as well suspect him."

"I have investigated him too, Captain. He had neither the opportunity, nor motive, nor means to do this. He has witnesses, several men of noble lineage, who testify he was with them on that evening."

Penn arrived, and Tadswell was happy to let Edward remain there while he asked questions. "So: the horse was there for a considerable time?"

Penn nodded, "Horse droppings say so. And the first time was shorter."

"The first time?" asked Tadswell. And Penn was able to explain.

"It would seem to be the same individual," said Tadswell.

"Aye. And someone who knew the ground, your honor. Rode straight there."

When he had finished, Tadswell asked to see the groom who had tracked down Grove, and he asked the Captain to leave him to that.

Later Edward found out Tadswell had questioned Jem at length about where he had stayed and possible witnesses to that. "Like he thought I could have been here, Sunday morning," said Jem with a chuckle. "I says to him, not without wings." But he had taken the details of the ship's agent, and the tavern Grove had quit without paying his shot. After dinner, once they had all gone through to the drawing room, the family sat talking about it. "I wonder what 'men of noble lineage' were able to overawe Tadswell?" said John. "Mind you, in among the gamesters he mixes with, there are plenty of shuffling rogues with titles."

"Still, I see what he means about lack of motive. I mean: it's all Arthur's anyway."

"He might have wanted to inherit sooner," said his father.

"That won't fadge, Pater," said Edward, reluctantly. "Look, as little as we like Arthur, this was plainly an interrupted burglary, not an attempted murder. And it's a fair distance to London. Drat. I forgot to tell Tadswell about the snuff-boxes Winter has recovered. Oh well, either Winter will tell him, or he'll be back. I'm for an early night. I will be fishing tomorrow."

"I might come with you," said John.

"No, you jolly well won't!" Edward informed him.

They were all laughing at him. He'd told John about his meeting her at the river, and he was pretty sure John had told his mother... and, well...

His mother came and gave him a kiss on the cheek. "Sweet dreams, Son."

"Oh, he's having them," said John, shoulders shaking.

"Go to the devil, dear brother," said Edward, shaking his head and retreating in the face of familial laughter.

Chapter 11

Georgina had successfully persuaded Mary that now the house was full, well, fuller, she could be safely left to sleep in her own room, with the door locked. It was pale pre-dawn, with thin drifts of soft mist making oceans around the dark trees when she peeped out of her window. She put on her dressing-gown and checked on her grandfather. He was sleeping comfortably, so she dressed, wrestling a little with her conscience. That conscience said she was sneaking out of the house to meet a man: as bad a breach of maid-enly behavior as was imaginable. The pragmatic part of her mind said that it was barely a hundred yards down to the river... well, maybe a little more. She could pick up her skirts and run if need be. His leg would disadvantage him, if he chased her. And she was sure of one thing, her aunt would do her best to see they never got to speak to each other, except in company, otherwise. And... she wanted to talk to him. To ask him, bluntly... well, just what? She had no idea.

She dressed with some care, and took a bonnet, and a pelisse, and followed the same route out. She wondered if she was perhaps too early, this time. Perhaps the fish were still asleep. Everything was very quiet and still, just one cock-crow, and a grumpy one at that. The Bourne-water was dark, but she was comforted by a silvery ring out in the midstream. She was so busy looking at that, that she almost walked straight into him, coming the other way. "Oh. You gave me a fright!" she exclaimed, her composure that she'd been so certain of, shattered.

"That," he said, "Was never ever my intention. I... I am so glad to see you, Miss Ross." He had stopped a few feet off, making no attempt to come closer, just standing there, looking at her. In fact, both of them were standing, without saying anything. She was rather aware of her heart beating.

Eventually, she said: "Good... good morning. It looks as if it will be a beautiful day."

"It is a beautiful day," he said.

"Um, are you going to fish? I would like to watch again."

"The fish will just have to wait. I was very much hoping to see you, Miss Georgina Ross, to find out how... how you could possibly think I would say anything insulting of you. I assure you, from the bottom of my heart, I could not dream of doing so."

"But you did," she said, the meeting rapidly losing some of its enchantment.

"But... When?" he asked.

"I was sitting with my grandfather on the morning after I had arrived. You spoke to your mother in the passage. You were not aware I was able to hear you. Or you didn't care. You were abominably rude and unpleasant."

He paused, tugging his chin, as he did when in thought. "Ah," he said, finally. "I frequently am abominable. Gussie, my sister, says most of the time. I am afraid I did insult you terribly."

"Yes." She informed him, baldly.

"But not in the way you think. It was, in fact, far worse," he said, shaking his head, looking grave.

"What?" This was anything but what she expected.

"Yes. You see, I was under the impression, then, that you were your Cousin Elvira. And you are as far from her as the stars are from the earth," he said.

"You... thought I was Elvira?" she said incredulously.

"Yes, I missed the introduction. And I made the wrong assumption. Such a wrong assumption, that I can never apologize enough for it. You had spent all your time with your grandfather, gone up to him before I got there... and I did not catch her name, and thought that she was you, ignoring him, not even going up to him, demanding we dance attention around her. I was offended on his behalf."

The humor of the situation... and an enormous feeling of relief made her want to giggle. "You don't like my cousin?" she said, not quite managing to keep her voice even.

"No," he said, smiling at her in a most engaging fashion.

"But she's modish and pretty and..." she knew she was fishing. She knew it was beneath her. But she wanted that reassurance.

"My brother said it better than I can. You're a diamond, Miss Georgina Ross. She's a rhinestone, at best," he said sincerely. "There's no comparison."

"You're flattering me," she said, suddenly uncomfortable, although still rather wanting to encourage him.

"Not a bit of it," he said. "And I have said nothing to what I'd like to say. I could spend all morning at it, Miss Ross, I just don't have adequate words. I'm not much good at flummery."

"Well, Captain Kelling," she said, bracingly, trying for a lighter tone, unsure of the ground she was on. Was this flirtation? He seemed quite serious. "It seems like flummery to me. And if all other words fail you, there's always 'insufferable baggage'. I shall not take it personally, in future."

He smiled. "And I will never live it down, I think. But at least you did not ask me how much money my father has, on first acquaintance. Which was rather what gave me a disgust of your cousin, and made me exclaim in that fashion. Would you consider, Miss Ross, calling me Edward? Or Ned? My friends do, and... and I earnestly desire to be your friend."

Actually, Edward Kelling thought to himself, he was a terrible liar. He did not want to be her friend. He had entirely different ambitions which started with wanting to take her in his arms and kiss her. But he'd sensed her nervousness, and instinctively held back.

"I am not sure that would be proper," she said, seriously. "After all, you call me 'Miss Ross.' I am also very sure my meeting you here is very improper. But I am glad to... to have cleared up that misunderstanding. I had better go now. I need to get back before anyone wakes."

He bowed. "May I call later? And... I would not presume to call you Georgina, without your permission. But I should like to."

"My aunt would have a fit," said Georgina. "She called me a forward, designing woman for talking to the priest without a chaperon. I really must go... Captain Edward."

He bowed again. "Until later, Miss Georgina. And the devil fly away with your aunt. The priest is at least seventy years old."

"Oh, not that one. The one who is staying with us. You will meet him when you call."

The country grapevine had brought the news that Arthur Weatherly had arrived and installed himself at Westmead House. The priest was news he had not heard, and Edward wondered what he was doing there. He didn't pay much attention to it, but instead walked on, whistling cheerfully enough to startle the birds who had just started their chorus, and found a spot to cast a line. The concentration required for doing fishing well was rather lacking, but he managed to catch a brace of fish, before sitting down to have coffee and a fry-up with Penn at the shed.

"You're looking uncommon cheerful for a man what only caught two fish, Captain," said Penn, pushing a pair of eggs onto his plate."

"And you're fishing, Penn." He sighed. "And I've a lot of casts to make and mend, but I hope I haven't frightened her off the rise, at least. One day, my man, my dream is you'll make this breakfast for both me and your new mistress. I've a notion she'd enjoy it. But... well, if that comes to be I'll have to take a job, likely in the city, so I won't be fishing here. Probably won't be fishing here anyway. The place will be sold."

"You think the old man has had his notice to quit, Master?"

"No, I don't," said Edward, knowing how quickly talk could spread in the country-districts. "It will happen eventually though."

"They say some priest-fellow come yesterday, over at Westmead House and is staying. I wondered."

"I'll satisfy your curiosity later. In the meantime, pass the coffee, will you?"

They sat and ate and drank coffee in companionable silence, with the sounds of a peaceful country around them, occasional cows, birds telling the world of how beautiful they were and how even a day like this was lucky to have them, and the song of the flowing water. Edward was already working on his strategy for the day, and thoughts for the future. He knew that would mean less mornings on the river, and most likely work in an office of some sort. Well, if he must, he must. He'd even been thinking towards emigration, before. He wondered how she'd feel about that?

On his return home, he set about his plan of campaign, buttonholing his brother. "I need a drag-man to take the pack off me, brother,"

John laughed. "They'll have the hide off me. Besides, I was planning to exercise my new horse..."

"You can do that later. We're going to go over to Westmead House to enquire how Mr. Frederick goes on, and your job is to fascinate the hounds."

"While you talk to your girl? I think that is a pretty poor bargain for me. I mean, Elvira told me I was a much better matrimonial prize than you, brother," said John, grinning.

"On first name terms, eh? Famous. You should keep them busy."

"I must love you dearly, brother, to go at all," said John, resignedly.

They went over to pay a morning call, to be loftily welcomed by Mrs. Salmonds. "And how is dear Lady Elizabeth today?" she asked, as if they were bosom-bows.

"A touch of goal-fever, but otherwise fine," said John.

"Good, good," said Mrs. Salmonds. "We have the pleasure of Mr. Arthur Weatherly visiting, as well as a man from my late half-brother's mission society, here to see my niece. Poor girl. Her parents left her in a most unfortunate way."

John cast a fulminating look at his brother. "Arthur. How delightful," he said.

"Yes, my daughters are in transports," announced Mrs. Salmonds. "Come through to the drawing room. We are having something of an impromptu soiree."

This, Edward found, was the case. Maude was seated at the piano-forte, and playing, while Arthur turned the pages for her, and they were unable to escape. "You owe me, brother," muttered John. "I could be out riding."

And of Georgina there was no sign. However, when the tune ended, the party exchanged greetings, and Edward decided that maybe, for once, Mrs. Salmond was not entirely wrong. Reverend Donald McLeod was clothed with parsonly respectability. But he was a commanding man, and a handsome one. And either totally oblivious to the barbs flung his way by Mrs. Salmonds or so above them as not to notice.

At the first chance, Edward got, he asked: "But where is Miss Ross, this morning? My mother said something of her musical ability."

"She is sitting with her grandfather," said Mrs. Salmond. "She has no idea what is due to our guests."

"I shall wander up to go and sit with Mr. Frederick myself," said Edward. "He likes to see me." John might forgive him eventually.

"Excellent," said Arthur. "If you sit with him, Cousin Georgina can come and play for us."

"Hers is the loyalty of Ruth," said Reverend McLeod. "But I will play for you, in the meanwhile."

"I shall escort you upstairs," said Mrs. Salmonds.

"Please don't put yourself to such trouble," said Edward.

"It is no trouble, Captain Kelling," said Mrs. Salmonds, "Elvira will take you up."

And with that Edward had to be content. Well, accepting. He learned, on the walk upstairs, that the priest from the mission society was paying attention to poor Georgina. "And I daresay it will suit her very well. It is what she is accustomed to, after all. He is ever so good-looking," confided Elvira.

The best Edward could manage to this was: "Ah." Not one of his greatest conversational gambits, he thought.

"Oh, Georgina," Elvira said. "The Captain has said he will come and sit with Mr. Frederick so you can come and play for us."

"Good morning, Miss Georgina," said Edward. He'd been rehearsing that all morning. And it did produce a dimple for a moment in her cheek. She bowed her head slightly. "Good morning... Captain Edward. How was your fishing this morning?"

"How do you know he went fishing this morning?" asked Elvira.

"An educated guess," said Edward. "I fish most mornings at this time of year. Yesterday, today, tomorrow the same again. I was hoping you would stay for a little, Miss Georgina."

"I had better go," she said. "I feel I have left my aunt to entertain my guest."

"Your Aunt Edith?" said Frederick Weatherly. "Is she here?" Then he was distracted by Edward. "Morning, Edward. How are you, young man?" he asked.

"Bearing up, sir. All the better for a good morning on the river," said Edward. "I have come to talk to you and to play you a game of chess, if that takes your fancy."

"It does, indeed."

So, the girls left, and Edward was left alone with the master of Westmead House. After a few moves, he said, "I wish to ask you something, sir."

The old man took a pawn. "Ask away."

"I would like your permission to ask your granddaughter if she will marry me."

The old man nodded. "You know, it has been my wish for an alliance between our houses for many years."

"Thank you, sir," said Edward, reflecting to himself that he wasn't sure what he'd have said, if he'd got a 'no'. Probably gone ahead anyway. He was not sure how much Frederick Weatherly was fully compos but, well, he'd asked. And frankly, no matter what anyone said, Weatherly's permission had been more important to him than that aunt. And if both said no, he would still have tried.

When the old man fell asleep, he rang the bell, and the little maid that Jem had fetched up from Southampton came. He put his finger to his lips and pointed to Frederick Weatherly, asleep in his chair, the sun creeping in the window onto his veined hands, and got up and went down to the drawing-room. Someone was playing the piano-forte with some skill, now.

He expected it to be either the visiting priest, or Georgina. He was somewhat taken aback to find that it was the priest and Georgina, playing a duet on one instrument, her face intent with concentration. When they finished and the audience clapped, Georgina – quite pink with pleasure and the praise, bowed to her fellow-player. "Thank you. I enjoyed that so much! I used to play duets with my mother. I have missed it."

"It was my great pleasure, Miss Ross. You are a tribute to your mother's teaching."

Edward, who knew himself to have the musical talent of a brick, allowed himself a faint pang of jealousy. Well, he'd have to try harder. He just wasn't sure how.

They took their leave, and Edward braced himself for his brother's wrath. He was feeling a little low about it all.

"You know," his brother said, "You're not in a two-horse race brother. Arthur is being remarkable charming and solicitous to your girl."

"Arthur?" Edward felt his hackles rise.

"Yes," said John. "It made up for the music, watching that Mrs. Salmonds trying to play bodkin and insert those daughters of hers into the mix."

"Wonder if anyone has told her his local history?" Edward said, savagely. Women did seem to like Arthur. He was fashionable, talked of all the *on dits* of the London scene.

"Don't do it, boy," said John. "Nothing like a bit of resistance to make the game more attractive for them."

"I wasn't planning to," said Edward. "I might plant him a facer, though. I'm just surprised, because she's very popular with the servants."

"And then she'd think you a brute, sympathize with him, and tend his hurts. Women," said his brother. "They make horses look simple."

Edward could only nod in agreement.

Georgina's expedition that morning had not escaped notice. Mary picked up on the damp hem to the walking dress. She confessed to having escaped the house to walk alone. "I'm quite used to being able to be alone, Mary."

"That aunt of yours will have a fit," Mary informed her, speaking of Aunt Louisa as if she was a total stranger and had never been her employer. Georgina found the staff of Westmead House had closed ranks around her, to the point of awkwardness. It was touching, however, that they considered her theirs. Well, she wasn't. Dr. Selby had been frank with her. He was of the opinion, now, that besides the head injury and the damage that had inflicted, that her grandfather had suffered some form of apoplexy. "When I get him to squeeze both hands there is a marked weakness on the right, which was not there before. Miss Ross, these things are seldom solitary, I am afraid. It may well recur. There is no way of knowing when. His recovery has been remarkable. I recommend a gradual approach. Encourage him to walk short distances."

"He is dragging one foot a little too," she'd told him. That had made him look grave again.

One thing that she liked about the Reverend Donald McLeod, was that he was forceful enough to ride absolute roughshod over Aunt Louisa. Confident in himself, and the rightness of God's purpose for him, he was able to stare her down, and continue with what he set out to do. It worked with an angry and disapproving aunt, but... thinking of her own father, not always with those intent on murder and rapine. He shared many traits with her late father, she realized. And now he had formally asked her if she would be willing to marry him.

"I cannot leave my grandfather, sir," she'd answered, not knowing if that was with regret or not. She certainly had not – like her mother, tumbled headlong into love with this charismatic Scot. But she found him to be likeable and, well, he was something familiar.

"Indeed, I should not have asked had you shown any intent of doing so. But I too have spoken to the Doctor. And I believe you would be a great help to my mission. It is something we believe in. It is something we are called to."

She'd had to think about how to reply to this. Finally, she decided honesty was the best path. "It is something my father was called to. My mother... was called to love him so much that she went with him. I was just taken along. I was a child, and went where they went. I must be direct, Reverend McLeod. I do not know that I feel the same calling. Indeed, my father often called me frivolous and... well, I don't think he thought I was devout enough for it. And the truth be told, I don't know that I am! I loved certain aspects of Africa, but I also knew nothing else. And there is a part of me that really does not wish to go back. I am not my mother, sir. We are alike in some ways, but, but she loved my father, and knew him well, before they married."

"And this is not true of us," said McLeod regretfully. "You are perhaps seduced by the worldly trapping of this situation..."

"I doubt that," she said caustically. "I have almost nothing, and I am very aware of that. My time here is quite possibly fleeting. I know well enough I cannot depend on my aunt. I will have to seek a paid situation somewhere, which I know is not easy for a woman in my circumstances. Anyway, however comfortable it is here, I have been very happy with fairly little before. I believe I will learn to be again. I don't know, Reverend McLeod. I am indeed tempted by your offer, but I would be accepting it for what I believe are the wrong reasons."

He nodded slowly. "I cannot truthfully say that I love you, Miss Ross. But I do believe that love could grow between us. Should you change your mind, Miss Ross... I would be honored. The Society would certainly be willing to help in any way it can. There are few paid positions in our ranks: we offer our service as our gift to God. It may be however that we can put you in the way of a situation of some kind. We would be happy to commend you. Anyway, I shall be taking my leave of you. There is the night-mail to London..."

"I do not wish you to feel you must rush to leave, Reverend McLeod," said Georgina. To some extent this was heartfelt. He talked of things she was familiar with. Her aunt and cousins did not.

———※———

Arthur buttonholed her after lunch, suggesting a turn around the gardens. After a meal of platitudes and barbs interspersed with good country food, which really was not lobsters and caviar – which apparently, according to her aunt, should be served in a gentleman's house – even for breakfast, it seemed a welcome interlude.

Arthur took the opportunity, too, to press his suit. "Cousin Georgina," he said, having picked a quick posy of spring blooms and pressed them on her, "I have been waiting this age to have some time alone with you. As charming as your cousins are, I only have eyes for you."

Georgina smelled the flowers, looking for a suitable reply.

So, he went on, "The longer I spend with you, Cousin Georgina, the more certain I am that you are the only woman I wish to spend the rest of my life with. Please, smile on me Georgina? It is midsummer madness with me and it's only April."

Confused and rather alarmed by this, Georgina retreated into: "You hardly know me, cousin."

"I feel I have known you all my life," he declared. "I long to take you away from here, from waiting hand and foot on an old man. To make you mine. To let you enjoy life!"

If anything he had said set her against him, it was the idea of taking her away. Her grandfather might have improved, but he still needed her. "I can't go anywhere, Cousin Arthur. I must stay with my grandfather," she informed him.

He sighed. "Look, forgive me for being so impatient, but my Uncle Frederick has somewhat recovered. As much as he is likely to, Selby tells me. From what you say, he doesn't even know who you are, Georgina. And if he dies, well, it is plain to me that your aunt will not use you well. You told me yourself, that your circumstances are not good. Let me make all of that irrelevant, and you secure and comfortable, which you cannot be now. As my wife you'd enjoy a considerable independence and status. Married, there'd be no need for a chaperon."

"I know he's confused, but my mother would have wished me to stay with him," she said, resolutely. "And... and I know what Selby says, but I think he grows less confused. He has moments of some current memory. He knows Captain Kelling."

Arthur scowled. "I am surprised the fellow dares to go into his presence."

"He's been very kind. I think you are wrong about him," said Georgina, happy, honestly, to talk about anything else. She really did not know her feelings about her handsome cousin. He was just the sort of man every girl dreamed of. Elvira and Maude had said as much to her, so she wasn't alone in that. Only, when dreaming met up with reality... she somehow found herself less sure.

"I've known him all my life. He is a violent man."

Just at this point, they were interrupted by the arrival of Elvira and Maude, walking through the shrubbery. "La, Mr. Weatherly," said Elvira. "Lessing told us you were out here. For shame, Georgina. To think of your coming out here without a parasol."

"No wonder your complexion is so brown, Cousin," said Maude. "By the way, your grandfather is awake and asking for you."

"I must go," said Georgina. "Excuse me, Cousin," and she set off back to the house. She asked Lessing, when he opened the door, how long her grandfather had been calling for her for.

He shook his head. "I'd have sent a footman if he was, Miss."

She smiled mechanically at him, and went on in, anyway. If Maude wanted to chase her off from speaking to her cousin, she was not going back out to dispute with her about it. Besides, she found herself in an awkward position with Captain Edward Kelling. He'd shown himself willing to rise to her defense, and, in every contact but the first, had been nothing but a gentleman. And the first was... understandable, she thought. But for all she knew he might be a violent man. The servants were very full of stories about him climbing into the house and rescuing her grandfather, and saving the house from burning down. But then, they'd known him from a little boy. And she had had the story of Edward having a fist-fight with Arthur. They would have been children, then, but perhaps bad feelings endured.

She hadn't actually turned Arthur down. Well. She'd never thought much about a proposal of marriage, before. She'd daydreamed a bit, but out in the wilds of British Kaffraria it was likely to have been Hobson's choice, if it was anyone at all. And then with the war, father being stabbed, and his lingering illness and death, well, there had been little opportunity to think of such things. And now she had had two proposals in one day, and had, for reasons she was unwilling to confront entirely, not accepted either. Oh well, she had a book upstairs.

Later that day, Captain Edward Kelling did call, but he failed to be violent. She had had time to think about what she decided was his flirtatious behavior this morning, as she knew little of the same, and had decided to keep him at a distance and maybe give him something of a set-down. But the opportunity was not granted her. He was out of her social order, and really had no excuse for amusing himself at her expense, she thought, rather angrily.

They bade farewell to the Reverend McLeod late that afternoon. He pressed his card on her, saying that if she should reconsider – or if he could help in any way, to write to him as well as the mission society. By the time Georgina came up to bed she was heartily sick of her aunt lecturing her on throwing away her chances – while throwing her daughters at Cousin Arthur's head. She thought her day could get no worse... but it did.

"Miss," said Mary, eyes narrow, daggers being stared. "Someone has been rifling through your drawers!"

"What!" exclaimed Georgina, shocked, and it was to be admitted, both slightly frightened and wrathful.

Silently, Mary showed her. Mary had insisted on everything being neatly and precisely packed. The disorder was not huge, but definite. A sudden instinct made her look for the little tin box. It was missing. There was nothing much in it but the papers that Mr. Winter had thought irrelevant, and a lot of letters. It upset her, none-the-less.

"Who could it be?" said Georgina, looking at the door, instinctively. It had a key, but she had only locked it at night, and that only after the burglary.

Mary plainly read her thoughts. "No one climbing in the window, Miss. It has to be someone inside the house."

"But... what are they looking for? I mean, even my money is locked into the safe, and I have the key with me all the time. My trinkets... they're not worth anything really."

"We will check them, anyway," said Mary.

They did. Nothing was missing.

"When could they have done this? And who? It must be one of the servants... but, but I like them. I thought... they liked me?" said Georgina, feeling rather plaintive.

"They do, by the talk downstairs. And Mrs. Lessing, she'll have someone's head on a platter if she catches them," Mary informed her.

"I suppose it could be that... Elvira again."

"Again, Miss?" asked Mary.

So, Georgina had to tell the story. And then restrain the outraged Mary from going straight out and tugging caps with her. "We'll just have to keep the room locked if one of us is not in it. I suppose she could have just been looking for something to make mischief with. I can't think I have anything else of value to steal."

"I'd like to bend the poker over her head. Or hit her with me smoothing iron," said Mary, crossly. "I'll just be going to get me things, Miss." Mary's determined 'my' disappeared when she was worked up. "I'll spend the night in the truckle bed in the dressing room."

"But Mary, I will lock the door," protested Georgina.

"And it is no use thinking that'll disturb your walk in the early morning, because I am under strict orders to go with you. He says it's not decent," said Mary primly.

"Who said?" demanded Georgina. "Who did you tell, Mary?" she was quite angry at being betrayed.

"Not a word to a soul did I breathe, Miss," said Mary, righteously. "It was that Penn that told me I ought to be with you! And a rare trimming he give me for letting you go without me!"

"What?" she exclaimed, incredulously.

"Oh yes," said Mary, "when they come over today, he calls me aside. He stands there with his hands on his hips and tells me he'll not have his future mistress spoken of as if she was some light-skirt when you gets caught, which you was bound to."

"It was purely an accident, and E... Captain Kelling was the perfect gentleman."

Mary nodded. "He would be, I reckon," she said, approvingly.

"Mary, I am not making up to... or... or setting my cap to Captain Kelling. He's well above my station," she said, sternly.

Mary laughed. "Lawks, Miss. It's him making up to you. They're complaining that he never brings any fish back to the big house nowadays."

Georgina blushed. "I did say I liked fish. But it is unsuitable, Mary. I have nothing, and his parents would be most upset. And they... especially Lady Elizabeth, have been so kind to me. Anyway, I am sure he means nothing by it. He is just being kind. Not another word," she said, sternly, seeing Mary's lips open to challenge this one. "Or I'll have to ask what you mean by being alone with Penn."

She was surprised and amused to see Mary color. "We was just talking," she said gruffly. "And now I'll get me things."

Georgina, who had been more than a little uncertain about going on what seemed like an arranged assignation – even with her maid, resolved that she'd have to have words with Captain Edward Kelling about his groom. It gave her something else to think about, besides the missing tin box. But, why take that? Maybe to search it at their leisure?

Chapter 12

The morning dawned foggy enough for bed to seem tempting to Edward. He said as much to Penn, who had everything ready in the stables.

His groom shook his head. "I promised I'd have you at the water, Captain. Yon giglet would have my tripes out if I got her up at this time o' day for nowt."

"Who are you referring to?" said Edward, looking at him askance. "I hope you are not..."

"Mary. Her maid," said Penn, interrupting. "Now we need to mount and go, Captain. I wants to have the fire burning nicely."

"You've been conspiring, Penn," said Edward, following instructions.

"Aye. Someone has to," said Penn with a nod, urging his horse into a trot.

Edward, torn somewhat between annoyance at having his affairs interfered with, and gratitude that, obviously, Penn had arranged for

Georgina to come down to the water, rode with him through the curling fog.

When they got to the little shed, Edward noticed that Penn had brought, instead of just having the food in a little flat box in a saddle-bag, a basket, and had two saddlebags as well. "What's this Penn? A feast?" He was amused and a little surprised, but also... well, Penn could hardly have organized this on his own. Someone in the kitchens had to know.

Penn nodded. "Just fit to set before a lady, Captain. Now I'll get to the fire, if you'll be so good as to set out the cushions."

"Cushions, Penn?"

"Aye. Jem's rib said you can't have a lady sit on them rough benches," said Penn, working expertly with his tinder-box.

"How many of you are in this?" asked Edward, taking two cushions out, and realizing there was a white cloth to set on their rough table.

"About half of us, I reckon," said Penn. "Of course, we wouldn't have done it without your lady mother's say so, Captain."

Edward could only stare at his groom, now setting out plates and knives, forks and spoons on the table. "My mother?"

"Oh aye. Betty says she thought it was charming."

"Does everyone know my business?" asked Edward, some edge in his voice.

"Now, Master. I didn't squeak beef on you. Happen your brother did. He told your mother. And then Betty sets Jem on me. What am I to do? We was thinking you were finding the way pretty rough, so we'd help. Her maid will come down with her, so it's all respectable like."

"You could have told me. I could have dressed for the occasion."

"You'd not have slept," said his groom. "And we want you at your best."

Edward had to laugh. "What is she going to say to this?"

Penn cocked his head. "Well, you'll find out soon enough."

Georgina found that Mary had beaten her into wakefulness, and had brought a small brazier up so she could wash. Mary insisted on dressing her hair, too. "This is hardly a formal dinner, Mary."

"You'd better take a shawl, Miss. It's cold and dark at this heathenish hour. Well, let us be off then."

"It's to be hoped we can get out."

"I've seen to that, Miss," Mary informed her.

They locked the bedroom door behind them, and Mary led her to the front door, produced the key from her apron, let them out, and carefully locked the door behind them. There was barely a breath of wind and the fog clung about the dark shadows of the trees as they walked down the drive and onto the path to the river.

"How did you get the key?" Georgina asked.

"I had it from Lessing. That Penn..." Mary shook her head.

"Goodness. Does Lessing know about this?"

"He says he doesn't want to," admitted Mary. "My, it's half-dark and quiet, Miss. I'd be affrighted on my own."

She sounded as if she was, anyway. "Take my hand," Georgina said. "It's getting lighter."

They passed the section of water where she'd seen Edward the twice before. There was no-one there. "I think we might be before them. This is a good twenty minutes earlier than I was here before," said Georgina.

"Indeed, I'll be killing that Penn if they're not here," said Mary. "My, it's cold."

"Well, that looks like firelight ahead," said Georgina, comforted by the idea of it, herself.

They came around the bend in the path, to see a dark structure, and someone kneeling at the fire. And Edward Kelling, feeling his collar. "Good morning Miss Georgina," he said. "I'll have you know this is not my idea... but I am still very glad to see you."

She blinked at the scene, the fire, a laid table with a white cloth and crockery and cutlery set on it, tasseled cushions on the rough bench. There were even flowers in a vase on the table. "G...Good morning, Captain Edward." Feeling she had to say something, and feeling rather overwhelmed. "This looks very, um, nice, for, for you fishermen."

He laughed. "Penn and I have been known to eat out of the pan. This is for you, Miss Georgina."

She bit her lip, looking at it. She was, despite herself, deeply touched by it all. No one had ever done anything even vaguely like this for her. "It is just so lovely. I... don't know what to say."

"Spanking good, I calls it," said Mary, approvingly, moving over to the fire and warming her hands.

"Will you let me seat you, Miss Georgina?" Edward asked, taking her elbow, and leading her to the bench.

Georgina was aware that it had been set up to charm her. Perhaps even to seduce her. Well, she wasn't about to be seduced, but she was charmed. She might have been ill at ease, had she been alone, had Captain Kelling sat next to her or something. But he sat down opposite, and smiled at her in the most disturbing way. The sky was paling, but the mist still hung over the river. Somewhere in the copse behind them a lark began a few trial notes.

"Coffee, Miss?" asked Penn, rising from the fire with a blackened coffee-pot, that had plainly seen much service. It was so familiar that it brought a lump to her throat. All she could do was nod.

"What's wrong?" asked Edward, noticing.

She swallowed. "Nothing is wrong. It is just the coffee-pot... we had one just like that for the trips back to Grahamstown. It took a few days with the wagon. I... I loved it. It was very exciting when I was a little girl. It just brought back so many memories."

"My dear Georgina... I wish you will tell me."

"What, Captain Edward?" She ignored the familiarity because of his obvious concern.

"Well, everything, really. But about your life, your family," he said.

And somehow, she found herself talking about the emptiness, the sky full of stars, the vast thunderstorms, of the sounds of lions somewhere off in the darkness. Of her parents, of the singing in the little stone and thatch Church up against the mountain. Of the teaching that was such a part of their lives. Of little things. She found him easy to talk to. He spoke a little of Spain, which he said helped him to understand. She did not touch on the killing, devastation and death. He did not, except peripherally, touch on the war he'd been sent to serve in, or his wounding. Instead he brought up several incidents that made her laugh. Somehow, they had wandered onto talk about books.

Penn brought strawberries and cream to follow the coffee, and then set to frying bacon and mushrooms and fish – ordering poor Mary around. She was smiling – and giving as good as she got, Georgina noticed.

Georgina found she had discovered someone she hadn't even known she needed. A friend. Someone that it was no effort to talk to, that she felt no particular need to keep at a distance, or fear her ignorance of this world would make her a target. With that trust established talk moved onto the worst parts. Not all of it, yet, but things she just had not talked of.

"You've been through the mill, and back again," he said sympathetically, having listened. "I can tell... there's more."

"Being alone and scared," she said. "A far cry from this." The sun had burned off the fog, and the day was as bright and full of spring promise as could be.

"Ah, but you might still get murdered in your bed, according to your aunt" said Edward with a smile. "Really, though, it's normally very tranquil out here."

"Well, I had someone rifle through my possessions, and steal the little tin box from my trunk, yesterday. It only has my mother's letters in it, so they are bound to be disappointed, but it was still upsetting to Mary and I."

He looked completely nonplussed. "Who could have... I mean I am sorry, but it must be one of your new staff. The older ones... look, around here, they'd sooner starve than steal."

"We think it must be that... Elvira. She's... done that to me before."

"Good gracious. The sooner you can send your relations packing the better," said Edward, crossly.

Georgina pulled a wry face. "It is awkward because her mother is my legal guardian, until I come of age. But I must admit I wish she had not come up from Southampton."

"Well, lock your door, and try not to hit her with the poker, Georgina, tempting though it may be! We'd rather not have any murders in beds here."

"I lock the door now. It must have been when we went down to dinner. And I do sleep with the poker at my bedside, Edward," she informed him. Somehow, they'd slipped into being 'Edward' and 'Georgina'. "So, I am more ready there, than elsewhere. If, of course, we were to be murdered in the breakfast parlor, I might not have a poker to hand. I might be forced to take after them with a fish."

He gave a shout of laughter. "I will have to see you always have a fish to hand."

"Well, I think it is a bit late for fish, judging by what my grandfather has said of it," she said, looking at the sparkling water. "We had better get back, before the household is all up."

"Old Lessing promised me he'd send the footman if your grandfather stirred. That other lot don't get up before ten," Penn informed her, as she stood up, and Edward hastened around the table to offer his arm.

She could only gape at the groom. "What?"

He looked at her, righteously. "You don't think we'd be doing something havey-cavey do you, Miss?"

"There is nothing quite as sanctimonious as an ex-poacher turned respectable," said Edward, laughing. "And they have all conspired against us, Georgina. Or rather, for us."

"I'm just looking after the reputation of my master's wife," Penn informed her in lofty tones. "Or I would be, if he'd get around to asking you."

Startled by this, Georgina took a couple of steps back, which proved her undoing, as the table and rough benches were set on a low bank above the Bourne. She realized the ground under her was giving way, and there was nothing metaphorical about that. Plainly, Edward, who was standing nearest to her, saw what was happening, and threw himself to her aid. Unfortunately, that just made the subsiding bank collapse completely, depositing the two of them into the water.

It was fortunately not very deep water – a few inches, and, as she landed on top of her substantial would-be rescuer, she was barely wet, beyond her feet and the bottom edge of her petticoats and dress. The water was very cold and the fall a shock – which was why she lay safe in his protecting arms for a moment.

"Are you all right, Georgina?" he asked.

"I... I am fine," she said, looking down into his concerned face.

"Then perhaps we should get out of the river. There is cold water coming down my back," he said, not actually showing any signs of letting go.

"I would, but then you would have to stop holding me," she said, still looking down at him, unable to move, and... not entirely wanting to.

"Ah. Well, we'll just have to stay here, then," he said as Penn splashed down into the stream too, to help them out. "Hang on, let me sit up." He managed to do that, putting her onto his lap. "Don't get up. You'll get as wet as I am! Put your arms around my neck. Here, Penn, help me up."

And he stood up, Penn lending him aid, with her in his arms. He stood there, feeling for balance, looking at the collapsed bank, and then looking at her.

"I could walk," she said. "My shoes are rather wet already, and it seems quite shallow. Unless you plan to wade out into midstream and drop me in as punishment for getting you so wet?"

That made him laugh. And hold her a little tighter. "Never. Well, I did push Gussie in, when we were toddlers, my mother will inform you. But she took my little bucket. And I don't have a bucket any more."

That made her laugh, despite the situation. "None-the-less," Edward continued, "Penn is right. I have been trying to find a way to ask you... I didn't want to frighten you off... you seem very like a shy bird, my dear Georgina. Look, I have wanted to ask you to marry me since... since you came upon me fishing. And well, the more I have come to know you, the better I like you. I want to spend my life doing that," he said awkwardly, but still not letting go of her. "I want to ask if you would consider marrying me, even if I am the sort of big oaf who falls into a stream with you. I will try to understand if you say no. And I know you can't leave your grandfather, and I would not ask that. But I would ask you to be my wife, one day, when you are ready." He swallowed. "I don't have a great deal to offer but my heart, but you have all of that. Georgina, please say yes?"

This was quite a different proposal from the other two, and not just because he was holding her above the water. There was an enormous earnestness in his voice, and his eyes were fixed on her... well, as if he was quite unaware that he was standing in a river.

"Yes," she said, wondering quite what had come over her.

"I am the happiest man on earth," he announced, and kissed her.

"Captain! Come out of the river!" said Penn, impatiently.

"And you shouldn't be kissing Miss Georgina!" exclaimed Mary from the bank.

"Why not?" asked Edward. "We have just become betrothed. It is customary to kiss on that occasion. Besides, I have been wanting to do so for days. I hope she gets used to it, because I would like to do it again." And he did, and she found that she'd raised her face to be kissed.

"Come out of the river and to the fire, Captain," said Penn. "I've a towel, for my lady's feet."

He nodded. "Give me your arm, and we'll get up the bank over there. I don't want to drop Georgina in the mud too. She might change her mind."

They struggled ashore, and he carried her over to the fire, where Penn and Mary had hastily set one of the benches, and put her down, and sat next to her, taking her hand, as Mary made haste to dry her feet with the rough towel Penn had run to fetch from a hook in the shed.

Gathering her wits, Georgina looked at him and made a brave speech, not quite bringing herself to let go of his hand. "Edward. I cannot possibly marry you. You know my circumstances. I am just a poor mission-station girl. What would your parents say?"

"Well," he said, "As my mother was behind Penn's organizing of this picnic breakfast, and I told her I had fallen headlong in love with you, and she approved, very much, I don't see a problem. And your grandfather gave me his blessing... family should not stand in our way, my love."

He paused. "But... My circumstances may," he said awkwardly. "I will understand if you cry off because of that. I must be honest. I am not a man of any great means. Our estate was left to my father grossly encumbered. He's done his best to bring it about, but we're not wealthy, and my inheritance is likely to be small. And, frankly, I hope I don't see it for many years. But I promise I will find some form of employment. I have already directed a few letters to contacts of father's, making enquiries." He grimaced. "I am afraid it will probably mean the city. But I should manage to have the means to support a wife, if not in the style I would like to give you, at least in reasonable comfort."

She understood perfectly well that he planned to do this, so she could enjoy a life of relative wealth. She was shocked by the idea. "No," she informed him firmly. "You must not give up your way of life for me."

"I don't have that many other options, Georgina. I am rather large for a laborer's cottage," he said regretfully. "And I must provide a reasonable life for you, and I will not live on charity. And we can come down on visits."

She shook her head at him. "My mother packed and followed my father to Africa. We lived very humbly, Edward. I have never in my life lived as I have here. I do not expect it. And I can cook and clean and wash and iron too. I do not wish you to live somewhere and do something you disliked, just for me. You, I think, are a country man, just as my Cousin Arthur is a city man. I... I do not think I am a city person myself. I remember my horror in Southampton. So many people, and I didn't know any of them. I like living where I know people, and they know me."

"And you'd like getting home and getting properly dry before you catch your death," said Mary, firmly. "Master Edward and you can argue about this... tomorrow. I'll bring you down. But you need dry shoes and petticoats."

"She's right, you know," said Edward, still not letting go of her. "We'll sort it out. Together. Together, I believe we can do anything. I never quite understood what a difference it could make. You've made me a very happy man. May I tell my mother?"

"You can tell anyone you please," said Mary, tugging at Georgina's arm. "But I'm taking her away afore she gets an infection of the lungs."

"I'll walk with you," said Edward, "Unless, unless we mount you on my horse. Thing is, I don't have a side-saddle."

"The sun is out. It's barely three hundred yards," said Georgina. "We will walk. And there is no need to accompany us. You should get dry before you get sick, Edward."

He laughed and let go of her hand, and stood up. She felt oddly bereft. How had she got used to something like that so quickly? But he helped her up, and took her arm instead. "I get wet all the time. I fall in the river regularly."

"I had been wanting to learn to fish," she said, smiling up at him. "But now I am less keen. It was cold."

"Ah, but the catches you can make," he said, squeezing her hand. "Look at what I got today."

She'd discovered his humor was catching. She looked mischievously up at him. "I can catch that kind of fish regularly, without getting wet, or muddy. I caught two, only yesterday. Not ones I wanted to keep, though," she said hastily.

"My brother said he thought I wasn't the only fish in your stream, Georgina. Well now. That flatters me a great deal. I was very sad I wasn't musical. And Arthur too. Well, I am very glad you didn't take him."

"He says you are very violent. And he is quite right. You break stream-banks," she informed him.

"I haven't punched him for years," said Edward. "But he plainly remembers it. I did darken both his daylights for him, but he made my nose bleed. I must have been about nine or ten. He was a little older and larger than me back then. But it amazes me that you got here without a dozen proposals."

"I had never had one before. Well, Arthur. He even got a special license!"

He shook his head. "Tch. They must be a slow bunch down in Africa. Or your father was a very frightening man."

That made her laugh again. "He could be alarming, I suppose. He was a big man and, well, when he was aroused, loud. But he was the gentlest person you could ever meet. A bit like Mr. Tadswell, you just had to say a word in Greek and he would be distracted."

"Ah, Tadswell. I wonder if he still thinks I did it," said Edward, shaking his head. "I will follow various leads on that matter, my darling. And I shall come and visit later, when I am dry and dressed, with my mother, I suspect. If I had the foresight of Arthur, and had a special license we could have made use of your priest-visitor. But I think it better if we are just betrothed, and do everything in the fullness of time, as little as I want to wait."

"Reverend McLeod left last night, on the night mail. I think you would have liked him, Edward. He is a good man, if somewhat driven."

"If you say he's a good man, I'll accept it," said Edward. "Now, do we sound the knocker and wake the house?"

"I have the key," said Mary.

But that too proved un-needed. Lessing opened the door as they mounted the last step, throwing it open, regally. "Good morning, Miss. Captain Edward."

Mary looked at the key in her hand. "Two keys," said Lessing, with a benevolent smile, looking at the fact that Georgina still had her hand holding Edward's as well as her arm locked in his. He looked enquiringly at the two of them. "May I have the honor of wishing you both very happy?"

"You may, but we'll not sound it out, yet, Lessing." Edward pointed upstairs. "There's those who might make things difficult for Miss Ross. And I won't have that."

Lessing nodded. "Mum is the word, Captain. But I can say there's no-one below-stairs who would wish you anything but the very best." He looked at the step, behind Edward: "You appear a little wet, Captain. Can we...

"I took a little dunk in the Bourne. A baptism, you might say," he said with a grin. "I will be off home, and get dry and changed." He released her arm and bowed over her hand and kissed it. "Until later, Georgina."

"Good-bye, Edward," she said, looking up at his broad, smiling face, and smiling back at him. And then, suddenly she found herself leaning in and kissing him. In front of them all! She quite shocked herself, but she found that none of the small audience seemed to feel the same way, especially not the man she kissed. So, this was what being in love was like. She quite understood why her mother had left her comfortable life, and gone off to Africa. "I will see you soon?" she asked, blushing fiercely.

"As soon as I can," he reassured her. "But I will have to go and talk to my dear family now. It will probably be this afternoon, as my father has a landowners meeting for the Hunt, and m'mother has to be there to do the pretty. I'll get myself home now, though, and see."

"And do get dry and warm," she said.

"Yes," said Mary, suddenly reminded of her duties. "Both of you. Come Miss. We need to get you changed."

Upstairs, she heard him whistling cheerfully and loudly as he walked down the drive to where Penn, following, had led the horses. He probably didn't even know he was whistling, she realized. He just sounded happy, and most likely all of Westmead House could hear him.

She submitted to being washed and dried and dressed by a Mary who was quite overcome by the excitement of it all, and wanted to repeat every moment of it, and, actually she wanted to talk about it too. She didn't think the chances of Mary being able to keep all the drama to herself were very high. But as it sounded like Lessing at least was in on it, which would mean his wife likely was, as well as some of the staff at Bournelea, keeping it secret was probably impossible.

She went in to her grandfather. His valet had already been in attendance, and he was awake and looking, she thought, better. "Would you like to sit in your chair again?" she asked.

"You're looking very happy this morning," he said, a faint crease between his eyebrows, as if he was struggling to think of something.

"Oh I am. It's just the most beautiful morning," and she bent over and kissed his cheek. She was feeling very like kissing people, this morning, she reflected.

That made him smile. Then suddenly he said: "You're not Dorothea, are you?"

Her heart fell. Was this where she was turned out of the house? She did not wish to leave him, but if he was recovering his memory, he would no longer need her, and would be in good hands. And, well, she would be free to marry. "No sir. Dorothea was my mother. I am your granddaughter."

He looked at her, long and hard. And then sighed. "This memory of mine is so cloudy still. I keep feeling I must remember..."

She could see it was agitating him, so she set about soothing him, talking calmly. "It is a great deal better than it was, sir. Dr. Selby will be very pleased with you."

His eyes narrowed slightly. "You are Georgina, aren't you?"

"Yes, sir. That is my name," she admitted.

"She wrote to me about you," he said, and closed his eyes, and rubbed his head, touching on the fierce scar. "I should have..."

"Everything will be all right," she said as calmingly as she could.

His answer was: "Winter!"

It puzzled her for a moment, as it was bright sunlight outside. Then it occurred to her. "You mean Mr. Winter, sir?"

"Thaddeus Winter. Yes. He'll know what to do," he said.

"I will send for him directly, Grandfather. He has been to visit you twice."

"I will write to him," he said. "He's the right man. Knows how to keep his tongue between his teeth. I don't want it getting out." He sighed. "A judgement on me, I think. Let me rest a bit, girl. I need to think. And send that man of mine to me. I'll go down to my study."

"Should, should you go so far? I can bring anything you need up to you," she asked.

"I could never write in bed."

There was a tap on the door, and one of the footmen came in with a breakfast tray, closely followed by the valet. "The master seems more alert today," that individual commented.

"My head is still half full of cloud. But some things are clearer now, Sanders. Now girl, stand over there, let me have a look at you."

So, she did, conscious of being stared at. At length, he said: "Like... but unlike. Is your mother here, girl? I think I remember her being here?"

She shook her head, and said in a quiet voice: "My mother is dead, sir. There's only me. You...you thought I was her, when I was caring for you. It seemed to comfort you."

He stared at her again. Eventually he sighed. "Never leave things until it is too late."

"Can I pour you some coffee, sir?" she asked more to try and stop him staring, than anything else.

It did bring a slight smile to his lined face. "You're a good girl, but Sanders will serve me. You will go and have your own breakfast. You're too thin."

So, Georgina took herself away. She was not in the least hungry, but to completely absent herself from the breakfast parlor would occasion comment, so she went down.

Only Arthur was there, which was something of a surprise, because he was not an early riser. "Good morning, Cousin Arthur."

He waved from around a piece of sirloin. Then, when he had finished chewing, he greeted her. He seemed somewhat abstracted, but asked how his uncle did.

"So very much better this morning. He seems to be regaining his memory."

Arthur looked grave. "That is very worrying. I have tried to be tactful about it, but his bitterness about your mother has always concerned me. He never forgave her for marrying your father, against his wishes. Never forgave his sister, my sainted aunt, either. They had been quite close. Georgina... I must renew my suit. Should he turn you out... it is a very harsh world out there, for a penniless young woman. Please, for your own sake, marry me. I have the special license. We could be married today and I could protect you, provide for your security. What are you going to do if he turns you out? It is no use thinking Mrs. Salmonds would care for you. It so unfortunate she came here, and I cannot think why she did. She will plague you, use you as a servant or throw you out. As my wife you would be secure. Safe from her."

She took a firm hold of the coffee pot. "Thank you for your concern," she said coldly, wondering if she should tell him that, actually, she was an affianced woman now. "But I do not believe we would suit."

"You're hanging out for something better with Edward Kelling! Let me tell you its not marriage he means. He's a philanderer and..."

At this point, Lessing entered. She had the comforting notion that he had done so on purpose, for he did not seem to have any reason, except to enquire if she wanted anything further. A quick glance at the table and she saw the opening. "Could I have some of that excellent marmalade, Lessing. The toast looks to be still warm."

"You shall have it in an ant's foot, Miss. And I shall send the footman in to lay a fresh place."

There was no need for that, but the effect was to make Arthur leave his plate and storm out.

"Goodness," said Maude, coming in, as he brushed past. "Have you had a tiff with him? I am so terribly bored, and he's the only thing that makes this place habitable. I wanted to have him to show me some dance steps, if you will come and play for us later." She had no compunction about speaking whatever was on her mind in front of the servants, treating them as if they were so much furniture.

"Mr. Arthur Weatherly has asked for a horse to be got ready for him. I believe it is his intent to ride into Winchester," Lessing informed her.

"Oh, that is just too bad of him. After he came to mama and said she must come and stay with you, so he could see more of us!"

"When did he do that?" asked Georgina, remembering something Maude had said about being visited, which just hadn't registered before.

"Why just after we got the note from Elvira, bragging that she was mixing with all sort of grand people. A hum, if you ask me! John Kelling was positively ignoring her yesterday. And Edward barely looked in. I thought there'd be parties and picnics."

"Picnics," said Georgina, digesting all of this, and unable to resist, with a quick glance to Lessing. "Can be very damp." Lessing turned his face hastily away.

"Yes," agreed Maude. "And the wind may blow and upset your hair. Do you like the new way I have dressed mine? It's the latest mode."

Georgina made suitable noises, and had a cup of tea and a sliver of toast, while Maude, and then her mother and Elvira enjoyed their breakfast.

Edward rode home with a song in his heart, not at all dampened by the fact he was almost wet through. He washed, changed, and went in search of his family. "Well, I have news for you," he informed them, cheerfully. "That was a capital scheme of yours, Mother. I must tell you Georgina and I are going to be married. And she is quite the most wonderful girl in the world. Not even dunking her in the Bourne put her off.

"So that's what I did wrong," said John, laughing, and coming to shake his hand. "You two will suit, I think."

"It is a bit early for champagne, but I still think it would be an excellent idea!" said his father. "That should finally make the old fellow happy."

"And it makes me very happy," said his mother, wiping away a tear before hugging him.

"Georgina was very worried you would not approve," he said.

"Well, I wouldn't, but it gets you out of the house," said his father, beaming. "When is this to happen?"

"You won't get rid of me quite yet. Georgina obviously wants to look after her grandfather, and I need to find some sort of gainful employment," said Edward.

His mother said: "That can wait. Now sit down. Get that champagne, Gerald. I want to hear ALL the details."

Edward spent the next half hour being grilled and reducing his family to a great deal of helpless laughter, and drinking several toasts. It was only when the butler came in to remind them that they were expecting morning guests that Edward was told by his father, that one of the tenants who lived next to the London road, had seen someone riding the chestnut on early Sunday morning. They did not recognize the person hunched in a riding cloak, but they knew the horse, and where it came from.

"Turns out Smedley knows the fellow that sold the nag, and who bought it, and went and asked if they still had it. They don't, but it was sold to the owner of the Green Boar near Overton."

That was about eight miles distant. Edward didn't know it, but John did. "It's popular with the cocking crowd. They'll even get a few people from London."

"I'll go and see if they can tell me who hired it," said Edward.

"You'll do nothing of the kind," his father informed him. "I have sent a note to Tadswell already. You'll stay away from it and not aggravate his suspicions! He doesn't need any help with that. I'll write a list of other contacts you can sound out about employment, Son. And it wouldn't hurt you to write to Mr. Winter. Firstly, he ought to know, and secondly he's a devilish canny fellow and knows a fair number of people."

So, Edward had a rather tiresome morning of writing letters that he really did not enjoy... and occasionally stopped to think of his early morning. It still made him smile, and made the letter writing seem worth-while.

He prepared himself with great care for the afternoon visit to Westmead House. His parents were primed not to make things difficult for Georgina with that woman who was, as far as the law was concerned, her guardian.

Georgina, on going back upstairs, got something more of a window into the kind of man her grandfather had been before being struck down. Before this, he had been confused but somewhat grateful for her care. Now... well, he was getting up.

"We can bring a desk up here," said Georgina, thinking that the loss of his precious snuff-boxes and this bowl, which he'd apparently cherished, might upset him. She was also worried about the exertion it would require of him, because she could tell he was not going to put up with being carried.

He looked at her from under his heavy brows, and shook his head. "Young lady, I know I've had my notice to quit. But there are things to be dealt with before the finishing post in this race. I will be going downstairs."

Georgina looked straight back at him, just as stern. "We have been trying to keep you alive and get you better. It has been a hard fight, and Dr. Selby did not think we'd win. Don't overdo things and make us lose now!" She stamped her foot.

It made him smile slightly. "You've inherited my temper by the looks of it, girl. Tell me, my daughter... did she speak well of me, ever?"

That took the wind out of her sails. "Yes," she said, quietly. "She wanted to see you again, very much."

He was silent for a while. And then said: "One makes mistakes. I need to go downstairs to my library. I have letters to write."

She recognized an implacable determination in him. "Very well, sir. But I insist you let me call the footman to assist you. It won't help you if you fall on the stairs."

He looked at her askance: "You insist, do you?"

"Yes. I do. Mother would never have forgiven me if I did not."

He snorted. "And that is important to you?"

"More than you will ever know." And here she was, getting into a brangle with him, getting him upset, which Selby had said not to do.

"You are wrong, you know. Well, call a footman, then."

So, she did, and in an anxious cavalcade they made their way down-stairs – slowly, with him leaning heavily on the footman, until they reached the library. He sat down in his chair with some relief, and barely had he done so than Lessing appeared, with a tray and some Madeira. "I am pleased to see you where you belong, sir," he said setting the tray down. "A very good day it has been, if I may say so."

The old man took a glass of wine, tasted it. "The seventeen? You must feel this an exceptional day, Lessing."

"It is, sir," said Lessing with a smile to Georgina.

The wine seemed to revive him, slightly. "Well, I am glad you think so, Lessing." He turned to Georgina. "I will just sit for a few moments, and then write some letters. No need for you to stay, my dear. Go out and enjoy the sunshine."

"I had a wonderful walk this morning, sir. If you have no objection, I will fetch my book and go and sit and read in the corner."

"Early riser, are you?"

"Yes, sir." Hoping to divert his mind, she said. "The river was beautiful. I saw some fish rising."

It did bring a reminiscent look to his eyes, but he said: "Still. No need for you to sit cooped up with an old man."

"It would make me happy, Grandfather. Please. I will be quiet."

He looked at her with just a hint of a wry smile. "You've a habit of getting your own way, have you? Very well, girl. But it's not what I intend for you."

She went and fetched her book, hoping that he might have dozed off, from the exertion. She was finding him very hard to read, in this recovery of his. Still, he had, so far, shown no signs of taking his conflict with her mother – or her father, out on her. On her return he was busily writing, and she said nothing, but found a straight-backed chair and settled into read, with just occasional glances out of the window, thinking of her early morning.

At length he finished. Sat there with his fingers steepled, looking at the table where the Chinese bowl had apparently stood. Then he sighed. "Call Lessing for me, girl. Georgina, eh? She and her brother George were very close."

She went and tinkled the bell, and said, "Yes, Mother talked to me a great deal about him. He wrote..."

"And I never did," her grandfather said. "Stubborn pride. A folly."

Lessing came, plainly feeling any calls from the master were far too important for a footman, and her grandfather handed him the sealed letter. "The groom is to take it to Winter immediately," he informed him.

After he left, her grandfather sat in his chair, with his eyes closed for a while. She wondered if he had gone to sleep. Then he opened his eyes and looked at her. "That footman. The one who helped me down the stairs. I can't remember him."

"He is new. I hired him, sir. On Mr. Winter's instructions."

"Hmm. Winter. So, you know him, do you?"

"I have met him several times. He's been to see you every time he has called."

"Excellent. He is a better man for the job than that old woman Lawrence. Mind you, I'll have to write to both."

"Can I get you some tea or something first?" she asked. "You need to rest and recover. It will wait." She wondered how she could explain that Dr. Selby at least would at least have to certify to the attorney that her grandfather was in full command of his faculties again. He certainly seemed to be, if tired.

"Mawdling my insides with tea... no. Oh, you would like some, would you, girl? Call for it."

"If you would have a cup with me?" she asked.

He assented and got her to sharpen his quill for him. But before the tea could arrive, so did her aunt, who walked in to the library without as much as a knock. "The footman said you were hiding out in here. Come to the drawing room at once and play for the girls. They are wanting to practice their dancing..."

"Who are you, and what do you mean by barging into my library, woman?" said her grandfather coldly, surveying her as if she were a black-beetle.

Aunt Louisa drew herself up. "I am Mrs. Salmonds."

"And who is that to me? How dare you just walk in to my library, and order my granddaughter around! Get out! No. Stop. Explain yourself. What are you doing here, woman?"

"I am here to chaperone my niece. And I find your tone offensive. I am her legal guardian."

Her grandfather stood up, and Georgina rushed over to him, worried by the alarming choler in his face. "She is my granddaughter. I, not you, am her guardian, and I will decide who is a suitable chaperone, and whether she needs one. Now get out!"

"Please sit down, Grandfather," said Georgina. "Please go away, Aunt Louisa. You are upsetting him."

"Shall I remove this... person, Master?" asked Lessing, in an arctic tone, from the doorway, where he and the housemaid bearing the tea-tray stood, as if rooted to the spot.

Aunt Louisa looked in horror at the butler. Then she turned on Georgina. "I have never been treated like this in my life! Thankless child! I will not spend another hour under this roof!" she shrieked, turning, almost sending the tea-tray flying, as she stormed out.

There was a moment of a frozen tableaux, for the rest of them. Then Georgina said, with as much calm as she could muster. "Please sit down, Grandfather. I won't let her upset you any further. And could you set the tea down, Sarah. That will be all, Lessing. Please close the door on your way out."

After the door closed, her grandfather still stood there, holding the edge of his desk. "Please sit down, grandfather," she said patting his arm.

He did, slowly. She poured tea. After a few moments he said. "Have I done ill, child? I have a terrible temper at times, something I have learned to regret. Shall I call her back and apologize? Did I misread the situation? Tell me, honestly."

She stood in thought, and then shook her head. "No. I think it would be a good thing if she left, and... well, I will go, just now, when we have drunk tea, and try and make peace, but I think we will go on famously without her."

"Has she been caring for you?" he asked.

"She did not quite throw me out onto the street, but she wanted to. Her husband... is a better sort of man. He stopped her, and arranged for me to send a letter to you."

"Is he here too? I would speak with him," said her grandfather.

"No. He's a sea-captain, and away at sea just now. I don't think he would have let her come here, by something the girls said." She passed him his tea.

He took a sip of it, and then said. "I think you have a great deal to tell me, Georgina. But yes, I will need to find a suitable chaperone for you. I am too old to go to London or to parties."

"I have no desire for either," she said, her heart beating rather fast. "I really don't want my aunt here. She, she was my father's half-sister and she always disliked him and resented his... his spending his inheritance the way he did."

"She is plainly unsuitable. I promised your mother I would see to it. No... Young Edward Kelling. I will get him to ask Lady Kelling if she knows of anyone suitable. A good sort of woman." He paused and looked thoughtful. "Edward... I have some memory of him being here." His forehead wrinkled with effort, thinking.

"Yes. He has been in to see you on most days, Grandfather. And, and he and his parents are coming to call this afternoon." She was aware that she was blushing to the roots of her hair. "And, and his mother cared for you when you were injured, after Edward carried you out of the house. You must thank her, sir."

He looked at her quizzically. "I don't know this part of my own story. Edward carried me out, eh?"

"Yes. He had gone fishing early in the morning, and saw this house on fire."

"My house on fire?" exclaimed her grandfather.

"Yes, someone had set fire to the front parlor. Edward came in through the library to try and get to your bedroom and found you on the floor, here. They were able to put the fire out. Grandfather, do you remember who attacked you? I should send for the magistrate. Tadswell has been several times and is investigating..."

"I have dealt with the matter," he said harshly. "I wish to hear no more of it. Now, tell me, I saw you color up. You have a liking for young Edward, eh?"

"I do like him very much, Grandfather," she said nervously. She worried that he might not approve, for all that Edward had said he'd asked his permission... that memory might not come to the fore.

He put his hand over his mouth, but it did not hide his eyes. Betraying creases showed he was smiling, and that relaxed her slightly. Then he said: "He's a younger son. Unless the older brother doesn't marry, he won't inherit much, you know."

"I cannot allow what does not weigh with him about my situation, to weigh with me about his. We will manage. I am accustomed to doing with very little, Sir. This will be no shock to me." She said rather stiffly. She held herself back from saying 'my parents managed'.

He looked at her, quizzically, plainly amused rather than angered. "You do know that I tried to arrange a marriage between his father and your mother?"

That did surprise her. "No! I mean, I knew mother went to Aunt Edith because, because she did not wish to be pushed into a marriage she did not want, but she never said to whom."

"One of my many mistakes," he said. "They knew each other well, the estates adjoin... anyway, tell me all about it."

She finished her tea. "I think I will leave that to Edward, Grandfather. But I have no intention of leaving you, while you need my care. He understands that, and indeed said he would never ask it. Now, I will go and talk to my aunt. I will come back."

He nodded. "I must write... two more letters."

She went out, and in search of her aunt – who she found packing, and harassing one of the maids who was assisting her. "You thankless girl! You deserve that your reputation will be ruined by living with that crazy old man," her aunt shouted at her, when she appeared in the doorway. "You'll never ever form an eligible connection. When he dies, you'll be brought down to size. And don't expect your Cousin to rescue you. He is torn between Elvira and Maude."

"Aunt Louisa, I do not wish to quarrel, and I am very grateful to the Captain..."

"Don't you speak to me unless I tell you to. You'll be well-served if he drops dead today. Don't think of darkening my doorway again if he does. You can starve on the street for all I care."

"Don't you dare speak to my mistress like that, you wicked old woman!" snapped the maid, tipping the trunk off the bed to scatter its contents. "Or wish ill on the master. You've been eating and drinking and being waited on at his expense, you and those daughters of yours, carrying on something scandalous. Pack your own things."

To Georgina's shock, that resulted in her aunt attempting to box the maid's ears, missing as she ducked, falling over the spilled clothes, and landing on the bed, yelling in rage. That brought her daughters, and several more servants. "Will you be quiet!" shouted Georgina. "Or I will indeed have the servants throw you and your baggage out."

"You... you wouldn't dare," said her aunt, suddenly shocked into quieter tones.

"Don't try me," snapped Georgina. "Please pack up your belongings. I will have Lessing order the carriage, for an hour from now. It can convey you to Whitchurch, from where you may take the Mail-coach to Southampton. I think that will be best."

"We didn't mean to..." said Elvira.

"I know, but my grandfather wants you to leave and so do I," she said and turned on her heel, clasping her hands tightly together to stop them shaking. She went back to her room, where Mary comforted and helped to compose her... partly by reliving all the best parts of the breakfast picnic by the river. Mary had by now convinced herself that it was the most romantic thing ever, and Georgina was in agreement with her, not that she had any more experience than Mary had.

A little later, she heard a timid tap at her door. It was Elvira. "We've packed. Cousin, mother is still in hysterics. I don't know what to do."

"Slap her," said Mary, pragmatically.

"I'll have the footmen carry your things to the carriage," said Georgina. "You and Maude can assist her down."

"She says you're never to come near her again. And you'll end up alone, starving and dead in a ditch."

"I will endeavor not to cut up her peace," said Georgina as tactfully as she could.

"Anyway," said Mary, "My lady's getting married. She'll be well-cared for, and don't need your mother nor no-one else. Now get along with you." And she closed the door in Elvira's startled face.

"You didn't have to tell her that, Mary," said Georgina as the sound of Elvira's footsteps faded.

"A little repayment for the nasty things she said about you, Miss. She's never even had a proposal. It'll teach her," said Mary from the lofty height of what Georgina had discovered to be 'gone sixteen'. "Payback too. She made me life a misery, often enough. Boxed my ears a couple of times."

"A good thing she does not know I have had three proposals, then."

"Three!" exclaimed Mary. "That'd be the Reverend, and?"

"Cousin Arthur."

Mary blinked. "Oh, you wouldn't want him, Miss. I heard bad things about him."

"What?" asked Georgina, rather surprised.

"Not fit to sully your ears with, Miss," said Mary primly. "The master was very angry about it, they say. Would you like me to go and call the footmen to carry their trunks?"

Georgina accepted that offer, and went back down to her grandfather. He was looking tired, but was just finishing a letter. He dusted it with sand, sealed it up and said, "There, that should do it all right-and-tight."

"And my aunt should have left. I was going to ask her to remain at least for luncheon, sir, to try and heal the breach, but she... she is bad-tempered."

"Hmph. It's a fault. Still, I think you are glad to have her gone. Now, Puss, if you can see these two conveyed to the posting-house. One is for Winter, again, but that groom will not be back. I'll have a little rest here, before we have lunch."

"Would you like to go back upstairs to bed, grandfather?" she asked, holding the letters.

"No, I've dozed in this chair for many a year," he said. "It is more comfortable for my hip, sometimes."

So, she left him, found Lessing, discovered her aunt and cousins were outside, their baggage and selves being loaded, and gave the letters into his care, to give to John Coachman to see handed in.

That being done she had a little time to return to her book, and a few daydreams of the future, and memories of her morning, before luncheon. She was happy to take her grandfather through to the morning room, and to eat quietly with him there. Conversation was desultory, he seemed a little pre-occupied. After the meal, he told her he was going to doze again, but to be sure to wake him when the party from Bournelea arrived.

"Would it worry you if I went and played on the piano-forte?" she asked.

"Now, that would be lovely," he informed her. "So many memories. Your grandmother played, and your mother."

She went and played, enjoying her time on the instrument, thinking of her future in something of a happy daze – and watching the clock. Just a little.

They arrived just after three. Georgina had great plans to wait in the drawing room in a ladylike and decorous fashion, but those went out the window when she heard the knocker. She had no idea what got her to run, but she did, and arrived as Lessing threw open the doors.

Edward decided that if this glowing girl wanted to hold his hand, tightly, he for one, was not going to gainsay it. "What of your aunt?" he asked, looking for her, and ready to stand buff.

"She has left!" Georgina informed him, happily. "She had a tiff with my grandfather, and he told her he was my guardian and he was the only chaperone I needed."

"Champion! So, he is doing better is he?"

"I think so much better. He knows who I am at least. He keeps saying he's on borrowed time, and struggling to remember some things, especially the last few weeks, but he is quite changed. The servants all say he's so much more like himself. I promised I would wake him when you came. I... I haven't told him yet, but he has guessed. Unless you want to change your mind?" she said, sudden doubt entering her voice.

"Never," said Edward.

"I shall wake the master," said Lessing, beaming avuncularly at them. "If you would give me a few moments."

"You might let me welcome my new daughter," said Sir Gerald.

Georgina looked somewhat nervously at her prospective parents-in-law. "I do hope... you don't mind?"

"Well, m'dear," said Sir Gerald, coming over and kissing her cheek. "You could have done better, but if it is Edward you want, well, we're grateful for this one fault in your taste."

"Oh, nonsense," said his mother, "Let go, Edward so she can give me a proper hug. I've been wanting to give you a hug since you arrived, looking so worried and forlorn. Now I can," she said embracing her.

John came and kissed her cheek too. "Welcome to our family," he said gruffly. "I'm glad for both of you. Ned and you shall suit."

Lessing returned to say that Mr. Frederick asked if they could please step into the library. He also informed them the master had ordered him to fetch up the best burgundy, but if the ladies would prefer something else?

They were ushered in, and Edward had possessed himself of Georgina's hand. He stepped forward, and wasted no time: "Mr. Weatherly, your granddaughter Georgina has agreed to accept my proposal of marriage. We would like your blessing, sir."

Frederick Weatherly looked at them with a broad smile. "And if I said 'No'?"

"I'd have to wait, because I promised Georgina she could look after you for as long as you needed her, sir. Otherwise I'd have her on the way to Gretna before you could say 'Jack Adams'. If I must wait, I must wait. But we will marry."

"Determined eh. I could cut her off without a penny you know," said Frederick Weatherly, still smiling.

"I don't have any pennies," said Georgina. "Please stop this, Grandfather. I don't have a father any more, and you are standing in for him. I want your blessing. I know you like Edward, and this means a lot to me."

He nodded. "Come and shake my hand, Edward, and give me a kiss, Granddaughter. Of course, you have my blessing. I could not ask for better man for you, Puss."

After the handshaking, and a few tears, Lessing brought in the burgundy and a toast was drunk. Frederick Weatherly patted his granddaughter's hand. "You will have a little pin-money from me, my dear. I'd like the wedding to be soon, that I may be there to see it."

"Well, sir, I need to see you established in good health first," Georgina informed him.

"Yes. And I am looking for some form of employment, which may take a little time," Edward told him.

"I should have asked you about your prospects," said Weatherly, chuckling. "Seeing as I am filling in for Georgina's father. He was a stiff-rumped man, you know, Edward. He stood up to me in a rage. So, what are your prospects, young man? How do you plan to support my granddaughter in a style I deem appropriate?"

"I cannot go back to my old profession, sir," Edward admitted. "But there are several possibilities. I have approached various people by letter. I shall go up to London next week to call on some possible employers. I am going to find something, sir. You've known me all my life. I'll give it my best. I will succeed."

"Hmm," said her grandfather. "You are still managing my estate?"

"Yes, sir. But I will have to give that away. But I will find someone reliable for you."

"We'll discuss this, along with a settlement, later. My granddaughter will not be entirely dowerless, you know. Although," He looked at Edward's father. "Things have changed a little, eh Gerald?"

"A little," his father acknowledged. "And Edward is acting as if he won't have a shirt. But there is some provision for him."

"I'll find something," said Edward, feeling decidedly awkward. "The important thing is that Georgina and I will be married. We can talk about the details later. And at least you are on the mend."

"I have achieved all I have ever hoped to achieve," said Frederick Weatherly, tiredly.

"You're tired, sir," said Edward. "I shall come over tomorrow morning, hopefully with a few fish."

"Ah. Now that I would enjoy! Now come here, both of you." He took both of their hands. Edward noticed the tremble and rather weak grip in the hand that took his, but the old man squeezed. "You have both made me very happy. My blessing on both of you."

"And to a generation of great grandchildren, sir."

"Those too," he said "My only sorrow is that Dorothea is not here to see it."

"She's watching, Grandfather. I know it," said Georgina. "Now. I will see them off and you are going upstairs to bed. But me no buts. It's been a long and wonderful day."

They bade their farewells and walked out onto the step while the carriage and the gentlemen's horses were brought around. Georgina really did not want them to leave. The one thing she realized that she'd always had out on the Mission Station was a family. She had not realized how very much she had missed it.

The door was wide open behind them – and suddenly from inside, came the oddest sound. It was incoherent, but loud, almost a roar. For a cold moment Georgina forgot she was now in England and thought it was a lion. And the next moment Edward, standing next to her, was running in, closely followed by his brother, who had been at the foot of the outside stair. She ran behind them, as fast as she could, for the library. In the short passage between it and the morning room, Arthur came dodging between them. He dodged Edward, but was not quite so successful with John, who put an elbow into his solar plexus and sent him staggering into the wall. Georgina had barely time to say "What is wrong?"

"Uncle collapsed," he gasped, "Coming to call..."

Then she heard Edward yell. "Georgina! Quick!"

She ran into the library, where her grandfather was sprawled on the floor, his face a purplish white. She knelt beside him, felt for a pulse, and to her relief found it. It was tumultuous, but there. By now half a dozen more people had arrived. "Help me sit him up," she said. "We need Dr. Selby, quickly!"

"I'll get him," said John. "Stay with her, Ned."

By the time Dr. Selby arrived they had moved Frederick Weatherly upstairs to his bed. He was still not conscious, but his color had slightly improved. Selby examined him, pinched his lips and shook his head. "It is as I feared," he said. "He has had a fit of apoplexy, affecting his brain."

"Will he recover? He was doing so well." Georgina wrung her hands.

"It is possible. But he may well have some lost movement, or have his brain further impaired. Or... he may have more incidents. It is rare for there only to be one. Do you know what triggered this?"

"Arthur was there. We can ask him," said Edward.

"I did not even know he had come in," said Georgina.

Lessing, who was hovering, said: "Yes, Miss. He came in while you were talking to the master. I... informed him you were busy, and that the Salmonds ladies – he asked where they were – had left."

"Go and fetch him," said Edward, tersely.

The butler returned with a shaken-looking Arthur. "I have no idea. I was heading into the morning room when I heard the noise and ran to look," he informed them. "Cousin, where has your aunt gone?" he was looking at her and, she realized, Edward, who had his arm protectively around her.

"Back to Southampton. My grandfather said she was no longer needed here," Georgina told him.

"But now she is. You cannot stay here without a chaperone!" said Arthur.

"I shall see to it," said Lady Elizabeth, coolly. "In the meanwhile, why don't you remove yourself?"

"I shall. I shall rack up at an inn tonight," announced Arthur.

"Off you go," said John, helpfully.

"I don't believe him," said Edward as he left.

"Neither do I," said his father, "but what is to be done? Dr. Selby, what can we do?"

"Watch and wait," said Selby, grimly.

"Very well," said Lady Elizabeth. "Gerald, you will take yourself home, get Betty to pack my night-gear. Georgina, I will stay with you. Edward..."

"I can sit with him as well as you can, Mama," he said. "And I will not leave Georgina to face this alone."

It was a long, long night's vigil. They took it in shifts, with Lady Elizabeth telling them she'd sleep first. All that was good about it, Georgina thought, was that she did not face it alone. At some stage she fell asleep on Edward's shoulder, and was faintly aware of being carried to bed and Mary fussing.

She woke to Mary telling her that she should come. It was pale predawn, and a yawning Edward had also obviously just been awakened. Lady Elizabeth and the valet were there already. "I am sorry to call you dear, but his breathing has got worse."

Edward turned to Mary. "Get the groom to go for Selby, and then ride on for the priest." Then he came and put his arm around Georgina. "I'm sorry, dear. I saw this several times in Spain. He's slipping away."

She nodded. "I have seen it twice myself now. I did not want a third time." She buried her face in his shoulder.

And just as the sun began to rise, as the birds began their singing, and the fish must have been sipping their first mayflies, Frederick Weatherly joined the morning rise, while the priest prayed over him and his granddaughter wept.

Chapter 13

G eorgina was glad of some help with the task of laying out her grandfather. Edward left first, promising to go to the undertaker and arrange for the coffin, and to ask his father to let Weatherly's attorney and man of business know and compose a notice for the Gazette for her.

Once they had finished, Lady Elizabeth took an affectionate leave of her, promising to come over later that afternoon. Mrs. Lessing wanted a few confirmations of her plans to show the master was dead, but as soon as Georgina had agreed to the hatchment being set above the door, and the knocker being tied up with black crepe, she was free to seek her own bed. She was tired enough to sleep deeply for some hours.

She was wakened by Mary, who came to tell her that Mr. Arthur Weatherly had arrived and demanded speech of her. "In high croak, he is," said Mary, disdainfully. "Telling Lessing it's him who is master here, now. Seen the hatchment above the door, he did. The stories they tell me about that man! You're not to be anywhere alone with him,

Miss. Why he give some poor girl a slip on the shoulder, and she killed herself, when he wouldn't do what he'd promised."

Georgina was somewhat stunned by that. Plainly, Mary at least believed the tale. She was just as shocked by what Arthur had apparently said, for all that it was true.

When she came downstairs, Arthur was in the library, looking in drawers. "Ah," he said. "You'd better get your pelisse. Your maid can pack your things. I'll take you across to Bournelea, immediately. You obviously can't remain here. Do you know where the old fool kept the safe key?"

She drew herself up, knowing the key to be hanging against her skin. "He never told me where he kept it."

"I'll have to do a proper search later. Get your pelisse. I have the curricle standing outside."

Right now, the idea of seeking refuge at Bournelea was extremely attractive. But she felt that it would be an imposition just to arrive without notice. So, she said that perhaps she should send a message, first.

"I did that as soon as I knew he was dead," said Arthur. "Get your pelisse. I haven't got all day."

"I need to pack," said Georgina.

"I'll see your trunks sent over. Your maid can pack for you," Arthur informed her.

"My maid will come with me," said Georgina, firmly, Mary's story in her ears.

"Very well. Mrs. Lessing can pack, or one of these other maids you've filled the place with. But you have to go, now."

Reluctantly, Georgina assented. He hadn't even conveyed any sympathies for the loss of her grandfather. It occurred to her, just then, that in the time she'd nursed her grandfather, he'd never as much as set foot in his sick-room. She went to find Mary and her pelisse, comforting herself with the thought of Edward and the kindness of his family.

One of the stable-boys was walking the horses hitched to the curricle from Westmead's own coach-house. She supposed it was his now. The step was let down, and Mary got up onto the tiger's seat, clutching her hat, and Georgina was seated next to Arthur. He set the horses in motion, and they went off down the drive toward the main London road.

When they got there, it took Georgina a minute to realize they were going towards London, not Bournelea. "We're going the wrong way!"

The curricle was now bowling along at a spanking pace. "I am going exactly where I plan to go," he said.

"Stop at once!" she demanded.

"I will, in a moment," said Arthur, looking about. It was an empty section of roadway. "Well, this should do," and he pulled the curricle to a stop. How silly and petty, thought Georgina. He was going to strand them at the roadside. Well. It wasn't that far to Bournelea. They could walk. But she was very wrong. Arthur had reached into the pocket of his frieze coat and produced a pistol. He turned and pointed it at Mary. "Get off."

"The devil with you!" said Mary.

"I can shoot you and leave you here dead, just as easily," said Arthur coldly. "They'd make nothing of a shot out here."

"Get down, Mary," said Georgina. "Please."

"I can't leave you with this black spy, Miss!"

"I will cope. I will not cope with you dead, dearest Mary. I could not bear that."

"I can't, Miss," said Mary, plainly afraid, but obdurate.

"Please, Mary." She pleaded. "He's mad. He'll kill you."

"He'll kill you too, Miss." Mary replied.

She lifted her lip. "No, I think he has something else in mind." She mouthed 'get help' hoping Mary would understand and get off.

"You are quite right," said Arthur. "Now, you pestilential little doxy, get down. I'll give you to the count of three. One..."

Georgina braced herself. On two, Mary started getting down. Arthur set the horses in motion before she was down, and she fell onto the roadway.

"She's fallen! Stop!" yelled Georgina

"She's just a servant," said Arthur, urging the horses into a canter. "The longer she takes to get up the better. She'll try and set someone on our tail, no doubt. But we'll be off the main road in a few minutes. They won't find us."

Georgina looked for her chance. She knew full well what her abductor had in mind. The idea terrified her... but it made her more determined to get away. She looked back, trying to see Mary, but that was a bend away. Arthur wasn't springing his horses, but they were moving a good deal too fast to consider jumping... If they slowed, she must be ready.

"Why are you doing this?" she asked, looking for an opening, anything that could give her an opportunity.

"Needs must," he said. "I tried to get you willingly, so this is all that is left to me. I'll enjoy breaking you to bridle. You will have to marry me, when I've done with you."

"I am affianced to be married, Cousin," said Georgina.

"Edward the cripple," he said with a snort. "Yes, I saw. Aiming high, for a missionary brat, aren't you? Well, he'll not take damaged goods, so your only option is marriage to me. It's a pity you're so skinny. Your cousins were more timbered up to my frame."

"Why don't you marry them then? They both wanted you."

"Marry one of them? Ha. My luck has been out for too long for anything but a cream-pot. If that old fool of an uncle of mine had not come down, and been stupid enough to tell me what he'd done, the first I'd have known about it would have been too late. Well, I think it is in his safe. But at least this way..."

They'd come to a fairly sharp corner, and he slowed slightly, concentrating on feathering it.

She seized her chance, and grabbed the near rein and hauled hard. The curricle swayed and veered wildly as he fought her for control of the rein. Then it bounded over the edge of the roadway with a wheel in the ditch. Georgina went flying off, and crashed into the dense bushes on the other side of the ditch. They broke her fall, but clawed at her as she tried to get up and run. The tangle of brambles gave her abductor precious seconds to pull himself upright from the ditch and lurch to grab her and pull her out. She hit him with all her strength, but it was not enough to break his hold. "You hell-bitch. I'll have to tie you up," he snarled.

He started to drag her, fighting every inch, back towards the struggling horses.

Edward had himself slept for a while that morning, but he had got up, shaved and decided he'd borrow his brother's curricle, and go across to Westmead and take Georgina for an airing, just to get her out of the house for a bit, and to give her mind a little tranquility. Well, and to see her and just to spend time with her. He was, he admitted, a man deeply in love, and last night had merely cemented in his mind that he had finally found the right girl, the one he never really believed existed.

They were just maneuvering the curricle around onto the drive when Will, the groom from Westmead, came up at a spanking pace. Edward pulled up and the groom pulled to a halt beside him. "Heard you was looking for a chestnut nag, Captain."

"Yes. Have you seen one?" he asked.

"Aye. That Mr. Arthur just rode in on one. I thought to come tell you. He took one of our horses yesterday. Salman. He was favoring his left fore. I tried to tell him, but he weren't listening. Reckon he went lame."

"Let's get across to Westmead, Penn." He asked Will, "How long ago was this?"

"Must have been all of twenty minutes ago. He made me get the curricle out, afore I could go. Said he was master there now, and I'd best do it, or be sent packing."

"Nonsense! The will's not been read yet," said Edward, as he flicked his whip, urging the horses into a brisk trot and out onto the London road. The distance to Westmead's turn was not great, less than a mile, and Edward was just slowing for the bend, when Penn shouted: "Captain! Up ahead. It's that little maid of Miss Georgina's!"

And indeed, there she was, running towards them down the high-road waving her arms. Instead of turning they drove towards her. "Chase!" she gasped out, pointing down the road. She was scratched and bloody, and panting desperately.

"Pull her up, Penn," said Edward. "Chase who?" he asked, in sudden fear.

She panted out: "Miss...Georg... ina," which sent his heart to his boots, and his whip to the horses.

"How long ago?" he asked keeping his eyes on the road.

"Just... now..." she managed. "Arthur... has... gun!"

If he had not already set the horses moving at a thundering pace, that would have done it. His entire focus was on the road, thinking ahead. There was a cross-road about two miles off. If Arthur – who would know the back-roads as well as Edward did, turned there, they might lose track. There were some cottages there... but asking would cost time, and they might not have taken heed.

"Seen a glimpse of 'em, Captain," said Penn. "Couple of sharp bends coming."

"Teach your grandmother..." said Edward, knowing the road, judging the distances, and not slacking his pace one iota.

And then, starting into the bend, he saw the curricle, in the ditch, and beside that, his love, wrestling desperately with her abductor.

She was alive, at least, and fighting like a wild-cat. Arthur was struggling to drag her, but looked up at the sound of their arrival. Edward left managing the curricle's horses to Penn. He, whip in hand, had got down and was closing on Arthur and Georgina. Arthur let go of one of her hands, and she hit him. She was wrenching at his grasp, to try and get the other hand free, before even seeing Edward.

But Arthur had drawn a pistol from his pocket. "Back off! Back off or the girl dies."

"If she dies, so do you," said Edward. The ever-ingenious Penn had handed holding the horses' heads to the maid, and was slipping around the other curricle to get behind Arthur. Edward knew it was a deadly situation, but if he could get close enough... if Penn could get behind them... but he dared not risk her. Himself, that was a chance he'd take. "Your kind only fight girls," he said, to nettle the man. "I'm going to turn your pretty face to pulp, this time. And you won't have a pistol to stop me."

"Then I'll kill you first!" snarled Arthur, shifting his aim to Edward. "I can deal with her. And I can't miss at this range." Edward could see Penn, closing. And Edward had a whip, and his love safe. He...

He misjudged Georgina.

She chose not to break away, but to seize Arthur's gun arm. She threw all her weight onto it, falling, dragging his arm down. Penn rushed. Edward's whip slashed.

In the screaming chaos, the pistol boomed. Penn floored Arthur with a stick he'd seized up. Edward charged in. He wasted no time on Arthur, but left that to Penn. Instead, he knelt next to Georgina. "Are you hit?"

Her face was white with shock, but her eyes were still open and she did say his name, before swooning. He picked her up and carried her to the curricle. She stirred in his arms. He was vaguely aware of her maid shouting at someone, and glanced to see if it was another attack on his love. But it was just the groom from Westmead, who must have followed them. That meant Georgina's maid was able to come to his aid. He could feel a warm wetness on his left hand. She must be bleeding, he realized. His first instinct was to get her up into the curricle and drive like fury for help. But the experience of the conflict in Spain said otherwise. He must staunch the bleeding as soon as possible. He set her down on the roadway, cradling her head, as she lay on his lap. His hand was indeed bloody. "We need to find the wound, and stop the bleeding," he said to the white-faced Mary.

Georgina opened her eyes and looked up into his face. "So sorry, Edward," she said, struggling to sit.

"Lie still, my darling. We just need to stop the bleeding and I'll take you to the Doctor. Where does it hurt?"

She closed her eyes briefly. "I just felt it hit. I love you, Edward. I am sorry I'm dying."

"Well you ain't," said Mary, hauling dress and petticoats aside. "We won't let you!"

"Ow. My leg!"

"Penn," shouted Edward.

His groom came running, and knelt next to her now exposed leg, looking at what Edward could see was a long, torn, bloody gash across her thigh, starting just short of her hip. "Well, she's not pumping blood, Master."

It was bloody enough, but, true, not spurting. "I think you'll be fine," said Edward, trying to insert all the confidence he could muster into his voice.

"Oh," she said with a wince. "I'm sorry. I had no idea being shot was so sore. I've never been shot before. I'll get up then."

"You'll stay still, Miss!" said Mary. "Won't she Master... I mean Captain?"

"She will indeed. And I hope you'll stay with us for always, when we're married. If it hadn't been for you, we'd have been well behind," said Edward.

"Oh Mary! Are you all right?" said Georgina, reaching out for her. "I saw you fall, but he wouldn't stop."

"Nothing beyond scrapes and bruises, Miss," said Mary gruffly. "Now let's get you made decent, and taken to a doctor."

"He's getting away! That bastard is getting away!" yelled Will, from his post at the horses' heads. Edward looked up and saw Arthur, staggering, but pushing his way through the brambles to where the horses from his curricle were still trying to free themselves. By the look of the traces, that would not happen quickly. "Leave him," said Edward. "Get a few strips of petticoat around that leg, Mary. Penn, you'll take Will's horse and ride to fetch Selby. I'll take Georgina home to my mother. Will, can you sort out that curricle? We can't leave the horses like that."

"Quicker if both of us do it, Will," said Penn. "And you can go on to the Priors and see if Doctor Selby's there. I know old Widow Haswell is poorly."

The two of them got to work as Mary hastily bound up the wound.

Will knew his work, and gave the greys and his horse to Penn, and had managed to calm Arthur's horses, and be a fair way toward pulling the curricle out of the ditch, by the time Edward could lift Georgina into the curricle. He boosted Mary onto the tiger's seat, climbed up himself, and Penn let go of the horses' heads. "I'll go to the crossroads and turn," he called to the groom, already running to help Will. It was barely a quarter-mile to the bend, and there was a donkey cart, but he coped with that quite well, seeing his hands were still trembling a little with reaction.

Georgina said nothing for the first part of the journey, but pressed close against him. "Poor little love!" he said, comfortingly. "I'll have you tucked up in bed in a trice. You'll be all right."

"I was very afraid. I thought I was going to see another person I loved die."

"You were a tiger, Miss," said Mary admiringly. "To do that!"

"Yes," agreed Edward. "But please don't ever do it again! I've never had a worse moment, my love. You are very precious to me."

"Oh, Edward," she plainly too was rallying. "You mean I'm not an insufferable baggage anymore?"

"You never were. You must have misheard," he said, slightly eased by her tone. "I might have called you an adorable baggage, but I wish to withdraw the 'baggage' part.

She was silent for a few moments. Then she said quietly: "I understand now why my mother was willing to pack and follow my father
to Africa. Edward..."

"Yes, my adorable one?" he asked.

"Nothing. Just... I am so glad you came to just then."

"My love, not half as glad as I am. And not half as sorry as Arthur
is going to be, if I ever catch up with him."

"Let someone else deal with him," she said urgently.

"It may work out that way," he said. "I cannot think what came
over him. Did he think inheriting made him invulnerable? It's not
that big an estate, and you are no defenseless, friendless girl." He held
himself back from saying 'like his prior victim'. That would be a tale
for another time.

She shuddered. "He was going to... He said I'd have to marry him
then. That you'd not take damaged goods."

"I'd have stretched him out for the undertaker. And he was wrong
too. You could never be that in my eyes," said Edward grimly. "Well, he
never could bear being thwarted. But put that behind you now. You're
with me and safe."

"Safe. He wanted to get into the safe... He said something about if
my grandfather hadn't come down... I think he was the one who hit
him."

"I'm sure of it," said Edward. "Proving it may be harder, but you at
least are safe. And he'll not walk free of it as easily as he did last time."

"Last time? He has done this before?"

There was no avoiding it. "Yes, a village girl, but she was willing
enough, we think. He was down visiting your grandfather, bored, fell
into a bit of dalliance. Promised... much. Only when he got her with
child... his promises came to nothing. She killed herself."

"That's the story I heard," said Mary. "And I do believe it now."

"But... but why didn't anyone do anything?"

"Well, your grandfather threw him out of the house, when it came to his ears," said Edward. "But there was not a lot he could do, really."

"Surely more," said Georgina, indignantly.

"I'd agree with you, particularly right now. He's not going to be welcome in the neighborhood, even if somehow he springs free of the charges I plan to press. But it's likely he'll just sell up. My brother says he's neck-deep with the gull-gropers – the money lenders. Ah, here is our drive. Your jolting is near an end, my love. I'll have you in a comfortable bed in a trivet."

Georgina was in more pain than she cared to admit, but had put on a brave face to comfort her rescuers. Edward might have no idea what an open, readable face he had, but his worry and distress had been obvious to her. Mary too, poor thing, was plainly badly shaken. So: she put in a brave effort. It seemed to help her too. Her wounded arrival at Bournelea, carried in in Edward's arms, caused an enormous stir. But she was very glad to have her injury, and Mary's scratches, washed and seen to, and to have the comfort of Dr. Selby examining it and telling her she was unlikely to die, and yes she would have quite an ugly scar, by the time he had finished sewing the wound closed.

"Nothing to touch Captain Kelling's one, but you two will make a pair. I would say the ball hit your femur at a steep angle, and that'll be the source of much of your pain. It did not break it, though, and you will heal. Now, you will probably become a little feverish. I am going to prepare a saline draught for you which my man will bring around shortly, and I also recommend a few drops of laudanum in water, to help you to sleep. I know Captain Kelling refuses to take it, but it will help you to sleep, and rest is what your body needs. You've been through a horrid time, Miss Ross. You will elevate that leg on a cushion, and rest. Now, brace yourself, you'll want something to bite on, because I shall be practicing my seamstress skills."

Edward came in to see her, as soon as Selby had left. He sat beside her, holding her hand, his mind plainly set somewhat at rest by the Doctor's visit. "I've sent Jem and his wife over to Westmead to fetch your trunks, and to reassure them. You're staying right here where I can watch over you." he said with a loving smile. "I'll be here, at your beck and call."

"Even in the early morning?" she asked. "I've made you miss one dawn rise. What a poor wife I would be should I deprive you of those."

"My lady, when you're up and well, we'll go and fish them together," he promised.

"I would love to go down to the river again with you," she said, unexpected tears welling up in her eyes. "Before it is sold."

"There are other rivers, my love. We'll find ours."

He was shooed out by Lady Elizabeth and Mary, who wanted to see Georgina made comfortable, and told him to go away instead of making her cry. He did, but only after drying her tears, and kissing her.

He came back later, when Lady Elizabeth was sitting there, with both of them peacefully engrossed in books – with the saline draught, the laudanum and chock full of news. "Well," he said: "Who do you think turned up at your grandfather's house?"

"I don't know?" said Georgina.

"For one: The magistrate. Tadswell. I was thinking we'd send for him tomorrow, and have a charge brought against Arthur, before Arthur fabricated one against you. That's what he'd likely do, you know."

She nodded. "Besides... something must be done about him. I am sure it was Arthur who tried to rob the house, who attacked my grandfather, and who tried to set fire to it. He might have killed everyone in it. He does not seem to think of others, just himself."

Edward beamed at her. "And fortunately, it seems Tadswell now agrees with you. He had a warrant for Arthur's arrest. He had a rumor about a bowl being offered to certain buyers, relayed him by Winter, as well as the fact of the snuff-boxes recovered from various files in London. It seems that he was able to follow certain leads about a chestnut horse, back to the Green Boar, and find Arthur a known visitor, and to establish that he had hired that particular horse on the relevant evening – to go and visit a friend, he said. Again, he hired the same horse, late on a Saturday night – and returned it on the Sunday that you had a burglar. My love, if you'd just hit him with the poker then..." She had to laugh. "From there, Tadswell went to the Capital and secured the co-operation of the metropolitan police in conducting a search of Arthur's chambers – and found several of your grandfather's snuff-boxes, and the Ming bowl, which he had obviously not disposed of yet. It was valuable, but not easy for him to sell."

He quelled her startled exclamation, with a raised hand. "But Tadswell was after the fair. Very put out he was, I gather, to find Arthur had been there, and had hopped the twig. Yes, he showed up at Westmead, much the worse for wear, claiming he'd had a curricle accident, demanding entry."

"Is there no limit to his effrontery?" Lady Elizabeth asked.

"Not much, I'd say," said Edward. "He always had a glib tongue and could seize the main chance. Fortunately, Will, stout fellow, had got there before him, and told them the story, and what I had said to him about your grandfather's will not yet being read. So, Lessing refused

Arthur entry, for all he cried he was master of the house, and he'd give them all notice to quit upon the instanter, if he was not let in."

"Good gracious! Well, even if he's locked up... the house will still be his, I suppose," said Lady Elizabeth. "We shall have to see what we can do for Lessing. Although it is a pity he didn't let him in, and get him arrested. Not that you'd want your cousin on trial and in all the papers, Georgina, but he needs to go."

"He has," said Edward. "He went around to the stables, and demanded they saddle him a horse. Informed them he was going to fetch the constable to have Lessing clapped up, if you please. But Will heard him abusing the stable-boy, went out and milled him down. I am so envious."

"So... what happened then?" asked Georgina, quite forgiving him his pugilistic desires.

"Well, Will was all for locking him in the store-room and calling here, but when he went to get the key, Arthur slipped off again. Will looked about, but couldn't find him. He might have made for the Priors. And yes, Mother. We'll be soundly locked up tonight, and there will be several of John's badly-behaved dogs loose in the house."

"For once I approve of them spannelling up the floors," said Lady Elizabeth. "Do you like dogs, Georgina dear?"

She nodded. "We had one for many years in the Mission Station. She was..." she choked slightly, swallowed, "My particular friend when I was a little girl. She was killed... when, when we were attacked."

Edward nodded and squeezed her hand. "I'll get a pup and train him properly for you, my Love, if you'd like that? Anyway, John's dogs are not going to like people wandering around, so that's all right and tight. Now. Here, my Love, is your medication, and the laudanum. Drink up, and I shall see you in the morning. If I know Selby's draughts it will be so nasty that you will want to recover, so you do not have to drink any more of them. I hope you have eaten, because all of it sits better on a full stomach."

"I have. And I am very tired." She took the medication, and it was quite as described.

He kissed her goodnight, and remarkably soon thereafter she was asleep.

Chapter 14

E dward went downstairs, wondering just how soon he might seek his own bed. His leg was a great deal better than six months back, but it ached now. He found that Mr. Tadswell was there, and waiting to speak with him. "I heard of the terrible happenings, abduction, grievous wounding, when I went to Westmead House," he said, gravely. "How is Miss Ross?"

"Selby takes a very comforting view of it all," said Edward. "We have just given her a saline draught from him, and some laudanum drops, so I think she will be asleep soon. She's had a dreadful time of it."

Tadswell nodded in agreement. "There will be additional charges flowing from that, but we already have quite enough to arrest Mr. Arthur Weatherly. He hired a horse in Hurstbourne Priors and set off in the direction of Southampton. I have set matters in motion to have him arrested." He clasped his hands together. He paused. "It seems I must offer you an apology, Captain Kelling," he said, awkwardly.

"Let us shake hands, and have a glass of wine together, Mr. Tadswell," said Edward, ending the man's discomfort. "My wife-to-be admires your scholarship, so I would rather we were friends.

"My goodness!" said Tadswell, beaming at him. "Had I but known that... Yes, yes. I would love to drink a toast your future happiness, Captain Kelling," he said, shaking Edward's hand warmly. "A remarkable young lady. And her father could have been a great man in academia, but made the choice to follow what he thought was his calling instead. Not many like that, Captain. Not many."

They sat, over the glass of wine, and Edward's brother joined them, after a few minutes.

"The part I don't get is what his motive was," said John. "I mean, the robbery..."

"He was deeply in debt," said Tadswell. "The story he told me of you, Captain, was far more accurate of him. It appears those 'witnesses' of his, for all their noble titles, are a set of ramshackle fellows – or so I was told by the police in the Capital. But I do not fully understand it, myself. I have spoken to the attorney... but I must say no more."

It was only the following morning, after a peaceful night only interrupted by a dog who wished to sleep in his chamber, that that, and other mysteries were to be solved.

The morning brought the arrival of Mr. Winter. The dapper little man was much shocked on arriving at Westmead House that morning, and having heard of the events of the previous day, including the arrival of the magistrate – and two constables, apparently, searching for Arthur Weatherly. He greeted Edward with what, for him, passed as great pleasure. "A s...sad business, Captain. And shocking too. I was unfortunately up in London yesterday, seeing – or in some cases trying to see to Mr. Frederick Weatherly's business. Now, I was h...hoping to see Miss Ross. A matter of some of the business which Mr. Frederick instructed me to pursue in his letter. Would that be possible?"

"I think so," said Edward. "I was up there a few minutes ago. She is reposing on the chaise lounge. You may however have to enter into a den of sewing women. My mother has half the country engaged in preparing clothes for her."

"I am s...sure they can spare us a few minutes," said Winter.

And this was indeed the case. Edward walked him up to the small drawing room now full of fabric, and emptying of women... and was about to leave when Winter asked him if he could remain. "Perhaps you too, Lady Elizabeth," he said with a twinkle. "As you are somewhat *in loco parentis* for Miss Ross, I gather, from my late principal's letter."

"My rudimentary Spanish suggest that means 'as the mad parent', Mother," said Edward helpfully.

"It is hereditary, I see," said his mother. "I will be happy to stay, and Georgina will indeed be my daughter."

"I know," said Winter. "And that is partially why I have come down to see you. Anyway, good morning, Miss Ross. M...my condolences. I...I am very sorry to learn of your loss, and of your shocking injury yesterday. I trust you are feeling in better pin today?"

"Much better, Mr. Winter," said Georgina, being restrained, gently, from rising, by Edward's hand on her shoulder. "It is just very sad that it happened, that's all. I thought he was recovering."

Winter nodded. "If it is any c...comfort, his last letter to me indicated that it was something he expected, and he was trying to tie up all the loose ends he could. And that in p...part is what I wish to speak with you about. He asked me to go up to London with a letter indicating his consent as your legal guardian, and to procure a special license so that you could m...marry Captain Edward Kelling. He informed me of your betrothal, and wished to see the knot tied

before he died. He plainly expected that to be soon, as he directed
me to act with urgency." He paused. "And he said that it was the best
achievement of a life not entirely well-spent. His w...words, not mine,"
Winter apologized. "He was very pleased about it. I hope you are still
of the same mind?"

"Oh yes," Georgina said, squeezing Edward's hand.

"As soon as possible," said Edward. "But the funeral is tomorrow.
It is too late to grant him his wish."

"I quite agree th...that would be unseemly," said Winter.

"But I do think that means that they do not need to wait a year," said
Lady Elizabeth. "But it will give me time to organize. Bride-clothes...
black..."

"I would marry you right now, in this room, Edward!" Georgina
informed him. "And Mama – as you said I was to call you, I don't care
a button for bride-clothes. My father said it wasn't the ceremony but
the life after it that was important."

"You know, my love, I am coming more and more to regret I never
met my father-in-law," said Edward. "First, he impressed Tadswell, to
the extent that he said if he'd known I was marrying you, he would
never have suspected me, and now this! But I think you deserve a
splendid send off. Things will be fairly plain fare after that."

"I would far rather spend the money on setting up home together,"
said Georgina with a firm set to her chin.

Winter coughed. "Ahem. May I suggest, anyway, that you delay
until after the funeral. You will have time to discuss this," he looked
over his glasses, "At more leisure. But your comment on Mr. Tadswell
does raise another of the issues that my principal had me trying to
address, yesterday. To no avail, because Arthur Weatherly was not at
his residence." He paused. "You see, my client did remember who
assaulted him, and w...what transpired. He told me. And the last

thing he wanted was his family name dragged through the courts, particularly in the light of his granddaughter's upcoming marriage. He thought you might cry off, Captain."

"Well, that is not going to happen," said Edward.

"I...I am glad to hear it, and never thought otherwise," said Winter. "I...I was instructed to offer certain inducement to Mr. Arthur Weatherly to have him remove himself from the country. In this I failed my former employer, but I did w...wonder if it might be necessary to clear your name, Captain. I was in a quandary about how to do so. We did track down the locksmith who made the duplicate key. Arthur Weatherly owed him money for it, and he had his signature and address."

"Good gracious me!" said Lady Elizabeth, fanning herself with her book. "I presume he planted the original for himself to lead you to find, Georgina?"

"I do not wish to bring disgrace onto your family, Edward," said Georgina.

"Nonsense. We all have some odd nabs as relations," said Edward. "And most people around would be glad to have Awful Arthur clapped up. But I daresay he's got away. He spent a fair bit of time on the continent before."

Georgina sighed. "I thought he was my friend, my rescuer. I just don't understand his motivation for all this. He could have left me with my aunt."

"I am very glad he didn't," said Edward. "And it is too late now, Winter. There is an attainder for his arrest."

"I know, and I f...feel it was in part my fault that occurred. But I wanted the miscreant who had done that to my friend and c...client dealt with. Anyway, that is as may be. Now, Miss Ross, you are not to concern yourself with the affairs of Westmead House. It will all be dealt with. Mrs. Lessing very much desired to consult with you about the funeral meats and preparations. I have provided her with funds for that. We have arranged carriages for the mourners. Everything is in hand."

"I suppose it is not really my concern, any more," admitted Georgina. "Oh. I have the safe key. Arthur wanted it... but, well, some instinct made me not provide it to him. I should have, I suppose."

"You should most definitely not have," said Winter firmly. "You should turn it over to Mr. Lawrence, who will be here tomorrow, for the funeral."

"But, Mr. Winter, I have my little money in there, as well as what you gave to me for running the house. I kept very careful account of what I spent, and I hope you approve, but the remainder must be returned to you."

"I assure you, M...Miss Ross, that can all be dealt with perfectly easily. Your funds are completely safe. Both I and Mr. Lawrence have no c...cause for complaint of the handling of the funds entrusted to you." He turned to Edward. "Now, C...Captain. May I rely on you to care for the estate, until probate is granted? There are monies provided for that."

Edward had to laugh. "I'm sorry, Mr. Winter. That'll be a frosty Friday in hell. I assume it will be sold for Arthur, wherever he turns up, in jail or out of reach in some foreign country. I'm not much inclined to enrich him, after what he tried to do to Georgina. Besides, getting myself a job now becomes a matter of far more urgency. I've a letter this morning from father's bankers, indicating they'd like to interview me..."

"I...I would hold off from that for the m...moment," said Winter. "You approached me, and I have certain prospects, w...which, Captain, would suit you far better than working in a bank in the metropolis. These things take a little time. I will be discussing your merits for the land-management task in the next week, I believe. And whoever the new owner of Westmead is, may wish to engage you."

"It would hardly pay them, or me, to do so, Mr. Winter. You pay me far more than is justified, and I still do not believe it would be sufficient for me to support my wife. They would have to be more realistic than you have been."

"Quite so," said Winter. "But I know you had no particularly l...large expectations, from your letter. Anyway, we will discuss this further after the funeral, young man. I seriously recommend that you do not accept any offers just yet. Trust me. I...I am working remarkably hard on your behalf. I know how m...much you meant to my client in his last months."

He soon took his leave, saying he had a great deal of work to wrap up. When he'd gone, Lady Elizabeth said: "What an inscrutable little man he is, isn't he? You can't quite tell what he is thinking."

"I suppose that is useful for business," said Edward.

"Well," said Georgina. "He has always been very kind to me. And he does sound as if he has some prospect of a country job for you, Edward. I don't... I don't think you'd be very happy in the city."

That afternoon, Mrs. Lessing came over, officially to enquire on behalf of all the staff at Westmead House as to how Miss Ross was doing, and less officially to tell of the preparations she'd made for the funeral, which she wished to dwell on in morbid detail. It wasn't really surprising, Georgina reflected. For her, her entire life had been working at Westmead, and now, despite the fact that Mr. Winter had been very reassuring and promised that there was no need for alarm, she and the other retainers knew that this was the end of an era for them. They'd be seeking work, which, as Mrs. Lessing said, at her time of life, was not something she be wanting to be doing. Georgina wished she could give her some real comfort, but Edward was good at it, saying that they knew the Squire would be batting for them, and that he and Georgina would recommend each and every one of them to the buyers. It was of course not that certain that anyone would live there, but some staff would have to keep the place from going to rack and ruin.

She also brought with her Georgina's mother's little tin box. The lock had been forced. "Wasn't us, Miss," explained Mrs. Lessing. "It was under the bed in Master Arthur's rooms. Back against the wall."

It was hard for Georgina to determine if anything was missing. She still had to wonder what he'd been looking for. It now mostly held letters, that her mother had tied up in bunches with ribbons. The ones from her Uncle George were well-read. They were just about country life, the life of a country gentleman, her mother's world, a world that she'd left for love. Well. It wasn't her world. It was Edward's, and she would have to, somehow, make sure that he did not end up too much like her mother, longing for the life she'd left. Well, Winter seemed hopeful it could be done in some way. And she did not need much. Edward too was a man of simple tastes, she found, happy with a book or a rod, or even solving agricultural issues of which she knew so little. She would have to learn more of them.

The next day brought flurries of rain and the funeral. Georgina was glad of Edward's support at the graveside, and surprised and touched by the number of people who had turned out for her grandfather at the little Church of St Andrew the Apostle. People were very considerate, and brought her a chair to sit on, even at the grave. The cortege returned to Westmead house where Mrs. Lessing had endeavored to set out a cold collation that would reflect well on her late master. A chaise-lounge had been provided for Georgina to recline on, and she was polite and received commiserations from far more people than she would ever remember the names of.

When most of the visitors had left, Mr. Winter, and a thin, elderly man, came across the room to her. "Mr. Lawrence would like to speak with you, Miss Ross," said Winter. "You w...were introduced earlier, but in the press of people..."

"Please do not get up, Miss Ross," the attorney said in a creaky, old voice. "You must forgive me not coming to call on you before. I have not been well. Had I known my client was this close to his end..." he sighed. "Anyway, there is some business we need to transact. Could we possibly adjourn to somewhere more private? The library perhaps? And would it be possible to have one of your footmen summon to join us, these people," he drew a list from his pocket. "Mr. Frederick's valet, Michael Sanders, Mr. and Mrs. Lessing, the Cook, Thomas Sneddon, and a groom by the name of William Morton, and a gardener by the name of Edward Brown?"

"I'll arrange it," said Edward. "Stay sitting, dearest."

"Could you accompany, M...Miss Ross, Captain?" said Winter. "There are matters in which she may need your support."

Edward nodded. "I'm always there to support her, Mr. Winter. She will be my wife, after all."

Edward limped off to speak to the footmen, and his parents, who were still there.

Mr. Lawrence said: "I knew your mother as a young girl. Your resemblance to her is striking. I would have known you even if Winter had not produced the supporting documentation. Interestingly, I had a visit from a rather... dodgy lawyer... a fellow called Chade – who informed me – on behalf of your cousin, Arthur Weatherly, that you were an imposter and had no documentation to prove your identity. I was happy to have my clerk show him the door." He reached into his pocket and produced a somewhat battered letter. "Pardon its appearance," he said. "It has been on rather a long journey – to Africa and back again. It is addressed to your mother, from your grandfather. I believe it got to Grahamstown the day you sailed. Captain Smith saw that it was sent after you. It came to me, yesterday."

"It would have meant so much to her," she said, sadly. "Well. If it was a nice letter. I am rather scared to read it, now. I have...good memories of his last day. And while he was confused he called me by my mother's name."

"I think you may safely read it," said the attorney.

Edward had returned and gave her his arm and they went through to the library, where they were joined by the servants who had been called. They huddled rather nervously behind Mrs. Lessing, looking uncomfortable. The attorney took his place in her grandfather's seat, something Georgina might have resented more had he not been so old and obviously in pain walking, himself. A chair had been brought for her. The rest of them stood.

"Oh," said Georgina. "I do have the safe key. Do you need it now, sir?"

"Not just yet," the attorney said, waving a hand at her, as he drew forth yet more papers from an inner pocket. "I have asked you to attend here for the reading of the Last Will and Testament of Frederick James Weatherly."

Edward had been sure it would be the reading of the will, and was rather pleased that obviously old man Weatherly had provided for the servants who had been with him for so many years. It was nice Georgina was there too. The estate itself would be entailed, and go to Arthur. But perhaps there would be some bequest for Georgina. It would be a good thing if she had some pin-money of her own. He knew she felt her poverty keenly, and he'd been determined to make up for it for her.

The attorney droned through the 'of' and signed at, and witnessed by details. Winter, and Doctor Selby were the witnesses. Each of the servants got bequests – quite generous ones, and old Lessing and his wife a pension.

His surprise, to have his name read next, was more than considerable. "To Captain Edward William Kelling of Bournelea Hall, the sum of five hundred pounds, in thanks for the kindness and unasked generosity of spirit he displayed in attending to my land and playing chess with me. You were in many ways the son to me that I had lost."

"Five hundred pounds!" exclaimed his love, looking up at him. "Oh, Edward! That is such good news, Mr. Lawrence! I'm so pleased. I'm so glad!"

"A r...reward well deserved," agreed Winter, "For that, and for rescuing him, so he at least got the opportunity, however brief, to know his granddaughter. And he was very fond of you, Captain Kelling. He missed his son, greatly, and y...you provided him with something of an alternative."

"Well!" said Edward. "That was unexpected! That'll give us a helping hand. I see why you were telling me to hold off, Mr. Winter. It'll make quite a difference."

"Excuse me," said the attorney, dryly. "May I proceed?"

"Oh, yes, certainly sir," said Edward, somewhat abashed.

The attorney nodded. "The residue of my estate is left to my daughter, Dorothea Althea Ross. Failing her, it is left to her child, Georgina Hermione Ross."

He cleared his throat in the sudden silence. "I have a further instruction, dated from the day before his unfortunate demise, requesting that I and my friend Mr. Winter should act as trustees until Miss Ross achieves majority, or until she is married to Captain Edward Kelling."

Georgina was the first to speak. "But... but what of Arthur?" It was not really so much speak, as squeak.

The attorney looked at her, and steepled his fingers. "In the will I drafted some seven years ago, after the death of Frederick Weatherly's son, his nephew Arthur Weatherly was the principle heir, although there was a considerable sum left to his daughter Dorothea, and her child or children. But I was called in just after Christmas, to assist Mr. Frederick in re-drafting his will. He was extremely angry with Mr. Arthur, and determined to cut him off without a penny. I did try to dissuade him, but he was adamant. He was extremely excited about the possibility of his daughter's return, and made his will in her favor." He coughed. "That will had some terms to prevent the money being spent on the mission society, and would have been complex to administer. Then, early in March, I was called in again, and the will was considerably simplified, merely leaving the residue of the estate to her or failing her, her child. He had received word that your father had died, Miss Ross."

"But," said Edward, finding his voice at last. "Isn't the estate entailed?"

The attorney shook his head. "No. While they are, usually, they do not have to be, Captain Kelling, and in this case, it was not."

"Did Arthur know?" asked Edward, suddenly joining things to-gether.

Winter answered that. "In his l...letter Mr. Frederick informed me that he told Arthur on the night he caught him breaking in and stealing his snuff-boxes. They really were of trivial worth, compared to the estate. Mr. Frederick was not given to any displays of wealth, you know. He lived very frugally. He had no need to do so. Appearances can deceive."

"They certainly deceived me," admitted Edward. "I mean, father said he had a fair bit, back when, well, he tried to get my father to marry his daughter. But we assumed his windmill had dwindled to a nutshell."

"In fact, very much the opposite c...case," said Mr. Winter, smiling broadly for the first time that Edward could think of. He waved at the servants. "P...Perhaps these gentlemen and you, Mrs. Lessing, could adjourn? We have a little further business to discuss with Miss Ross." He looked at Edward. "Strictly speaking, I should ask you to leave too, Captain. Seeing as you refused to contemplate being the agent for the heir."

Georgina clutched his arm. "No." She said firmly. "I don't quite understand all this, but I need Edward. Do you mean to say... this house is mine?"

"Yes. And c...considerable other assets besides. Some of the values are quite hard to determine, as they are such things as property held in the c...colonies, and shares in vessels. But the rest comes to the better part of a quarter of a million pounds, by the least computation. I will be going through it all with you," said Winter. "But it may take me a few days. Mr. Frederick Weatherly's holdings were extensive. The land is the smallest part of it, although he had instructed me to initiate the purchase of at least a thousand more acres, with the stated intent of keeping his granddaughter and new husband c...close to home, a process I have begun. I am sorry, but I was not at liberty to tell you, until Mr. Lawrence had read the will."

"You must have laughed a great deal at us, Mr. Winter," said Edward. "Well, Georgina." He braced himself. "I... I don't think I can marry you. You are a very wealthy woman now, and..."

"Don't you love me?" she asked, incredulously, and looking utterly forlorn.

"More than anything else. But... but you could have anyone. I have nothing to offer you."

He found his cravat being seized and a very angry young woman staring into his eyes. "You... would have me, when I had nothing."

"But I had nothing too. Nothing much anyway," he protested.

"You were always everything I ever wanted. Leave me and I will... I will... I will pine away," she informed him.

Aware that his love's face was upturned and mere inches from his, he leaned in and kissed her. And then kissed her tears away, and gave her his handkerchief. And then firmly informed Winter that he could wait on Georgina tomorrow, because right now he was taking her home, as the priest had already left, and they couldn't use that special license right then.

Georgina said: "We could marry tomorrow?"

"We'll talk to my mother. I know my little sister will kill me if I get married without her. We may have to wait until she can be fetched."

Later, when they got back to Bournelea, and his love finally allowed herself to be parted from him – after making him promise, earnestly, that he would not let her inheritance stand between them. "After all,"

she said. "I was over the moon about your five hundred pounds. Why should my money be any different?"

He knew why. Because hers amounted to, from what Winter said, a substantial fortune. But... well, Georgina. The girl who had fallen into the river with him. Who had got herself shot to save him. Who wanted to come and fish with him. Who had worried that she was too poor for him. Who, from what Winter had now told him, had been carefully husbanding her pennies, looking to find some form of employment, but had turned down an offer of marriage from Arthur, who had told her that would make her wealthy, for her to instead accept him, who had so little to offer. Marrying Arthur would have made her rich, in a way, he reflected.

Well, if Arthur ever turned up he might save the hangman some work, he thought. But he had a visit from Tadswell, late that afternoon. "He arrived at his chambers in London. The officers assigned to watch them failed to apprehend him. It would seem he has lost an eye, and was looking very seedy, and they were looking for a gentleman of the first stare. Anyway, he managed to embark on a ship bound for Brazil and be away before they found him. The warrant will remain open, of course. Attempted murder, two counts of robbery, attempted rape, attempted manslaughter..."

"You can add to that, that he probably killed the old man, if not directly, from apoplexy," said Edward, grimly. "It would be hard to prove, but I think he sneaked into the library, not knowing Frederick Weatherly was in there. He believed the new will to be in there, from what he said to Georgina. And it seems the original attack was an interrupted theft, in which Frederick Weatherly caught him, and then informed him he'd cut him out of his will. It was rage I think, that was behind the attack, and he set the fire to cover his tracks. Arthur had been living on that expectation for a while, I think.

Tadswell nodded. "I must admit the fact – which I had from the attorney – that he was not the heir – led me astray. He had no motive for murder, I thought. I did not know that he had assumed he was the heir."

"Well, it is a good thing the attorney didn't tell you I was to inherit five hundred pounds! Mind you, it was as big a surprise to me, as it is to you!" said Edward. "Or I would have been even more of a suspect."

"Well, that is a well-deserved windfall," said Tadswell, handsomely.

"It'll a help a little with the wedding," said Edward. "Which will be private, because of her bereavement, but I should like to invite you to attend."

"I would be delighted!"

"I have to warn you, that as we're being married by special license, and that can be done anywhere, Georgina wants it at dawn on the river."

The expression on Tadswell's face was sufficient repayment for his doubts about Edward fishing the dawn rise. But Edward couldn't keep a straight face for very long. "Be easy, sir. You wouldn't get my mother or sister down there, either."

Georgina waited until she was alone that evening to read the letter her grandfather had sent to mother. It did make her weep. It was a letter full of the longing of an old man for reconciliation, and indeed, expressed regret. It set out his plans for her to stay with him, and his plans to introduce his granddaughter to society. It would have meant a great deal to her mother, Georgina knew. And it meant a great deal to her.

Two days later, when she was a little more comfortable walking again, Edward did take her to the Bourne, just the two of them, to watch the perfect circles of the rising fish in the clear water, and the sun coming up on a new morning, for both of them.

Also By

Alfred's journey to Harrogate was comfortably conducted in fine style in one of his well-sprung travelling carriages, as he had decided the weather was too inclement to enjoy driving up in his phaeton.

Mark had expressed some disappointment at this. "Yes, I know, Mark. You would have looked so wistful I should have been beguiled into giving you the reins and you would have had both of us in a ditch."

"It was a pond!" protested his secretary. "Besides, you were rather bosky... m'lord. Yelling at me to spring 'em. And we were both some-what younger then."

"I," his lordship informed him, austerely, "Have grown up since my Cambridge days. The fact that you have not is merely confirmed by what you doubtless consider a natty waistcoat."

"All the crack," his secretary assured him, being well armored against this particular from of ribbing.

"Perhaps in Bond street. Yorkshire may be different."

"I'll start a fashion among the provincials," said Mark Latham.

"Or at least have less people to shock," said Alfred. "But on the whole, I think you may be right. It'll give their minds a new turn, and stop them looking at me. You have great value, Mark."

"The things I nobly do for my employer," said his secretary.

"In practical fact, Ness and couple of the grooms are bringing my cattle and the Phaeton up, as well as a few hacks. It's pretty country, if rather bleak, and if you fancy to take the chariot or one of the horses out, they are at your disposal. This is to be something of a holiday for you, which you need after collating all those reports."

"It's a mess, isn't it?"

"A damned mess. And they tell us our fleet will keep us safe. I'm more likely to be surprised that they don't mutiny."

"Some do, of course."

"Yes. An argument that will be made, I foresee."

They arrived in the town late in the afternoon. The trees on the Stray were still in young leaf and the town looked its best, spring flowers out in many gardens, and of course on the Stray. The sun had made a late afternoon effort and shone on some young women and their swains, walking to look at the flowers, no doubt. "The town putting on its best show for you, Mark," said Alfred, amused by his friend's praise of the scene. "Having this belt of greenery does help thought. It's quite 200 acres of public land. Mother's little domicile does front onto the park, which, I may tell you, means there are people about at all hours of the morning."

"After wild nights of northern revelry, no doubt," said his secretary.

"Well, in the Season – May through to September, there are entertainments every night. And the George and the Queen hotels can get quite lively. No, it's the bands. They provide something to listen to while people drink the waters. I have a wholly unproven theory that the worse the water, the more discordant and louder the band."

"But then you are so musical, m'lord," commented Mark, who was.

Alfred was not.

"They start up by half past seven. I am even less musically inclined at that hour. St John's well, Mother's nearest, is thank heavens, considered 'the sweet spaw'. There's even more mineral in the ones down in Bogs field, on the way to Low Harrogate."

"I can hardly wait for the treats in store for me," said Mark, grinning.

"I am sure they will feel the same way about your waistcoats, Mark. Ah, here we are," he said as John Coachman drew up at the imposing three story house fronting onto Park Parade. He noticed his secretary sticking a finger in his carefully starched collar, before pasting a smile on his face.

As it was, his nervousness was misplaced. Arabella and his mother had gone across to Low Harrogate in the landaulet, not expecting them for some hours. So, Alfred was able to get comfortably emplaced before his sister burst into his room, and hugged him fiercely. Bella was some seven years younger than he was, and, since the death of their father, he'd been a stand-in, as well just an elder brother. She was definitely growing up.

She held onto his arms and leaned back. "My, brother. You are looking remarkably fine," she said, mischievously: "Mother is not going to approve of your neck-cloth."

"I brought a shield. She will be so distracted by Mark's natty waistcoats as to barely notice my existence."

Made in United States
Orlando, FL
23 December 2022